A TRIAL IN VENICE

A TRIAL IN VENICE

ROBERTA RICH

DOUBLEDAY CANADA

Doubleday Canada and colophon are registered trademarks of Random House of Canada Limited

LIBRARY AND ARCHIVES CANADA CATALOGUING IN PUBLICATION

Rich, Roberta, author
A trial in Venice / Roberta Rich.

Issued in print and electronic formats.
ISBN 978-0-385-67669-4 (paperback).--ISBN 978-0-385-67670-0 (epub)

I. Title.

PS8635.I249T75 2017   C813'.6   C2016-903000-8
                                               C2016-903001-6

This book is a work of fiction. Names, characters, places and incidents are products of the author's imagination or are used fictitiously. Any resemblance to actual events or locales or persons, living or dead, is entirely coincidental.

Cover design: Rachel Cooper

Cover images: (top) Rest, 1879 (oil on fabric), Bouguereau, William-Adolphe (1825-1905) / Cleveland Museum of Art, OH, USA / Hinman B. Hurlbut Collection / Bridgeman Images; (bottom) The Entrance to the Grand Canal, Venice, c.1730 (oil on canvas), Canaletto, (Giovanni Antonio Canal) (1697-1768) / Museum of Fine Arts, Houston, Texas, USA / The Robert Lee Blaffer Memorial Collection, gift of Sarah Campbell Blaffer / Bridgeman Images; (rope) © Blackslide, (paper) © Engin Korkmaz and (large stained paper) © Marpalusz all from Dreamstime.com

Printed and bound in the USA

Published in Canada by Doubleday Canada,
a division of Random House of Canada Limited,
a Penguin Random House company.

www.penguinrandomhouse.ca

10 9 8 7 6 5 4 3 2 1

 Penguin
Random House
DOUBLEDAY CANADA

To Martha, Sam and Ben.

Pozzi Prison,
Venice
1580

THE WALLS OF HER CELL wept with moisture. *If I could keep dry,* thought Hannah, cupping her belly, trying to ignore the wet straw bedding poking through her cotton shift.

Only the present matters. I am alive. I have kept myself safe for weeks. By the force of my will and the fierce constitution God has blessed me with, my heart continues to beat. I breathe. My head throbs, but it is still attached to my shoulders. My baby moves within me. My strong, courageous baby. If a boy, I shall name him Daniel, who showed such bravery in the lions' den. If a girl, I shall name her Esther, in memory of Queen Esther, who saved the Jews from King Xerxes.

Rats scurried across her cheek. Her waste bucket had no lid. Daily she heard the tinkle of silver, the rattle of fine china and the pop of wine corks—noblemen imprisoned for sodomy or debts, consuming the delicacies they paid the guards to fetch them. From the next cell wafted the stench of gangrenous human flesh and the screams of other prisoners.

Unable to endure the wet pallet any longer, Hannah rose and began to clean a wound on her forearm. With the clumsiness of pregnancy, she had fallen and gashed her arm. She poured salt water over it then bound it with the only thing she had: a filthy rag.

The guard Guido pressed his pockmarked face, mouth caved in from lack of teeth, to the bars of her cell.

"Close to your confinement, are you? How long, do you reckon, till the baby comes?"

Guido was no worse than the other guards, but she hadn't the heart to answer, unwilling to acknowledge she would be giving birth to her precious, long-awaited child on a dirty pallet in a prison, surrounded by leering guards, instead of on clean sheets in a bright, airy room at home, comforted by other women and a competent midwife.

Hannah was imprisoned for the most serious of crimes. Had it not been for her belly, the Doge's soldiers would have hanged her soon after they arrested her. If she did not die of the plague or starvation first, she would deliver in the spring—scant months away. Once the baby was born, soldiers would drag her from her cell to the *strappado*. Wrists bound behind her, she would be suspended from a rope thrown over a beam. Weights added to her ankles would intensify the pain, and she would suffer unbearable agony until the breath left her body. Because she was a Jew, she would be quartered, her parts scattered throughout the city. Her baby would be cast into a canal. That is how it was done in Venice.

How distraught Isaac would be if he could see her. If only she could turn into a puff of smoke, drift out the tiny barred window set high in the wall and float back to him.

Isaac. She repeated his name over and over to give herself courage, a caress in this prison of harsh blows on soft backs, of deafening shouts and jeers.

From her linen bag, among a handful of *scudi*, she fished out the oyster shell button that had once decorated Isaac's shirt. She remembered a warm, sunny day with gulls wheeling overhead. She and Isaac had been walking on a beach with Matteo and baby Jessica when they found it. She took it home and with an awl and coping saw fashioned a button out of it. Isaac had laughed with pleasure and said how resourceful she was.

Hannah stroked it against her cheek, taking pleasure in its coolness, its tiny ridges. And then she recalled Isaac's letter and was overcome with a sadness so profound she felt unable to move. What had possessed her to sail across the sea, leaving behind the person who loved her most in the world? She could no longer remember.

This is what she had become: a friendless woman hunched in the corner of a fetid prison cell, back braced against the wall, as she clung to a button.

In spite of Hannah's sleepless nights and poor food, the baby continued to kick her insides energetically—staying the executioner's hand. Just as her unborn child protected her, she would protect it, because what is the use of a mother who cannot keep her child alive? And so she forced down the stale bread and thin gruel Guido's wife, the prison cook, provided her. Bianca was gaunt with washed-out blue eyes and the wishbone legs of a woman who had endured too many pregnancies. At night Hannah wrapped herself tightly to prevent rat bites, and avoided prisoners who suffered from coughing fits and infected sores.

The thought of her own death frightened her. She would be a fool if it did not. But what gave her no peace, made her stomach clench and her mind restless, was the knowledge she had failed Matteo.

Hannah had risked her life—but worse, risked the life of her unborn child. And for what? Matteo might be dead. Strangling a five-year-old would be an easy task. But they needed him, didn't they?

Or would *any* little red-haired boy serve their purpose just as well?

CHAPTER I

Constantinople
1579

I N LESS TIME than was needed to recite the Shema, the Jewish morning and evening prayer, they had taken Matteo.

The day began like any other. Hannah rose, prepared her son's breakfast of maize soup and a sweet bun, and then kneaded bread dough and placed it in a wooden trough to proof. When she checked the larder, she found there were no carrots to braise in the pan with the Shabbat chicken. She put on her shawl, fastened Matteo's jacket around his stout middle, took him by the hand and headed for the market. He skipped along next to her, his chubby legs pumping to keep up.

She strolled past the vendors at the marketplace until she found the stall where she bought her vegetables. One moment she was haggling over a half-dozen aubergines, Matteo's fingers folded in hers; the next she was racing through packed aisles, knocking over tables laden with fruit, shoving past merchants and housewives, shouting at strangers, "Have you seen my son? Red hair? Five years old? Tall for his age? Wearing a blue jacket with a patch of yellow on the sleeve?"

She hurried to the main road. Perhaps a Gypsy with a dancing bear, or a troupe of acrobats or some other diversion had caught her son's eye and he had elbowed his way into the crowds, exploring as curious boys do. Perhaps an Arab camel caravan. The Arab drivers were often inattentive—drunk on date wine, dazed from eating opium or exhausted from months traversing the White Desert.

But the road was empty.

Hannah stopped in the spice market; she paused at the stalls of the apothecaries, their carboys filled with leeches. Shielding her eyes against the sun, she pushed her way to the yoghurt vendor, hoping to find Matteo there, begging for a cup of sheep's yoghurt sweetened with honey.

But there was no small boy among the white-turbaned sellers, no fair-skinned child with a blue jacket among the Gypsies and urchins.

She dodged a worker grunting under a load of bricks and nearly skidded on the entrails of a dead dog. She raced on, sucking for air that would not come, feeling stabs of pain under her ribs. Too many turbaned men pressed into her. Too many veiled women in voluminous skirts blocked her passage. The smells of camel dung, cardamom and rotting fruit overwhelmed her. Shouts of the *simit* vendors and the colicky cries of donkeys struggling under mountains of firewood rang out. Breathless, she slowed her pace. She would go home and return with Isaac. He would know what to do. They would find Matteo together.

Hannah sped back, dizzy and panting so hard she could barely get out the words to her husband. They searched for hours, then days, then weeks, before they were forced to acknowledge what Hannah had known all along: Matteo did not wander off. He did not slip out of her grasp in a moment of excitement to watch a Gypsy leading a dancing bear or a wandering juggler or a fire eater. What she had most feared, from the moment she realized her hand was clasping empty air instead of Matteo's hand, had come to pass.

After all this time, they had returned for him. Hannah was a fool to suppose they had given up.

Following several anguished weeks of wakeful nights and tear-filled days, Isaac insisted they get rid of the grey parrot, Güzel. Matteo had not yet mastered the sound of the letter *m*. Although he could press his lips together with great concentration and say *mmm* well, he could not couple the sound with a word. So *Mama* emerged as "Ama." For the pleasure of seeing Hannah burst into tears, the hateful bird would mimic Matteo with cruel clarity, calling from the mulberry tree in the garden, "Ama! Ama! Where are you?"

Isaac hauled the parrot off to the market, where he traded the screeching creature to a jeweller from North Africa in exchange for a lapis lazuli necklace for Hannah.

Hannah and Isaac set about the task of mourning. At night in bed they held each other and wept, neither saying a word. As the Torah said, "The greater the sorrow, the less tongue it hath." But they had no body to wash, no small tombstone in the Jewish cemetery in Hasköy to place a stone on once a year, no one to bring food to their door.

Even Jessica, young as she was, grieved for Matteo. She stood next to his bed, patting the blankets, her face contorted with worry, glaring at Hannah as though her mother were responsible for her brother's disappearance. She would peer under his bed then shout his name the way she did when the two of them played hide-and-seek. "Matteo? Matteo?" She would look down the long hallway, expecting him to burst upon her with a whoop and gather her into a bear hug. When he did not, Jessica cried and struggled out of Isaac's arms as he tried to comfort her.

For Hannah, grief took the form of a lump under her breastbone—a hard bolus of sorrow that no amount of weeping could dissolve.

CHAPTER 2

Villa di Padovani, San Lorenzo, the Veneto

*H*OLY MOTHER OF GOD, Cesca thought, thrusting open the front door of the villa, *I am as near the gates of paradise as I am ever likely to be.* The lock had long ago separated from the door; it lay on the ground, rusted and in pieces. Standing in the entranceway, feeling the sun-warmed floor through her thin-soled shoes, Cesca dropped her valise. With Matteo's hand tucked into hers, she tiptoed into the reception room, wanting to weep from the sheer gorgeousness of the room.

Cesca, raised on thin gruel and cabbage soup when living with her mother and four other whores, was starved for beauty the way a rose growing in a cow shed is starved

for the sun. As a child Cesca had grown practised at closing her ears to the grunts of pigs foraging for refuse in the
streets and her mother feigning pleasure with men in the
curtained-off section of their room. Cesca had schooled
herself to ignore the crumbling mud-packed walls, blind
beggars and scrofulous dogs, and had instead pretended to
be a fairy tale princess captured by wicked pirates.

Leaving Matteo to play by himself, she made her way
through to the drawing room, afraid that if she trod too
loudly, everything would vanish like a lark snatched in
mid-song by a hawk. Butter yellow sunlight poured through
the shutters, warming the terrazzo floor, a mottled expanse
of crushed green, brown and yellow marble set in cement.
Some areas of the floor were badly scratched, others
smooth, with a lustre. From a distance the floor had the
beautiful monotony of a newly sprouted wheat field; up
close it was a cunning multiplicity of hue and texture.
Cesca flung open the shutters, releasing a million motes
that danced in the light. She knelt and ran her fingertips
along the floor. Something quickened in her nether regions.
If she spent every waking moment in this room for the rest
of her life, she would never tire of the ceiling high enough
to fly a kite in or the ivory doorknobs as white and as
glossy as meringue.

Leaning against the wall, she fumbled her rosary out of
her pocket. She kissed it, thanking the Holy Virgin for her
good fortune. Was it absurd to turn misty eyed over a
floor? Of course it was, but the wood hut in Rome where
Cesca had grown up had a badly tamped dirt floor that

became slick with mud in the spring and lively with insects in the summer.

And the drawing room walls! Cesca had never before seen plaster as fine as the inside of an oyster shell. *Entaco*— cool to the touch, and lime-washed the colour of fresh goat cheese. Such beauty inflamed her. She pressed the back of her hand to the plaster then trailed it back and forth. Then, hiking her skirts above her knees, she threw her head back, twisting and turning as though dancing the *ballo del capello*, preening in the sunlight, arching and yielding, feeling the sun's heat like a lover's tongue licking golden honey down her neck and breasts. She danced over to the Istrian marble fireplace, dodging a hay cart lying on its side and missing two of its wheels, and kissed the lions flanking it, the stone smooth and cold to her lips.

Foscari, whom she had left behind in Venice to attend to legal matters, was not present to spoil her bliss. He would see only a neglected villa, the shutters falling off their hinges, broken glass in the tall windows, debris left behind by vagrants. These shortcomings were trifles. With hard work and money all would be put right.

Foscari was jealous if anything, other than his company, gave her pleasure. He was due to arrive in a few days with the court order tucked under his arm, and as a reward she would lead him upstairs to the bedchamber for one of her playlets. Although these dramas gave her little enjoyment, they provided Foscari with a great deal. The sight of his body—his pubic hair, what little there was of it coarse and grey, migrating southward to fleck his shanks like pond scum—repelled her. But she was as good an actress as any woman on the stage at the Teatro La Bel Canto. His insistent plowings cost her nothing and made him so biddable. Often, she tried to envision what coupling with a young, virile, playful man her own age would be like, one whose skin did not hang in curtains from his arms like wrinkled, yellowed linen; one whose scrotum did not dangle halfway to his knees. It might be agreeable. Some women found it so. Perhaps when she was rich, she would invite a sturdy young peasant to her bed, but until that happy day she was yoked to Foscari and he to her. Without his position in society—he was from a noble family—and his knowledge of the law, Cesca hadn't a prayer of obtaining her share of the immense di Padovani fortune. Foscari, in turn, needed her knowledge of Matteo's past life with Hannah and Isaac in Constantinople to concoct convincing testimony for the court.

If not for Cesca and her familiarity with Hannah's daily routine, they would never have found the boy in that jumbled market. Now that they had snatched him—their second attempt—Foscari also needed her ongoing help in caring for Matteo, who had taken an unfortunate dislike to Foscari.

Any affection Cesca might once have had for Foscari had vanished last year in Constantinople when they made their first attempt to spirit Matteo away from Hannah. Foscari blamed the entire fiasco on Cesca. Yet, there had been no reason to denounce her. A true nobleman would have accepted the blame. Foscari had not. She had tried to forget his perfidy, but it kept floating to the surface of her mind like a piece of excrement in a chamber pot.

The Valide, the Sultan's mother, had ordered them banished. The Sultan's personal guards, the Janissaries, escorted them to the docks to put them on the first ship leaving port.

Despite this, at Cesca's suggestion they had hidden month after dreary month in a felt maker's shack in a tiny village on the Bosphorus until Hannah and Isaac let down their guard, believing their son to be safe. The fault had been Hannah's. She should have known Cesca would persevere. Matteo's estate was the largest in the Venetian Republic. Such a prize was worth a few months of eating nothing but sheep's cheese, lentil soup and flat bread, not to mention enduring Foscari's unwanted attentions.

Matteo had followed Cesca into the drawing room, and was giggling and racing about, arms outstretched, boots echoing on the floor. What a dear little lamb he could be when Foscari was not around. On the voyage from Constantinople to Venice, he had wept so long and hard for Hannah that Cesca feared he would never be consoled. His hiccupping and the snot dripping from his nose had driven her mad. But once she allowed him to sleep with her in her snug berth aboard the *Il Baldone*, he had finally settled down.

At the moment, Matteo was spinning his wooden top on the floor, shouting with disappointment when it teetered and fell on its side. His cheeks were flushed from the excitement of the canal ride from Venice and seeing their new dwelling for the first time. Later, after she had explored the villa and grounds, she would coax him to take a nap. But not now. Now she wanted to daydream about her plans to restore the villa to its former splendour. Soon it would be hers to do with as she wished.

"Are you as happy as I am, *mi amore?*" Cesca asked.

Instead of answering, Matteo put his arms around her waist and nestled against her. Cesca patted his head and ran her fingers through his glossy hair. His little body pressed against hers in a way that was rather agreeable at first but soon grew wearisome. Cesca disentangled herself and sent Matteo out to play, cautioning him not to get too close to the canal.

Cesca took a great lungful of air, and caught the slightly eggy odour of tempera. She lifted her eyes to the west wall of the drawing room—and was unable to believe she had missed seeing this when she had first entered the room. Her mouth fell open and a gasp of amazement escaped her lips.

Frescoes in dusty pinks, in purples and gold and silvery greens, covered the wall from floor to ceiling with scenes of hunting, peasant women knitting and weaving, children unravelling silk cocoons, noblemen gazing with admiration into the eyes of beautiful women. Painted cupids kicked their fat legs and giggled down at her from the ceiling.

Housemaids dangled plump babies; pageboys peered from behind half-opened doors. A mélange of fruits and flowers—tulips, roses, carnations, apples, melons, grapes, oranges—arranged in an overflowing basket balanced on the top of the door jamb. Grapevines trailed down both sides of the door, as tantalizing as a woman's unbound hair.

On the palms of their hands valets proffered trays covered with cakes and savouries. Cesca could almost smell the mince and cinnamon and goose pâté.

Most intriguing of all was the figure of the *castellana*, the mistress of the villa. She leaned over a balcony, full of bosom and wide of skirt, so artfully painted that for a moment Cesca feared the woman might topple over the railing to her death. Behind the *castellana*, who wore a green velvet skirt with silk blouse and pearl necklace, stood a wet nurse clasping a gurgling infant. The *castellana* appeared in command of the household, the sort of mistress capable of dealing with saucy parlour maids and colicky babies but also one who was kind to servants and animals.

Cesca's mother had once worked as a scullery maid for such a *castellana* and was full of tales of her efficient domestic management. Cesca must quickly acquire these skills. To seduce a man, all one needed was a wet cunny and a clean bed, but to keep him—and she very much wanted to keep Foscari, at least for the time being—a woman must provide a well-run household.

Cesca skipped and bowed and fluffed her skirts in front of the *castellana*, picturing new frocks and a house full of servants tripping over one another to do her bidding. Very soon, the villa's next mistress would appear in Cesca's own looking glass.

She walked to an open window and fanned her flushed face. Feeling giddy, ears ringing, she dropped to a crouch, her head bent, and hugged her knees, grateful that Foscari, with his arch smile and perfect self-possession, radiating *sprezzatura* from every pore, was not here to mock her for what he would consider vapid sentimentality. The Marquis possessed impeccably good taste and made instructive, albeit sometimes hurtful, comments on her dress and accent. Without such instruction she could not hope to improve herself. And his connections! He was received in every drawing room in Venice.

Since birth Foscari had had a houseful of servants tending to his every need. As a result, he had not the slightest notion how clean clothes appeared in his dressing room each morning or by what process his muddy boots were transformed into clean, shiny ones. All he saw was Cesca smiling as she held out his waistcoat, brushed and sponged, waiting for him to raise his arms and slip them into the perfectly tailored sleeves. Foscari was as impractical as one would expect of a nobleman. He would be of no help in improving the villa.

From the window leading to the portico, Matteo peeked in, his lips parted, his spinning top hanging by its string, banging against the frame. Then he took flight, racing up and down the portico. His little legs moved so quickly they seemed a blur as he disappeared down the stairs to the front lawn toward the canal.

Cesca stood, straightened her skirts and pinched her cheeks, as she often did to give them colour. The fresh breeze through the window played with the tendrils of her hair. She slowed her breathing, trying to control the frisson of ecstasy that came with knowing the villa would soon be legally hers.

Wonder of wonders, Venetian women were permitted to own land. A friend of her mother's had put enough money aside from whoring to purchase a bawdy house. The property was registered in the friend's name and upon her death would devolve to her daughter. The first time Cesca had heard this story she had not believed it, but it was true.

Cesca eased open the doors to the garden, which were set with glass, now mostly broken. The fragility of the substance rendered it so costly that the thought of replacing the doors made her wince. And so did the sight before her. A small grove of olive trees stood unpruned; the row of espaliered orange trees along the fence was overgrown and shapeless. Greenish rainwater filled the nyphaneum, a marvellously huge fountain sizable enough for a dozen nymphs to gambol in, its catch pool surrounded by statues of pagan gods. A barn swallow dared to swoop for a drink then fluttered away. The weeds, the crumbling mortar, the rutted roads, the footpaths littered with human dung from tramps who had evidently camped for weeks on end, were of no importance. The villa would soon be hers and she'd recapture its brilliance.

In truth, Cesca had no greater right to occupy the villa than did a tramp dossing down for the night. Foscari, with his quick wit and clever tongue, had convinced the mayor of San Lorenzo, a man given to drink and the company of whores, both tastes readily satisfied, that Cesca's occupation of the villa was necessary for the well-being of the little heir. She was not clear why the mayor had power over a property he neither owned nor leased nor rented, simply because it was located within the boundaries of his village, but what did it matter? Cesca had in her pocket a parchment signed by both the mayor and Foscari and impressed with red sealing wax.

Under her ownership, the villa would be transformed into a home where a mother did not sell her daughter's virtue, where the larder was always stuffed with freshly baked bread and where she and Matteo, this robust little boy she had become rather fond of, would live together in harmony.

CHAPTER 3

Villa di Padovani,
San Lorenzo, the Veneto

B Y THE BLOOD OF THE *Holy Mother, let Foscari have triumphed,* Cesca prayed, stirring her cooking pot and peering out the window of the summer kitchen. All that was left in the larder were turnips and a hunk of mouldy pecorino, more rind than cheese. The cow she had found wandering in the south pasture was no cow at all, just a wall-eyed ancient creature with caved-in sides, which had not been freshened in years. She grazed along the canal, breaking down the clay embankment with hooves the size of dinner plates. There were no hens and hence no eggs, just a crepe-necked old rooster, which would soon fall under the axe and into the soup pot—if Cesca could find an axe in the stable, a cauldron in the pantry and enough wood to lay a fire in the hearth. But no matter. Under her management, swampland would be drained, tenant farmers would resume paying their rents and the villa would sparkle with fresh whitewash and new glass. The lands would produce again. She would see to that. Soon she would have no need to purchase wine or olive oil or flour. And wasn't that the very definition of the true aristocrat?

Foscari, for all his faults, was wise in the ways of the world, familiar with courts and judges and nobles and the sophisticated modes of commerce in Venice. He could read and write, and reckon as fast as any Jew moneylender. He knew everyone in the district—even Andrea Palladio, whom Foscari had pronounced the finest architect in the whole of the Veneto.

From the window she watched the Brenta flow gently. To drift along by barge on it was as soothing as being carried in a mother's arms. The Brenta never acted rudely— never overflowed its banks, flooded houses, carried off people and cows and feather beds and chickens, as did the Tiber River in Rome, where she was born. There were many vessels on the Brenta today—*burci* loaded with produce; *burchielli* filled with nobles on their way to their villas; boys in fishing boats, poles upraised. But there was no sign of Foscari's lean figure in the bow of a vessel, his face turned into the breeze, his eyes impatient for the sight of her. What in God's name was keeping him?

As Cesca stirred the poultice she was concocting for Foscari—he suffered from gout—she kept her face close to the window. It was always best to keep busy. Idleness left time for worry. Activity would take her mind off what might have happened in Venice. Foscari had been certain the judge would grant the order, but how could one be sure of anything in this world?

A number of luxurious *burchielli* drifted by, looking like grand floating rooms. The wealthy—she would soon number among them—travelled in barges overloaded with the furnishings for their villas during the spring and summer. In autumn they gathered it all up and returned to Venice. Barges filled with tapestries and carpets and tufted sofas, feather beds, ball gowns, wigs, horsehair mattresses and gilded chairs. A bargeman had told Cesca that nobles travelling along the Brenta made a *villeggiatura*, a pleasure, of it by staying in villas along the way, attending parties, meeting old friends.

Just when Cesca had given up hope, a canal boat pulled up to the villa's dock. The captain wrapped the bowline around a mooring cleat on the dock, and Foscari disembarked and started up the untended lawn toward the house. He was favouring his right foot; his gout must be paining him. With a wave of his hand, he bid the stout boatman to carry his four huge valises up the stairs of the portico.

Cesca called to him out the open window. After looking around to see where her voice came from, Foscari limped toward her, his cloak billowing behind him. He had to duck to enter the low-ceilinged kitchen. Then he extended his hands to her so she could tug off his scented gloves— the latest in fashion from Paris—finger by finger, releasing the fragrance of Parma violets. Seeing no dry, uncluttered spot to set down the gloves—the kitchen was filled with cook pots and water casks and sacks of this and that—she handed them back to him. He cradled them in one hand, wary, she assumed, of creasing the fine kid.

She kissed him chastely on both cheeks, eager to hear his news. His silver nose felt warm as it brushed her cheek. He had once told her the tip of his real nose had been sliced off in a duel. But she had long ago discovered he had a perfectly serviceable nose, just that it pleased him to cover it with an engraved masterpiece a silversmith must have charged him dearly for. His silver nose was one of his many affectations. It amused her that smiling made the nose ride up on his face.

When she dropped her arms and stepped back, his face gave her no clue how matters had gone in court. "What a pleasure to see you," she said. "I am flattered. This must be the first time in your life you have ever been in a kitchen." How tall Foscari was—in the way all nobles were—thin limbed, loose jointed and confident; the top of Cesca's head barely grazed his shoulder. The poor were never tall. How could a body grow to any height on stale bread, beans and pork scrapple?

"So lovely to see you, my dove." He watched as she turned back to stir the brackish mixture before it burned. He swept off his hat—an elegant affair of red felt and pheasant feathers, with three corners and a wide brim— then ran a finger along the back of her neck.

"You have never looked more beautiful, Cesca. Look at

the colour in your cheeks! How well you have adjusted to country life. All the cream and fresh sausage these *contadini* make so admirably has rounded out your figure."

She faced him. "Bah!" The comment annoyed her. "Anyone can see my dress hangs on me, that the bodice is slack from all the flesh I have lost."

"Think of the future," he went on, as though she had not spoken. "What a life of luxury is ahead of you. Soon you, like the ancient Sybarites, will stuff your mattress with rose petals." He laughed and gave her a pat on the bottom. "Just imagine! You will someday own this villa designed by Palladio, the same genius who designed the church of Il Redentore."

"*Molto gentile,* Foscari, thank you. I am glad to see you, too." *Just tell me now—good news or bad?* "And you? How did you fare in Venice?" she inquired. *Never mind the well-chosen phrases,* parola guista, *the gracefully constructed sentences. Just spit it out!*

"I cannot seem to adapt to the malodorous air of Venice. I felt perpetually ill. I walked around with a handkerchief held to my nose. The city necessitated several variations to my health regime. I found an apothecary who is gifted in compounding various tisanes, elixirs and infusions. I tried them all." He made a face and pursed his lips. "Some of them very nasty, indeed."

"Do they help?" Cesca was also skilled at compounding. She had learned from her mother, who was adept at ridding the district of unwanted curs and rats.

He shrugged and tapped her playfully on the cheek with his gloves. "Who can say?"

Cesca smiled up at him, which he took as an invitation to place both hands on her waist, undaunted by the evil, pungent smell of linseed oil. Evidently the slender column of her neck was sufficiently alluring for him to overcome his usual fussiness.

"I must devote a great deal of time to looking after myself. Some men in my position have trading ventures. I have my health regime."

At any other time Foscari's remark would have amused her. Now she gave a sigh of impatience. "What do you think of my villa? When I finish heating your poultice, I shall give you a tour."

"I saw enough, walking from the canal to the house, to know that it is a morass of neglect. No wonder the mayor was delighted to find someone to occupy the place and keep out the vandals."

"But you must see the stables and the pastures and—"

"I do not need to eat an entire egg to know it is rotten." He nibbled at her nape. "It would be quite impossible for someone of my sensibilities to live here."

"I am sorry to hear you say that." What a relief. Brief visits were fine, even the occasional grappling in bed was tolerable. Anything longer than a few days would be trying.

She did wish the villa and grounds were in tidier condition, but she had been so preoccupied with feeding herself and Matteo since they arrived two months ago. She and the boy spent a great deal of time foraging in the countryside for berries, roots, an unlucky hen and, once, a rabbit in someone's snare. There were doves from the dovecote and carp from the canal, but without a few ducats, God help her when winter descended. "Be of good cheer, Foscari. You will feel better once you have rested from your trip."

"And such an ordeal it was! Three entire days on a leaky boat."

"Poor darling." Cesca arched one eyebrow in a way she knew Foscari envied. She had caught him once, practising in a looking glass. But in truth, although she knew herself to be a good actress, sustaining this role of enchantress was difficult when the issue she wanted to talk about was so pressing. If she insisted, Foscari would brush her off with a phrase like "All in good time." Then he would punish her by making her wait even longer.

Cesca said, "I found it a delightful and relaxing trip, with nothing to do but trail my hand in the water and gaze at the charming sights on both banks of the canal—well-tended villas, grazing cattle, robust gleaners merrily scything the fields. But you are so sensitive and in such delicate health. You could hardly appreciate such things."

He smiled at her and ran his finger along the ridge of her nose. "Never mind whatever you are stirring in that pot. Make us some tea and then come to the garden." He started to leave then paused mid-step. "And Matteo? He is well?"

"Healthy as a tick, may the Virgin be blessed. He is napping in his room."

Foscari hobbled to the portico and down the stairs to the garden behind the villa.

"I shall be out in a moment with our tea and bread and butter," she called out from the kitchen. The bread had been left to cool by a careless farmer's wife on her kitchen window, there for the taking, along with a crock of butter.

Cesca hunted about the summer kitchen until she came across an elaborate teapot in a back cupboard that must have been original to the house, but of course no precious tea. She picked a handful of lemon balm she found growing in an overgrown kitchen garden near the back door and steeped it in boiling water. Then she arranged the pot and a couple of cracked mugs on a tray and walked out to the nyphaneum to meet Foscari. He was perched on the low balustrade of the pool, shifting his weight from buttock to buttock. There being nowhere else to sit, she set the tray beside him and arranged herself cross-legged on the ground facing him.

He studied the pot—the spout was shaped like a dragon's mouth, the handle its tail—as though trying to puzzle out how on earth the steaming liquid could be persuaded to emerge and fill their mugs. He reached toward the spout as if to grasp it. Before he could scald his hand, Cesca seized the pot by its handle, her fingers protected with a cloth. "Allow me," she said, and poured him a cup. "Have some bread and butter." She passed him the plate, watching him help himself to a piece, slather it liberally with butter, then chew, his jaw swinging sideways like a goat's.

"You have grown attached to the boy," he said between bites.

Foscari's words were so unexpected, uttered so seriously, without his usual bantering tone, that she startled. "*Perché no?* Of course I am. Fond as I would be of a lap dog or a prize lamb to be slaughtered in the autumn."

"You pretend to be impatient with me," he said, "and my little illnesses, but it gives you an opportunity to fuss and carry on about me—or rather it did before you became so infatuated with that child."

"You make 'that child' sound like a heavy object dropped on a hard floor." She took a sip of the lemon balm. "Let us not quarrel. There is room in my heart for both of you."

The truth was Matteo detested Foscari with all the ferocious energy of a five-year-old. He blamed the Marquis for taking him from Hannah and Isaac. He hated him for sometimes making Cesca cry.

Cesca was about to run her finger down Foscari's nose, but feared dislodging it because then would follow the elaborate regluing Foscari was compelled to go through to keep it in place. Instead she squeezed his thigh. "Am I not cooking up a hideous brew to relieve your gout?"

All this chatter was getting on her nerves. She could stand it no more. "Tell me how your petition was received in court."

Foscari picked up his hat, which he had brought with him from the kitchen, and pinched a pheasant feather between his fingers. "I appeared before Judge Abarbanel, a man I know slightly—he is married to the daughter of an old friend. I explained to him I am first cousin to Matteo's late father, the Conte di Padovani."

Perhaps it was true. Were not all noble families related either by blood or marriage?

"I assumed the order appointing me guardian would be granted readily. What more was required? A child in need of a guardian and here was I—a respectable, trustworthy relative, albeit a distant one—willing to assume the task. The judge proved obstinate. Although I explained the case to him, attested to my relationship to the Conte, and showed him the child's christening blanket, do you know what he said?"

The blanket with the di Padovani crest worked in gold thread was Matteo's favourite. He had sobbed when Foscari seized it from him during their voyage.

Foscari flicked the tip of the feather back and forth across his chin, gazing at the ground in remembered humiliation. "He said the evidence was sorely lacking. His very words, 'sorely lacking'! What more had I, he demanded in the most peremptory way, than a ragged blanket with the family crest on it?"

Cesca listened with a growing sense of apprehension.

"'That threadbare scrap could be a lucky find from a rag picker's handcart,' the judge added. Calling me a liar, in other words. As for Matteo, the judge asked, why this miraculous appearance after so many years? Where on earth had he been hiding? When I explained that the midwife who had attended his birth had been raising him, he demanded to know why she was not present to testify. The judge said, 'She must explain to the court why she took him. Without her testimony there is no case.'"

Foscari did not meet Cesca's eye.

"I replied, 'But she is a Jew, my lord.' And he replied, 'Yes, it is unusual to accept evidence from Hebrews, but I can make an exception.'" Foscari cleared his throat. "I explained that she had kidnapped Matteo, a Christian, spirited him off to Constantinople, and had been raising him as a Jew until I rescued him, the poor mite. Why would you want to hear testimony from such a rogue of a woman, I asked the judge?"

How drawn Foscari suddenly looked, how rounded his shoulders, how sallow his complexion.

"I told the judge, 'The midwife has violated God's laws as well as the laws of the Venetian Republic. She will not come to Venice knowing she will be arrested.'"

Foscari got to his feet and began to pace—if his halting gait could be termed pacing. "Instead of congratulating me for saving the boy's immortal soul, the judge said, 'That is a problem you must deal with. The midwife must identify the boy as the child the Contessa gave birth to. She must explain to this court where the boy has been all these years and why she has not claimed the di Padovani fortune on his behalf. I should tell you, sir'—he called me 'sir' as though I was nothing more than a tradesman—'they say the heir to the di Padovani fortune perished along with his parents in the plague of 1575. You know how servants gossip. A di Padovani servant is married to one of my footmen. Now you claim the boy is alive. I cannot take your word alone.'" Foscari grew very red in the face. "'You have a heavy evidentiary burden before you, sir,' said the judge. 'I suggest you get on with it.'"

Cesca wanted to clap her hands over her ears. It was as though Foscari was relating the details of a tragic shipwreck.

"I replied, 'May I at least write the midwife, Hannah Levi, that if she comes to testify, she will not be arrested for raising this boy as a Jew?' 'You may not,' the judge replied. 'I shall make that decision once I have heard what she has to say for herself.'" Foscari mopped his forehead. "And then he said the most hurtful thing of all. 'This midwife must identify the child. You, sir, might pluck any child off the streets and then, like a conjurer pulling a rabbit out of a hat, shout, "Whoosh! Here is the boy."' The judge snapped his fingers. 'No, sir, I knew the Conte and the Contessa. Out of respect for their memory, I insist on the strictest proof that the child is who you claim. I won't have any tricks in my courtroom. You find that midwife, Jew or gentile. Bring her before me. Without her, I shall not make your order.' Then he slammed his record book closed."

Could Foscari have foreseen any of this? Was something missing from his account? What had he done to make such an unfavourable impression on the judge? But Cesca could raise none of these questions without sounding as though she was making an accusation. "And if you cannot produce Hannah?" Cesca asked.

"This is the worst part. The judge said, 'If you fail to find this midwife, then I have no choice but to allow the di Padovani estate to pass to the residuary legatee, the Monasterio San Francisco de Rosas. They commenced a claim on the estate some time ago. Their advocates will summon the family servant—Giovanna, I believe her name is—to testify she last saw the boy covered with buboes and lesions, more dead than alive in the arms of the midwife. Most unlikely, sir, that an infant could recover from the plague, would you not agree?'" Foscari looked down at his boots. "It was mortifying, my dove. I have never felt such a fool."

"But Hannah will not—"

"We have two steps to take. The first is to present Matteo to the judge, which is easy enough. The second is the hurdle. How to persuade Hannah to come to Venice?" Foscari drew a brandy flask from his pocket and poured a healthy dollop into his tea. Cesca had never seen him so agitated. His mouth was tight, a line of white around it. His eyes had lost their customary confident lustre.

"Of what possible use is the testimony of a five-year-old boy?" Cesca said.

"Exactly what I asked Judge Abarbanel. He replied, 'The boy can identify his blanket. All children can do as much. They are as attached to their blankets as men are to mistresses.'" Foscari gave an unpleasant laugh. "And then he said, 'I must see the boy with my own eyes. I knew his mother, the Contessa Lucia. Perhaps the boy inherited her flaming red hair.'"

"To which you replied?"

Foscari had anticipated the di Padovani fortune would fall into his lap like an apple from a tree. Had he tried to answer the judge's objections or had he just stood there saying nothing? No, she was sure he had spoken eloquently. He was adroit with words, quick with a classical quote or a line of Greek poetry.

"'Red as a winter apple,' I replied. Then the judge bashed on as though I had not spoken. 'I met the Contessa years ago—a remarkably beautiful woman. I might recognize her features in her son.' Then he signalled the bailiff to call the next case." Foscari straightened his nose with such force she was afraid it would leave his face. "Utter rubbish. I resembled neither of my parents. What about you? I suspect you cannot answer because you don't know who your father was."

Foscari could be wounding, but she was developing some quick-wittedness herself. "From whom else would I have acquired my good looks and gracious demeanour?"

He had the good grace to smile. "I do not mind confiding, my dear, that I am discouraged. If the estate were not so vast—the palazzo, the two brigantines, this villa, the thousands of ducats in the Fugger bank in Augsburg—I would depart the field of battle and let the monks prevail—"

"Stop! We are not defeated yet."

"And God bless them. But what is to be done?"

Cesca willed herself to smile and tilt her head in a becoming way. "I know how to persuade Hannah and I shall do so, but in the meantime I need money to run the villa. I have to hire servants and buy provisions for the winter."

"What makes you think I have anything to give you?"

"I am poor, Foscari. I have always been poor. I do not require you and your silver nose to be poor. I can be poor all by myself." Cesca's voice rose. "If you wish me to continue as your partner—" she held up a hand to stop him from interrupting "—yes, *partner*, you must give me some money. So far, I have nothing to show for my unceasing labour but an aching back and unbecoming muscles in my arms."

Foscari began to walk around the garden. He was wearing a new pair of breeches tailored to make his buttocks look less like empty flour sacks and more like the ripe haunches of a young man.

"Credit, my dove," said Foscari. "Convince the local tradesmen to extend you credit." But he reached into the purse around his waist and fished out a few small coins, which he placed in her outstretched palm.

"This is not enough to keep the wolf from my door." But she closed her fingers around them.

"Now," Foscari said, "fetch me pen and paper. I shall write Hannah."

"Leave the letter to me," said Cesca. "I know what to say. The priest will pen it for me."

I have already left too much in your hands, Foscari. If Hannah must be part of our scheme, so be it. She is easy to outfox. It is you, Foscari, who worries me.

CHAPTER 4

*Port of Eminönü,
Constantinople*

SISTER ASSUNTA STOMPED into the bedchamber, wearing only her billowing black robe. Without her wimple, she was an alarming sight. Bunches of cropped brown hair framed her broad face, bringing to mind the clumps of wool that dangled from the hind end of a ewe. With her hands on her wide hips, she announced, "There is no help for it, my girl. Pregnant or not, it is laundry day. Zephra is ill. The other servants are busy in the silk workshop. May God be thanked, there are silk orders to fill. Isaac claims he doesn't need my assistance. With your help, I will see to the washing."

The nun had been living with them for seven long weeks,

performing chores Hannah could not muster the will to do. Assunta had been a tremendous help, which made Hannah feel obligated to like her. So far she had not succeeded.

Hannah rolled over, trying to ignore the imposing figure looming above her in a flour-streaked apron, the smell of wood smoke on her robes. Assunta tugged the coverlet off. The state of the house was appalling. Dirty linen over-flowed in rush baskets lining the hallway. Isaac had not had a clean shirt in days. The underarms of all Hannah's dresses bore perspiration rings. The bodices of her cotton dresses were stained with baby pap, which she had been feeding to Jessica, the daughter of Leah, a young slave girl from the Sultan's harem who had died in childbirth. Hannah had regretted naming the baby Jessica because the name was coupled with the memory of her sister, Jessica, who had died so violently in Hannah's arms. How long it had taken her and Isaac to cease calling the child *zisele*, sweetie, or *ketzele*, kitten, and start thinking of her not as the ghost of Jessica but as a person in her own right.

Hannah and Isaac had adopted Jessica and were raising her as their daughter. Now there were only two clean nap-pies left for the infant.

"There is not a scrap of soap the size of a baby's finger-nail anywhere to be found," said Assunta.

If Hannah did not rise promptly, Assunta would drag her from bed to make soap, a chore Hannah approached with dread each autumn when, at the height of slaughter-ing season, there was plenty of rendered, pure white kidney fat to be had from the butchers.

Barefoot—Assunta detested shoes and wore them as seldom as possible—she hovered while Hannah removed her shift. "The job is half finished. I prepared the lye. You shall deal with the rest."

Just the type of remark to provoke Hannah, as Assunta well knew. For Hannah, a half-finished job was an abomination. To her, action and deed were as twins, hands linked, floating in the same womb. Hannah's mother had been a non-completer of chores and as a child Hannah vowed not to follow in her footsteps. The house of Hannah's childhood had been strewn with knitted sweaters missing one sleeve; sheets covered with embroidered roses missing their petals; one little brother dressed only in a shirt, another only in a pair of breeches. Half-cooked vegetables languished over a fire smouldering for lack of kindling. Her mother had died in childbirth when Jessica, Hannah's sister, was half emerged from her womb, leaving the midwife to wrap a cloth around the baby's head and tug her the rest of the way.

"Give me a moment," said Hannah, glancing at Assunta's feet, which were planted on the floor in front of her. The feet both fascinated and repelled Hannah. Still bearing pink striations from the seams of Assunta's leather boots, they were long and wide. Standing on such feet must be like standing on a platform. How comforting to be the owner of such substantial feet.

When Hannah finished washing her face, she brushed her hair into a neat coil at the back of her neck, dressed and padded downstairs after Assunta. The nun watched critically as Hannah poured the lye water from the bucket into the fat and stirred the mixture with a long-handled paddle. Hannah stood well back as the mixture heated and fumes rose.

"Faster—the soap will not thicken without hard stirring." Assunta wrested the paddle from Hannah and commenced a violent motion, which soon had the ground around the cauldron ringed in a greasy mess. "Soap making is a perversely satisfying task, is it not? Just imagine! From two repellent things—grease and lye—we make something pleasant and useful." She chuckled, pleased with her observation.

Assunta was right. It was no good lying in bed feeling sorry for herself. The sight of several pounds of soap cut into rectangles would give Hannah a feeling of accomplishment. The servants could have performed the task, but they were busy unreeling silk cocoons, and besides, they would not take care to get the correct proportions of fat and lye.

Hannah wiped a trickle of sweat from her face and stretched forward, a hand on the small of her aching back, to reclaim the paddle. "Calmness, Assunta. Watch me. Do it like this." Hannah stirred, trying not to splatter the caustic grease onto her hands. Her skirts were already full of holes burned by the harsh liquid. She waited for the emulsion to come to trace. To test it, she dribbled Matteo's name to see if it would form a pattern on the surface. The letters held their shape. This was a hopeful portent. Hannah often worried whether her mourning over the loss of Matteo was affecting her unborn child. She would take the neat letters as a sign her baby was healthy.

Not only had Matteo vanished last year—Cesca and Foscari, she was certain it was them, had come back for him—but within a few weeks of his first disappearance, Hannah had suffered a miscarriage.

One rainy night the infant had ripped its way out—tearing and slithering and leaving a snail trail of bloody mucus behind. The pain had been almost unendurable—not the physical agony, which had been bad enough, but the pain of losing a child she had carried for three months. When the spasms subsided, Isaac buried the contents of the basin in the garden under a mulberry tree.

Throughout the gut-wrenching ordeal Hannah knew with certainty she had herself to blame for both misfortunes. If she had been paying better attention, Cesca and Foscari would never have been able to snatch Matteo. The grief and guilt she felt as a consequence had smothered the tender life growing within her; it had withered and died.

Isaac tried to persuade her to have hope. For the first time since her marriage, he pointed out, she had conceived a child, proving her body was receptive to his seed. Heartened by his words, as soon as she felt ready, Hannah encouraged Isaac to make love to her. Now she was, with God's punishment behind her, once again pregnant.

In order to enjoy warmth, one must feel cold; in order to enjoy food, one must know hunger; and in order to cherish the sensation of a baby stirring under one's heart, one must have known loss of a child who grew hardly big enough to make its presence known. This new infant nestled inside her, not restive, not impatient to be born. This baby curled up in her matrix, unfurling gently, reaching out like the bud of a rose seeking the light. And when he—Isaac spoke of the baby as a boy—emerged, he would be as brilliant as the sun.

Since this pregnancy, Isaac had changed as well. It was not her imagination: his belly was rounder, his cheeks fuller. It suited him. He had always been too lean. Although he still had dark smudges under his eyes and muttered and tossed in his sleep, he seemed less sorrowful. He ate with pleasure and did not avoid the company of their neighbours who had a son the same age as Matteo.

Hannah poured the hot soap into wooden moulds. When it was cool, she took up a wide-bladed knife and, with the blunt side of it, scored the soap into white rectangles, precise as coffins lined up in a coffin maker's workshop.

Just as she was covering the bars with a tattered blanket to retain the heat, the front doorbell rang. One of the maids answered. A young boy with a wind-scoured look to his cheeks came into the garden. The maid followed close behind him, wiping up his dirty footprints with a mop. By the marlin spike dangling from his waist and the way he eyed Zephra's loaves of bread cooling on the rack on the kitchen window ledge, it was clear the boy was from the docks, just off a ship—a Venetian ship, to be sure, for he wore a cap with a crudely embroidered lion of Venice.

In the boy's hand was a letter. "Greetings," he said. "Are you the mistress of the house?" When Hannah nodded, he walked over to her, holding it out—a grubby-looking affair of sheep's parchment, the edges bound together with a piece of rawhide. Likely it had been laced and unlaced countless times by greedy fingers probing the corners for a coin as it made its way by whatever route it had travelled to Constantinople.

Hannah wanted to grab the letter from his hands, hoping it contained news of Matteo. She forced herself to be calm. What a foolish thought. Cesca and Foscari would never wish her to know where Matteo was, never wish her to have the comfort of knowing if he was dead or alive. No, it was, no doubt, a letter for Isaac from Leghorn or some such city. An offer of a new variety of silkworms, perhaps, or a shipment of printed cotton from Bellagio. It might be an order for silk from Venice or a bill of lading for a recent shipment.

Assunta marched over to the boy. Hannah seized the letter from him before Assunta could reach for it. Hannah pressed it to her breast, trying to divine its contents.

After what seemed like an eternity but was likely a few minutes, Hannah heard the rear door open and then close. Isaac, back from the palace, made his way into the garden. Without a word, Hannah held the letter out to him. Isaac handed the boy a coin for his trouble and sent him to the kitchen for a bowl of soup. Isaac turned the envelope over, studying the crossing-outs, the blots, the smudges. Isaac could read anything—no word was too obscure, no script too difficult for him to decipher. He squinted at the envelope.

Please, God, may the letter say Matteo is well and happy, and that I must come and fetch him. She allowed herself to imagine Matteo sitting at his customary place at the breakfast table, spooning in his barley soup, great, sticky globs of it falling on the floor for the cat to lick up; or practising on his tightrope in the back garden, barefoot, stubby toes gripping the rope, hands holding the balance pole parallel to his chest.

Hannah peered over Isaac's shoulder to see their shakily written address covered with blots of ink and spotted with greasy drips from a candle. "A letter from an associate?" Hannah asked. The parchment was of that peculiar Venetian variety, fashioned from the hide of fat-tailed sheep, the pores so big the script was forced to detour around them like an ox cart avoiding holes and ruts in the road.

"It is palimpsest," he said in the lecturing tone he sometimes affected to tease her when she was tense.

Isaac's jesting was his way of saying, 'Do not hope, my darling, for what can never be. Matteo is not coming back to us no matter how fiercely we wish it. Think of Jessica and our new child and be content. Hope makes our lives more difficult.'

"Please, Isaac, open it." Even the best of husbands could be provoking.

He unlaced the strips of rawhide binding it fast. As he turned the envelope upside down, a sketch fell to the floor. Hannah bent over and snatched it up. It was a simple charcoal drawing of a little boy wearing a hat and a jacket, sitting astride a fat pony. Next to him, holding the bridle, stood a curly-haired woman. Hannah took a deep gulp of air. It felt like the first time she had taken a proper breath since Matteo disappeared.

Isaac took the drawing from her, glanced at it, and all the humour drained from his face. He handed it back, saying nothing. Smoothing open the letter, he studied it then looked up. "It is from that daughter of a whore," he said. "Cesca—or Grazia, as she called herself here in Constantinople when she had pretended to be my sister-in-law. Written, it would appear, by a scribe without much regard for the niceties of ox gall ink and fresh parchment."

Hannah clenched her hands so tightly her nails left crescents in her palms. But her fury was mixed with relief. Her son might be alive. Isaac, his handsome face intent, pondered the letter. The script had a mean-spirited look to it, uneven, extending to the very edge of the parchment, not leaving enough of a margin to thrust a pin through without landing in the middle of a letter.

"The writing is so tiny I need a jeweller's loupe," said Isaac.

"Take it into the garden, where the light is better," said Assunta.

The three of them walked into the garden and sat under the grape arbour.

Isaac studied the letter, Hannah sitting close to him. She would have grabbed it from him if she could read, but although she could sign her name—more than most women could manage—and, after a fashion, could add and subtract—she could not read.

Isaac stood and walked a few paces past the row of vegetables, into a patch of sunlight. Hannah and Assunta trailed behind. He held the letter with his back to the sun, the better to see. He began:

4 September 1579

Dear Hannah,
You must have apprehended by now that Foscari and I took
Matteo from you that day in the market. You have no reason to
love me, but believe me when I say I am deeply troubled I have
injured you so grievously. I thought I was doing my duty by
bringing him to Venice to raise him as a Christian, but I fear I
have done both you and Matteo, who cries for you piteously, a
terrible wrong.

I wish I could write Matteo is thriving, but he is not. The
doctors say he has consumption and only a few weeks to live. I
know you will want to say goodbye to him before God, in His
wisdom, gathers him to His bosom.

I beg you, board the next ship to Venice. Matteo and I are
living in the Villa di Padovani on the Brenta River. All the
boatmen know the estate. The mooring posts are yellow and red.
Two orange trees grow on the front lawn.

Please come for Matteo's sake, whom we both cherish.
Godspeed,
Cesca

Matteo was alive! Sick, yes, but alive—or he had been
when the letter was written. Hannah could nurse him back
to health. She would pour her strength into him. Under
her care, he would survive. "The letter is dated more than
six weeks ago," said Isaac. Hannah put her arms around
Isaac, resting her head on his chest, and held him close, so
close she could feel his heat on her neck and his heart

beating in unison with hers. "We must go to him, Isaac. There is time. The baby will not come before the spring."

Isaac stood, the letter in one hand, his other arm around Hannah.

"For the first time we know where he is."

He pulled her to his chest, resting his chin on the top of her head. She felt his chin move side to side. A firm no.

"Please, Isaac, we must be together—you, me, Matteo and Jessica. We are like a collection of precious porcelain dishes. Leave one behind and always there will be an empty place at the table where the plate should be."

"God has once again planted a child in you, a hearty one, who clings to you like a spider monkey to its mother's back."

He did not articulate what they were both thinking: you have miscarried. You must not risk this baby. God may not smile upon us again.

He said, "Stormy seas prevail this time of year. There will be no ships sailing this late in the season."

"We will go to the port. We will find a ship. By next week we can be sailing to Venice."

"Stop and think, Hannah. Cesca has lied to us about so many things. How do you know she is not lying about Matteo?"

"Not even Cesca would be so cruel," said Hannah.

Isaac gave a snort. "She would grind Matteo's bones to make her bread."

"Then isn't her cruelty one more reason to rescue Matteo? Don't you see? We can bring him home. We shall be like the family we used to be."

"Oh, Hannah." There was a terrible tenderness in his voice that made her sadder than anything he could have said. Her husband often scolded her for her innocence. There were those in the world, he would explain, who appeared like other people, who talked, laughed, ate and slept like normal men and women, yet had no fear of God, no love or respect for their fellow humans. Isaac contended that Foscari was such a man, a beast who had learned to walk upright.

"Do you not realize the true purpose of this letter?" said Isaac.

"No, I do not."

"We have spoken of Cesca and Foscari many times and you have seen firsthand what they are capable of, but still you cannot believe in their wickedness."

"I do not understand why they want to deprive Matteo of the only mother and father he has ever known. Is it to raise him as a Christian? Is it because we are Jews?"

"Foscari and Cesca would not care a fig if wolves were raising Matteo, the way wolves raised Romulus and Remus. They wish to steal his fortune."

"But how does one steal a villa, a palazzo and trading vessels by kidnapping an innocent child?"

"To steal with a pen is more deadly than to steal with a sword. They will find a way to plunder his fortune, no doubt, with the help of a complicit judge. Foscari must have some scheme to convince a court to appoint him guardian of the di Padovani estate."

"But suppose Matteo *is* ill?"

"I would wager he is in perfect health." Isaac spoke in a

warm, coaxing tone. "Be sensible, Hannah. Do not let them be in command of you as though you were a puppet and they were your puppet masters."

"Please, Isaac." But she knew it was useless to argue. Once Isaac had set his mind against an idea there was no convincing him otherwise. She might as well try to persuade the kindling in the fireplace to ignite of its own accord, or the cook pot to recite poetry.

"I know Jessica needs me here, and you need me here, but . . . God entrusted Matteo to me. I saved his life at birth. I saved him from his uncle, who wanted to murder him. I saved him from starvation on the ship sailing here. Once you save a life you are responsible for that life."

"And me," Isaac said, "you saved me, as well."

"And do we not have a special bond of love between us that can never be broken? Years of living and working together have made us like a pair of dancers, with an instinctive knowledge of the other's needs and rhythms."

She went over to the rain barrel in the corner of the garden and filled a mug. Her reflection stared back at her, her dark curly hair falling forward around her face, fuller now with her pregnancy. She thought about Matteo, about his blue eyes, his red hair, his arms around her neck like a rope of precious pearls. "If I do not go, I will never be at peace." She held up the mug for Isaac to take a drink. "I would do the same for you, Isaac, if you were ill in a faraway country."

"This is what I love most about you, Hannah—your steadfast heart." He smiled to take the sting out of his next words. "It is also what most exasperates me about you."

She slammed down the mug on a rock next to the arbour with such force it shattered to the ground. "And you, Isaac? Do you know what exasperates me most about you? Your stubbornness. Your bloody-mindedness. Your refusal to compromise." This was the first time they had argued since Matteo's disappearance. For the past months they had tiptoed around each other, each treating the other like a fragile vase balanced on a narrow ledge. To shout at him, to unleash her anger, brought a peculiar relief. There was a chilly comfort in speaking her mind, though she knew she would later regret it. Arguing was tacit recognition they were both stronger now and could withstand each other's fury.

Assunta tried to draw Hannah out of the garden and back to the kitchen. "Let us see to the soap, Hannah. It is time to put it in the sun to dry."

"Damn the soap. Damn Isaac and damn you!" She kicked at the shards of broken cup. "I will go alone to Venice."

"I forbid you," said Isaac.

"Are you mad?" Assunta said. "A woman travelling alone?" She tried to take Hannah in her arms. "Do not fret so. Our Lord Jesus is watching over Matteo."

Hannah said, "Did not your Jesus preach that if you have a hundred sheep and have lost one, you must leave the remaining ninety-nine and go into the wilderness to seek out the one that is lost? And when you have found it, return home, bearing it on your shoulders, rejoicing?"

For once Assunta was silent.

Isaac followed the two women into the kitchen. "Hannah,

let us not quarrel." He tried to take her hand, but she wrenched it away.

That night Hannah tossed and turned, unable to sleep as she replayed the quarrel. Isaac had not mentioned, because he did not know, the most important reason she must not make the journey. Hannah had killed a man in Venice. Walking up the gangplank onto a ship bound for Venice would be like walking up the steps of a scaffold to be hanged.

CHAPTER 5

On board the Fortuna,
Mediterranean Sea

H ANNAH LEFT LIKE a thief in the night. While Isaac slept, she arose early, eager to be off before her resolve deserted her. She looked in on the nursery, where baby Jessica slept in the arms of the wet nurse. The infant would survive under Isaac's watchful eye and the wet nurse's rich milk.

Very softly, so as not to waken her, Hannah kissed the top of Jessica's head. Hannah owed a great debt to this child, born in the Circassian Mountains to a mother captured in a raid by a Yürük nomad and sold to the Sultan as a concubine. After many years of being barren, Hannah had conceived because of Jessica, of this she was certain.

The batting at her breast, the tender gaze in Jessica's green eyes, the little girl's sweet baby scent, had persuaded Hannah's womb to welcome Isaac's seed. Hannah ran a finger down Jessica's cheek, a new surge of love and gratitude overwhelming her. She would miss this baby girl who had been such an unexpected gift.

With all her heart Hannah wished she had been able to make peace with Isaac. They had argued until late in the night. Finally, hearing the anger in both their voices, Assunta had drawn Hannah aside and said resignedly, "I shall accompany you as far as Malta. It is time I returned to my convent. I know of a late-sailing ship, the *Fortuna*. She was delayed in port for repairs. Tomorrow she leaves for the Veneto. Have you money enough for the voyage and your stay in Venice?"

Hannah had told no one, not even Isaac, about the loose floorboard in their bedroom under which she had stashed coins—twenty hard-earned ducats and a few dozen silver coins, working as midwife in the Sultan's harem.

If only Isaac could walk her to the docks, kiss her goodbye and give her his blessing. She returned to the bedroom one last time and brushed his cheek as he slept, then she went to find Assunta.

Sister Assunta heaved the valise Hannah had packed hurriedly and her own onto her back and off she marched to the Port of Eminönü, Hannah trailing behind. To Hannah's surprise the captain of the *Fortuna*, a brigantine out of Brindisi, consented to take them on as passengers. If he thought two women travelling alone was unusual, he showed no sign of it; he barely glanced up at them, his eyes riveted on the six ducats Hannah placed in front of him. They hastened to their cabin, no bigger than a miser's larder, left their valises and returned to the deck. There they stood watching as Kiz Kulesi, the Maiden's Tower, the lead-clad domes of the Imperial Palace, and the minarets of Hagia Sophia grew smaller and smaller in the distance. When the land fell from sight, Hannah and Assunta went shivering and windblown down to their cabin. Innne was light. It was far too late in the season to be sailing; the winds were cold and unforgiving.

While Sister Assunta prepared a pot of tea on a brazier in the cabin, Hannah lay under a quilt in her berth, averting her eyes, feeling nauseous as the wooden crucifix dangling from Assunta's waist swayed in time with the pitching ship. What would Isaac think when he woke up and found her gone? He would be furious, of course, but would he understand? Would he follow her on the next ship if he could find one?

Assunta handed her a mug of tea. "Where will you stay in Venice?" Hannah had been too preoccupied with getting to the docks and finding the *Fortuna* to reflect on that. The Council of Ten, the governing body of Venice, did not permit Jews to reside—even for short periods—outside the Jewish ghetto. Her only remaining relative in the ghetto was her brother, Asher, and theirs was a troubled relationship. Showing up unannounced and asking for shelter even for a few days was nothing short of risky. And yet, she must. She had no other place to go.

"With my brother, I hope."

"You will need kinfolk at a time like this. How fortunate you have family to help you."

"It will not be as easy as you suppose. Years ago Asher and I quarrelled."

"About what?"

"Nothing of significance. We Jews are a fractious people," said Hannah, forcing a light note into her voice, hoping it would be enough to satisfy Assunta's curiosity. In an effort to further divert her, Hannah said, "Shall I fetch a small cask of fresh water for washing from one of the sailors or will you?"

"Christians, Jews, it makes no difference. To be human is to be fractious. What was the fight about?"

Assunta could be as relentless as a magistrate. Hannah knew from experience that the nun would give her no peace until she had divulged the whole unhappy story.

"It shames me to tell you, Assunta. After our father of blessed memory died, Asher, who had once been my favourite brother, sent me a letter accusing me of stealing Papa's violin. It was a beautiful instrument made of cherry wood by a violin maker in Cremona, with a fine horsehair bow. When we were children, Papa played it at night at the foot of our beds to coax us to sleep." Hannah thought she had put her resentment about Asher's false accusation behind her, but she felt it rising in her again as she recounted the wretched details.

"Go on."

"With Isaac's help, I wrote a letter denying any wrongdoing. Asher sent another letter, refusing to believe me, calling me a liar as well as a thief. No amount of reasoning could convince him I was innocent."

"So your dispute has not been resolved?"

"When I see him, I hope to convince him he was mistaken."

"Perhaps." Assunta looked as doubtful as Hannah felt. "Your brother sounds like an obstinate man."

"All men are obstinate." *Especially my husband. The person dearest to my heart would not give me his blessing to sail for Venice. I may not have a husband when I return to Constantinople. Many wives have received the get, the Jewish divorce document, for less.* "If Asher will have me, I will remain with him for a day or two until I can find a boat to take me to the di Padovani villa, a journey of three days."

"I worry for your safety. A Jewess travelling alone will attract unwanted attention from ruffians and Jew baiters. You know as well as I, Jews are not allowed to travel outside the city limits without permission."

Within the ghetto, dressed as she was—in blue *cioppà* and red head scarf—Hannah would appear as any other Jewish matron. Outside the confines of the tiny island of two thousand souls she would be conspicuous. "But what can be done?"

"If only you could move about as freely as me."

Assunta was lying on her berth, half naked, wearing only a shift. Hannah was amused by the dark tufts under Assunta's arms, as dense as mouse nests.

"You move about freely because you are bigger and stronger than most men."

"True enough, but that is not what I meant. A nun is freer than most women to come and go. Out of respect for our habit, men do not regard us as objects of prey. Even pickpockets and cutpurses leave us alone, assuming rightly we have nothing of value to steal."

"How I envy you, Assunta. Oh, to be a nun! To live in a dusty cell in a convent, praying five times a day, eating nothing but polenta and stale bread donated by a munificent baker. I wish devoutly for such a life." Hannah spoke in jest, but she could tell from Assunta's face that she took the words literally.

"And so you can!"

Assunta gave Hannah a great slap on the back that nearly knocked her off the edge of her berth, where she was sitting.

"You must disguise yourself as a nun." Assunta rummaged in her bag and brought out a length of black gabardine. "Here," she said, handing the cloth to Hannah. "Sew yourself a nun's habit. I was going to make a new robe for myself during the voyage, but you need this more than I. Take my wooden rosary. String this crucifix around your neck." She dropped the articles beside Hannah. "Learn the Pater Noster." Assunta fumbled around in her valise until she found a swatch of white linen. "For the wimple and cornette," she said, passing the swatch to Hannah. "They will protect you from the rudeness of men who have nothing better to do than pester unaccompanied women."

Hannah was so startled at the thought of pretending to be someone else, in particular a nun, that she needed a moment to collect herself. "But is it not a crime to disguise oneself as a nun?"

"What do you care? All you have to do is learn a few prayers and rules of comportment and no one will be the wiser."

"I am with child, or have you forgotten? How can I pass myself off as a nun?"

"By making the robe very full and the veil and wimple very long." She leaned over to whisper in Hannah's ear. "You would not be the first nun to carry a child. They say the convents in Florence are little better than brothels. It is scandalous what those sisters get up to."

Hannah said, "God would never forgive me."

"And if you are caught travelling about Venice and the Veneto without permission? If you are discovered to have raised a Christian child as a Jew?"

"The idea of such a disguise is grotesque."

"No, the sight of you swinging from a rope would be grotesque." Assunta gave Hannah a shake. "You are a Jew regardless of whether you have a rosary and crucifix swishing at your waist. God knows what is in your heart. Is not being a Jew more than just wearing a . . . what do you call the men's prayer shawl?"

"*Tallit.*"

"And those little black boxes containing the Scripture?"

"Phylacteries."

Assunta sat down next to Hannah on her berth, which groaned under her weight. "Am I not right?"

"Outward manifestations demonstrate inner faith." How pompous Hannah sounded to herself.

Assunta said, "It is to find your son. Can't you pretend for his sake? God knows you are a Jew. You know you are a Jew. Other Jews know you are a Jew. What else matters?"

Hannah thought of her role in the world: Jewess, wife, mother. Take away her faith and her entire being would cease to be, like a clock from which a cog has been removed. But in refusing to accept Assunta's advice wasn't Hannah guilty of what she had accused Isaac of: stubbornness?

Hannah smoothed the gabardine over her knees. What harm would there be in at least having a nun's habit in her bag? "Why are you being so generous to me?" It was a blunt question, one Assunta herself might have asked.

"Before your husband washed up on the shores of Malta years ago with his silkworm eggs and his clever ideas, our convent was so poor it seemed we would need to send our Sisters back to their families and shut our doors forever. Now, thanks to Isaac, we have a full workshop, with orders coming from Venice and Leghorn. The Grand Master of Malta orders his robes from us. We twist the silk thread Isaac weaves into tents for the ladies of the Sultan's harem to picnic in. What I am doing for you is little enough compared with what your husband did for my convent."

"But to masquerade as a nun?"

"Hannah, do you remember the story of the Venetian merchants who stole the body of Saint Mark from Alexandria in the year 828 and returned it to Venice? It was a *furta sacra*, a holy theft."

"I would not be much of a Venetian if I did not."

"They abducted his body from the very heart of the mausoleum and placed it aboard a cargo ship bound for Venice. To escape detection by Muslim customs authorities, they concealed Saint Mark's body in a barrel of raw pork."

Hannah shuddered. "Please stop."

"The Muslim inspectors were so repulsed when they lifted the lid and saw the pork that they immediately replaced the lid and waved the merchants on their way."

"But would God forgive me?"

"Is God such a simpleton as to be deceived by a black robe and a wimple?" Assunta said. "My point is, Hannah, sometimes we must do things against our nature to accomplish a higher purpose."

The image of Matteo as she had last seen him came to Hannah: he was trotting through the market, his hand clasped in hers. "I will do as you suggest."

"Good girl." Assunta smiled, which transformed her broad face into one filled with intelligence and character.

"You are kind," Hannah said, unfolding the fabric and shaking out the wrinkles. Hannah reached for the sewing articles in her valise: scissors, needle, thread and thimble. She took up the scissors and with Assunta's help cut out two halves of a simple robe. Before she could change her mind, she picked up the needle, threaded it and began to baste the seams in place. How horrified Isaac—indeed, everyone she knew—would be if they could see her now.

Hannah remained in her cabin day and night, stitching a robe from Assunta's fabric. It was a simple matter to sew, not much different from any long robe. But the wimple? Hannah had no clear idea how to construct such a headdress. Assunta had little aptitude for sewing. However, demonstrating with her own wimple, she pointed out that it must be high in the front like the prow of a ship and longish in the back to cover the neck.

Hannah had come to admire Assunta, the woman she now shared this cabin with, but how alone she still felt. The swell of the waves and the rocking of the boat, the slamming of her body from one side of her berth to the other, made her nauseous. Isaac would have held her hand, encouraged her to go on deck and stare at the horizon until her stomach grew accustomed to the violent sea, but he was not here. She must fend for herself.

"It is not just a simple matter of sewing a habit, though, Hannah. You must learn to act like a nun," said Assunta a few days later.

"I know. Latin prayers, and standing and bowing, and singing, and prostrating myself before God. There are no doubt a thousand tiny, daily acts of piety that are part of a nun's life. So many opportunities for mistakes. A mispronounced word, a false gesture or remark and I will be exposed as a fraud."

"Let us have a lesson. Put down that needle."

As Hannah pushed her half-sewn habit to the back of the berth, the ship heaved so forcefully she was nearly knocked to the floor. To give herself courage in rough weather, Hannah reminded herself that each swell carried her closer to Matteo.

"I will provoke you as you will be provoked," said Assunta. She thought a moment then said, "You are in the Rialto market to buy a snapper. The fishwife demands an outrageous price. You offer her half of what she asks. She

says, 'You bargain worse than a dirty Jew.' Your response?"
Assunta waited. When Hannah said nothing, Assunta
jabbed her arm.

"You are an ignorant piece of human waste," Hannah
began. "As for your fish, I have seen livelier specimens
floating belly up in the canal, poisoned by the pig tanners'
filth. You are— "

"Do not play the fool."

Hannah laughed. "I would say, 'My convent is a poor one,
dear lady. I can afford three *scudi* and no more.' Then I would
pause a moment, and if she did not accept, I would turn on
my heel and walk away, my eyes meekly fixed on the ground."

"Suppose our fishwife says to you, 'Take pity, Sister. I
have five children to feed and a husband who is bent and
crippled and unable to work.'"

Hannah said, "I would tell her, 'God bless you and your
children. We at the convent work for God's wages and He
is a poor paymaster.'"

"Well put, Hannah. I am proud of you."

Hannah bowed her head, holding her palms together
under her chin as though in prayer. "Thank you, Sister."

"What shall you call yourself?"

"I am Sister Benedicta of the Holy Order of—"

"Say you are from Malta. Few people have been there."

"Saint Ursula of Valletta." This was Assunta's convent.

"A wise choice. Did you know Saint Ursula's breasts
were torn off because she refused to marry the chieftain of
a band of Huns?"

"A woman after my own heart."

"Next lesson. Take up my Book of Hours."

Hannah accepted the prayer book reluctantly, as if the gold tooling on the worn leather cover might scorch her hand.

"Hold it more naturally." Assunta shoved Hannah's hand across her belly as though closing a troublesome gate. "Like that. And now the rosary. Let me fix it around your waist." She tied it fast, with a square knot any sailor on the *Fortuna* would have been proud of.

There was a knock at their cabin door. Hannah opened the door, ready to say *"Shalom Aleichem,"* but caught herself in time. A cabin boy was standing there. In his hands was a plate of something pale, iridescent with fat, glistening with blood. "For you, Sister, for your blessing on me and the ship and our safe voyage."

"Sausage!" Assunta said. "What a timely gift. Thank you, my son. Sister Benedicta, give this boy our blessing."

Hannah made the sign of the cross then kissed her thumb as she had seen Assunta do countless times, but she did not take the plate from the boy, waiting, instead, for Assunta to step forward. Vileness in the form of a sausage—a sausage fashioned of the most odious parts of the swine: eyeballs, lips, intestines, testicles, anus. A feeling of nausea swept over her. She clasped the post of her berth for support.

The boy thrust the plate at Hannah, who had no choice but to accept the meat. She held it as far as possible from her body. Assunta remained seated. Hannah said, "May the Holy Virgin—" she expected her tongue to fall from her head, but it did not "—bless you, and all whom you hold dear. Thank you for this gift." She closed the cabin door with a shove of her hip and placed the plate behind the door.

"You are making splendid progress," said Assunta. She retrieved the sausage and was soon fussing with the small charcoal brazier. Within moments the small cabin filled with the stink of pork. "While I am cooking, you practise your prayers."

Hannah opened the Book of Hours. She could not read a word, and suspected that neither could Assunta, but she bowed her head, lowered her eyes and moved her lips. She knew no Latin; however, she was acquainted with Osmanlica, the language of the Ottomans, so she mumbled a few words, pretending to pray.

"Very convincing, Hannah. I am proud of you. You will fool all but the most devout. What are you reciting so solemnly?"

"A shopping list—eggs, lentils, butter, milk, bread and radishes."

Assunta laughed as she flipped the sausage on the brazier, let it cook for several minutes and then forked a fat piece onto a plate. "You have one more test."

"I cannot," Hannah said, putting the Book of Hours on the table.

Assunta sliced off a morsel from the great lump. "Start with this." She speared the piece and held it out to Hannah. "Eat."

"This is not necessary."

"Do not make a drama out of a simple act."

Hannah pressed her lips closed, rather like Matteo when she would try to feed him salted cod.

"And you think your Isaac is stubborn?"

Hannah took the pork between her fingers. She stood at the porthole. With no effort at all she could open her fingers and the hateful piece would fall into the sea.

"Are all Jews as mulish as you?"

"I cannot do it."

"You mean you *will* not do it." Assunta took the meat from Hannah and held it to her lips, making the kind of jiggling gesture mothers use to encourage a child to eat. Hannah shuddered at the smell. She would gag if Assunta did not remove the meat. She closed her eyes.

"Then I shall have my Book of Hours and rosary back. Oh, and that habit you are so busily sewing, please."

Assunta ate the morsel with great satisfaction, rolling her eyes and patting her stomach. Once she had swallowed, she said, "I wash my hands of you."

Hannah cut off a piece. It stuck to her fingers. Greasy, of course, with the stench of pigpens and snouts and grunting. Pigs—eaters of garbage, creators of filth.

"Anyone would think you are holding excrement between your fingers."

The meat hovered close to Hannah's mouth. Assunta sighed. "All this work for naught." She untied the rosary from Hannah's waist, then retrieved the Book of Hours from the table and put it back in her valise. "Now my habit, if you please."

"Wait." Hannah, still holding the meat, bent her elbow, which now felt as stiff as an iron rod. Her hand met her lips and she popped the sausage in. The morsel seemed much larger on her tongue than it had in her hand. When she bit into it, it stuck to the roof of her mouth. She manoeuvred the morsel around, chewing as fast as she could.

"Swallow and be done with it."

Hannah began to gag. Assunta slapped her on the back and offered a mug of water. "Now another piece."

And so it went until Hannah had choked down three bites. Her belly swirled in protest. If, may God not be listening, she was ever forced to eat human flesh, it would taste very much like this fat-glistening, shimmering sausage.

CHAPTER 6

Villa di Padovani,
San Lorenzo, the Veneto

FROM THE GARDEN came the warbling of sky-larks. Cesca's dozen snares, made of horsehair and weighted down with pebbles, awaited them under the overgrown rose bushes. Such tasty little birds when well cooked, but yes, she must admit, a little too bony. She cracked two brown eggs into a chipped blue bowl to prepare an omelette for Matteo, which she would serve him when he finished his lessons with Foscari. Every day, upstairs in his study with the shutters closed, Foscari interrogated Matteo about every aspect of his life with Hannah and Isaac so that the boy could answer any questions the judge might ask him. Chastened by his humiliation in court, Foscari was leaving nothing to chance. But from Matteo's sullen replies and Foscari's badgering tone, the sessions were not going well.

Cesca had also tried. Matteo, instead of being cooperative, refused to give more than a few curt words in reply to her questions. For example, the other day when she asked him whether the blanket belonged to him, he pursed his lips and refused to speak. He would relent in time, Cesca was sure. But it was taking far too long.

There was a speck of blood in one of the yolks, a bad portent. Was Hannah not coming in spite of Cesca's letter? It had been two months and still no sign of her cloud of dark, curly hair and flat bosom.

Cesca glanced out the window toward the canal. A boat drew up to the dock; a man, accompanied by an enormous dog, disembarked. He handed the boatman some coins, hesitated for a moment, studying the villa, then began to walk up the lawn toward her.

The man paused again, as though he had spied her through the window. Was he entranced by her? Most men were. But his eyes jumped from roof to portico to loggia. It was the villa, not her neat waist and blond hair, that mesmerized him. As he drew closer with his extravagant white beard and moustache, the brindle mastiff lumbering behind him, Cesca realized who he was.

She raced upstairs to gaze into her looking glass. She fiddled with a lock of hair, tossing it this way and that. If only she had some gum arabic to hold the errant lock in place. If only she had ivory combs and this new device she had heard of—a parting instrument. She pinched her cheeks and bit her lips to give them colour then ran back downstairs.

Foscari was an admirer of Palladio, who had designed *her* villa—as she had come to consider it—many years before. Cesca had listened to Foscari, transfixed by the inspiring tale of Palladio's rise through the ranks of society.

Once a stone mason, Palladio had been taken up by a wealthy nobleman, Trissino—humanist, lover of the poet Plutarch—who, recognizing Palladio's talents, had sent him no less than five times to study the classical buildings of Rome and Athens. In turn Palladio, the son of a humble miller, became a legend. Who had not heard his amusing quip, 'I prefer the whiteness of stone dust to the whiteness of flour'? What gentleman had not read, or at least claimed to have read, *I Quattro Libri dell'Architettura*? The humblest peasants to the most distinguished nobles spoke of him with admiration and affection—a mason who had bounded up the slippery social ladder with nary a stumble. In spite of his exalted position he had not taken on airs. He was that rarest of men: one who could converse with ease with anyone from poorest tenant farmer to the Doge of Venice.

And here he was, striding up Cesca's lawn, hands clasped behind his back, jaw squared, chest thrust forward as though bracing himself to enter battle. He was older than she had expected, but his arms, still muscular, strained against the seams of his jacket. With its nipped-in waist and long coattails, the green jacket was not a style in the least flattering to his stocky build. Either his wife—if he was possessed of one—thought it becoming, or he had fallen into the hands of an impish tailor. He mounted the stairs, pushed open the door without knocking and strode inside. "Pippo," he called, and turning patted his thigh. The mastiff ambled in after him. In contrast to his master, the dog seemed in no particular hurry and leisurely sniffed the floor and furniture once inside. From his dewlaps hung a ribbon of slobber, which, when he jerked up his head to look at a buzzing fly, arced in Cesca's direction and attached itself to her skirts.

Palladio carried a silver-headed walking stick of the type men carry for show rather than function. His meaty thumb, hooked over the top, looked as though it should have been clasping the handle of a stone chisel rather than the delicately worked silver head of a gargoyle. Judging by the thumb's flattened tip, it had suffered the blow of a hammer more than once.

Cesca's mother—a whore and therefore well-positioned to make such comparisons—used to say a woman could gauge the measure of a man's member by the size of his thumbs.

A sobering thought occurred to Cesca as she eyed this august man. She had not the faintest whiff of a connection to the di Padovani family or any right to be making herself at home. There was only the letter from the San Lorenzo mayor, whom Foscari had probably bribed so he would grant Cesca occupation.

"*Signora.*"

"Please, do come in," Cesca said.

Palladio took Cesca's hand in his and gave it a hearty kiss. "I am your neighbour, Andrea Palladio."

After dropping her hand, Palladio proceeded to stride up and down her reception room as though he had not merely designed it but owned it, occupied it, collected the incomings and paid the outgoings on it.

"I am Francesca . . ." To her embarrassment, her voice trailed off while she considered the many family names she had used over the years. "Trevare," she said, after too long a pause. It had been her mother's surname. Of her father, she had no knowledge. Not his name, his occupation or even the colour of his hair.

"I was passing by and thought that if you would grant me the indulgence, I would give the villa a proper inspection. I designed it many years ago. Conte di Padovani provided me with a simple country farmhouse to work on. I transformed it into the crowning jewel of the district." He spoke matter-of-factly, without a hint of boasting, his eyes still focused on the floor. He strode back to the grand portal of the main entrance.

Cesca knew Palladio and the Conte, Matteo's father, had become friends during the construction. Was Palladio's visit a pretext for checking on Matteo's welfare? She intended to keep Palladio on the topic of malfunctioning fountains and leaking roofs to avoid questions regarding her legitimacy as mistress of the household.

"The neighbours tell me you are making everything ship-shape. I have come to see for myself."

"I have worked like a skivvy. The villa was so neglected when we arrived."

"Indeed," he said. He surveyed the weed-choked lawns, the overgrown boxwood topiary, the listing portico and, in the distance, the peeling paint of the stables.

Cesca, who was reluctant to rinse out her own teacup if she could find someone to perform the task for her, had found herself scrubbing floors and statues, pruning back the errant grapevines that threatened to engulf the east loggia and even, may God be watching, mucking out the barn. In spite of all this toil her hands, which should have been as red and coarse as a washerwoman's, were soft and pliant, thanks to the Holy Virgin, who sent a black lamb scuttling into the courtyard every morning. Cesca would run her hands several times through its greasy wool. The lanolin that coated them provided protection from the harsh well water and lye soap.

"Forgive my curiosity, but what is your connection to the di Padovani family?" Palladio asked.

Dare she try to pass herself off as a relative of this noble family? She had been told often enough by Foscari that her accent was wrong, her attitudes plebeian, her deportment—whatever that might be—atrocious. She was struggling to acquire the graces of a lady of birth and refinement, but did her manners and speech still betray her for what she was—"an ambitious tart," in Foscari's words?

"Yes," she said, flicking a crumb from her dress and tidying her hair, "I am a cousin of the Contessa's, from Rome." Cesca gave him her most dazzling smile, the one that deepened her dimples and showed her pretty teeth. "I live here with Matteo, the Conte's son."

"So you have taken on the task of raising him?" His brown eyes crinkled at the corners.

Palladio was possessed of such a genial air that Cesca relaxed. She returned his smile, thinking no more of her muddy hems, tangled hair and stained work dress. "Yes," she answered with a frankness meant to disarm. Then she told him the same tale she had told everyone in the district: Foscari was the guardian of the di Padovani estate—it would be true soon enough—and Matteo, lawful heir to the grandest fortune in the Veneto, was his ward. She was Matteo's governess, as well as a cousin to the late Contessa Lucia.

"How fortunate the boy has someone like Foscari to manage his affairs. It is not an easy matter to lose one's parents. I should like to meet Matteo. I was fond of the Conte. Such a fine-looking man, with a good seat on a horse and a well-turned leg. And, when it came to building this villa, an open purse."

Cesca cocked her head to listen for sounds of Matteo upstairs, but everything was silent. Foscari must have fallen asleep from all the brandy he drank during their lessons and, sensing an opportunity, Matteo must have dashed out the back entrance to run as wild as a savage.

Just then she heard the clomp of horse's hooves. She walked to the window. "Matteo is out there, riding his fat little pony, Apollo." The pony belonged to one of the tenant farmers. She pointed to the path leading to the canal. "Look, there he is. Isn't he the most perfect little darling?" Cesca enjoyed the boy when he was outside and when he was tired from playing. At such times he would lie quietly in her bed as she told him stories. She would pretend he was her natural child. But when she broached the topic of the blanket, he would say, "I hate Foscari. I will not say what he wants me to say. He stole me from Ama and Papa and he stole my blanket." At such times she would grow weary of him and wish he would go away.

Palladio studied Matteo as the boy gripped the reins and hugged the pony's middle with his sturdy legs. "The very image of his mother. He has her eyes and round little chin."

How reassuring to hear this physical resemblance confirmed, Cesca thought.

Just then Matteo, perhaps feeling their gazes, turned, grinned at them, let go of the reins and waved with both hands.

"Hold fast, Matteo," Cesca called to him.

"An enthusiastic horseman, isn't he?" Palladio noted.

"A tad reckless, I would say," Cesca replied.

Then she gestured for Palladio to take a seat in the reception room, which was empty of furnishings other than a couple of rickety chairs and an unsteady table.

"Foscari shall manage the estate with prudence until Matteo comes of age." How pious and false she sounded. Prudent management? She feared that with his new-found riches Foscari would be as rash as a sailor. All those bright, shiny ducats would line the pockets of the casino owners in Venice and fatten the wine merchants and butchers of Castello unless she could think of a way to prevent it. "Would you like a liquor made with fruit from my own trees?"

He nodded.

"Give me a moment to fetch it."

Cesca went to the larder to get a bottle, then returned to the reception room carrying Majolica cups of blue and yellow.

Palladio accepted a cup. "Where is Foscari? Am I to have the pleasure of his company? I have some business to discuss with him."

The mention of "business" caused her a moment of unease. What commerce could he have with Foscari? As far as she knew, Foscari had met Palladio only once, and briefly. "Foscari is upstairs—indisposed, I fear." The word "indisposed," which Cesca had learned from Foscari, covered a number of maladies, from brandy sickness to the grippe to the French pox. It was also a word that did not invite further inquiry. Better to leave Foscari where he was, as Cesca preferred to have Palladio all to herself. Tonight at dinner she could regale Foscari with details of her visit from the famous Palladio.

"The Conte was an interesting man. A humanist, like my patron, Trissino. Kind and generous to my workers and not above sharing a jug of black wine with them on payday. But, God rest his soul, he was an obstinate man. I warned him the ground was unstable at the northwest corner and we should position the entire structure to the west at least four paces. Nevertheless, he insisted on having this particular view of the canal. Now look." He flung a hand toward the walls and ceiling. "See the crack and that heaving stone at the base of the column? Shoring up that pillar is going to be an expensive job." Pausing for a breath, he took a child's marble from his pocket and placed it on the floor. They watched as the marble hesitated, uncertain what direction to travel, then rolled into a corner. So there were problems beyond unkempt trees and tangled vines. Another expense, another claim on money she did not possess.

"But why should I trouble you with these irksome problems? You are fortunate to have only Matteo to tend to and, I expect, meals to cook and other household chores."

So he thought her a needy relation working for the privilege of a square meal and a place to rest her head. Cesca did not know whether to be insulted or relieved. Palladio sipped the thick, syrupy liquor. He might have come from a humble family, but he had a natural dignity and elegance about him, a refined way of holding his cup, a benign manner of cocking his head when he spoke.

"Delicious," he said, putting his cup on the floor.

His eyes moved from floor to ceiling and back again. He dropped to his knees with the agility of a much younger man—she judged him to be in his sixties—to examine the terrazzo. He squinted at it from all angles, first with the light and then against the light, which streamed through the central arched window and the two smaller windows flanking it. He ran a hand over the surface, checking for roughness.

A hen had found her way inside and was now clucking crossly, trapped between the crossed paws of the mastiff, which was covering her in streamers of drool. Palladio removed his wide-brimmed hat, shooed the hen outside and then proceeded to pace the length and breadth of the reception room.

Flirting was a habit Cesca could not seem to break. She said in a teasing voice, "Why, sir, do you expel my favourite tenant, the red hen? Is the chicken not one of God's most useful creatures?" Whenever she met any man, she felt bound to captivate him, even an old man like Palladio.

"Not when it's shitting in the most elegant room on the Brenta."

"If you had seen the filth and disorder when I arrived, you would not be confounded by the presence of a little red hen." She wanted the attention of this man, who seemed more interested in the cracks in the terrazzo floor than in conversing with her and admiring her clear blue eyes and translucent skin. "I do not think you appreciate the improvements I have made." Cesca knew any man watching her would find her enchanting—by turns charming, then petulant. One such display of coquetry was certain to captivate Palladio.

But he continued to move about. His boundless vitality fascinated her. He was like an aging stallion cantering round and round a paddock. He touched a plinth with a bust of Pallas Athena. "Please, have a seat," said Cesca, with no expectation that he would plop into a chair and settle there for any length of time.

His face was flushed and circles of sweat marked his jacket.

"Feel free to remove your jacket. You will be more comfortable." Cesca held out her hand to take the garment. He shrugged it off with the appearance of relief and handed it to her. As he did, he stretched his shirt over his broad chest and a whorl of chest hair escaped. His voice had a deep, mellow quality that resonated through the room like a church organ.

Had he been younger, he might have induced in her certain feelings of wantonness. Again she wondered if he had a wife, and if so, whether he was fond of her. It behooved her to know, for such an important, powerful man was sure to be useful.

Cesca followed him as he walked to the drawing room, where she planned to drape his jacket over a small marble statue of Bacchus, his crown of vines and grapes in need of a good scrubbing. When Palladio glanced up at the east wall, he stopped so abruptly she nearly knocked into him.

"*Che cazzo!*" Palladio swore.

Cesca giggled. It was a strong oath. She had heard it many times in the slums of Rome, but she hardly expected to hear it in her own drawing room. Palladio stood staring, hands clenching and unclenching at his sides.

"Whatever is the matter?"

"Did you have this *trompe l'oeil* painted?"

Cesca must have appeared blank, for he bellowed, "The frescoes, woman! The frescoes! This wretched flim-flammery—those overfed cupids on the ceiling, the maid-servant poking her fleshy nose out of a false door. The artist could not even paint the entablature. Look at the top-heavy travesty! Completely out of proportion to the columns."

The painted door, meant to imitate white Istrian marble, with a tracery of black veins, seemed beautiful to her—two thin columns topped with a horizontal piece painted to mimic an ornate frieze.

"And that!" He waved at her favourite section of the fresco. "The *castellana*, with a barely contained bosom! Most undignified."

The *castellana* had taken on the role of the Virgin Mary in Cesca's eyes. Each morning after breaking fast, she entered the room and stood before the *castellana* to ask for guidance. Once, she caught herself genuflecting, and was glad Foscari was not present to ridicule her. How reassuring the *castellana's* painted bosom, the gentle smile playing around her lips, the appearance of command and the competence in the set of her shoulders. Here was a noblewoman who would have no difficulty finding the best chefs to roast her joints of beef, the most skilled seamstresses to embroider her initials on the bed linens and the most graceful way to arrange guests at formal dinners.

"'The sight of these frescoes is enough to make the dead weep with pleasure. These paintings are a sublime combination of the grand and the homely, the sacred and the profane,'" she said, echoing Foscari's words upon seeing the artwork for the first time. How elegant she had thought his words, how impressed she had been by them. "But," Cesca continued, "I cannot accept credit. The murals were painted long before I arrived."

"I am sorry. Yes, you look like a sensible woman."

How on earth did he know whether she was sensible? "I hope to God I am not," she replied. "A sensible woman would never undertake the challenge of setting this ruin to rights."

Before Palladio could inquire why Cesca would repair so much as a pig's sty, she said, "I am told these frescoes were painted by the great Bordolini." *And,* she wanted to add, *I have derived more pleasure from this Bordolini, whoever he may be, and his frescoes, than I have from any man either in or out of the bedchamber.*

As if he could tolerate no more of the sight, Palladio plopped into a chair and stretched out his legs with his back to the paintings. His mastiff settled his head, solid as a block of black granite, on Palladio's left foot. The dog closed his eyes and gave himself over to the pleasure of his master scratching his flank, which caused his hind legs to work as though he was chasing imaginary rabbits through the forest.

"Things must not pretend to be what they are not. Paint is paint and should not resemble marble. Lime wash is lime wash and should not look like tempera. To paint a wall to resemble a doorway is a deception—blasphemy. Throw a pot of whitewash at this fakery."

When my body has turned to dust and the worms have eaten my eyes. "Nothing pleases me more than what you call 'fakery.' I love this wall precisely because it is a delicious illusion."

"Remedying it would be a simple matter. I will do the job faster than a sheep can jump a stile. Have you a good-sized bucket and some lime?"

Palladio's look made her realize he was teasing.

"I wish you could see the expression on your face."

He was the same age as Foscari, but unlike Foscari, Palladio had a contagious energy that made her feel young—which she was, for heaven's sake. With Foscari, she had to walk slowly to match his pace. She ate with less gusto when she saw him transferring a bite of baked meadow lark from one cheek to the other, anxious about swallowing for fear of choking on a bone. She even caught herself hesitating, as Foscari did, about biting into an apple and maybe breaking a tooth.

She studied Palladio's smooth skin, muscular thighs, barrel chest, shrewd blue eyes and mason-spatulate thumbs. No question, he was a handsome old dog. But one old man in her bed was sufficient. Foscari came to her at night with his fly already unbuttoned, so impatient was he to possess her. Sometimes, God help her, he did not trouble himself to remove his green kid boots but wore them the entire time, bracing them against the footboard of the bed as he had his way with her. His seed, although it had a sour and goatish smell, might not be too old to cause mischief. It would not do to fall pregnant, of course, but she had a remedy for such a nuisance. In Rome, whores tucked sea sponges soaked in musk, amber and civet up their passages—a strategy that, so far, had worked equally well for her.

"I must see Foscari," Palladio said. "I hope to work out some of the fine points of our arrangement."

Cesca stared at him, disconcerted.

"I have the endurance for one more undertaking before God calls me. My wife wishes to live in a villa such as this."

Well, she can find her own.

"Her doctors tell me she needs a change of surroundings. As for me, I need a new project, one that will engage my heart and mind. This villa looks as though it will do nicely."

Cesca sat very still. "What do you mean?"

"Foscari hasn't mentioned our agreement?"

Cesca shook her head.

"He has promised me the villa."

Cesca could not imagine what Palladio was talking about. The only villa she could think of was the Villa Francesca. It took her a moment to work the matter out. Then she understood, and it was as if Palladio had dumped a barrel of live eels over her head.

CHAPTER 7

Port of Venice

Venice. the city Hannah had abandoned so reluctantly and now returned to so eagerly had never looked more beautiful. It rose up from the lagoon like a fairy tale kingdom, its shimmering collection of islands strung together by bridges like pearls on a necklace. It was like a much-loved, familiar face seen with renewed affection after a long absence. With the salty spray wetting her face and the sun glinting off the water; the cerulean blue of the lagoon; the wind toying with the water, teasing wavelets into performing glittering dances; gondolas skimming along, as graceful as dragonflies; and the Piazza San Marco coming into sight—she wondered:

how had she convinced herself she had conquered her need for Venice?

Hannah had never felt at home in Constantinople, a city of half-barbarous Mussulmen. She had never become fluent in Osmanlica, the inelegant, disjointed language of the Turks; or understood their customs; or felt comfortable among her neighbours in the Jewish quarter. Most were Sephardim, Jews from Spain, who hardly seemed like Jews at all but rather some pleasure-loving variant of Christian.

How fitting, how right it would be, to give birth to her child in Venice. But suppose Isaac remained behind in Constantinople? Suppose he had been so furious when he discovered her missing he had gone to the Rabbi? Isaac would have no trouble convincing him that her disobedience, her flight from bed and household, was grounds for divorce.

The *Fortuna* had not docked in Malta due to a fierce storm that had blown the ship off course and so Assunta had voyaged the entire way. She would have to find another vessel to transport her back to her convent. The ship dropped anchor as a tender flying the Venetian flag pulled alongside. Two customs inspectors came on board. Short, bustling men wearing caps with the Venetian lion stencilled on the brims. Hannah's heart sank.

"What is happening?" asked Assunta, nodding at the gesticulating and shouting going on between the inspectors and the captain.

Why had Hannah not anticipated this? All she had thought of was disembarking and finding Matteo. Now she told Assunta, "During outbreaks of plague, the custom inspectors require ships to unload passengers and crew onto Lazzareto Nuovo for forty days of quarantine to ensure no one is infected. All ships entering the harbour must do the same. We might be sequestered with hundreds of other angry travellers on that tiny island, unless our captain can convince the inspectors otherwise." She rubbed together her index finger and thumb. "Sometimes a few ducats can persuade them to relax the rules." A delay of forty days might mean the end of her chance to find Matteo alive. She watched from a distance as the captain and inspectors continued to argue. Finally, one of the inspectors accepted a handkerchief, lumpy with coins, from the captain and shoved it in his pocket. They got back into the tender and rowed off. Hannah breathed a sigh of relief as the captain ordered the anchor raised and they glided into harbour.

When Hannah alighted on the wharf, she and the other passengers dropped to their knees and kissed the broad planks. She inhaled the pine pitch, breathed in the scent of damp earth and flowers and trees from the shore. But the ground continued to shift under her feet. Hannah had proven to be no better a sailor on this voyage than she had been years ago on her journey from Venice to Constantinople. After several storm-tossed weeks, she was grey with fatigue and bone thin. There was no Isaac—a husband all the more precious for his absence—to help her. How she missed his grin, his nimble wit, his steady calmness in much the way an amputee must miss his limb. At times during her journey when she had been struck by a sight such as the sails luffing in the wind, or confounded by the miserable, constant diet of double-baked biscuits and dried fish, she would turn to make a comment to Isaac—and find herself addressing the empty air. Other times she would turn to admire his handsome features and instead find herself staring at Assunta's broad face.

But she had much to be grateful for. The baby within her seemed unperturbed by the voyage and moved vigorously. Thanks to the kindness of God, she no longer suffered the usual afflictions of pregnancy: headache and swollen ankles.

The wharf was crowded with dock workers and porters, men with legs like wishbones from lugging their heavy burdens. Hawkers were selling the bounty of the lagoon from pushcarts: tiny shrimp, sprats, eels and snails, clams, squid, sardines, mussels, *rumba*, a delicacy found only in the lagoon, and *branzino*, a fish of incomparable flavour. The lagoon tossed all these and more into the fisherman's nets. Flocks of white pelicans hoping for a sardine surrounded their boats, squawking and flapping their wings, like a pack of raucous hunting dogs begging at a rich man's table.

A peasant woman from the Terra Firma, judging by her sombre dress and embroidered head scarf, sat with a large tub anchored between her knees. She was harping sheep's milk to make pecorino.

"The soonest worn, the soonest you become accustomed to it," Assunta had said earlier, watching Hannah stuff the nun's habit into her valise.

Hannah had shaken her head. "I cannot wear such a garment to enter the ghetto."

"As you wish," Assunta had said.

Now she adjusted on Hannah's head the red scarf that all Jewesses were obliged to wear then tucked in a stray lock of curly dark hair. "Be well. I hope you make peace with Asher."

"I must. My brother is a moneylender. Few secrets are safe from him. If anyone can find out what Foscari and Cesca are plotting, Asher can. He has a spider's web of spies—Jew and gentile, other moneylenders, and men servants and porters in the palazzi along the Grand Canal, perhaps even law clerks and bailiffs. He used to say, 'An informant in the right place is worth any number of soldiers in the field.' My letter from Cesca was written many months ago. I need fresh news." Hannah gave Assunta a hug. "We shall meet again, my friend. Thank you for travelling with me. May you find a ship to Malta soon and have a smooth sail onward."

Assunta held fast in her strong arms. Hannah would miss this fierce Bride of Christ.

"With God's help, you will find your son."

Hannah blinked away tears. "Thank you for your lessons. If I succeed in passing myself off as a nun, it will be due to your good tutoring."

"You were an apt pupil." Sister Assunta paused. "For a heretic."

"Nonsense, your Latin prayers refused to stay in my head, tumbling in one ear and out the other like stones through a chute," said Hannah. "I am grateful for the pleasure of your company. It would have been a lonely voyage without you."

Hannah had grown fond of this brusque woman, who had not only instructed her in the ways of Christian prayers but also bossed about the *Fortuna's* crew. She had shouted at them between cupped hands to reef in the sails. She had given the cabin boys advice on how best to climb the rigging and demonstrated with her long, curved needle and leather palm the most efficient method of mending wind-torn sails.

"I hope you will think about what I have said. Do not turn your face from the teachings of the Lord. Put aside your heathen beliefs. Bend your knee to Jesus."

"Thank you for your concern about my soul."

It was an exchange they had had many times. Sister Assunta gave Hannah's shoulder a hearty thump and they parted.

Hannah found a porter to carry her valise. As she walked through the streets, the porter behind her, her *cioppà* barely flapped in the stiff breezes coming off the lagoon. The hem was weighted down with the fourteen ducats left after paying her passage. A woman, whether in broad daylight or blackest night, was an easy prey for thieves. In her pocket she had a number of *scudi* to cover her daily expenses.

A large puddle soaked her shoes. The piazza was awash in water. It was the time of *alta aqua*, high tide, which sloshed into the streets and *piazzi*, making them impossible to cross dry shod. How easy to imagine Matteo at her side, stomping in the pools of salty lagoon water, making the water arc and glisten in the sun. In the eddying puddles he would sail the little red boat Isaac had carved for him.

A former neighbour, wearing the obligatory red hat for Jewish men, marched along the Fondamenta toward her.

Hannah ducked her head and pulled her head scarf lower on her forehead. It was not modest for an unrelated man and woman to greet each other in public. Some people crossed a bridge or ducked behind a building to avoid such encounters.

Her dark dress and red scarf grew hotter as the sun rose overhead. How uncomfortable a nun's habit would have been and yet, perhaps a wiser choice. The city swarmed with two-legged rats who hung about eavesdropping, trying to pick up sellable information—the price of wheat in Sicily, the number of boots the navy ordered, the cost of printed silk in Bellagio—or the sudden reappearance of the Jewish midwife who had disappeared the night the nobleman Niccolò di Padovani had been murdered.

CHAPTER 8

Jewish Ghetto,
Venice

To BEG A FAVOUR of a foe is to disarm him. Or
so they say. Hannah had no bed, no food, no
heat, and no pillow upon which to lay her head.
Her other siblings had left the ghetto long ago—one
brother to Macedonia, another to Palestine; her sister,
Jessica, of blessed memory, was dead.

Hannah could not sleep rough on the street and risk
being beaten and robbed or worse by one of the numerous
gangs that roamed the streets and canals at night. Her ducats
were all she had. There was the baby to protect. Sleeping on
damp ground could bring on her travail. She did not want
to give God an excuse to take *this* unborn child.

A public inn was out of the question. Such establishments were far too dangerous for a woman travelling alone. Share a bed with a stranger, perhaps a man and surely a Christian? Unthinkable. She must go to the ghetto, seek out Asher, beg for shelter.

The words of her brother's letter still resounded in her memory: "You have stolen from me and from our family. You should have your right hand cut off like a common thief. You are dead to me. In my heart, I have sat *shiva* for you." But he was, after all, her brother. With his help, she would save Matteo from whatever scheme Foscari and Cesca had devised. Asher would know about the law courts, know how to approach the clerks to find out if, as Isaac suspected, Foscari had petitioned to be appointed guardian.

Many families had members who did not bring credit upon them—a lazy son, a lecherous uncle, a shiftless cousin, a headstrong girl. Asher was not ill-intentioned, merely impulsive, prone to bouts of anger that came and went as quickly as drifts of snow on the lagoon in January. His temper tantrums as a child had been legendary. In the ghetto, where everyone knew everything about the neighbours— from what the wife cooked for dinner, to how many times a week couples made love in their creaky beds shoved against thin walls—it was rumoured he was too eager to take chances. The other moneylenders were uneasy about his willingness to advance large sums to disreputable borrowers in exchange for interest rates higher than those permitted by law. These loans did not appear in Asher's ledger for inspection by officials from the Ministero delle Finanze.

Hannah and the porter headed north toward the ghetto. An hour or so before sunset they drew near the tiny island that had once been her home. The air was redolent with the smell of sugar caramelizing in the bakeries and yeast working in dough for *challah*. As she crossed the Ponte delle Guglie, she glanced up at her former building, her apartment, four rickety floors above the *campo*. Around her people chatted in Veneziano, the dialect of her childhood, and Hebrew and Ladino, the language of the Sephardim, and Yiddish, spoken by Jews from the Germanic countries. Every syllable, every word, every phrase was as clear as Murano glass. Here there would be no need for clumsy hand gestures, no fumbling for the right verb or noun, no reluctance to speak for fear of making a fool of herself. Her old frustrations—crying herself to sleep nights from homesickness, struggling in vain to learn the customs and language of the Ottomans—were forgotten.

To return to the city of one's birth is to flirt with the notion of becoming a child again. When she had departed Venice, Hannah had left her young self behind. Now she reunited with it—the toddler clinging to the sides of her crib; the bride in Isaac's arms; the young matron blessing the Shabbat candles; the woman sitting in the women's gallery, the *mechitza*, in the synagogue, listening to the men below chanting and singing God's praises. She had longed for Venice in the way she yearned for her youth—yearned for it without being aware she was yearning.

In front of the heavy wooden gates leading to the ghetto, Hannah reflexively stood to one side so the gentiles who had come to shop could proceed first. There were a few nuns in the crowd, shopping for second-hand garments to clothe their orphans.

No one paid her the slightest attention. Hannah was amused to see Vicente, the gatekeeper, having a snooze, a jug of wine nestled between his feet. It was his task to unlock the gates at dawn and lock them at sunset.

Seeing Vicente made Hannah recall the cozy suffocation of ghetto life—the gossip around the wellhead in the morning with the women, the smell of bread baking in the communal ovens, the children running through the *soto-portegi*, playing hide-and-go-seek or find-the-slipper. She inhaled—cinnamon, rotting refuse, perfume, bread baking, chicken roasting.

The frantic swishing of dozens of brooms interrupted her reverie. How could she have forgotten? Sunset would mark the beginning of Shabbat. The women were preparing.

The porter unloaded Hannah's valise from his handcart and dropped it by her side next to the wellhead in the centre of the *campo*. Hannah gave him a few *scudi*. He stooped, tipped his hat and clattered past Vicente, out the gates and over the bridge, dragging his handcart behind him.

The square of the Ghetto Nuovo was hardly more spacious than the deck of the *Fortuna*. When Hannah was a child, it had seemed immense. She had imagined it to be a miniature of the entire world and pretended her family's house was Nueva España and her friend Raisl's house on the other side of the square was darkest Africa. The *campo* was a vast ocean that must be traversed to get from one country to the other. From within the ghetto she had had no view of the glittering Venice. Her dwelling, with its peculiar haphazard windows, like all the others in the ghetto, faced inward toward the *campo*. The Council of Ten had ordered that any windows looking out on the city be bricked up. It would be unseemly for Jews to observe a Christian from a position of height, nor must a Christian be offended by the sight of Jews at worship. There had been talk of having the interior windows, those overlooking the *campo*, bricked up as well, but kinder souls had prevailed and they were left open to admit whatever breeze and light there was. The ghetto was an uneasy compromise between Rome and the Republic of Venice. The Church wished the Jews expelled; the government tolerated them for their moneylending and trade connections with the Levant.

How different her old *loghetto* was from her spacious, sunny house in Constantinople, with the generous garden filled with flowers and fruit trees. Although the ghetto teemed with people and livestock and carts like ants on a piece of honeyed bread, it was so shadowy it was as though the sun itself had been banished. Even now, an hour before sunset, oil lamps were hanging from the doorways of the bakery and the goldsmith and from under the archways of staircases leading to *loghetti*.

When she had lived here, Hannah had been able to look out her apartment window and spot the top of Asher's head, hair as tangled as a skein of black yarn curling out from under his red hat. He sat at his table in the untidy row near the Banco Rosso with the other moneylenders, in stalls no wider than the breadth of their shoulders. Some had a jeweller's loupe screwed into one eye; some sat stroking their beards, chatting with passersby, waiting for customers. Piles of odds and ends taken in pledge sat at their feet.

Now Hannah ran her eye down the familiar line of pale, dark men and yes, there was Asher, the handsomest of her brothers, four years younger than she was, holding a gemstone up between pincers the size of a mouse's whiskers and squinting through a jeweller's loupe. His good looks had got him into trouble as a young man. Perhaps they continued to do so, though he was married now to a keen-eyed, sharp-tongued woman.

Asher's profits were modest, while the risk he would not be repaid was great. His customers came from all classes— farmers from the countryside in need of a few ducats to get them through the winter without starving, matrons who required money to pay for a daughter's wedding, noblewomen who had overspent at their dressmaker's and young nobles who proved unlucky at the baccarat and roulette tables. The Church of Rome forbids Christians to lend money. The book of Leviticus says: "And if thy brother be waxen poor and fall in decay with thee; then thou shall relieve him: yea, though he be a stranger or a sojourner; that he may live with thee. Yet, take thou no usury of him, or increase: but fear God, that thy brother may live with thee. Thou shall not give him thy money on usury, nor lend him thy victuals for increase."

Jewish law, as set out in the Mishnah, allowed interest to be charged on loans to non-Jews. And so the Council of Ten permitted Jews to lend money but with strict regulations. The maximum interest Asher could charge, by annual decree, was five percent, regardless of the risk of default or the demand for money. He and his family would always live in a simple room on the top floor of a rickety building in the Ghetto Nuovo. His wife, Tzipporah, would always worry about the price of their Shabbat chicken and always struggle to find the money for their sons' Hebrew lessons. She would never put a joint of lamb on her Passover table. They would always eat bread pudding and not seed cake. Every pregnancy would be a cause for worry about another mouth at the table.

The customer in front of Asher shifted his weight from one foot to the next, awaiting Asher's decision on whether the stone would suffice as a pledge. Not wanting to draw attention to herself, Hannah circled the two and waited behind a pillar, standing at such an angle that she could observe both men's faces without being seen. She need not have bothered to be so discreet. They were so engrossed in conversation they paid no attention to those around them.

The stone in Asher's hand—Hannah remembered his hands, butter soft in this city of callus-handed men—was a square-cut beryl. He held it up the better to study it. Asher nodded at the client, a middle-aged nobleman wearing a fox-trimmed cloak. The man was robust and well-fed and waited impatiently, patting his huge belly. He bent toward Asher and whispered something Hannah could not hear. The intimacy of their posture, Asher's bantering reply and the man's smile suggested a familiarity beyond money-lender and customer.

"My tailor and butcher press me to satisfy my accounts," the nobleman said.

"It is not a perfect stone—there is a flaw in the middle. But because you are an old client, I will advance you two ducats. Only for thirty days, mind." Asher waved a hand to shoo away a fly that had settled on his tiny scales.

"Five ducats," said the nobleman.

Asher performed the traditional pantomime of honest outrage by bunching up his fingers, holding them to his left eye socket, twisting his wrist and pretending to pluck out his eye and place it on the table in front of him. "Do you want my right eye, as well?" He put the beryl on the velvet cushion in front of him. "I'll give you three ducats for your audacity."

"Come, let us settle on an amount that will make us both wretched. What say you to four?"

"Three," said Asher, "but I will throw in for nothing a little something else." He winked. The customer nodded.

So Asher was still playing the informer. Hannah caught the glint as Asher handed the gold coins to him. The nobleman was too grand to carry his own purse. He beckoned to his manservant. After picking up the coins, the nobleman dropped them into his purse, which he handed back to his servant.

Asher said, "Sir, here is your little nugget."

As her brother had once explained, all knowledge was a precious commodity if one knew the proper ear to whisper it in. The notion that ordinary household secrets and miscellaneous facts were articles of trade like silk, mace and freshwater pearls had come as a surprise to Hannah. So great was Asher's motley collection of spies he was welcome in every palazzo in Venice without troubling himself to make an appointment, or so he claimed.

The portly man nodded and motioned his servant to leave them. Asher passed him a folded piece of paper. The nobleman opened it, read it and then tucked it into the pocket of his shirt.

"Interesting information, my friend." The nobleman smiled. "You Jews have your uses. Is there anything that happens in this world you do not know?"

"Yes," said Asher, "as a matter of fact there is. Deep in the heart of the Circassian Mountains, beyond the Black Sea, in a deep cave on the westerly side of the mountain, lives the tribal chieftain of the Yürüks. I do not know him or the number of sons he has, or the ages of his wives, or his name or the size of his flock of sheep."

The nobleman laughed. "And while we are gossiping, what news of our mutual friend?"

"A fortnight ago I lent him fifty ducats." Asher inclined his chin toward the moneylenders down the aisle. "All the others turned him down, but for the interest rate he offered, I decided to take a chance. Sixty days only. I pray I do not regret it."

Tread carefully on this particular knife's edge, my brother. Do not be too bold with your loans, or too easeful with this nobleman with a paunch as rounded as a woman nearing her confinement. Powerful, debt-ridden, money-owing noblemen are obsequious when they come, hands outstretched, for loans, but when they cannot pay, they cry for the blood of the Jewish moneylenders. When the lender dies, the debt is extinguished. It does not serve you, Asher, to gamble everything if your life is forfeit.

"Mmm, no small amount," said the nobleman.

"He claimed it was for gaming debts," Asher replied.

"I think not. No one sees him at the casinos anymore."

"A woman?"

"Is it not either one or the other?" said the nobleman. They grinned at each other in the conspiratorial manner of men.

Once the nobleman and Asher shook hands, bidding each other farewell, Hannah moved from behind the pillar. Asher, still sitting, glanced up and looked straight at her without recognition, seeing no doubt an ordinary Jewish matron.

How best to approach a brother carrying an old grudge and possessed of a volatile temper? As a boy, her brother had had an unforgiving nature, seeking out slights in innocent remarks, taking umbrage at nothing, holding grudges over long-forgotten trivialities. In Asher's nature, goodness was at war with pride; kindness and generosity struggled with arrogance. The benevolent side of Asher won more often than did the wicked. This was why she had loved him as a child and had continued to love him in spite of the hurt she felt over his letter.

Hannah walked closer to him, giving Asher a moment more to recognize her. They had both changed. It had been years since they had last seen each other. "Don't you remember your sister Hannah?" she asked. He studied her face. Then he tried to spring to his feet, but Hannah held him in his chair with her hand on his shoulder.

"Hannahlah!" He whispered her childhood nickname and rose to embrace her. "I cannot believe you are here."

Sometimes the heart responds before memory can intrude.

"How wonderful to see you," he said.

A second went by as she waited for Asher to recall their ugly dispute. When he was a child, she had been able to read his thoughts, which reflected openly on his face. But now there was a shifting aspect to his expression that she could not decipher—first a look of joy; then, as he recalled their quarrel, a look of anger; then—what? Joy again?

Asher grinned, showing his strong teeth. His fine dark eyes shone. He glanced around. "Where is Isaac?"

"Isaac is ill. He will be joining me as soon as he can." Hannah would not tell Asher the truth until she was sure where matters stood between them. If Asher thought it odd she had made such a long voyage on her own, he did not show it.

He stood and hugged her. "What a sight we must be—curmudgeonly brother and prodigal sister embracing." His beard scratched her cheek; he smelled of lemons and baby artichokes fried in butter and garlic and last night's soup. "What brings you back to Venice?"

"I have come to fetch my son, Matteo."

"You have a son? But I thought . . ." He did not voice what he was thinking: that she had been barren for years.

"He is not a child I gave birth to but a child Isaac and I have raised as though he were our own."

"We did hear rumours of a baby after you left." He spoke in a low voice.

Hannah explained she had fled the ghetto after rescuing Matteo from his uncle Niccolò. "Matteo has been taken by a woman named Francesca and the Marquis Foscari. I must find my son before he comes to harm." The expression on Asher's face, half startled, half alarmed, prompted her to ask, "Do you know them?"

Asher considered her question. "Foscari, yes. Francesca? No." He squeezed her upper arm in sympathy. "I am sorry to hear about your son's disappearance. I am sure you love him as much as if you had birthed him yourself."

Hannah wanted to inquire what Asher knew of Foscari, but first she must secure shelter. "May I stay with you tonight?"

"Now that you are in trouble you come to me?" His words were said in jest, but not far below their surface was another emotion altogether. Resentment? Anger? She was having trouble reading the mood of this brother she had once been so close to.

"Come here a moment." Asher pulled her deeper under the *sotoportego*, where the sun did not penetrate even on the brightest days. The stones gave off a clammy smell. "I have something to tell you." Not meeting her eyes, Asher said, "Hannah, I owe you an apology. After you left for Constantinople, Rivka came over. You remember her? A squint in one eye? Sells eel pies in the market? Wife of old Emmanuel, the knife sharpener?"

Hannah nodded.

"It was Emmanuel who stole Papa's violin. He was not himself, Rivka said. His mind wandered . . . he could not remember his own name some days. He just ambled into our house and grabbed it from the cupboard. Rivka was so ashamed she needed months to work up the courage to return it to me. By that time I had already written that letter to you. I wanted to send an apology, but, God forgive me, my pride would not allow me."

Accept the olive branch, she told herself; do not question the spirit in which it is offered. The old Asher, the one she remembered from long ago, would not have been so quick to apologize even when wrong. Yet it seemed his regret was heartfelt. Hannah put a hand on his arm. "Asher, I forgive you." But did she? He had accused her of being a thief. "Do you remember that night you fought with our brother Chaim over a toy and Mama begged you to stop? She took the broom and started smacking both of you, trying to separate you, but you were worse than street mongrels and would not stop. She began to cry. Papa picked up his violin and started to play. He played and played all through the screaming and crying and snotty noses and Mama weeping and trying to get close enough to thump you with the broom." Hannah had hated Asher for making her mother cry in such a pitiful, helpless way.

She could tell by his face, now relaxed, that he, too, remembered that night. "He played so sweetly, better than any of the *klezmorim*."

"You stopped fighting to listen. Papa kept playing song after song. We girls danced. You danced with Mama."

"I miss Papa," Asher said.

"Not a day goes by that I do not think of him with his fiddle in one arm, his bow in the other, tapping his foot in time to 'La Brandôlina,'" Hannah said. "I cannot hear a violin without tearing up."

"Now I have Papa's violin back, but I do not know how to play it."

"One of your sons will learn."

"They are all savages, more interested in brandishing swords than violin bows. Besides, where would the money come from for lessons?"

They laughed together.

"Of course you shall stay with us," Asher said.

"Are you sure? I do not want to put you and Tzipporah—" She was about to say "in danger" but instead said, "I do not want to inconvenience you." She left unsaid her thoughts: *I killed a nobleman and might be arrested, bringing death to myself and danger to the ghetto. I have raised a Christian child, and not just any Christian child but the heir to the di Padovani fortune, as a Jew. That alone is enough to see me hanged.*

"Nonsense. We would be delighted."

Hannah let out a sigh of relief. With Asher's words it was as though her raging fever had at last broken. Her anger toward her brother drained away, but had peace been too easily achieved?

"Come, we must go. The sun is nearly down." Asher gathered up the tools of his trade—scales, pincers, strong-box and purse—and the articles he had taken in pledge that day. "To arrive from such a distance in time for Shabbat is a *mitzvah*, a blessing." He bid goodbye to the moneylender at the next table, a reedy-looking young man, then made to leave. "Come upstairs. The boys have grown so since you saw them last. You will not recognize them. And—" he dropped his voice "—Tzipporah has grown large again." He rolled his eyes heavenward. "May it be a girl. I never thought I would say such a thing, but to have five boys is like living with a pack of noisy dogs."

Hannah said, "I can imagine." But she could not. Matteo was a studious boy who played with his friends and excelled at his lessons. He was a chess player, a solemn walker of the tightrope, a boy who loved stories, a boy who loved his mother. From the moment they emerged from Tzipporah's womb, Asher's sons had been boisterous. Not fond of their Hebrew lessons, incapable of sitting still for the old Rabbi's sermons, they tossed their *kippot* into the air the moment they left the class. They were fond of practising their archery skills on the occasional bird foolhardy enough to fly into the ghetto, and threatened to toss down the well little girls who ventured into their part of the *campo*. "Five? I don't understand. You had . . ." Her voice trailed off.

"We lost Jacob and Saul to the pestilence last year."

Hannah felt tears form in her eyes.

"The plague arrived in the Ghetto Nuovo on the Day of Atonement. Like a terrible fire, it licked its way through every household and left heartbreak and misery behind. We were fortunate to lose only two children. Some families?" He shook his head. "Parents dead. The children forced to wander the streets, living on scraps. The authorities decided the epidemic was the fault of the Jews. As punishment we were forbidden to buy, sell or trade for six months. No one earned as much as a *scudo*. Many families survived the pestilence only to die of starvation."

Hannah touched Asher's cheek. "How old were your sons?"

Asher glanced away. "Jacob was seven. Saul, old enough to become bar mitzvah."

"I am so sorry."

"So you see—" he smiled wryly "—death is thinning the ranks of our family fast enough without me helping matters along with quarrels."

"Not all families sing in harmony, especially quarrelsome Jewish ones. I accept your apology. Even as I read your letter, I prayed that someday we would be reconciled."

"We shall speak no more of the matter." He cleared his throat and recited a passage familiar to them both: "'Let melancholy and passion born of spleen and bile be banished from our hearts on the Sabbath day.'"

Looking around to make sure no one was observing them, Hannah took him by the shoulders. "Now give me a kiss to welcome me back." Asher proffered his cheek. Always he was the one who presented the cheek, never the one who gave the kiss. Would Asher have eventually written a letter of reconciliation or would they have remained forever estranged if she had not come to Venice? Would she forget his letter or was their relationship like a broken mug, whose mended crack would always be visible?

Asher reached for her arm and steered her across the *campo* to the staircase leading to his *loghetto*. "Tzipporah has always been fond of you."

"I will help her with the cooking and the children." Asher assumed his wife would welcome Hannah, but he did not spend most of his day trying to keep a dark, musty apartment clean and the boys fed and clothed. Five boys and another baby on the way—all crammed into a space barely big enough to contain sleeping pallets and a charcoal brazier. A house guest who would stay who knows how long? No, Hannah did not expect an ecstatic welcome.

"We can always squeeze one more pickle into the barrel." They stopped in front of Asher's building.

"I hope you are right."

CHAPTER 9

Villa di Padovani,
San Lorenzo, the Veneto

FOSCARI USED FALSE PROMISES to conceal his intentions the way grand ladies used beauty marks to hide their smallpox scars. Any remaining trust Cesca had in him vanished with Palladio's visit. She lay in bed, staring up at the ceiling, hands clenched at her side, humiliation washing over her. What a fool to have trusted him again after he had betrayed her in Constantinople.

Cesca had fantasized about a beautiful, safe place, a villa where nothing bad could ever happen. It was now as if a loaded miller's cart had barrelled out of nowhere without so much as a wheel creak of warning and crushed her. This is what occurs when a woman trusts a man.

Foscari rolled over in bed, his face looking naked without the silver nose. His plague amulet of hessonite garnet and sapphire hung from a gold chain around his neck. He flung an arm over her hip. She moved away. The way he breathed! Why had she never noticed? He snorted like a spavined old canal pony pulling a barge laden with firewood. Worst of all, his tapering white fingers were unstained by ink, which signified he had still not visited the notary. If Foscari's promises were diamonds, there would be a necklace of blinding brightness hanging from Cesca's neck.

Before he could awaken and grope for her, Cesca threw back the covers, rose and tugged out his velvet purse from where he, the simpleton, always hid it: under his commode.

Months ago, when they had been dallying in bed, Foscari promised that if he was successful with the moneylenders, he would give her half of whatever he could borrow. The selfish pig had managed to borrow a great deal, as was evident from his new jacket, velvet breeches and embroidered handkerchief. What an innocent goose she was not to realize a plain fact: the promises of a man with an erect member are as worthless as a sailor begging for God's mercy on a storm-tossed sea. Once the sailor is on dry land, the tempest a distant memory, the pledge of a lifetime of devotion is forgotten.

Foscari had given her scarcely enough to keep her and Matteo fed and warm. The price of his jacket alone would have paid for retiling the roof over the kitchen so she wouldn't get rained on every time she boiled rice. But what did he care? Once the court case was completed and he had his order, he would toss her aside.

She loosened the silk drawstrings and thrust her hand in the purse. Delicious. Gold coins—hard yet soft, cool yet hot. And so many of them. She did not need to hold one up to the moonlight streaming in through the window to know they were Venetian ducats. Any hesitation Cesca had about stealing melted away as the coins dropped through her fingers and into the pocket of her dressing gown. Now she could hire a servant girl from the village to help with the cooking and cleaning. She tucked his purse, considerably lighter, back under the commode and started to walk to a small room under the stairs; she could conceal the ducats behind a loose brick there. Halfway down the stairs, however, she turned and retraced her steps to the commode.

Perhaps she was being too greedy. To be fair, Foscari had saved her that day in Constantinople when the Janissaries had marched them in disgrace toward the docks to sail back to Venice. He had shoved a handful of gold coins into the fist of the Janissary in charge. The soldier had unshackled her and Foscari then looked the other way while they melted into the crowd. Because of Foscari, they were able to escape and hide until the time was right.

She reached under the commode and fished out his purse for the second time, and from her pocket she extracted a few ducats. Regretfully, she dropped them back into the purse.

Foscari. The pompous old fraud. She studied his face as he slept. The silvery moonlight from the bedchamber window should have been kind to his cheeks and chin, but it was not. If only Palladio could grout, sand and plaster Foscari's face, filling in the creases, mortaring the furrows in his forehead, chiselling off his warts, until he looked as young and handsome as the statue of Hercules in the nyphaneum. Before Palladio's announcement that he would purchase the villa, Cesca had thought Foscari a reliable means to an end. The recollection made her feel naive.

Palladio owning *her* villa? Not while there was breath in her body. But what to do? Though Cesca wished vengeance on Foscari with all her heart, a woman could not exact vengeance in the time-honoured way of males. Not for Cesca the agreeable thud of steel against bone, blood pooling on stones, intestines spilling out of bellies, the breastbone split asunder.

Men fired cannons over the bowsprits of brigantines or shot muskets from the parapets of fortresses or duelled in an open field. Cesca's theatre of war was the kitchen and the bed chamber. There was a delicacy to a woman's revenge: menstrual blood in the soup, pubic hair in the bread, lice harvested from bedding and pinched into the crotch of breeches—any of these measures, along with a few incantations, would bring on fever, diphtheria, smallpox or the plague. Dried snake excrement under the pillow, the desiccated heart of a toad in the breeches, a broken knife under the bed, would cause impotence.

Cesca walked down the hall to Matteo's room. She climbed into bed with him and slept until late morning. When she awoke, it was cold enough to see her breath in the air. She threw on an old dress and shawl and went downstairs to start the fire. Squatting in front of the hearth, she gave the embers a puff of air with a pair of leaky bellows.

She would pretend all was well between her and Foscari. She would continue to bathe his gouty foot with her special potion of aloes wood, oak fern, musk, sienna and honey. She would warm his brandy between her breasts. Her naughty bedchamber tricks would continue, although touching his flesh now would be as inviting as plunging her hands into a bed of stinging nettles.

Cesca's mind worked best when her hands were occupied. She dumped some calves' brains—a gift from a neighbour—into the pot, with such force water splashed onto the floor. From outside the kitchen door came the squawk of a stray chicken. She glanced up to study it scrabbling among the stones in the yard—too skinny to roast, too old to lay. She ripped open a burlap sack and rooted through it until she found a cabbage the size of a man's head. She had liberated it from a field on one of her midnight walks. She thought of Matteo. He detested cabbage as much as she did. Raw, boiled, steamed or braised in butter, cooked in a soup or stew—it made no difference. He would wrinkle his nose in his stubborn fashion and push her hand away when she held a spoonful to his lips. "No, Ama Cesca," he would protest, clamping his lips and turning his head.

Cesca hefted the bag of flour in her hand, just enough to make a skinflint's loaf of bread. When she opened the sack, a rat jumped out, nearly hitting her in the face. She wrenched off her shoe and flung it, but the filthy creature scampered away unhurt.

If Matteo were here in the kitchen instead of cavorting about outside, he would be standing on a chair next to her, prattling about dragons and ponies and getting underfoot as she cooked, poking his fingers into her ingredients and making a sticky mess of her dough, begging for a piece to make his own bread and then trying to braid it as he must have seen Hannah do when twisting ropes of dough for *challah*. Hannah had encouraged him to believe that the sun rose and set on him. When he did not get his own way, he pouted and flung himself about. When he was in a good mood, he was entertaining.

Cesca placed the dough in a crockery bowl to proof then draped a cloth over it. She added kindling to the fire in the oven. The more she considered Foscari's betrayal—there was no other word for it—the angrier she grew. Rage heated her blood like a spicy stew. As the dough rose in the bowl, she put a dry willow leaf into the oven. When it curled and turned the right shade of brown, her oven was the correct temperature for the bread.

For the present, she could not dispense with Foscari, but a scheme began to take shape in her mind—a clever, elegant scheme. It might work, but her execution must be perfect. She slammed the cabbage onto the table and then reached for the iron cleaver hanging on the wall. Imagining it was Foscari's head, she raised the cleaver above her head with both hands. With a blow she chopped the cabbage in two. Each half tumbled to opposite edges of the table and rocked back and forth. She slashed at the halves. A wedge of cabbage flew off the table and onto the floor.

Cesca heard the hissing of swans from her neighbour's property. She looked out the window. There was Foscari in his dressing gown, cane in hand as he walked across the lawn. He kicked a couple of hapless cygnets that happened to waddle in front of him, which sent them squawking, breast-flopping into the canal. A barge tied up to the dock. Foscari accepted a letter from the bargeman. Strolling back toward the villa, Foscari opened it and began to read. After a moment he smiled, refolded the letter and tucked it into the pocket of his gown.

He pushed open the door to the kitchen and strode in. "Cesca, put down that cleaver."

She lowered the kitchen tool to her side.

"I have news of the midwife," said Foscari.

"She is coming?" Cesca tossed the cleaver onto the table.

Foscari leaned on his cane. "My informant tells me she has arrived in Venice. She is staying in the ghetto with her brother the moneylender. She will be here at the villa in three days."

Cesca nodded. "I knew Hannah would come."

"The credit is due to you, Cesca, for your cunningly worded letter to her." As he bent over to kiss her, he dropped his cane. It clattered to the floor.

She picked it up and handed it back to him. "All the pieces of our puzzle have fallen into place—the boy, the blanket, the midwife."

"Not quite. The child cannot be trusted to say his lines."

"Speaking of Matteo," said Cesca, "where is the boy?" She glanced around worriedly.

"He's practising on his tightrope. Pietro is with him." Pietro was a tenant farmer's son who had taken a liking to the child and strung up a rope between two larch trees for Matteo to use.

Cesca peered at Foscari in alarm. "Nothing dangerous, I trust?"

"He is fine. Much safer than riding his pony." The rope was so high above the ground that it required either Pietro to lift him onto it, or Matteo to climb the makeshift ladder of wine barrel staves nailed to the tree trunk and hop on by himself.

Cesca retrieved the cleaver and balanced it in one hand, wondering idly if she was strong enough to split Foscari's skull in a single blow. "Shall I pour tea?" He nodded and watched her as she pinched a few leaves of tea, a recent present from a neighbour, into the pot then poured in water. She waved him to a chair. Better he not loom over her from his great height. She poured the tea and they sat at opposite ends of the long pine trestle table.

He took a sip. "Is there any brandy?" He held his mug up and waved it. "This tea is bitter."

"It is too early for brandy." But she went to fetch the jug and portioned out some into his mug.

"Hannah is coming! How delightfully everything is working out." Foscari began to hum a sprightly peasant tune he must have heard in the village. The Marquis seemed as content with the world as a dog with two cocks.

What use was it to Cesca that Hannah was on her way? Her arrival would bring Cesca no closer to having the villa. She pushed herself to her feet and picked up her cleaver once more. *Thwack! Thwack!* More tiny pieces of cabbage to join the growing pile. Frustration rose up, and before she could stop herself, she said, "I had a visit from Palladio. He told me you were selling him my villa." She had not meant to speak of it, but the words shot out of her mouth like a molten lead ball out of a musket.

Foscari stopped humming. From the twitching of his jaw muscle she knew he was trying to think of a plausible lie.

"With his own lips." *Talk your way out of this, you rat-faced son-of-a-whore.*

"Palladio?" said Foscari. "An excellent fellow. Very gifted. A genius. He told you that? I cannot think why. Yes, he and I had some vague discussions when I bumped into him in Venice. But I thought his interest was feigned. He wanted an excuse to visit the place—inspect his handiwork, see how the foundations and the roof were holding up. That kind of thing. You know what architects are like. He struck me as a bit of a fusspot, truth be told." When he was nervous, Foscari had the unattractive habit of stretching his upper lip over his front teeth.

"Why would an esteemed gentleman like Palladio need an excuse to pay a social call?"

"Or perhaps—" a sly look came over his face "—he has heard rumours of your beauty and wanted to see for himself."

"You are talking nonsense."

"How suspicious you are. It was a brief chat, Cesca, which

I had for your benefit. Nothing more. He will be useful to you in restoring the villa to its former glory. Hire him! Who knows better than Palladio how repairs should proceed?"

A hand on her hip, Cesca stood listening while Foscari's silver nose moved up and down as he bunched and unbunched his cheeks. It was rather like watching a rat trying to nose its way through a small chink in the wainscoting.

"I cultivated Palladio for your sake, my dove," said Foscari, growing more confident. "I hinted I might sell him the villa at a favourable price because of his . . ." Foscari paused, lowering his voice. "Special knowledge of secret rooms that do not appear in the original drawings."

"What are you talking about?"

Foscari said, "All these old villas along the Brenta were built with a strong room no one knew about except the architect and the workers, all of whom were sworn to secrecy."

Cesca said, "I have been through this place a thousand times, inspecting every corner." *Looking for items of value I might sell to buy food for me and Matteo because you have given me so little money.*

"How do you suppose rich and noble families hang on to their gold and gems? Through carelessness? I assure you not. Every villa has a clandestine room that contains an iron-clad strongbox and heavy oaken cupboards with pad-locks as sturdy as anvils."

Foscari had a nimble tongue.

He fingered the amulet at his throat. "When the plague arrives in the Veneto, would you rather stay in Venice and burn wormwood, juniper, ox horn, sulphur and lavender in your hearth to repel the disease or flee to the country?"

Sciocchezza! I don't believe a word coming out of your mouth.

"The rich need access to their money in the country just as much as in the city." He cleared his throat. "And when their creditors grow impatient and insist on inspecting the strongboxes in Venice? Or," he said, warming to the subject, "poor relatives come calling with greedy hands outstretched?"

"I don't believe a word." And yet . . . suppose he was telling the truth and there was a hidden room with a forgotten cache of gold? "Let us put an end to this argument." She rapped the wooden board with her cleaver, then scraped the onions and cabbage into the steaming pot of calves' brains. "Today, in fact right this instant, you march down to the notary's office in the village. Instruct him to draw up a paper promising to transfer the villa to me after you are named guardian." *And if you do not, I will hide Matteo so well that not even a pack of hunting hounds can find him. Hidden he will remain until I see a nice, fresh piece of parchment with my name at the top and your signature and seal at the bottom.*

"Anything to put your mind at rest, my dove." He stood up and reached for her. "You have the brains of a man in the head of a woman. This must be why I adore you so."

"You are the most charming of men." Cesca wound her arms around Foscari's neck, feeling the leathery touch of his cheek, trying not to inhale the fusty scent of his skin. For the present, she was bound to him as tightly as a goshawk is tethered to a falconer's wrist. Unless she could find another falconer.

CHAPTER 10

Villa di Padovani,
San Lorenzo, the Veneto

F OSCARI'S SCREAMS of rage and Matteo's hysteri-
cal weeping rang from the library. There was the
sound of boots as Matteo stomped down the hallway and raced out the front door before he slammed it so
hard one of the precious panes shattered. Cesca wanted to
run after him, grab him by the shoulders and shake him
so fiercely his teeth rattled.

Foscari chased after him, pausing only long enough to
wave Matteo's blanket under Cesca's nose. She knew what
was coming. Foscari would lay the blame on her for this
latest tantrum, like a cat depositing a limp rat at its mistress's feet.

"I fault you for this outburst, Cesca. You have spoiled the boy beyond all reason. I have tried everything—gentle coaxing, bribery, threats, beating him with this." He brandished a willow switch then flung it to the floor, where it scuttled along the marble and bounced to a halt in the corner. "He is as obstinate as a donkey. He shakes his head at every question I put to him, lips pursed. Just now he screamed at me that he would tell the judge I am a bad man who steals innocent little boys from their mothers. Nothing I say has the slightest effect. I have had many talks with him and each time I have emerged the loser in this battle of wills." Foscari drove a fist into his palm. "A rude child no bigger than a flower pot stands between me and the richest fortune in Venice."

Cesca was not unsympathetic. Matteo could be difficult.

"He says he will tell the judge he never saw the blanket before and that I stole it off a washerwoman's clothesline." Foscari was spitting with anger. "He shouts epithets at me. He throws his toys out of the window, expensive toys that I brought him from the finest toymaker in Venice. Why does he thwart me at every turn?"

"Shall I try to reason with him?"

"And why do you undermine my authority by coddling him, preparing special dishes and exclaiming over every scraped knee and bruise? Coaxing him to sleep by singing to him?" he sputtered, his face purpled with rage.

Matteo would not sleep, and without sleep he was impossibly irritable the next day. Cesca spent hours singing to him at night and telling him stories, but he refused to settle down. When he finally fell asleep, he would awaken an hour or so later and thrash about, demanding water, his bed linen soaked with sweat. It was all very discouraging. And exhausting. Most annoying of all, even after his long absence from Hannah Matteo still called for her in the most pitiful manner. "Let me try."

"It would do no good," said Foscari. "The child must be choleric. If by tomorrow he is not better behaved, I shall summon the local surgeon, Tagliacozzi, who will no doubt diagnose the boy as suffering from an abundance of yellow bile. He will bleed Matteo with one of those nasty-looking fleams."

Bleed him? Cesca tried to push from her mind the vision of a lancet with the curved hook inserted into Matteo's arm, probing for a vein; the basin catching the droplets of his blood. The boy writhing on the bed in fear and pain.

"Do not look so upset. Tagliacozzi is a graduate of the University of Bologna. If Matteo still does not improve, he will apply leeches. That should put the whole thing right."

"The boy is fond of me. And sometimes I can make him behave." Cesca suspected Matteo loved her only because there was no one else. Every child, even a sturdy little dumpling like Matteo, needed love. She herself needed love, for heaven's sake. When she was rich and had the villa securely in her name, she would find it.

"You deceive yourself." Foscari gave a bark of laughter. "It is that Jewess he loves. He blames us both for her loss."

"All he must say is that the blanket is his?"

"Which he will not do."

This is what it came down to: her happiness rested on the tractability of one small, insignificant, annoyingly stubborn child. Without Matteo, Foscari could not obtain his order. The villa would not be transferred to her. Cesca would spend the rest of her life grieving, like a swan for its dead mate, for terrazzo floors, Murano glass and her beloved *castellana*.

"The boy is a rock in the middle of a field. I cannot shift him." Pausing, Foscari said slowly, "Perhaps, like a farmer, I must plow around him."

Cesca went to the kitchen and commenced stirring linseed oil, olive oil, pine resin, rosemary and wormwood. Then she sprinkled in oats to form a thick paste. It was another poultice for Foscari's gouty foot. The hot linseed was so acrid it filled the room with a stink like that of burned hair. No herb, not even rosemary, was strong enough to mask the stench.

Together they walked out into the garden and sat under a holm oak. Cesca placed the basin filled with the mixture on the ground. Foscari perched sulkily next to a statue of Dionysius and rested his back against the tree trunk. "The boy's outburst could not have happened at a worse time."

"What if you told the judge that Matteo is ill?" Cesca said. "Then wouldn't Hannah's testimony be sufficient?"

"Abarbanel made it clear that without both Hannah and Matteo, he would give the estate to the Franciscan monks for their wretched monastery and we will have not a *scudo* to show for our efforts." In his impatience, a little puff of air escaped his lips. "The monks will strip the ducats from the estate faster than a butcher singeing the bristles off a pig's hide."

"When must you return to court?" Cesca pulled off Foscari's boot and helped him to ease his foot into the steaming basin.

He winced with the heat of it. "In a fortnight."

"Postpone the trial. With God's grace and my instruction, Matteo will come around, but it will take time." Foscari had managed to bungle the simple task of persuading the boy to acknowledge the blanket. Five minutes of testimony was all that was required of Matteo.

"I have already explained a delay is impossible."

"But why?"

"Judge Abarbanel may have all the time in the world, but I do not. My creditors circle like wolves bringing down a stag." He shifted his foot in the basin, wiggling his toes. "I tell you, I have nothing left, and without the prospect of an imminent court date, no moneylender will lend me another *scudo*."

Nothing left? What a liar you are, Foscari. I left you with a fat purse even after helping myself to a few of your ducats.

"I *shall* be in court with Matteo. If I must, I will beat him until his bottom is raw."

Through the upstairs window, she heard Matteo calling for her. For once Cesca welcomed his summons. She needed a few minutes alone. "Excuse me while I go inside to check on him." She got up and went in the house.

As she passed through the upstairs hallway, she noticed marks on a door jamb where a previous occupant—perhaps

Matteo's father—had measured the height of a child over many years. What child? A neighbour's boy? A nephew? She touched the marks. The stone felt cool on her hand. She pressed her cheek against it as she thought of what she should do next. Would there be another set of marks for Matteo—another slash of candle soot, Matteo wriggling in protest, as her hand pressed his red curls to get an accurate measurement? He exasperated her with his crying and his refusal to cooperate, yet Foscari's fury with the child worried her.

She found Matteo in bed, eyes open as he thrashed about in his usual restless manner. He must have snuck in the back way and flopped into bed—fully clothed, judging by the bunched-up covers. His chest, so defenceless, like the breast of a plucked pullet, rose and fell with shallow breaths. She kissed his forehead and pushed damp hair off his cheek. Then she helped him off with his clothes. There were red stripes on his back. She drew the coverlet over him. In the morning she would apply an unguent. *Please relent, Matteo. Your future and mine are entwined like a grapevine on an arbour. I am trying to be a good mother to you. Now you try to be a good and obedient child to me.*

She returned to the garden.

"There, you see?" said Foscari when she settled back under the oak. "This is the troublesome way of children. In an absolute passion one moment then fast asleep the next."

"It is hard to fall asleep when you are in pain. You should not have thrashed him."

Foscari continued in what was for him a humble tone.

"Perhaps you are right. You take over the duty of instructing him. I am sure he will then be letter perfect by the court date."

"You have made my task more difficult by antagonizing him. If only I had had charge of him right from the start. Now I must undo the damage you have done by screaming at him and whipping him. You cannot break a child the way you would an unruly horse." To Cesca's surprise and embarrassment, her voice started to falter—she had also seen welts on Matteo's bottom after some of his sessions with Foscari—and she had trouble finishing her sentence. "Cruelty only makes him more resolute." She pretended to cough, and bent to brush a rose petal off her skirts. "Your ill treatment provokes him to be sulky and ill-tempered." She adjusted the position of Foscari's foot in the poultice. "If only you had obtained that order months ago when you first went to court."

"Is that so?" He shot her a look of annoyance. "And if only you had persuaded the boy to be more agreeable."

It was all Cesca could do not to pick up the rusty scythe lying in the grass and strike him. "I have done my best."

"My dear, of course you have." A long moment of silence followed as Foscari moved his foot to and fro in the basin. "I see a way out of our difficulty, but I need your help."

This time, Cesca decided, he would not inveigle her into doing his bidding then stab her in the back. She crossed her arms over her bosom. "When will you go to the notary?" Weeks had elapsed since Foscari's promise, but there was still no letter of intent.

"Oh, that. Never fear. I shall arrange to visit the notary straightaway. It's just that I have been so consumed with worry about the boy, I have had no time to think of anything else." Foscari cleared his throat. "An idea has occurred to me, though."

"And what is that?"

"If Matteo cannot testify properly, I must find a boy who can."

"I don't understand."

"You have said yourself. Matteo is disobedient and wilful. I am not convinced even under your guidance he will ever be cooperative."

Foscari was going to suggest something she would not care for. Cesca could tell by the way he tugged at his earlobe as though milking a miniature cow.

Foscari said, "I know where I can find a compliant, healthy child of about the right age."

"But then what will become of Matteo?"

Foscari glanced at her, an unreadable expression on his face. "Well, he is of no further use to us, is he?"

CHAPTER 11

Jewish Ghetto,
Venice

BEFORE HER PREGNANCY Hannah would have bounded up the steep staircase to Asher's apartment ahead of him, as nimble as a mountain goat. Now, the skirts of her *cioppà* bunched in one hand, she was slow and clumsy. By the time they reached the third floor, Hannah was panting and holding her sides.

Through the apartment door came the yells of boys and Tzipporah's shouts. Hannah recalled her sister-in-law as a very improving kind of woman. Improving of herself, improving of Asher, improving of everyone around her whether they wished to be improved or not. But that had been five years ago. Perhaps grief had smoothed the rough edges of her nature.

From inside the apartment came the sound of a heavy object crashing to the floor. Without waiting for Hannah to catch her breath, Asher flung open the door and, standing to one side, made a sweeping bow as though ushering her through the portals of a palazzo on the Grand Canal.

All apartments in the ghetto vibrated with industry—sewing, soap making, carpentry, hat making and boot repair. When Hannah and Isaac had lived in the ghetto, they considered themselves fortunate to inhabit a cramped, airless place not unlike Asher's. Hannah had owned a pair of brown hens, which roosted in the cook pots at night for lack of a nest. But in this apartment was chaos of a different order. The scene within Asher's dwelling recalled the destruction of King Solomon's temple. The two narrow rooms overflowed with stacks of books and papers, clock mechanisms, embroidery hoops, thimbles, thread, a tortoiseshell cat batting spools of blue yarn along the floor, a small loom, the hull of a half-carved toy boat.

Suspended from the sill of the only window was a wooden rack. Damp breeches and shirts flapped in the breeze. Open baskets hung from the ceiling bulging with second-hand clothing and quilts taken by Asher in pledge. Heavier articles sat stored in sacks on the floor, which overflowed with brass candlesticks, Turkish carpets, paintings, tapestries and God knows what else. The boys, all miniature replicas of Asher, were everywhere, the smaller two playing with *dreidels*. They seemed to be all sharp elbows and scabby knees poking through mended shirts and breeches. They were much too thin. Hannah glanced at Asher, noticing for the first time his jacket was worn at the elbows and his shirt cuffs tattered.

Hannah remembered only the friendliness of the ghetto. The street vendors, the smell of pickled herring and the winter peaches arranged in a pyramid on the vendor's table, the bakery fragrant with yeast and sugar and raisins and precious cinnamon. Now, looking around the *loghetto*, Hannah realized her mind had winnowed out the bad memories, leaving only the good behind. She had forgotten the dim rooms bursting with large families, with no place for storage, no place to escape on summer nights so hot the pine pitch between the boards of the building stank and oozed—if one brushed against them, they would leave streaks of sticky, black pitch on clothes and skin.

Of course, there were no glass panes in the windows, no *cristallo*, the clear glass the glass-makers on the island of Murano were so famous for. The ghetto windows were covered with oiled parchment, which as time went on ripped and let in the fever-making vapours of the night air. What a contrast to her airy, spacious, well-appointed house in Constantinople, with its gardens, summer kitchen, mulberry orchard and, most of all, her beloved Isaac.

Since she had left Constantinople, sleep had not come easily without Isaac next to her. Hannah would remember their nights together and grow hot and restless, thrashing in a way that had nothing to do with the thinness of her mattress or her threadbare covers. She would throw a leg out then bring it back under the quilt, trying not to think of him: the smoothness of his chest; the areola of hair around his nipples; his long, strong back arched toward her; the salty taste of his skin; the way he grabbed a handful of her hair and tilted her head back to kiss her throat; her nightgown a silky pool on the floor in the morning.

In the midst of Asher's tiny apartment, like a large-prowed ship in the calm eye of a storm, stood Tzipporah. Hannah walked to her, trying not to hit her head on the low ceiling or trip on a sack. She felt giddy from the climb up the stairs and from the heavenly odour wafting from a pot on the brazier.

"*Shalom aleichem*, Hannah," Tzipporah said, thrusting aside a sheet drying from a rope suspended from the rafters. Her belly was protuberant—she was at least seven months along, Hannah judged. Her sister-in-law stirred something on the charcoal brazier. Hannah inhaled and sighed with pleasure at the floral fragrance. Lily of the valley. Her favourite scent, one that brought back memories of her mother arranging a few delicate white-belled stems in a vase on the Shabbat table.

"*Aleichem shalom*, Tzipporah." Hannah gave her sister-in-law a hug. Tzipporah must have felt the thrust of Hannah's pregnancy in the embrace. She grinned and pinched Hannah's cheek.

"At last! I am so happy for you."

Tzipporah was a handsome woman, as tall and straight as a glassmaker's *borsello* with a wide, generous mouth that still boasted all its teeth. She flailed her arms like a windmill, as she admonished the boys for shouting, rocked the youngest one, slicked down a cowlick and stirred the concoction on the stove.

Tzipporah had acquired creases around her mouth and eyes, but her skin was otherwise unwrinkled and free of pox scars. Hannah reached up to stroke it; it was soft as a baby's. Tzipporah smiled and tilted her head into Hannah's caress.

"Still so thin! In another month you will look like the snake that swallowed the elephant!"

Tzipporah let out an embarrassed chortle as she realized how tactless her remark sounded. The giggle made her seem younger than her thirty-five years but sounded odd coming from so stern a mouth.

"So sorry, Hannah. You look pretty. Pregnancy has made you radiant." She clasped Hannah's hands in her own and drew her closer to the small window. Tzipporah took her chin and turned her face this way and that, running a thumb along Hannah's cheek. "How was your journey? No, do not tell me. I can read it in your skin. Your face and neck are chapped from the wind. Your hair is coarse from the sea air."

Tzipporah's fondness for Hannah was genuine. Asher must have complained to his wife about the missing violin, but such accusations had not diminished Tzipporah's affection for her sister-in-law.

"The journey was long and tiring." Hannah peered over Tzipporah's shoulder to see what was in the pot. Something thick, honey coloured and smooth, with a lovely lustre to it.

Asher was trying to separate two of the boys who were wrestling near the brazier. Tzipporah ignored them. "What are you cooking?" asked Hannah, standing as far from the brazier as she could in case one of the boys overturned it as they shoved each other.

"The very thing you should be rubbing on your skin. Cream made of beeswax, almond oil and lanolin. Here— hold out your hand." Tzipporah drizzled an amount the size of a small coin onto Hannah's palm. "Smooth it on those rough cheeks."

Hannah did as she was told. First Assunta, now Tzipporah. To be surrounded by good-hearted, bossy women seemed to be Hannah's destiny. The cream was rich and fragrant. It absorbed into her skin, leaving a rich sheen behind.

Asher glanced up, holding the two boys at arm's length. "Tzipporah is famous for her potions. Her coltsfoot salve sells before it is off the stove and poured into jars," he said.

"The rich noblewomen in the grand palazzi send their ladies' maids to buy it from me." Tzipporah nudged Hannah with her elbow. "It also works as dubbin on Asher's old leather boots."

Hannah took a deep breath. "I would be grateful for your hospitality. I need a place for a few nights before I leave for San Lorenzo."

The affable look left Tzipporah's face. "I thought you would be staying at a public inn. We cannot . . ."

Hannah waited for her to continue, but Tzipporah, turning to Asher, said, "Send the boys out."

"Before I do that," said Asher, "let me introduce you— Samuel, Tubal, Solomon, Benjamin and—" he gestured to a crib in the corner, from which a fist waved "—Elijah, the youngest, aged three. Come, boys. Say hello to your aunt Hannah."

"What lovely boys. So handsome, so strong."

"And who could they take after not to be handsome?" asked Asher, grinning.

Hannah smiled in agreement. Elijah was the best looking, with wide-set black eyes and an impish expression on his face. The others might be too thin, but this clever child had somehow managed to acquire a nice layer of flesh.

"And may we also remember little Jacob and Saul, of blessed memory, who will never grow up to be strong or handsome but who will always be in our hearts," said Tzipporah.

Asher nodded.

Hannah pressed her lips together and looked at the floor.

Just then one of the boys—Tubal, Hannah thought—punched Samuel in the arm, making him howl with fury then retaliate by thumping Tubal on the back.

"Enough! All of you! Outside this minute," Asher said.

There was a stampede of footsteps on the staircase as the boys raced out. Matteo would take pleasure in the fierce camaraderie of his cousins. They would race around the *campo*, playing tag and wheedling oranges from the fruit vendor. In the midst of such good spirits and hilarity, Matteo's grave nature would give way to playfulness.

"Good," declared Asher, as the last boy clattered down the stairs. He closed the door. "Peace at last."

Hannah turned toward her sister-in-law. "I understand your reluctance about me staying, Tzipporah, but I have nowhere else." A pleading tone crept into her voice, shaming her. "I know I am one more mouth to feed, another body taking up space in a crowded house." When Tzipporah just stood and shook her head, Hannah went on, "Just until I can find my son, Matteo."

"Food and space are not the problem." Tzipporah shot Asher a glare. "You didn't write her?"

Asher looked as though he wanted to follow his sons out the door.

Tzipporah said, "Bah, too busy worrying about your father's miserable old fiddle."

"Placing such news in a letter, which anyone with a knife could unfasten and read, would not have been wise."

"Tell her," said Tzipporah.

Asher turned to Hannah. "You know how people gossip in Venice. A servant of the di Padovani household put out the rumour that the Conte gave you two hundred ducats for delivering his heir. When you left Venice so abruptly, everyone assumed you had sailed to Malta to ransom Isaac."

Hannah's stomach tightened. Sometimes the body senses disaster before the mind comprehends it. "And so I did." There was more; she could tell by the hesitation on Asher's face.

"You left in the middle of the worst outbreak of the plague," said Tzipporah. "All was death and confusion. Thousands died. The city stank with the rotting flesh. And not just the poor died. Nobles, as well, including one of the di Padovani brothers, Niccolò. Some say he died of the plague, but others say he was murdered."

Hannah would not ask if Niccolò's body had been discovered. She did not want to arouse curiosity by showing an interest.

Tzipporah glanced at Asher as though seeking his support. "Some said the Conte's baby died of the plague soon after his birth. Some said you stole him."

Hannah twisted the fringes of her red head scarf between her fingers. "Matteo was alive. I took him with me." A long while ago, in another lifetime or so it seemed, Hannah had been summoned in the middle of the night to deliver the child of the Conte di Padovani. The baby refused to leave the comfort of the Contessa's womb and was murdering her with his obstinacy Hannah managed, with the help of her birthing spoons, a pair of joined soup ladles fitted around his head, to coax Matteo out. Several weeks later, when his parents perished in the plague, Matteo became hers—hers and Isaac's.

"Now the gossip is the boy is back under the protection of a nobleman, a relative of the Conte's, who is raising him in a manner befitting the heir to a great fortune. The gentiles say this nobleman rescued the boy from the Jewish midwife who delivered him."

"I see." Hannah was astonished so much was known about her actions that terrible day when she boarded the ship for Constantinople, Matteo in her arms.

Tzipporah said, "You cannot raise a gentile child. Not only is it against the law, but—"

"There are murmurings of the ancient libel," said Asher.

"I don't understand." Hannah did understand but needed to be sure.

"You know as well as I do," said Asher, "that for hundreds of years Christians have held the belief that Jews perform ritual murder of Christian children, from a compulsion to re-enact the Crucifixion. Only yesterday I saw a crude drawing on a church wall in Dorsoduro of a hooked-nosed Jew with a knife upraised, about to slit a baby's throat. Underneath was a basin to collect the baby's blood. To the right was a Jewess rolling out dough for matzah."

Hannah walked to the window and flung it open, letting in the cold air. "Fanning the embers of blood libel, bringing it to full flame, is a task the fanatical preachers are only too willing to perform."

"I agree. The rabble is always eager for an excuse to spill Jewish blood," said Asher.

"Matteo is my son. I love him."

"He is not your son," said Tzipporah. To soften the harshness of her words, she put an arm around Hannah. "The child is Christian. It is not right for you to raise him."

"You must give Matteo up," Asher said. "If you do not, you will bring slaughter and destruction not only to our family but to the entire ghetto."

CHAPTER 12

Jewish Ghetto,
Venice

"I CANNOT," SAID HANNAH. "He is my son."

Tzipporah was unmoved. "After you left Venice, soldiers from the Prosecuti arrived, making inquiries."

If only Asher had put aside his petty grievances and warned her. But would it have made any difference? Would she not still have come?

"They wanted to know about a baby belonging to the di Padovani family."

Many years before, when Matteo was only a few months old, Hannah had followed his uncle, Niccolò di Padovani, into the ghetto. The nobleman had carried a basket containing Matteo. Niccolò planned to kill the child and nail his corpse to the doors of the church of Sant'Alvise just outside the ghetto. With one slice of the knife across Matteo's throat Niccolò's position as heir to the family fortune would have been secured and the Jews blamed for Matteo's death.

"They gave old Vicente, the watchman, a drubbing, trying to get information. Vicente insisted he had been drunk and saw nothing." Tzipporah stirred her cream and then faced Hannah. "The old Rabbi came forward. He convinced the soldiers you had sailed for Malta to ransom your husband and that yes, there had been a baby—a fact that could not be denied, because there were deckhands and porters at the dock who verified that—but that the child was a Jew, an orphan whose parents had perished in the plague."

"Without Rabbi Ibrahim's intervention, you know what would have happened next," said Asher. "Our friends and neighbours would have been dragged from their beds and beaten until someone confessed to what the Prosecuti were so keen to hear."

To be beholden to her old foe the Rabbi, who had once counselled Isaac to divorce her, was an unhappy thought.

"And Matteo? Did they discover I had taken him?"

"When the soldiers returned the next day, they reported that a servant at the Conte's palazzo had told them the Conte's baby was dead," said Asher.

"It must have been Giovanna." Another old enemy she must feel grateful to—Giovanna, the midwife who had tried to oust Hannah from the Contessa's bedchamber the night Matteo was born. After Hannah had rescued Matteo, she had run back to the palazzo to return him to the Conte and Contessa. Hannah had—as a ruse to escape the soldiers who were after her—painted him in convincing plague buboes and lesions. Giovanna had slammed the door in her face before Hannah could explain the baby's horrific appearance.

Tzipporah said, "If the soldiers of the Prosecuti come calling again, even our quick-witted Rabbi will not be able to defend you. The two who have taken Matteo will step forward to condemn you. You understand now why it is impossible for you to stay."

"But I have nowhere else and it is nearly sundown." Hannah hoped Asher would speak up for her, as she had so many times for him when he had gotten into trouble as a youth for staying out late, fighting, being rude to his elders, keeping company with courtesans and gambling in the casinos on the Rialto. To her dismay, he remained silent.

Tzipporah gestured with her wooden paddle, leaving a trail of cream on the floor. "Your presence endangers all of us," she said. "The ghetto is so small I would not be surprised if half the people in the *campo* recognized you today and have already told the other half."

"Do these gossipmongers also say that Foscari and Cesca are scoundrels?" Hannah asked. "Once Foscari has his hands on Matteo's fortune, who knows what he will do to him?"

"Why would they harm your son?" Asher said. "It is in their interests to keep him alive. Matteo will be raised in a manner befitting the son of a nobleman. Foscari will hire nursemaids to care for him. When he is older, tutors and fine scholars will educate him. When he is of age, he will take his place on the Council of Ten, serving the government. You and Isaac cannot offer him anything so fine."

"If only Isaac and I could be his legal guardians," said Hannah.

Asher laughed. "As if a Jew could ever be appointed in such a capacity. Or a woman, for that matter. A widow cannot even be guardian of her own children."

"Isaac told me of a boy from Siena whose uncle was appointed guardian. By the time the boy reached adulthood, his so-called protector had laid bare his estate—the timber felled, the house in disrepair, the fields laid to waste, the cattle slaughtered. The ward, penniless, petitioned the court for redress but got no satisfaction. His guardian had already squandered the entire estate."

"No doubt there can be evil in the custom of wardship. Many children are taken advantage of, but Foscari is from an old and noble family," said Asher.

"That does not make him less of a rogue." Hannah could see her brother was not convinced, so she changed her approach. "It is easy for you who have been blessed with so many sons to advise me to give up Matteo, but I cannot."

"Hannah." Asher put his hand on her arm. "Whether Foscari is a rogue or not, murderer or not, villain or not, makes no difference. The heart of the matter is this: if you are discovered with a Christian child, you will be hanged and the ghetto will be burned to the ground."

"But my son?" said Hannah.

Tzipporah said, "*Your* son? What about my sons? And my husband? And my neighbours? There are two thousand

Jews living here. How long will we be safe if you are arrested?"

From the crib, Elijah gave a sharp little cry of distress then fell back to sleep.

"I have made trouble," said Hannah. "I am sorry. That was not my intention. I will leave now." To where she did not know.

Asher moved some clothing off a chair. He gestured to Hannah to sit. "Tzipporah, give her some bread and broth before she goes. It is the least we can do."

Through the opened window could be heard the squeaking of hinges, the thud of gates shoved closed, the rasp of an iron bolt drawn across heavy wooden portals. They looked at one another. It was sundown. Vicente had locked the gates. Hannah was barely able to hide her relief.

Asher was the first to speak. "Tonight is Shabbat. You will celebrate with us." He shouted out the window for the boys to come in. Soon there was a clatter of footsteps on the stairs and then the four older boys trooped in. Solomon was carrying a covered dish, steaming hot, fragrant with the smell of meat and vegetables. He had been to the communal oven in the *campo*, where everyone's *cholent*, stew of chicken and parsnips, was baked for Shabbat dinner.

Asher cleared a space in the middle of the room and set up a makeshift table, a long board balanced on a couple of carpenter's sawhorses. Tzipporah picked up Elijah, tucked him under one arm as she slammed bowls on the table with such force Hannah was afraid they would shatter. Then she sat, holding him in her lap, barely concealing her anger.

Asher donned a *kippah* and took his position at the head of the table. He bowed his head and intoned, "'She watches over the ways of her household, and does not eat the bread of idleness.'" It was a verse from Eshet Chayil in the book of Proverbs. It was the blessing men made to their wives before each Shabbat meal.

How many times had Isaac recited all twenty-one verses when he returned from *shul*? "'A woman of valour,'" he would say. "'An accomplished woman, who can find her? Her value is far beyond pearls. Her husband's heart relies upon her and he shall lack no fortune.'"

Hannah sat with her head bowed and remembered her joy, not so long ago, as Isaac recited those familiar words, gazing at her lovingly with his dark eyes, Matteo restless in his chair, Jessica wiggling in her lap, pulling at the tablecloth, the Shabbat chicken steaming before them. The vision of them all gathered around the dinner table sailed through her mind, leaving in its wake a yearning for Isaac, before giving way to an ache. She was overwhelmed by a sudden longing to return to Constantinople, to put things right between her and Isaac, to beg his forgiveness for leaving without even a goodbye, to say, 'I am sorry. I was headstrong. I should have stayed with you and Jessica.'

Asher and the boys joined hands in prayer. Tzipporah covered her head with a scarf and blessed the candles and the *challah*. The boys were quiet except for the rumblings from their bellies, their eyes riveted on the earthenware dish containing *cholent*.

Asher began to serve. Everyone watched silently as Asher slid his spoon through the stew then put heaping portions in each bowl. Tzipporah cast him a look that said as eloquently as words that he should serve smaller portions, that this dish must do for several more meals before the last bones and gristle ended up in the soup pot. Asher handed around the bowls, first to Hannah, then Tzipporah, then proceeded from the oldest to youngest boy. "It grieves me to say this but . . ."

"Then don't say it, Asher," Tzipporah said. "The Torah tells us to say nothing on Shabbat that will draw tears."

Elijah, who had been sitting on Tzipporah's lap, began to cry. Tzipporah offered him a taste of *cholent* to quieten him, but Elijah would not be comforted. With a practised, unselfconscious motion, she drew a breast out of her bodice and nursed him, while Asher finished serving. Elijah was a rosyfaced child, with curly dark hair and a disconcerting way of glancing around the table, appraising his family face by face as though deciding whom he liked and whom he did not. When his black eyes settled on Hannah, he broke his suck on Tzipporah's breast, jerked his body toward Hannah and smiled. She let his tiny fingers clasp hers. He held out his arms and Hannah brought him into her lap.

"Hannah, I know you love Matteo as much as we love our sons," said Asher.

Hannah took a spoonful of stew. It was tasty, but glancing around the table at her brother's hollow-cheeked sons, she had no appetite. Still, she must eat for the sake of her unborn baby. She took another small taste. She would consume half her portion so one of the children could have the other half. "Say what is on your mind, Asher," said Hannah.

Asher began. "We are asking Hannah to give up her son, Tzipporah, but could we give up one of ours?"

To Hannah's surprise, instead of dismissing the idea outright Tzipporah pondered the question. Then she replied, "I have been blessed with five fine sons. I have another baby on the way. God, in his wisdom, may send other children after this one."

Asher gestured to Elijah, now sleeping in Hannah's arms. "Elijah is healthy. He is a Jew. When you change his nappies, you will see he has made his first covenant with God. The *mohel* circumcised him on the eighth day as required by law."

"But . . ." Hannah was uncomfortable with where the conversation was heading.

Asher said, "Sometimes one family is wonderfully blessed with children and another family is not. There are many examples of adoption in the ghetto. Elijah would be happy with you. You and Isaac could give him a better future than we can."

Hannah looked at Tzipporah to gauge her reaction to Asher's words.

"Elijah is young. He will have no trouble adjusting to a new life with you and Isaac, but no." Tzipporah reached across the table and clasped Hannah's forearm. "But no, we could not give Elijah to you, any more than you can surrender Matteo to those two who stole him from you."

CHAPTER 13

Jewish Ghetto, Venice

ANNAH LAY ON HER sleeping pallet, her thoughts racing. She had never felt so alone as she did in this cramped *loghetto*, pressed in on all sides by the slumbering bodies of her nephews, sister-in-law and brother, all squeezed in so closely she smelled stewed chicken and parsnips on their breath. She belonged to no one; no one belonged to her. No one loved her as much as Isaac did. Without him, she had joined the great mass of people in this world who are unloved by anyone. Her longing for Isaac was as strong a sensation as the baby kicking within her, but she had trampled his love underfoot. She tried to remember what Isaac smelled like—the soap she washed his linen in, the fragrance of his hair when he returned from the barber. What he sounded like in sleep as his chest gently rose and fell when his breathing slowed. What the scratch of his black beard felt like.

She could describe these things to herself in words and she could summon the physicality of him—the warmth of his body, the robustness of his laughter. But the longer she and he were apart, the less vivid these details became.

After easing herself from between Tubal and Samuel, she rolled onto all fours. Then she rose to an upright position. She went to Elijah's crib. Lifting him in her arms, careful not to awaken him, she cupped one hand behind his head, the other on his bottom. He snored, turning his head and rooting in his sleep for her breast. How well he fitted in her arms. How easily she could grow to love him. How simple it would be to give up her search for Matteo and persuade Tzipporah to allow her to take this lovely boy back to Constantinople. She had a feeling that Asher would not object to one less mouth to feed if it meant his son was well raised. Even in his sleep Elijah seemed to smile at her, dark lashes fanning his cheeks. Her unborn baby moved as if in response. She placed Elijah back in his cradle.

Hannah fumbled her few possessions into her valise—her comb, nightdress and a pomegranate from Tzipporah's larder, careful not to drop anything. With her pregnancy she had grown so clumsy and absent-minded, dropping small items, forgetting to do the simplest things like fasten her dress or lace her boots. She rolled up her sleeping mat and tucked it under the table. After edging open the door of the *loghetto*, she crept down the creaky stairs. It would be at least three hours until Vicente, pockmarked face flushed from drinking through the night, would swing open the heavy gates of the ghetto. Asher and Tzipporah would waken to find her gone and be relieved by her departure.

At the bottom of the tiny stairwell, Hannah dug out the nun's habit from the bottom of her valise. Somehow it had become damp and had acquired the dank smell of sea water trapped too long without air. She struggled into it, banging her elbows in the narrow space as she tugged the robe over her head and smoothed down the skirts. The habit flapped around her as she moved, making her feel as if she had dead mackerels tied around her waist. Hannah fastened the wimple and *serre-tête*, the bands of linen, that framed her face. They were so tight she could look in no other direction than straight ahead. This, Assunta had explained, would prevent her from being tempted by the devil, who always crept up obliquely, from the left side. Avoiding the devil was all very well but what about the soldiers of the Prosecuti? They were a more likely danger. The massive headdress would soon make her neck ache. A renegade black curl escaped and she poked it back in. She stuffed the blue *cioppà* into her valise, fingering the hem first to assure herself the gold ducats were still there but they were not. After a moment of panic, she remembered she had sewn them into her nun's habit, hoping robbers would be less likely to steal from a nun.

Not a soul was in the *campo*, which the dark filled with shadows and unnameable sounds. She walked to the hut where Vicente slept and hunkered down out of sight behind it, waiting for dawn.

Her legs grew stiff from the night air. Bats whooshed close to her head, their squeaking making her recoil. At last the sun rose, sending fingers of light through the wide-spaced planks of the ghetto gates. As was his custom, Vicente opened the south gate first. When he left it propped open to unfasten the north gate, Hannah slipped out.

Hannah headed for the wharf, dragging her valise along the Fondamenta. The skirts of her habit billowed around her. The habit, now that she had worn it for a few hours, had trapped all the normal fragrances of her body and distilled them into an unfamiliar medley. It took her a moment to realize what was wrong. She did not smell like a Jew anymore. No garlic, no pickled herring, no honey cake. Just musty gabardine and the scent of Assunta's much-fingered rosary beads.

She passed a group of bystanders listening to a Franciscan monk. It was a common enough sight. The city had more than its share of fanatical preachers. The monk was a short, overfed man. Fat rolls creased his neck; his plump hand moved through the air as he gestured. He stood with his arm around a young chorister, a boy of about twelve with the fresh, clean look of the country and the brown, untroubled eyes of a fawn. The monk paused to make the sign of the cross over the boy's head. "Should the blood of an innocent child be spilled to satisfy the heretic Jew?"

People had gathered around the monk. Encouraged by the crowd, he shouted, "Drive the heathen from our city as our Lord and Saviour drove the moneylenders from the temple." He brushed back his brown hood, exposing a tonsured head. "You there, Sister," he called to Hannah. "Would not our fair city be a paradise on earth without the Jewish pestilence?"

How these fanatics caused Hannah's blood to boil! One would think a lifetime of hearing such rantings would have made her indifferent, yet she wanted to call back, *Ignorant pederast, you know nothing of Jews.* She took a deep breath. *Calmness,* she counselled herself. *This is my first test.*

A few dozen paces away stood a group of Jews, their red hats vivid amid the collection of sombre grey- and black-garbed people; the Jews glanced at the monk then walked swiftly toward the ghetto. She should ignore the monk's question and continue to the docks. But would her conscience allow her to stand cravenly silent or, worse, pretend to agree with him?

She wanted to yell over the murmurings of assent from the rabble, *Does not your Bible teach you to "Do unto others as you would have them do unto you"? Is that not the Golden Rule? The keystone upon which your religion rests? How would you feel if I preached against the Franciscan order? Would you want to be driven from Venice?* But she made a fist, held it to her mouth and bit down. *Rise above the petty insults of the world,* her father would have admonished. Her mission was to find Matteo. Nothing else mattered.

The monk chuckled, warming to his theme. "We all know the rumours of Jews poisoning wells. The plague was their handiwork, as well. With their incantations and dark ways, they summoned the pestilence. And who has not heard the stories of Jews snatching Christian babies and draining their blood to make their ritual bread? The city fathers have offered protection to this viperous lot, but the sooner they are driven from the city, the safer we Christians will be." The throng pressed closer to him. In spite of her disguise, Hannah began to feel fearful. What if someone recognized in her features the stamp of Jewish blood? *I must not toss oil on a fire that is already burning out of control. I must remain silent.*

A few drops of rain began to fall. *You want to drive the Jews from the city? Rumours of evildoing circulate with special vigour when the moneylenders ask for repayment of their loans. How much easier to banish a creditor than to pay him.*

One brave soul in the crowd, a carpenter from the look of his leather apron and tool belt, called out, "'Tis a cowardly thing to level accusations at a poor and defenceless people." There was an angry rumble. A few men bent down to pry up cobbles from the street.

Hannah felt like rushing over to the carpenter and throwing her arms around him. At least there was one virtuous gentile in the crowd.

"Poor and defenceless?" the monk asked. "The Jews are the richest of us all."

A stone hit the carpenter on the forehead. He strode off, his broad back soon lost in the mob. If she opened her mouth, Hannah would be their next target. She gathered up the skirts of her habit and hurried on. The monk called out to her, "What convent are you from, Sister? Come back. You have a comely face."

Turning away, Hannah moved on through the throng, mouth dry, her cheeks burning with rage and self-reproach. How she wanted to run, but she could not without attracting attention. She had not succumbed to the temptation of shouting at the monk; she had managed to keep quiet. This should have been a source of pride. But she had for years listened passively to hateful diatribes against the Jews. Now she wore a nun's habit, a shield from which she could voice her objections. Yet still she had not spoken out. She grew hot with shame. She knew she would relive this feeling of guilt many times before she could forgive herself.

From a distance Hannah glimpsed the di Padovani palazzo on the Grand Canal. It looked sad and neglected. The last time she had seen it the window glass sparkled and the stone facade had shone in the sunlight. Now no sleek black gondola was tied to the dock. The mooring posts, paint peeling, stood leaning toward each other for mutual support, like drunkards returning home from a tavern. But glass and stone facades and mooring posts could be repaired. This was Matteo's legacy—a grand palazzo and the life of a nobleman.

Hannah hurried on amid the sounds of halyards rattling against masts and the shouts of porters loading cargo. The smell of fish and seaweed grew stronger. At the wharf she found a boatman—an old man in a blue cap, with a mangy cat at his feet—who was loading a number of passengers onto his barge, about to cast off for the Brenta River. He tossed her valise into his wide-bottomed boat. Clutching her robes in one hand, Hannah climbed in, trying not to trip over the crates of turnips, cauliflower and beets lining the gunwales. She took a seat next to a large man with a silver-headed cane—a man far too well dressed to be travelling on this modest barge.

Soon they were in the middle of the lagoon, the domes of San Marco growing smaller in the distance. At another time Hannah might have enjoyed the ride, but she was still shaking from her encounter with the monk. She sat gripping the side of the barge with both hands, tense with impatience to see her son. Her valise lay slumped on the bench next to her, where she'd placed it to keep it out of the water sloshing in the bottom. Inside the valise was a small, wooden sailboat with two masts, which Isaac had carved for Matteo when he was a baby.

The boatman rowed from San Marco through the lagoon to Fusina, the first town on the Brenta; then he put up his oars and sturdy canal ponies took over the task of pulling the boat. The canal had a number of locks that raised and lowered the water so boats could pass. Each one had a small dwelling to shelter the lock keeper, who was obliged to be available at all times.

Hannah fidgeted on the hard seat of the boat, her growing belly making her uncomfortable. She wanted to shift her seat from the sunny part of the boat to the shaded, but she could not rise to her feet with ease. Her hand tightened on the gunwale. Suddenly she felt unwell. A feeling of heat and then cold passed over her. She bent low, clutching her belly. The pain was like her monthly pains. Like the cramping she had felt when she suffered the miscarriage. This child must remain nestled inside the sturdy cage of her ribs and sharing bones. This baby must emerge—plump and pink and shaking tiny fists at the world, staring at her with Isaac's black eyes and finding her satisfactory. The man next to her, noticing her distress, handed her a mug of water. Hannah nodded gratefully. She stroked her belly. Her muscles relaxed. *I will tell you when it is time, my child. We have many more weeks together, you and I.*

If one is tired enough, one can sleep anywhere, even sitting upright on a boat, jammed between a large, well-dressed man on one side and a burlap bag overflowing with beets from Burano on the other. As Hannah dozed, gratefully aware of the baby moving within her, she heard a groan from the man next to her. He rocked back and forth, clutching his hand to his chest, moaning in pain.

She wondered again why this prosperous-looking man was travelling in this uncomfortable barge when there were elegant *burchielli* to transport the wealthy back and forth on the Brenta. She was a little in awe of him. With his finely tailored waistcoat and jacket, he was clearly a man of importance, but he did not seem to be one of those haughty gentiles covered in velvet flounces and smelling of roasted meats and Malvasia wine.

"Your hand is troubling you, sir?"

He looked up at her—a leonine head of white hair and a face drawn with pain. "I was helping one of my masons position a stone lintel. Like a fool, I managed to smash my hand between lintel and jamb shaft. My fingers have throbbed like the devil ever since."

"May I see it? I have knowledge of simple remedies."

Mutely, he held out his hand.

Three of his fingers were swollen and red, the skin broken, the wound suppurating yellow pus. Gently Hannah moved the fingers back and forth. No bones broken, it seemed. "I will do what I can, sir, but you will not thank me for the discomfort I will cause. Left untreated, however, the wound will cause more mischief and your hand will never heal."

"You cannot make me feel any worse than I do now."

"Hold your hand over the side, sir. Let the water cleanse it."

He dangled his hand over the gunwale, creating a small wake alongside the boat. "I warn you I am a poor patient. The slightest pain sends me roaring in agony."

"The cold water will numb it." Men could not tolerate pain, even vigorous, healthy ones like this man. It was clear why God had given the task of birthing children to women.

Hannah took a pouch of salt from her linen bag and sprinkled some into the mug of water she had been drinking from. With her finger she swirled the salt around until it dissolved. She leaned over toward the man. "Place your fingers in here. It will sting, but the salt will drive out the poisons."

"*Grazie mille*," he said, grimacing as the salt bit into his wound. "I should introduce myself, Sister. I am Andrea Palladio."

"I am Ha— Sister Benedicta." His name meant nothing to her, although he said it in a way that suggested she should recognize it. "Do not thank me too soon. The worst is yet to come."

She opened her valise, picked up her linen bag and removed a sewing needle.

"I shall distract myself by looking at the scenery, studying the lovely villas with their graceful willows arching into the water. Very soon the most beautiful of these villas will be mine."

Hannah took his hand in hers. It felt like the paw of a lion's, rough and covered with wiry hair on the top of his fingers. Her needle was still threaded with the black silk she had used to sew her habit. "I will stitch the edges of the wound together then bind it tightly. You must keep it clean and dry for several weeks until it is healed."

He groaned but did not struggle. Soon the task was done. In the bottom of the bag was a round tin. She fished it out and pried off the top. The smell of pine pitch and coltsfoot drifted in the air. After covering his wound liberally with the black salve, she bound his hand in a clean square of cloth from her bag. "There you are. If we had been on dry land, I might have made a neater job of it, but this will have to do."

Palladio said, "You have a gentle touch. I am grateful."

They settled back on the bench of the barge and soon he was asleep, his elbow propped on his knee, his hand resting lightly on his cheek. Most encounters with gentiles made Hannah anxious, but this one with Palladio did not. He had a calm, reassuring demeanour.

At last, on the third day, just as the shadows of dusk were lengthening, she was awakened from her doze by the bargeman shaking her. "Here is the Villa di Padovani, Sister. The finest in the district."

The barge bumped against the dock. Seated next to her, Palladio dozed.

Hannah glanced up the lawn to the dwelling. This neglected edifice was not the fine villa she had expected. The facade was streaked green with algae. The horseshoe-shaped arches were in need of repointing. Once *cristallo* must have sparkled in the windows, but now many of the windows were as empty as the eye sockets of a blind man. Rubble lay scattered on the ground, covered with weeds and vines.

The boatman, who must have noticed her expression, said, "It's fallen on hard times. But it was the most magnificent estate on the river when the Conte was alive. And the largest. Twenty or so tenant farms, hundreds of hectares of land, dozens of outbuildings, barns and stables."

The main entranceway to the house faced the Brenta and was close enough to the canal that anyone in a boat could be seen. Which meant she might be able to see inside the villa from the boat. Hannah scrutinized the windows, looking for any signs of life. A tall, stooped figure seemed to pass inside, but she could not be certain.

Voices floated from a distant field, an indistinct mumble. Gleaners, perhaps, bringing in the winter wheat. Doves circled overhead, cooing to one another. She had forgotten how sounds carried in the country, unmuffled by the clatter and jostling of carts and people.

Surprise would be her greatest ally. Foscari and Cesca would be watching for her. She did not want to knock on the door and confront them. She was alone. They would have servants standing by if she caused difficulties. She had no idea what condition Matteo was in. If Isaac was right and their son was in perfect health, she could steal in when night fell and take him away on the next boat back to Venice. If he was ill, she did not know what she would do. "Please let me disembark farther along the shore. I want to surprise my cousin."

"As you wish," the boatman said.

They floated along for another few minutes until they were well past the villa. The boatman pulled ashore, took her valise and helped her out. Solid ground. How lovely. She resisted the desire to fall to her knees and kiss it as she had when she and Assunta arrived in Venice.

The boatman stood in front of her, his head bowed. Hannah rummaged in her bag for a coin. She smiled at him and pressed a five *scudo* piece into his hand. "Thank you for your services."

He continued to stand there, shifting his weight from one foot to the other. Finally, he said, "Your blessing, if you please."

Of course. "'*In nomine patris et filii . . .*'" Hannah placed her hands on his head and intoned the prayer that Assunta had taught her. "Go in peace," she said, feeling as fraudulent as a conjurer at a fair.

He nodded. "Thank you, *Sorella.*" He climbed back into his boat and cast off.

Hannah walked up the towpath, carrying her valise, grateful the sun was setting. She paused for a moment to study the ruin several hundred metres away. Somewhere in that vastness was Matteo. What would Isaac do in such circumstances? He would be stealthy, remain calm, reveal nothing, gather information, then act.

And so would she.

CHAPTER 14

Villa di Padovani,
San Lorenzo, the Veneto

ANNAH WOULD NOT change out of her habit and into her blue *cioppà* and shawl. Soon it would be dark. Her black habit would render her invisible, allowing her to sneak into the villa, find Matteo and abscond with him, a will-o'-the-wisp with a small boy tucked under its wing.

But if he was ill, how could she take an ailing, fretful child on a journey of three days back to Venice? She would need a place to hide—a nearby farmhouse, perhaps—where she could nurse him back to health. Unless God had forsaken her, as He had every right to, He would provide. Hannah walked up the bank of the canal to a stand of arching willow trees well concealed from the villa. She lay down, feeling as vulnerable as a small bird, ready to take flight at the sound of a twig breaking on the footpath. The long trip had exhausted her. She dozed, using her valise as a pillow, for once grateful for the warmth of her habit. When she awoke an hour later, startled by the hoot of an owl, the country-side was bathed in moonlight. From the Brenta came the shuffling of the canal ponies' restless hooves and the animals' gentle snorting.

Hannah stood and stretched, considering what to do. The moon was full, or nearly so. She walked around the villa. At the back was an uneven pathway with a plank thrown over a muddy, mosquito-ridden ditch. It led to a set of makeshift steps. Balancing on a tippy board, trying not to look down into the effluvia flowing underneath, she proceeded across, trying to imagine the elegant Contessa, with her ermine cloaks and velvet dresses, living in such an unhealthy place.

She climbed the steps and entered an area that appeared to be for the use of servants. She was grateful she wore shoes, not boots. Everything was still except for the lapping waves from the Brenta. She cocked her head to listen for sounds inside the villa. Echoing hallways and high-ceilinged rooms greeted her. The villa seemed deserted. No servants, no tenant farmers, no Cesca, no Foscari. This was as it should be. Most people, unless they were very rich and could afford candles, went to bed with the sun.

Hannah knew of the customary layout of a villa from the Conte's palazzo in Venice. The main floor would be devoted to commerce: workers hauling sacks of grain, peasants arriving to settle accounts, merchants selling seed for the spring planting. The second floor would be for family. The attic was the preserve of servants.

Hannah passed a small room filled with mouldy cleaning cloths and broken furniture. She felt hot and unclean. Her gabardine skirts mocked her, tangling around her legs as if trying to trip her. She proceeded along a hallway, through a dusty drawing room with high ceilings and a huge painting of an immodestly dressed *castellana* peering down. The woman had the imperious look of a wealthy Christian. The fine velvet of her square-cut bodice revealed an unseemly amount of pink flesh the colour of intestines. Mercifully, there were no paintings of Christ's Crucifixion or the Annunciation of the Virgin. Hannah crept along, staying close to the walls, avoiding open spaces.

The drawing room might once have been elegant but was now scattered with chicken droppings. A hen roosted in the cornice above the door, clucking softly to herself. Sacks of wheat and barley slumped against the wall. The broad staircase at the far end must lead to the family quarters. She shoved her valise behind a sack of wheat, kicked off her shoes and, carrying them in one hand, began to climb the stairs. The house remained silent. Had she ventured all this way only to find she was too late? Had Cesca and Foscari already left, taking Matteo with them?

Hannah paused to catch her breath on the stair landing— and heard from somewhere above her the scrape of a wooden chair on a terrazzo floor.

She continued upward. At the top of the stairs was a long hallway with three rooms on each side, all with closed doors. Little moonlight penetrated from the window at the far end. She glanced around, hoping to see a taper on the walnut table in the middle of the hall, but there was none. Perhaps it was just as well. Candles had a way of casting menacing shadows from the most innocent of objects before they smoked and sputtered out, leaving one to imagine the worst.

A breeze blew through the window. From downstairs came a noise. A muted footfall? The scuttling of a mouse? Leaning over the balustrade, she tried to locate the source.

Terrazzo floors lacked the comforting squeak of the pegged wooden floors she was accustomed to. Stone deadened noise. An army of men could march in the next room and there would be no revealing creak of floorboards. At home Hannah had always known where Isaac was—by the crack of the tread he was on as he climbed the stairs at night, the groan of their horsehair mattress when he was sleeping, the splash of water in the basin when he rose to make his morning ablutions before going to *shul*.

Hannah paused again, thinking she heard a sharp sound. A musket firing? A loose shutter banging? The sound did not repeat.

She cupped her ears. Noise came from outside—wings flapping, another owl hooting, murmurs from the boatmen on a passing barge. And again the scrape of an object being shifted, perhaps a chair, perhaps a wooden crate, and after that a muffled squeak like the cry of a baby animal.

She wanted to run to the canal and board the next boat

back to Venice, but she forced herself to be calm. She lowered her shoulders, which tensed when she was frightened. Her imagination provided her with scenarios: Matteo in bed, half dead of fever; Foscari standing over him with a bloody knife; Cesca holding his limp body.

She must act. Which door to try first? The one nearest to her. There was a click as she eased it open. The room was a bedchamber—but unoccupied, judging by the bed covered with a torn damask spread and by the tattered, once-splendid *padiglione* suspended from the ceiling.

Moonlight played on the walls in front of her, exposing a looming black figure. Hannah froze at the sight. Then she relaxed. How silly to be frightened by one's own silhouette.

From down the corridor came a noise so abrupt she could not identify it. When she tried to re-create it in her mind a moment later, she could not. A walking cane on a terrazzo floor? The heavy breathing of a man past his prime? A child struggling for breath? There was someone nearby. Her ears were not playing tricks on her.

She stood holding her breath, feeling the sweat dripping between her breasts. A crashing sound came, like someone stumbling into a cupboard full of china. Through an open window reverberated the tiny cries of night creatures.

Light appeared at the end of the hallway. But she had not heard flint striking steel to ignite a candle. A chill ran over her as she recalled her grandmother's tales of *menorah* candles igniting spontaneously on Passover, of witches hovering in trees outside the room of a birthing mother and of two-headed wolves howling in apple orchards.

Then, as suddenly as it had appeared, the light vanished. Hannah's mouth was so dry she inserted two fingers to stimulate the flow of saliva. It was like thrusting her fingers into a parchment twist of flour. She must put her grandmother's stories back into the dark box where they belonged.

The next four rooms were bare. The stairway beckoned her back to safety. Then a child coughed. There was no mistaking it. Matteo was close. She could feel his presence, almost smell his sweet scent. She reached the last room, and paused, unsure of what might be behind the door. This room must have been the source of the light.

Afraid she would find it as empty as the five other rooms, she pushed open the door. The hinges rasped with an unearthly sound. She stood in the threshold, hesitating. A slight breeze stirred up dust and blew it in her direction. She gave a small sneeze, peering around the edge of the door. There was an answering sneeze from within the room. A small figure in the middle of a bed sat hugging something. It was too dark to see more than a hazy outline, but the size and shape were right. If only she had a candle, even a rush taper, so she could drink in the sight of his handsome little face.

She ran over to the bed. "Matteo!" she whispered.

The child rubbed his eyes and blinked up at her. It was difficult to make out his features. "Matteo," she whispered again, this time more loudly. "It's Mama." She sat down on the side of the bed. Her heart was fluttering so wildly she thought it would give out. She felt dizzy. Eight weeks she had endured on the *Fortuna* for this moment. She had abandoned her husband, jeopardized her life and the life of her unborn child, all for this moment. "Hello, my darling boy. It has been so long."

The boy sprang out of bed, ran to the window and flung back the curtains. She heard a frightened intake of breath as he stared at her. Silvery moonlight streamed into the bedchamber.

Yes, the boy had blue eyes. Yes, his hair was red. But it was the red of beet root, not the rich red of a fox's pelt. His lips were thinner, the teeth small and regular. He had no dimples.

He was a lovely boy, healthy, slender, straight limbed, about the same age as her son.

But he was not Matteo.

CHAPTER 15

Villa di Padovani,
San Lorenzo, the Veneto

"SORRY TO DISAPPOINT YOU, my dear," a voice said behind her.

Hannah startled, and then turned to face Foscari. "I see you are masquerading as a nun. What an odd thing you are, or did you convert?"

Foscari had changed little since Constantinople—the old fawn jacket had been replaced by a new blue one with bone buttons and now he wore finely tailored breeches, but otherwise he was the same. The silver nose would have looked outlandish on a less patrician face. The nose piece was polished to a lustre and attached by nearly invisible silk threads wound around his ears. It caught the gleam of the candle in his hand. On his right cheek blossomed an angry-looking boil. He strode toward her so swiftly she stepped back, thinking he meant to strike her, but he simply stood close to her, close enough that she could smell the brandy on his breath. She wished she had something to defend herself with.

Foscari smiled, revealing a row of teeth unnaturally even and white. "I have been following you as you made yourself at home on my villa without having the courtesy to announce yourself. I was hunting for something in the attic—a stool to rest my poor foot upon—when I glanced out the window and caught you disembarking from that turnip-laden barge. And then hiding in the willows. Dear me! I have never seen such a thing. I had no idea what you were up to."

What had she been thinking, showing up here alone, pregnant, her nun's habit making her even more ungainly? She should have brought someone with her. But she had no one to bring. The thought of Foscari spying on her, perhaps as she slept, or performed her bodily functions, gave her gooseflesh.

"I am here at your invitation."

Foscari played the role of the fop, but he was a calculating, clever man. Isaac was right. Foscari was not human, merely an animal that had learned to walk upright.

"You kidnapped Matteo from me and spirited him off to Venice. I hardly think—"

"My dear, it is pointless to argue about the past."

"Who is this child?" Hannah pointed to the boy, who now stood in a corner, staring at her.

Foscari walked over to him. "Lucca is from Venice. Rather a pretty little thing, isn't he?" Foscari removed a handkerchief from his pocket and, wetting it with his tongue, wiped a smudge of dirt off the boy's cheek. "And healthy, to boot." He shook his head. "Which is remarkable, considering the air in Venice. That sulphurous, yellow cloud hanging over the canals every night." He gave a mock shiver. "Lucca is flourishing in the salubrious air of the countryside. He was a skinny lad, but now we are fattening him up like a Pasqua lamb."

"He is your son?" Lucca had high cheekbones and narrow shoulders like Foscari, but unlike Foscari, the child's eyes were not cold as well water. And they were an azure blue. His mouth did not look like the slot in a poor box, as did Foscari's, but was as pink as a flower petal.

"Can you not tell the difference between well born and low born? Do all Christians look the same to you? He is a beggar's bastard, plucked from the streets of Castello."

But there was none of the hard, coarse street Arab about the boy.

"I bought him from a woman who claimed to be his grandmother."

Bought? How does one buy a child? "What have you done with Matteo?"

"All in good time. First, I suggest you calm yourself. There is a solution to our dilemma, which will serve us both."

"*Our* dilemma? My only dilemma is getting my son back."

Lucca tugged on Foscari's arm. Holding the handkerchief once again to Lucca's face, Foscari looked down, patting the boy on the head. "Lucca, we will disturb you no longer. Hannah and I will make our way downstairs. Take yourself back to bed." Lucca's face fell. He seemed about to protest, but he climbed back into bed.

Hannah tucked the covers around him. Lucca appeared older than Matteo by about a year, but he did not have Matteo's stocky build. Only the sweet smell of little boy sweat was familiar. Lucca reached up as Hannah bent to smooth the sheet over his chest. He touched her face and stared at her. His gaze was nothing like Matteo's—which was slightly critical and appraising. This boy looked at her with the ardour of a hungry child gazing at a tray of marzipan in a confectionery shop. She wondered if he had ever slept in a bed before; whether anyone, a mother or grandmother, had told him a bedtime story or sung a lullaby to him. His smile moved her, and for an instant she clasped his bony chest to hers and rubbed a small circle on his back. He relaxed in her arms. "Good night, *tesoro.*"

Foscari beckoned her into the hallway and guided her down the staircase. His hand on her back felt as boneless as a glove filled with porridge. And yet, she suspected, if she tried to dash for the attic or the basement or the stable to look for Matteo, his hand could tighten on her neck with the strength of a blacksmith's.

Foscari settled her in a chair in a reception room so huge and with a ceiling so high that the entire Ghetto Nuovo could have fitted within its perimeters.

"Where is my son?" Hannah asked again.

"*Your* son? Matteo is not your son."

"Of course he is mine."

"Before I tell you where he is, let me offer you some refreshment. You must be exhausted after your trip from Venice." He rang a bell on the table next to him.

It was true. She *was* weary. The baby within her kicked, pressing onto her sharing bones, making her feel the need to use a commode. A servant, a stout country girl carrying a candle, brought mugs of spring water on a tray and, without glancing at Hannah, placed them on a small table.

The red boil on Foscari's cheek seemed to have grown bigger. Her fingers itched to prick it with a sewing needle and squeeze it until the blood ran. She shifted her chair so his face fell in shadows.

"What do you want of me?"

"We shall get to that in a moment." Foscari leaned forward and patted her hand. "First, I am going to have a brandy. Will you join me?"

Hannah shook her head. Foscari rang for the servant again, who returned with a bottle of the amber liquid and a glass, which she set down on the table. Foscari quickly poured himself some.

"It is simple." He steepled his fingers in a grotesque imitation of prayer. "I have petitioned the courts to appoint me the boy's guardian."

His words did not surprise her. It was as Isaac had suspected. "You are contriving to steal Matteo's fortune."

"Such an unpleasant word. I prefer *salvage*, or *save*, or *rescue*, even *retrieve*."

Hannah said, "You and Cesca are very persevering—I grant you that. You failed in your first attempt to snatch

Matteo from me in Constantinople. So you bided your time. Then you sank your talons into him and carried him off."

"Do you wish his estate to devolve to the Monasterio San Francisco de Rosas? Yes, don't look so startled. The monks, those filthy, brown-garbed reprobates, are the residuary legatees if no di Padovani heir can be found. Is that your wish?"

"Matteo's estate benefiting one of the most powerful enemies of the Jews? Of course not."

"Alternatively, there is the Office of the Public Trustee, so corrupt, so dishonest that—"

"It does not bear thinking of," she said. The Office of the Public Trustee was notorious for stealing, with the blessing of the state, the fortunes of widows and orphans with no male kin to protect them.

"This is what will happen unless I am appointed guardian. Fortunately for us, the courts work slowly. The monks have been trying to get their greedy hands on the estate ever since the Conte's death. They had nearly succeeded, when I intervened. You should thank me for saving Matteo's fortune, instead of sitting there glaring at me in your ridiculous nun's costume." Foscari swirled the brandy in his glass. "What have *you* done to safeguard the boy's wealth?"

"My husband and I planned to bring Matteo to Venice next year after the birth of my baby and hire a notary to claim his estate." It was untrue. She and Isaac had discussed it many times but had reached no conclusion about the best way to safeguard Matteo's inheritance.

"Oh? And what would be left of his riches by then?

The monks would be well on their way to squandering them. And who could be his guardian? Not you, not your husband."

Hannah opened her mouth to protest but thought better of it. Foscari only spoke the truth.

"I think you are forgetting how large the di Padovani estate is. All this land, the ships and the palazzo in Venice would keep the monks as fat and happy as fleas on a dog." Leaning over, he touched her shoulder. "The judge wants to hear you testify, my dear. You must explain you took Matteo from the di Padovani palazzo then fled with him to Constantinople, where you have been passing him off as a Hebrew. In short, the truth."

"But I will be hanged for raising him as a Jew." *Never mind my other crime.*

"The judge has promised me he will not charge you with any offence when you appear before him. You have nothing to worry about."

"I do not believe you," Hannah said.

"You have no choice."

He held up a finger as though an idea had just occurred to him. "But this is what I will promise you. If you testify Lucca is the heir, Matteo is yours to do with what you like."

Hannah said, "I do not understand. If you wanted to pass off Lucca as the heir, why did you steal Matteo?"

"Sometimes even the most carefully conceived plans must be altered. Matteo turned out to be entirely unsuitable. We have tried various methods to make him more compliant—to no avail."

Methods. What a bland, dangerous word. A word calculated to appease worry while concealing the truth. What had they done? Beaten Matteo? Withheld food? Confined him to his room? Hannah tried to control her voice. "What methods?"

"Cesca was confident she had won the boy's affection. She indulged him by giving him endless treats, petting and spoiling him. She arranged for a pony, persuaded a farmer to string up a tightrope between two trees so Matteo could practise his tightrope walking. It's nothing short of a miracle that he didn't fall and break his leg."

"What methods, Foscari?"

"The judicious use of a willow switch. Something you should have done a long time ago."

"You are a brute."

Foscari continued as though she had not spoken. "When the switch failed to convince, I came up with an easier solution. I happened upon Lucca—eager to please, sunny disposition, all the qualities your son lacks. I have been preparing him to give testimony."

Foscari crossed his long legs. "However, the judge wishes to hear from you, the Jewish midwife who delivered Matteo."

"And a substitute for me, I suspect, would not be so easy."

"Precisely. Another Jewish midwife who could describe not only the birth but when interrogated by the judge— and he is a very finicky type of a judge—the interior of the Conte's palazzo and his wife and family and so on? Not possible. Hence Cesca's letter summoning you."

"So my testimony is essential." If Isaac were here, he would tell her: *we Jews have a long history of negotiating with*

gentiles in circumstances where we have no power. Consider the con-
tratto, *the contract between the Venetian government and the Jewish
community in which the Jews purchase the right to live unmolested in
the city for a certain number of years. No one ever made a successful
bargain giving into hotheadedness. Leash your tongue as you would leash
a vicious dog.*

"One could put it that way."

"Take me to Matteo."

"Will you testify?"

Nothing would have given Hannah greater satisfaction
than to say: *you are mad to even dream I would be part of your
wicked scheme.*

But if Foscari refused to let her see Matteo, how could
she find him? The child could be hidden anywhere on this
estate of several hundred hectares.

"Why should I help you to steal my son's fortune?"

"Because if you testify Lucca is the rightful heir, then
Matteo is yours. You can roast him with rutabaga and
serve him for your Passover dinner." He sipped more
brandy. "I will take you to him right now. He is with one
of the tenant farmers."

"And if I refuse to testify?"

"Then I shall have him killed."

CHAPTER 16

Villa di Padovani,
San Lorenzo, the Veneto

H ANNAH AND FOSCARI entered a thatched cottage. In answer to Foscari's call, a plump woman emerged from bed, wearing a night-dress and rubbing the sleep from her eyes. She stood in front of the last embers in the hearth, shaking her head at Foscari's question.

"She took him away, sir, this very morning. I don't know where she went with him."

"It seems I cannot produce the boy at this instant," said Foscari.

"You must know where he is."

"Do not raise your voice to me. I have done nothing

with him. Cesca and I had a disagreement. She has disappeared with Matteo to punish me."

"To where? You must have some idea."

"I do not."

She was about to accuse him of lying, but the look on his face made her believe him. Despite his fury, Foscari appeared old and defeated. In the dim light of the cottage, his back was less erect, his forehead more deeply etched, his jowls more crepey. A sudden weariness swept over her. She could not do anything until morning. It was time for both of them to sleep. They walked back to the villa, Foscari dragging his gouty foot, Hannah drooping with fatigue.

Hannah climbed the attic stairs to the servant's quarters, where Foscari had given her a room. Her alcove contained only a bed with threadbare linens left behind by some long-forgotten cook or scullery maid.

Either from exhaustion or despair, Hannah felt overwhelmed at making the simplest decisions: whether to lie on her side or her back; to pull the covers around her chest or to leave them at her waist; to use the waste bucket now or wait until morning. She lay on the thin mattress, wearing only a shift, her nun's habit folded under her head as a pillow. She wrapped her arms around herself and rocked from side to side, wondering if she would ever again hold Matteo, wishing she had a warmer blanket against the cold night. From the willow tree outside came the cry of a bird—loud and monotonous. If only it would not repeat the same cry over and over. Hannah closed her eyes and tried to sleep. The sound ceased. There was a rush of wings then the squeal of a small animal. Then silence. She imagined an owl, its sharp beak piercing the soft grey breast of a mouse and ripping off the meat. She rolled over to her side, filling the alcove with the creak and rustle of her straw mattress.

As she often did just before falling asleep, Hannah thought of home. Jessica would be talking by now, and perhaps weaned. Isaac was a tender father. He would be showing Jessica how to form her letters with a piece of chalk on a blackboard, letting her play in the silk workshop, giving her a shuttlecock or a silk cocoon to hold in her fat little hand. Or maybe, as Hannah wished with all her heart, he had boarded a ship and was on his way to Venice. Was it possible to send thoughts through the air? If so, then she would say to Isaac: *come to Venice, my darling. Let us make everything right between us again. When I quarrel with you, it is as if I am quarrelling with myself. We are two halves of the same person, complete only when we are together.*

Finally, she drifted off into an uneasy sleep. She dreamed of the Marquis Foscari. He was bathing in a large copper tub set in the middle of the drawing room. When she entered the room, Cesca and Foscari turned to stare at her. Cesca was washing him, a towel draped over her shoulder. She was soaping Foscari's back, not with a sponge but with the still-beating heart of a lamb. His silver nose gleamed from the rays of the sun coming through the high window. The reflection blinded Hannah. Cesca and Foscari beckoned her to come closer. When she approached and peered into the tub, Foscari was bathing in human blood.

Hannah forced herself to wake up. Having such nightmares could result in a baby born with extra fingers or toes, or perhaps no ears.

Something touched her cheek. Hannah tried to brush it away, but it wrapped around her neck and shoulders, like the arms of a little monkey. The more she thrashed, the more it clung to her. Half asleep, half awake, Hannah sat up, to find a slender form pressed along the length of her, a leg thrown over her hip. Thin arms clasped her; a small hand patted her cheek.

"Don't cry," a child whispered in a voice that was not Matteo's.

"What are you doing here, Lucca?" Hannah whispered back, although they were far from anyone who might overhear them.

He sat up in her bed, silhouetted against the silver moonlight from the window. The back of his head was as flat as a pine board, giving him a neglected appearance, suggesting his mother had not troubled herself to turn him in his cradle but had left him to stare hour after hour at the ceiling. Hannah reached for him and coaxed him to lie down.

"I heard crying, so I followed the sound until I found you." He tossed the covers over both of them and then pressed against her again. "I cry at night sometimes, but when I lie on my back, my tears fall into my ears. If I *must* cry, I lie on my side."

"How old are you, Lucca?"

"I'm not sure. Six?"

"You are wise beyond your years."

"My grandmother used to say that, too."

Was this the grandmother who had sold him to Foscari for a handful of *scudi*? Hadn't she worried Foscari might use the child for unnatural purposes? Or had she been too hungry and desperate to care? Was compassion a luxury only the well-fed could afford? "I was crying because I miss my son, Matteo. I have not seen him for many months."

Lucca snuggled closer. He did not feel the least like Matteo, who had been plump with baby fat the last time she had seen him. Hannah tucked Lucca's head to her bosom and he lay in her arms. Matteo would not have submitted to such an embrace for more than an instant. This boy lay too still, trying to prove himself worthy of affection.

The night had turned colder still. The shutters had blown open, letting in unhealthy night air. "Are you warm enough?" Hannah asked.

She felt him nod against her shoulder.

"Are you Matteo's true mother?" Without waiting for a reply, he said, "Cesca is not my true mother. Matteo likes Cesca. Sometimes he calls her 'Ama Cesca,' and combs her hair in the back where she can't reach and helps her plait it."

Was it Hannah's curse to always be resentful of Cesca? Surely it was better for Matteo to feel fondness, even love for Cesca, than to be lonely and unhappy.

"Other times he kicks her and calls her names."

"Yes, I am Matteo's true mother. If only I could find him."

"Matteo and I never shared a bed. Cesca wouldn't let me." A note of indignation crept into his voice. "She said I might talk in my sleep and keep him awake, but I wouldn't have."

There was a worried, too-adult tone to his voice that saddened Hannah.

"I slept on the floor next to his bed. On cold nights I could see his breath in the air. I told him stories. I tied a string around my wrist and the other end around his wrist. When he was too tired to listen anymore, he would tug three times and I would be silent so he could sleep."

"What a good friend you are." She longed to ask him a thousand questions, but it was better if Lucca told her in his own way.

"Yes, I am, thank you. People are fond of you if you are kind."

An old man's head on a young boy's shoulders. Hannah stroked his hair, hoping Lucca was like one of those tough little weeds that flourish in spite of no mother beaming approval down upon them and no father ready with a patient word of encouragement. *I would like to help you*, tesoro, *but I do not see how.* "What kind of stories did you tell him?"

"About riding ponies together. He has a white one, but Apollo is too old to carry us both. Matteo told me he needed a young pony so he could search for you. He said we could search for my mama, too, except she's dead. I made up stories about trotting through forests and foraging rivers to find you, fighting bandits and dragons along the way. Then getting on a big boat, a galley. Do you know what a galley is?" he asked.

"Years ago my husband nearly died on such a vessel alongside thirty other slaves."

"Was it a Turkish galley or a Venetian?"

"Venetian."

"Made of oak? Lateen sails?"

"I do not know."

"A *galeotto* or a *galera grossa di mercato*?" Lucca squirmed out of her arms to sit up.

"Do not excite yourself." Hannah patted his back, settling his head back on her breast, but he struggled free again and looked up, trying to read her face in the moonlight.

"I could sail such a vessel. I am very strong. Cesca told me living in the country would make me grow taller. She feeds me eggs, and since the cow was freshened, I have mugs of milk. Sometimes at night my leg bones hurt from growing. When I lived with my grandmother, I mostly ate gruel." Lucca yawned.

Please, Lucca, do not go to sleep just yet. I know you have more to tell me. "When did you last see Matteo?"

Ignoring her question, Lucca pointed upward. "Can you see all the windows in this attic?"

The light was faint, but Hannah noticed for the first time the small square windows encircling the room, just below the line of the roof.

"Don't they look like the arrow slits in a fortress? You can see forever. Well, maybe not forever, but at least the distance of a day's ride on horseback. We pretended the attic was our fortress and we could spy enemy troops advancing. Matteo mostly played the king, but sometimes I did. We ran from window to window with our muskets. Not real muskets. Long sticks."

"What a good imagination you have."

"Yes, but it was no use thinking up games, because Matteo started wetting his bed, so Cesca got mad and sent him to live in a tenant's cottage."

"My poor Matteo."

"I am careful not to wet the bed." He rubbed his eyes. "I never had a friend before Matteo. I am small for my age, so when I was living on the streets, the other boys beat me and stole my food."

Please do not fall asleep just yet. "Do you know where Matteo is?"

"This morning I was in the attic looking out the window to see if I could spy Matteo. I watched Cesca—I call her 'Ama,' like Matteo does, even though she is not my mama— put Matteo into a boat. She sent him off with two men."

Cesca must have guessed Hannah was arriving today, fetched Matteo and hustled him off. "Do you know where the men were taking him?" Hannah tried to keep the anxiousness out of her voice.

"I shouted to Matteo from the attic, but he didn't look up. I guess he was too far away to hear me."

Lucca paused and frowned. Hannah could see his eyes rolling upward as he re-imagined the scene.

"Matteo was going to Venice. It's where that boat—the blue one with the bow that curves up like a Turk's slipper— always goes. Not a *burchiello*. It was the old one with the oak mast and a rope lashed to a canal pony."

"Venice?" What was Cesca thinking? Would she keep Matteo hidden until the trial?

Lucca stretched. "May I sleep with you? I am so tired."

"Cesca did not go with him?"

"Boat trips make her throw up."

"Lucca, can you tell me anything else?"

"Matteo was going to the same place I once stayed." Wretchedness crept into his voice. "My *nona* sent me there last winter when we had nothing to eat, nor any firewood. There were lots of children. Some of them were cruel. One boy hit me and tied me to a tree. The nuns were not nice, either, except one named Sister Magdalena, who gave me a wooden sailboat to play with."

"How do you know Matteo went there?"

"Because I heard Cesca telling him it was a wonderful place and that I enjoyed living there. But she was mistaken. It is a cold place with nasty food. It has statues of ogres on the roof staring down as though to eat you."

"Do you remember where it was?"

"From the dormitory where I slept with the other boys, I could smell the pine pitch the boat builders use to caulk the galley hulls. The flames of their fires rose so high in the sky they touched the stars. Whenever the old abbess preached about hell, I thought of the Arsenale fires, stinking of pitch. Did you know those boat builders are so skilled they can build a new galley every day?"

The shipyards of the Arsenale were in the poor *sestiere* of Castello in the southeast part of the city, as far from the Jewish ghetto as it was possible to be. It was a district Hannah had not the slightest familiarity with. Castello contained a half-dozen orphanages overflowing with foundlings and waifs.

"I want to be a ship's carpenter when I grow up, but the Marquis says I am to be a count, instead. My name will be Matteo di Padovani. I am to be the heir to a great fortune. I shall have this villa and my own ships to sail far and wide. Maybe to the Levant and back. I like ships." Then his voice faltered. "The Marquis calls me 'Matteo.'" Lucca spoke in a convincing imitation of Foscari's high-pitched voice. "He asks me, 'Matteo, what district did you live in in Constantinople?'"

"And what do you say?"

"I answer, 'Eminönü.'"

"And then he asks, 'What were your parents called?' And I say, 'Hannah and Isaac.'"

"How difficult for you," said Hannah. "So many things to remember."

"Yes, but if I am good and clever and answer everything correctly, the Marquis will buy me a blue-hulled boat with a stepped-in mast, a mainsail and a jib. A real boat, not a toy." Lucca wiggled his toes in excitement. "And I may give my boat any name I wish."

"Have you thought of one?"

"*Lucca*," he said without hesitation. "That way I will never forget who I am."

Villa di Padovani,
San Lorenzo, the Veneto

TWO DAYS AGO, when she saw Hannah struggling off the turnip barge, clad in an ill-sewn nun's habit, Cesca giggled so hard she had to hang on to a table to keep from falling down. How could Hannah think she would deceive anyone in that ridiculous garment, skirts flapping about her legs, the hem soaked with bilge water? The linen bands around her face distorted her mouth and nose as though her face were being squeezed in a vise.

Let Foscari, with his bottomless well of false promises, work his charm on Hannah. Let him come running to Cesca, begging her to reveal Matteo's whereabouts. She had not worked her fingers to the bone to be cheated of what was hers by right.

Now Hannah was off again to Venice in her horrid nun's costume. Well, she would never find Matteo and neither would Foscari.

Cesca had tried to reassure Matteo that his stay in Venice would not be for long, but he had cried and wrapped himself around her; refused to release her as she stood on the dock, waiting for the men to carry him into the boat.

"Please," he had pleaded. "You come, too."

Finally, one of the men had prised his arms from around Cesca's neck so they could load him in the boat and depart. Of course it had broken her heart to send the boy off with those two millers—strangers, really—who for a few *scudi* had agreed to keep an eye on him during the voyage, but what choice had she had? Foscari was more than capable of harming the boy. The trip to Venice was for Matteo's own protection.

Cesca washed. The water was hot and felt so much better than the leaf-filled water from the rain barrel she had been forced to use the past few mornings. She daubed goose grease on her hands, sore and scratched from picking berries in a nearby field.

After donning a clean frock, Cesca arranged her hair prettily on top of her head, allowing a few tendrils to escape. She rubbed some leaves of lemon balm from the garden—it was the best she could do—between her breasts and dabbed a bit of juice from crushed mulberries on her cheeks to give them colour.

Soon she was strolling down the towpath, swinging an empty wicker basket. She walked as though she had all the time in the world, even giving a little skip now and again, in case Foscari was spying on her out of the attic window. It would not do to have Foscari realize she was on her way to Palladio's. Her hat, filched from a neighbour's porch, was a floppy affair, with a wide blue ribbon that trailed fetchingly down her back.

The weather was mild for early winter, the scene before her pastoral. The sun shone and two mourning doves landed on the ground ahead of her, where they pecked in the dust. A barge floated by on the canal, piled high with timber. From the chapel in the village came the sound of a young boys' choir, voices raised in praise of God.

Once she was out of sight of the villa, Cesca set down her basket and stooped to pry a pebble out of her shoe. Then she straightened and began to march through the fallow fields, past washerwomen singing as they rinsed clothing. She passed an orchard of peach trees, their branches etched black against the blue sky. On the ground beneath one of the trees lay a blanket covered with peaches already pitted, which someone had left out to dry in the sun then forgotten. Nearby lay a tidy heap of kernels.

Looking around to make sure no one was about, she hopped over the fence and tipped the whole blanket of peaches into her basket.

Cesca had to stop herself from grabbing handfuls of the leathery globes of yellow fruit tinged with orange and stuffing them into her mouth. Peaches! How she loved them. So delicious with a dollop of cream, but the kernels so deadly. There was more than enough fruit for her. Even if she stuffed her face all afternoon, there would still be plenty left. She bit into a peach, the dried flesh so wonderfully sweet. Between mouthfuls, she gathered the kernels and tossed them into her pockets.

Still mindful of her purpose, she hopped back over the fence and continued along until Palladio's house appeared in the distance. The architect had made such an impression that Cesca could not gaze upon any building now, from coop to cottage to castle, without analyzing its structural flaws.

His dwelling looked more farmhouse than villa. Nothing so grand as the Villa Francesca. Palladio's residence was a squarish structure sitting on a fieldstone foundation, with a listing east wall and a brick *barchessa* in need of repointing. The house snuggled into the side of the hillock like a white puppy relaxing at its mother's flank. Wisps of grass sprouted from the tiled roof. A bleating black lamb was tethered to a pillar that supported one corner of the front porch. *The cobbler's children are not quite barefoot*, Cesca thought, *but they are wearing boots with tattered soles and flapping tongues.* Odd that a gentleman of such eminence did not live in grander style.

Lifting her skirts to avoid the chickens pecking among vegetable peelings, she walked to the front door. If Palladio's wife was not at home, it might make her mission much easier. Biting her lips to give them colour, she laced her bodice tighter to make her breasts rounder and firmer.

From the rear of the house came a series of barks. A black-domed head appeared, from which hung a pink tongue as long as a clapper. *"Buon giorno,"* Cesca called out. The mastiff, Pippo, shambled over, looked at her, poked his muzzle into her basket and, before Cesca could shove him away, gave the dried peaches a swipe with his tongue. Together Cesca and Pippo walked toward the farmhouse.

The words *Villa Allegra* were painted on a sign hanging from a plane tree to the left of the front door. That much of the sign she could decipher. Villa of happiness. *We shall see about that,* she mused.

It was midday. Her stomach gurgled for want of a meal. She glanced at the chimney, and was gratified to see smoke rising. The air was redolent with the fragrance of garlic and baking bread. With any luck, Palladio would invite her to stay for *un pranzo squisito*.

There was no bell, but the door was ajar. Cesca called out, and hearing no reply, she touched the door with her fingertips. To her surprise, the solid oak door was so skilfully crafted it opened. She squinted into the interior. Pippo pushed ahead of her, waving his tail.

Palladio sat at a huge table that took up most of the room. He was making a replica of a villa, an edifice so delicate it seemed to levitate above the table. He glanced up, evidently startled by the breeze that wafted through the open door. Then he rose, blinking, to greet her.

"I am not disturbing you?" Cesca said.

His shoulders were massive under his loose-fitting linen shirt, yet somewhat stooped, no doubt from his sitting at a workbench as he assembled his architectural models. "Please enter."

There was a cough from a corner of the room. A woman rose to her feet and came forward. She had the appearance of having been assembled by many sculptors, each with conflicting ideas about what the female form should look like. Nothing about her seemed harmonious. Her arms were too long, her legs too short, her neck too thick, her hips too narrow. Yet there was something so genial in the woman's countenance, something so appealing in the slope of her cheeks, the tilt of her head and the scrutiny of her gaze, that Cesca took an instant liking to her. If this was Palladio's wife, which the woman gave every sign of being, the architect cared more for balance and proportion in buildings than in the human figure.

Palladio said, "Allegra, this is Francesca. She is living in the Villa di Padovani, caring for the Conte's son, Matteo. Cesca, this is my wife, Allegradonna."

"How lovely to meet you. My husband has talked of you."

Allegra spoke in a mild voice that would have been better suited to a small, dainty woman. It made Cesca smile and reach for her hand. Allegra bent from the waist to clasp Cesca's hand. She was unsteady on her feet and held Cesca's hand as much in support as in greeting.

Still clasping Cesca's hand, she drew Cesca into the room. Allegra wore an ordinary brown loose-fitting dress with a linen bodice. A yellow shawl draped her shoulders. Palladio joined his wife, putting a hand on her waist. He patted away perspiration from her forehead with his handkerchief. They were oddly matched but, judging by the look of affection on Palladio's face, well suited.

"Will you have tea with us?" Allegra motioned Cesca to sit at the workbench.

Palladio pushed aside the tiny doors, windows and pillars he had not yet added to his model. Then he took the wicker basket of dried peaches Cesca held out to him and set it on the tamped earth floor.

"I do not want to interrupt your work," Cesca said to Palladio, smiling in a way that showed her dimples to good advantage.

"Please," Allegradonna said. "Have the kindness to sit awhile with us. We do not receive many visitors."

It was not difficult to see why. Of course, all farmhouses were cluttered with masses of equipment. Cesca had been in a farmhouse only last week to barter for some eggs and found they kept the plow and a pair of oxen in the kitchen. This room was a maze of maps, papers, trowels, planes, awls, drills, lathes, mallets of all sizes, plumb lines, screws and nails. Narrow pathways had been carved in the clutter to allow passage from the stove to the table, from the table to the hearth and from the hearth to the sleeping area. Such a contrast to the vast emptiness of her villa. No wonder Palladio coveted the spacious Villa di Padovani.

"I'll fetch the sugar." She walked from the room.

When Allegra returned, she lowered herself into a chair then gripped the arms, evidently suffering a spell of dizziness. Cesca poured a mug of water from the pitcher on the table and went to her. Cesca held the mug to the woman's lips so she could drink, Allegra's hands were shaking so.

I pat the ewe so that I may steal the ram.

"*Grazie*, Francesca, you are kind."

"*Prego*. It is nothing."

Palladio went to the hearth, stooped to reach the kettle and poured out three mugs of tea. He placed the bowl of sugar in front of Cesca and offered her a spoon. Then he returned to building his model. How rich he must be to afford sugar.

"We were wondering when you would pay us a visit," said Allegra.

"How are you getting on in the villa? Painted over those dreadful frescoes yet?" asked Palladio, looking up from affixing a series of tiny bricks to the wall of the miniature.

When Cesca shook her head, he said, "It is the first thing I will do when the property is mine."

Cesca forced herself to smile. "I am only now realizing what a great deal of labour is involved in keeping the place from going to ruin." *And money. I need a great deal of money.*

"The Conte liked to hunt wild boar in our woods. He was a dear man," said Allegra. And then, as though her store of small talk was exhausted, she struggled to her feet. "I shall retire to take a nap, if you will excuse me."

"It was a pleasure to meet you," said Cesca.

Allegra gave a slight nod and moved out the door, an embroidery hoop tucked under her arm.

Obtaining legal title to her villa might take longer than Cesca had at first conceived, but she had discovered in herself unexpected reservoirs of patience.

Pippo lumbered over and settled his head on his master's knee. "*Ragazzo cattivo*," Palladio said, stroking the greying muzzle. The dog stretched his neck and stared at Cesca, leaving a strand of drool on Palladio's breeches. A crunching sound came from the mastiff's mouth. "Spit it out," Palladio ordered. The dog looked at the ground and averted his head. Palladio seized the mastiff's muzzle and pried open the jaws. He reached in and extracted a tiny door, detailed in inlaid ebony and tortoiseshell. "Wicked boy. Go away, I am cross with you."

The dog resumed his place in the corner. Palladio wiped the door on a rag and placed it on the table. "Pippo is so old I should put him down, but my sons were so fond of him. They all rode on his back as children and learned to walk by holding on to his ears." He looked away, fumbling with a pair of pincers to reset the door in its proper place.

Cesca, who knew from neighbourhood gossip that Palladio had lost three sons to scarlet fever, did not wonder at the catch in his voice. "How skilled you are," she said to change the subject, as she studied his model building. "It is probably nonsense, but someone told me the old villas were built with secret rooms that no one but the architect and the family knew of. Can this be true?"

Palladio grinned. "If so, would I tell you?" But then he grew thoughtful. "No," he said, "though a commendable idea. I wonder I did not think of it myself. Perhaps I shall suggest it to future clients." He squinted at the replica of the villa as though trying to work out where he might tuck in such a room.

If there was a greater liar in the world than Foscari, Cesca had yet to meet him. "I am no judge, but to my eye this building is perfection just as it is." The roofline resembled the wings of a dove in flight and the arches of the portico were as graceful as a nun's wimple.

Palladio said, "I fashioned a similar model for the Villa di Padovani. It was made of thousands of *mattoni picholini*, tiny bricks. The Conte commissioned the villa as a wedding gift for his wife, Lucia. Never, during the many months I worked on the villa, did he permit her to view the construction. When the villa was finished and at last she saw it, she burst into tears of happiness."

"The Conte must have been a devoted husband," said Cesca.

"Some would say ridiculously fond. White orchids arrived for her from Sicily once a week," said Palladio. With a deft movement he fitted a tiny window into the opening of a wall.

"It is on the Conte's business I have come," Cesca said. "I hardly know what to do. I am beside myself with worry." She put her hand over Palladio's and gave it a squeeze. "The Marquis petitioned the court to appoint him guardian of the estate, but it seems God has other plans. I fear for his sanity. The poor darling has been hearing voices, pacing the grounds in his nightshirt at all hours. He has forgotten the names of friends. He wears his breeches backward. He grows rigid and his breath will not come. The whites of his eyes have turned as yellow as crocus petals." She lowered her voice. "He seems to have a profound disturbance of the mind."

Only the part about his eyes turning yellow was true—caused no doubt by the brandy he sipped from dawn to dusk. On and on Cesca prattled, reciting the symptoms of peach kernel poisoning as they flowed through her mind as swiftly as water over a miller's wheel. "I worry about Matteo. He is such a darling. The very image of his mother, as you say. But unless a guardian is appointed soon, his estate will be forfeited to the monks." She recounted the judge's stubbornness, his insistence on hearing testimony from Hannah and seeing the boy. "Without his patrimony what will become of him? The woman who was raising him, Hannah, is unsuitable."

"I am sorry to hear this."

"You were a good friend of the Conte's?"

"I admired him a great deal."

"He would have wanted his son to have what is rightfully his."

"I was delighted to have a chance to see Matteo at the villa last month. The Contessa would have been proud at how fine-looking he is."

"Yet Foscari in his present state . . ." Cesca said. "If only I knew a trustworthy man to take on the responsibility."

"Another relative, perhaps?" asked Palladio.

"You have put your finger on the problem. There are none. What is needed is an honourable man, a friend of the family's, someone mature . . ." Cesca stirred more sugar into her mug. "I wonder if *you* might be persuaded."

Palladio looked taken aback. "There must be someone else. I am ill-suited to the task. I am also preoccupied with this." He waved a hand to encompass his model. "The Villa Cressi must begin next month. All my time must be devoted to it."

Cesca dabbed her eyes with a corner of her handkerchief, careful not to displace the stain of mulberry juice blushing her cheeks. "You were a friend of the Conte's. He trusted you."

"You need someone with a head for commerce," Palladio said, picking up a tiny brass bracket designed to secure the roof and twiddling it between thumb and forefinger. "Many noblemen of a certain age suffer from episodes of clouded judgment. Maybe it is the result of noble families inter-marrying for generations. The blood grows thin." He patted her knee. "I'm certain Foscari will be as straight as a plumb line soon."

"The doctors tell me he is dying," said Cesca. *Or soon will be.* "I beg you to do it for the memory of your dear friend the Conte. It is an undertaking that requires a worthy man such as you."

"I would be a poor guardian."

Cesca tapped her chin in order to appear pensive. "You already intend to purchase the villa. This way you would have the pleasure of it with none of the expense. The estate would pay for the repairs." Another thought struck her. "And the frescoes. You could do as you liked with them." While it saddened her to think of her beloved *castellana* obliterated by a coat of whitewash, it could be scrubbed away after Palladio's death.

Palladio glanced up from attaching the brass bracket. "The duty of the guardian is to preserve the estate for his

ward. The fate of the frescoes will be Matteo's to decide when he comes of age."

"I will help. I have a good head for figures. I learned from my father, who managed a large estate outside Rome." It could have been true, she thought in her own defence.

"I arranged with Foscari to buy the villa because—" Palladio lowered his voice "—I wish it for my wife, who, as you might have guessed, is ill. She was a maid servant at the villa many years ago before we married. How wonderful it would be for her to spend her last days as its *castellana*. With a dressmaker from Venice to make her fine gowns, a house full of servants and a kitchen to manage, she will be happy in her final days." He shook his head. "No, you must find someone else. I simply wish to purchase the villa, not manage such a complex enterprise as the di Padovani fortune."

"There is no one else. Will you at least attend the trial so that you may see for yourself that Foscari has taken leave of his senses?"

"I cannot promise even that. Allegra needs me here."

Cesca allowed a pained look to cross her face. "Foscari, to put it bluntly, is quite deranged. He plans to substitute some street waif for Matteo. I cannot answer for what will happen to the boy if Foscari succeeds in his mad scheme."

Palladio stood and paced the length of the room. "Why would he do such a thing?"

Cesca lowered her voice. "To tell you the truth, I think this boy, Lucca, might be his natural son." The lie had sprung full blown to her lips, as so many of her clever lies did, but on reflection, perhaps it was true. Foscari did seem

uncharacteristically fond of Lucca. In the orchard one afternoon, she had seen them playing Hunt the Slipper, which had struck her as odd, since Foscari always professed to dislike children. "I have sent Matteo away for his own protection."

"I wish I could help, Francesca. But I want to be by Allegra's side during her illness. I am in the middle of several projects. I have no aptitude for managing such an estate. You must find someone else."

Cesca thought it would be easy to gaff him, net him and then haul him into her boat, but Palladio was proving an obstinate fish to land. The trial, when Judge Abarbanel would decide guardianship, was fast approaching. She had no choice but to continue with Foscari.

CHAPTER 18

Jewish Ghetto,
Venice

HANNAH TWISTED HER wedding band, now worn on her right hand as befitted a Bride of Christ. She recalled the day she and Isaac had stood under the *huppah* and he placed it on her left hand. How fortunate Isaac could not see her in this cumbersome nun's habit, the hem heavy with mud and her face hollow eyed from anxiety. As she walked along the familiar streets toward the ghetto, dodging the herky-jerky carts on cobblestones and ignoring the shouts of hawkers, the cries of beggars and the screams of seagulls circling overhead, she ached for him. He would know how to navigate these treacherous shoals between Cesca's duplicity and Foscari's demands.

The iron-rimmed wheels of the porter's cart resonated like rocks tumbled together in a barrel on the cobblestones. The tide was high. Hannah held up her skirts to keep them from getting soaked in water washing over the slippery cobblestones. More than ever she hated the nun's habit. Everywhere Hannah went, gentiles asked her to dispense blessings. She had to bow her head and genuflect when she passed every church. Children plucked at her skirts, begging for bread; old women smiled and nodded to her, crossing themselves, making her feel like a swindler. *If you knew I was a Jew*, she wanted to say, *you would not treat me with such reverence.*

As Hannah and the porter proceeded toward the Fondamenta di Ghetto Nuovo, she put both hands around her middle, giving her belly a gentle squeeze. The baby had not moved in days. Was the infant as fatigued as she was? Could an unborn child be tired from swimming through the dim waters of the womb? Or was it something more serious? She tried not to think of all the stillbirths she had delivered or, more worrisome, the cramping and bloody discharge that had swept away the baby last year before it had a chance to take on human form.

Forgetting for a moment she was wearing a nun's habit, Hannah said *"Buon giorno"* to Vicente. The gatekeeper was applying goose grease to keep the iron bolt free of rust. Without recognition, he nodded and waved her through the oaken portals.

As Hannah entered the ghetto, the strange world of the Christians—the world of worshipping paintings and statues and secreting away the fingers of long-dead saints and

splinters from the True Cross in reliquaries—fell away. The square looked as it had when she was here last. This morning the ghetto was noisy with the language of commerce and bargaining—the hand gestures, the exaggerated shrugs, the cries of dismay and delight, the theatrical lamentations of outrage and feigned heartbreak. Jewellers bargained for gems; farmers from the Terra Firma negotiated loans to get them through the wheat planting season. Noble ladies pawned their jewels to satisfy gambling debts.

This was the familiar world of Asher and Tzipporah, of Hannah's former neighbours, friends and the many children she had delivered over the years who were now young scholars in the *yeshiva* or betrothed in marriage. This was the world that, by insisting she must have Matteo, she placed in peril.

Under the *sotoportego*, squeezed between two other money-lenders, sat Asher, a loupe in his eye, squinting at something in front of him. She waited for his customer to depart, a muscular man, a farrier by the look of his heavy leather apron. Then she approached her brother.

"Why are you here dressed like that?" he whispered. "Change out of that habit at once."

I am in need of love and comfort, she wanted to say. "I need a place to stay while I search for Matteo."

"We can't talk here."

Hannah slipped into a shadowy corner and shrugged out of the habit, wimple and cornette. Underneath was her *cioppà*. She returned to Asher, who was packing up his scales, his loupe, his tweezers and pincers, plus a hefty bag of assorted candlesticks and silverware, judging by the clank they made as he hoisted the sack over his shoulder. "Come upstairs. The boys are having their lessons in the Rabbi's study. Our place will be quiet. No one will see you." They climbed the stairs together. Once in his apartment, Asher motioned Hannah to sit.

Tzipporah was lying on a rush mat, Elijah nestled against her. Both were sleeping.

"I have come from the villa in San Lorenzo," said Hannah. "They were keeping Matteo there, but now he is in an orphanage here in Venice. Once I find him I will sail back to Constantinople and never bother you again." Hannah spoke in a quiet voice so as not to wake Tzipporah and Elijah.

"Why is Matteo in an orphanage?"

"I suspect because Cesca is hiding him from Foscari. Matteo has proven too stubborn for them." *Good for you, Matteo.* "They found another boy they want to use in his place."

Asher said nothing as he brushed a skiff of dried mud off the cuff of his breeches.

"Foscari claims the judge will not have me arrested if I testify, but I am frightened, Asher. Frightened of being in prison when my baby is born." Hannah willed him to look up, to put his arms around her.

"So you want to find Matteo and simply flee to Constantinople?"

Hannah nodded.

"Hannah, you must do as Foscari wishes. If you find Matteo, for the love of God, hand him back to Foscari," Asher said.

"You don't understand. Foscari is asking me to lie in court." Hannah told of Foscari's insistence she identify Lucca as the di Padovani heir.

"All the better! Testify this other boy is the heir then take Matteo back to Constantinople. Isn't that what you want? To have your precious son returned? Spout whatever lies Foscari wants and be done with it."

"But I would be committing perjury."

"Since when do you care for the courts of the gentiles? Say whatever is required to get your son."

"It is not that simple," Hannah said. "Matteo is heir to a great fortune. Is it right for me to deprive him of a life of privilege and wealth?"

"You must choose. Either take him back to Constantinople and raise him as a Jew, or let Foscari have him."

"But—"

"I am weary of arguing with you. First you tell me you want Matteo back. You want to raise him as a Jew, even though such a criminal act, if discovered, would bring harm to me, to Tzipporah, to our sons, to all the Jews of the ghetto. Now you want him to have his estate."

"It is his right."

Asher's face grew dark, as it always did when he was angry. "Why did you come if you don't wish to take my advice? If all you want to do is debate? Are you a Rabbi that you are so all-knowing and wise? Can you read? Can you write?" He waved a hand impatiently. "Go away, grow a beard, read the Talmud. Then come back and we'll argue about whether you should perjure yourself in the Christian courts."

Hannah had never seen him so irate. "I had hoped for your sympathy. Matteo is my son, yes, but Foscari and Cesca are criminals. I cannot let them steal Matteo's estate."

"I might as well tell you, Hannah, I lent a great sum of ducats to Foscari. If he does not get the order for guardianship, I shall be ruined."

"Oh, Asher, no. Tell me you are not serious." But there was no jest in his face. "How could you have been so foolish?" She nearly asked the amount of the loan but decided she did not want to know.

"For my sake, do as Foscari says. He has another boy to serve his purposes? Perfect! You shall have your son back. I shall have my loan repaid with interest."

"I don't feel in my heart that is right."

There was a change in Asher's face, a shift in his posture, an almost imperceptible turning away from her. "I did not want to say this to you, but it seems I must."

"What do you mean?"

"I know what you did."

Five innocent words when uttered separately. A five-pointed star in her heart when spoken together. Hannah knew exactly what Asher meant. "How? How do you know?"

"Keep your voice down. I don't want to wake Tzipporah." He bent his head to her ear. "I was visiting a woman that night. Her name does not matter. Let us just say she was a married woman. Long after midnight I was walking home across the *campo* when I saw a man carrying a basket with a tiny fist waving above the sides. There was mewling from the basket. It was a strange sight—a well-dressed man, a nobleman I guessed from his fur-trimmed cloak—carrying a baby. A gentile in the ghetto long after the gates had been bolted and locked aroused my suspicion. I followed him, keeping well out of sight. I guessed this high and mighty nobleman had got his Jewish mistress with child and wanted to abandon the baby to her relatives."

"You are lying. You were home in bed that night curled up next to Tzipporah. Any other night of the week, yes, you might be out seducing married women, but not the Sabbath."

Asher continued. "When I saw *you* pursuing the nobleman, I was even more curious. You were so intent on keeping him in sight you didn't notice me. The nobleman entered the butcher's shop and you followed. In a trice, I heard shouts and screams. I peered in the window and watched as the man set the baby on a table and grabbed a filleting knife hanging on the wall. He held the knife to your throat then raised it above the baby's head. You and the nobleman fought, yelling, shoving each other. You wrested the knife from him. You tucked the baby under one arm and stabbed the nobleman. I watched you drag his body to the canal and heave it in."

Asher was telling the truth. All the details, from the filleting knife to Niccolò's upraised hand, were just as he had described. "How I could have used your help." Embers of anger glowed within her and threatened to burst into flame. "If you had come forward, together we could have overpowered Niccolò and I would not have his death on my conscience."

At first Hannah wanted to spring at her brother and rake her nails down his face. Wanted to feel his blood on her hands. Then a terrible sadness took hold of her. This brother she had loved and protected for so many years had deserted her. "You witnessed me being attacked and you did nothing?"

"We had quarrelled. I was angry with you." Asher drew out a handkerchief and wiped the sweat off his face. "I turned on my heel and hurried home."

"I cannot think anyone, even you, could be so cruel."

"I am not proud of myself."

And yet, were his actions so out of character? Whereas their father had been kind and gentle, her brother had always been quick to take offence, slow to forgive. He was a man who preserved ancient wounds in a brine of imagined offence and insults.

"You may think me heartless, but I was furious with you. I rejoiced in your trouble. Later that night, though, after I had had time to reflect, I was consumed with guilt. I rose before dawn, before even the fishermen were out. I returned to the butcher's shop. I was afraid the nobleman's body would be found floating by one of the Christian guards patrolling the island ghetto by boat."

Asher's mouth was dry. Hannah could tell by the tone of his voice.

"I borrowed a boat and searched the Rio del Ghetto until I found the corpse. I fished him out, stripped him naked so he could not be identified. I tied a burlap bag filled with cinder bricks around his torso and rowed out into the lagoon. When I was nearly to Burano, I pushed him out of the boat."

"So you concealed my crime."

"Yes, until now."

"Speak plainly."

"You tell whatever falsehoods are required. If you do not do everything in your power to help Foscari obtain his blasted order for guardianship, I will go to the Prosecuti and denounce you."

Before Hannah had time to react, she heard Tzipporah stir and the baby begin to fuss. Their quarrelling had awakened them. Tzipporah sat up, yawned and stared at Hannah in surprise. "You came back," she said.

"I am just leaving, Tzipporah," said Hannah. She felt ill. Needed fresh air. Needed to be away from Asher. Needed to be free of everything that reminded her of him.

Tzipporah rubbed her eyes. "Where will you go?"

Asher folded his arms across his chest. His face turned so red he looked as though he was being spit-roasted. "Hannah is not welcome here."

"Yes, she is for one night." Tzipporah put Elijah, who was beginning to cry, to breast.

"Another woman telling me what is right and what is not." Asher shot Tzipporah a furious look. He went to a cherry wood box with a hasp on it. "By the way, I have something for you, Hannah. A letter from Isaac, delivered yesterday."

He handed it to her with a look of satisfaction. The letter was unlaced; he had already read it. She recognized her name on the outside of the letter, which was addressed in Isaac's broad, confident strokes. She clasped the parchment to her breast and stroked it as though it was Isaac's back. He had touched this very paper with his hand, perhaps pressed it with a kiss before sealing it. Warmth seemed to radiate from the parchment as she tried to divine the contents. Words of love and forgiveness first. Then the news that he was coming to Venice. He might even be on a ship right now.

Relief swept over her. Kissing the letter, Hannah forgot Asher's threat for the moment. If it pleased God, may Isaac arrive in time for the baby's birth. She handed the letter back to Asher to read.

"*Yasher koach*—may you have strength! You will not like what Isaac writes." Asher unfolded the letter and smoothed the parchment out on his knee. He ran an eye over it, as if to assure himself the contents had not altered since he first read them, then cleared his throat and began. By the time he had read half of it, Hannah was begging him to stop, tears streaming down her face. The only bright words in Isaac's letter were "I pray every night you are well and that the baby will be born safely." The rest were hurtful, stinging; words that did not sound like anything Isaac was capable of thinking, let alone committing to paper. Were it not for the baby, Isaac wrote, he would divorce her for disobedience. He would come for the baby's birth. Then they would discuss their future. And the most hurtful sentence: "Since it is clear you no longer wish to be my wife and act as a wife should, I will release you from the bonds of marriage if that is what you wish, although it will grieve me. I have never loved anyone as I have loved you."

She hated Asher for reading this detestable letter in a quiet, solemn tone, taking pleasure in her grief. She hated him for having a handsome, fertile wife. Hated him for his healthy sons. She snatched the letter from his hand and tried to shred it, but the parchment was too strong and she managed only to smear the ink with her tears.

Tzipporah tried to put her arms around her, but Hannah shrugged her off. What did Hannah's anguish matter to Tzipporah? Why did she have that look of pity on her face? She had Asher and her sons. Hannah turned her face to the wall so they would not see her weeping.

Divorce? It was not possible. Isaac loved her. He had promised always to love her. They had met and married within a month. Isaac had taken her without a dowry. His love had never faltered during her long years of barrenness— the sad little cycles of hope and despair that followed the courses of the moon. He loved her still. He must.

She wanted to run from Asher's apartment and fling herself in the Rio di Ghetto Nuovo. And then she remembered the baby growing under her heart.

CHAPTER 19

Villa di Padovani,
San Lorenzo, the Veneto

FOSCARI WAS A TALL, ill-natured gander, neck extended, hissing at the sky, spitting and stomping back and forth on the lawn. His thin lips opened and closed. From the kitchen, Cesca heard him shout "Slut," "Whore," "Treacherous bitch."

Cesca marched outside.

"For the last time, where is Matteo?" Foscari demanded, as Cesca descended the steps of the portico.

"I've sent him away. Far from here, far from you, you double-dealing son of a pig."

"What you are playing at?"

How heartwarming to see his face contorted in rage, his

silver nose dangling on a single thread. Cesca had never seen him so agitated.

"I need Matteo," Foscari said, "as you well know. How can I force Hannah to testify if he is nowhere to be found? She is not an imbecile. She will insist on seeing him before she gives evidence. And she will want a share of his fortune. You know what greedy creatures Jews are."

"You should have thought of that before you decided to sell my villa."

He laughed. "*Your* villa?" He spoke in a tone he had never used—harsh and loud and vulgar. Then he recommenced pacing. Finally, after several lengths around the garden, he came to a halt in front of her, tired and panting. Cesca braced herself for a long tirade or even a blow, but he surprised her by taking a deep breath and saying, "I am sorry, my dear." He continued more calmly. "As a matter of fact, I have been to the notary." He patted his waistcoat pocket. "Here is my letter promising the villa will be yours once I am guardian."

Soon he had adopted his customary bantering tone. "For your happiness I would pluck the very stars out of the sky and tumble them into your lap. I would rearrange the constellations in the sky to better suit you. I would alter the beat of my heart."

All nonsense, of course, but how instructive to hear Foscari go on so, his elegant hands fluttering this way and that, tapping his breast to show his sincerity, pausing, then tugging his earlobe. He put so much effort into his performance the exertion seemed to weaken him and he had to lean against one of the pillars holding up the portico. "I know how you love this estate."

She nodded, waiting, admiring his self-control.

"And so," he went on, "my letter of intent." With thumb and forefinger, he dipped into his waistcoat pocket and extracted a folded piece of vellum. "This simple piece of paper shall seal our bargain and put your mind at rest. I shall sign it when you tell me where Matteo is."

Cesca took the vellum from him and studied it, feeling his eyes on her as she grew red with humiliation. She squinted at the vexing black squiggles, which to her looked like beetles chasing each other in circles across the page.

Foscari sighed and snatched the paper from her. "I am the son of one of the oldest and most noble families in the Veneto, the centre of my mother's universe, a graduate of the University of Bologna, a humanist and a lover of Petrarch's poems. I cannot believe I have fallen in love with a woman who cannot, even if a musket were held to her head, sign her own name other than with a sooty thumbprint."

His words had their desired effect. Cesca stared at the ground, hands clenched at her side, as she tried to conceal her mortification.

Foscari said, "Look, here is your name and there is the line for me to sign on. It's all very legal and proper. You have nothing to worry about."

She glanced at the document. Yes, she could see his name at the top and there was hers. But the rest was a puzzle. She took the document back from him and continued to stare at it until she surprised herself by recognizing a few words—*beef* and *lamb* and *chicken*. Such words appeared on butchers' signs over shop windows along with crude sketches of the various animals. Her eye ran down the page. There were a few numbers. This document must be a contract for the sale of livestock. She studied it for a moment, squinting anew at the dancing, inky marks. Then she set her face in a smile, revealing nothing of her discovery. On the bottom right-hand corner was an impressive-looking blue ribbon, fixed in place by a red wax seal.

"Very kind of you, Foscari. I knew I could trust you." At long last she understood the true value of literacy: being able to read allowed you to cheat and rob those who could not.

"Now, where is Matteo?" asked Foscari.

"He is with my aunt's cousin in Venice. Her house is Calle Balastro, 54, Dorsoduro." It was the first address that sprang to mind. "You need not worry, Foscari. He is well tended to. I will bring him to court so Hannah can see him. Use Lucca, if you wish. Hannah will cooperate."

"I am glad you have come around to my point of view."

"But what if the judge has Hannah executed for raising Matteo as a Jew? Have you thought of that? Then we will have two boys on our hands."

"Only one."

"Which one?"

"The obedient one, of course."

"Whatever you say." Their easy agreement seemed to please Foscari, who went upstairs to his study and returned with a pen and inkwell. He dipped the quill. With a flourish, he signed his name to the vellum document. "There you are," he said, waving the vellum about to let the ink dry. "I shall give you this letter once I have Matteo."

Foscari was an ass; he was a babbler. In signing the bogus document, he had signed his own death warrant.

CHAPTER 20

Oespedale della Pietà,
Castello, Venice

THE ARSENALE WAS the most heavily guarded
shipyard in Europe. Nothing was familiar about
it—not the sweet fragrance of fresh-cut timber, or
the scent of pitch used to caulk the ships, or the crackling
of the caulkers' fires, or the thud of axes bouncing off oak,
or the smell of turpentine. Flames shot like the unearthly
claws of the devil, staining the sky in shades of orange, red
and yellow. Hannah walked past sail makers hunched in
front of their huts, sewing by the light of candles, their
palm cushions blotchy with patches of blood.

The Oespedale della Pietà must be close. Hannah strode
on until she came to a convent with a grey, forbidding

aspect—a blank facade with a roundel like an eye embedded high on the wall, which depicted the figure of a nun. Tall gates, grated windows. No generous, embracing portico; no graceful arches; no ample loggia. Hannah glanced up at the roof. Sure enough, just as Lucca had said, stone gargoyles stared down as though to eat her. Assunta had described such places, so Hannah could imagine the chapel within—the shrouded Communion windows and the open mouths of nuns at Mass, parting their lips to receive Christ's body in the form of a wafer slipped though a slit in the curtain by an unseen priest. Then the whisk of skirts and the dusty odour of dried flowers as the nuns filed back to their bare cells.

The convent door was bolted. The night porter dozed with his arms wrapped around a large, hairy dog. Behind him, from the chapel, came the disembodied voices of nuns intoning a Gregorian chant. Their voices were so feather-light they floated before drifting down around Hannah, covering her like a red-and-blue silk shawl she had once owned, which was so finely made she could draw the entire garment through her wedding ring.

Slowly, Hannah slid the bolt open, crept through the door, and then fastened it behind her.

It was Matins, the service that took place in the middle of the night. It lasted, Hannah recalled from her lessons with Sister Assunta, an hour. There was little time to search this immense edifice of shifting shadows for a boy no taller than a wine barrel.

In her linen bag, banging against her leg, was the orange Hannah had brought for Matteo. She tiptoed past the watchman. She would announce neither her presence nor her intention. If she did, there was sure to be an interrogation, and what explanation could she provide? That she, a nun, was the child's mother? And what if the other nuns refused to believe her? Why would she, a Carmelite nun, be spiriting away a sleeping boy in the middle of the night? She could think of no plausible explanation.

The choir ceased their chant. There was a momentary silence and then they commenced to sing again, this time a madrigal, livelier and accompanied by a lute. Between verses, when silence prevailed, she could hear children thrashing in their sleep. Shoes in hand, down a corridor Hannah scurried, following the snores, night cries and stirrings of small bodies, until she found the boys' dormitory.

The room would have been as black as pitch if not for the tallow candle sputtering on a pottery shard on the floor—a candle too close to bedclothes and nightshirts, too close to children's bare skin and restless limbs. The long room was as narrow as a ribbon and lined on both sides with cots. Curtains—tattered sails salvaged from some long-ago sailing vessel—kept out the miasma of the pitch-filled night air. The nuns no doubt did their best with meagre donations, but the orphanage was a poor place—drafty, musty, with moss and lichens veiling floor and walls.

Hannah would not dwell on what the nuns probably fed the boys—gruel, and watery mutton broth with a few vegetables.

Her eyes adjusted to the gloom. Here were the luckless products of unfortunate couplings—superfluous, discarded children. The room was a jumble of skinny haunches, arms, legs crooked from lack of nourishment and covered by ragged bedclothes far beyond anything that could be darned. It was as though someone had dropped a bag of graveyard bones from the ceiling and let the bones bounce until somehow they arranged themselves on the cots. Had the light been better, she suspected she could have seen fleas leaping about and lice nesting in the bedclothes.

Thank God for Matteo's red hair and high-spirited giggle. He would be as easy to spot among these poor waifs as a copper coin on a robe of black velvet. Even in the darkness his hair would be a beacon.

Hannah picked up the candle, trying not to spill the tallow pooling on the shard, and began her search. The candle cast deep shadows and would not last more than a half hour. At least fifty cots stood lined up on either side of the room. All were occupied, some with as many as three or four boys. Some boys kicked phantom balls in their sleep, or lunged at ghosts or demons. Others were as still as death.

As Hannah walked down the aisle, she realized it would be easy to miss one small boy amid so many. The smell of infirmity—vomit, phlegm, dried blood—filled the air. How could Cesca have sent Matteo to such a place?

Hannah tripped on a loose floor stone. She caught herself before she fell on a cot with a boy about four years old. The child rolled over but did not wake. Sores covered his legs. Hannah bunched her fingers on one hand as if to make the sign of the cross. Feeling foolish, she stopped and let her hand drop to her side.

She reached down. The boy seemed the right size, but she could not see his hair. She touched his head. All she felt was stubble. She touched it again, her touch firmer this time. The boy turned over. Hannah scanned his face. Some feature was missing. At first she could not determine what it was.

She bent for a closer look; stared down, willing him to turn his head so she could see him better. His forehead was high and blankly white. She reviewed his features: neck, chin, mouth, nose and forehead. Something vital and obvious was missing. She lost precious seconds trying to figure out what the child lacked. And then she realized with horror: the boy had no eyes. His lids lay flat in their sockets.

She pressed a fist to her mouth, ashamed at her shock and disgust, then moved on to the other cots. A few paces later, she stopped and returned to the sightless boy. She bent over him again and placed a hand on his brow. So many boys, so much misery, so impossible to help them all. But did that mean she should help none? Out of her pocket she took the orange meant for Matteo. She found the boy's hand beneath the covers, placed the orange in his palm and closed his fingers around it.

She carried on from bed to bed, holding the cumbersome skirts of her habit in one hand, trying not to trip a second time. From one bed to the next she hurried, touching the heads of boys, searching in vain for a glimmer of red hair. Big boys, small boys, sleeping boys, groaning boys, some on their backs, some on their stomachs, some curled on their sides, faster and faster she went. She soon realized the difficulty. The boys' heads were all shaved, every last one, probably to control the spread of lice and ringworm. She continued, frantically now, stroking heads—most of them prickly with new growth, but some, the newest arrivals, she guessed, as smooth as a marble. How foolish she had been to think Matteo's red hair would guide her.

The singing in the chapel had ceased and she heard the swish of slippered feet on stone paving. Matins was over. She started to panic. She had examined only half the boys. There were at least another twenty beds she had not yet scrutinized. Hannah forced herself to breathe more slowly. The boys did not seem to be arranged oldest to youngest. Perhaps the most recent arrivals would be wedged in nearer to the door—

From the bed next to her came a cough from deep within the chest. A small hand caught her skirts. She touched it. The hand was too frail to be Matteo's pudgy fist. It felt hot. She tucked it under the child's thin blanket. What if Matteo was not here? What if he was in another orphanage or, may God not be listening, had already died of pox or diphtheria? The dankness of this ancient building would incite illness in all but the most robust child. *Merciful God*, she prayed, *if you help me to find him, I will never trouble you again.*

She scanned the remaining cots but still saw no boy the right size or shape. Lucca was mistaken. Matteo must be in one of the orphanages farther north of the harbour, each one no doubt as crowded as this.

But she could smell the pine pitch drifting through the windows, just as Lucca had said, and hear the shouts of the sawyers and carpenters as they worked, for when the demand for galleys was great, they worked around the clock. She tiptoed from bed to bed, hurriedly straightening blankets and pillows, touching heads, necks, foreheads, hands—whatever she could reach.

Footsteps approached. She stifled a groan of despair. Her mouth was so dry she could hardly part her lips, but she began to pray aloud: "'Hear, O Israel, the Lord is our God, the Lord is One.'" It was the Shema, the prayer she and Matteo had recited together each morning and night since he was an infant. She moved along the aisles, reciting the Shema over and over as loudly as she dared: "'*Shema Yisrael Adonai Eloheinu Adonai echad.*'"

One boy had fallen out of bed; his forehead showed a gash oozing blood—he had struck it on the iron frame of his cot. She wished she could settle him back into bed and tend to his wound, but she dared not take the time. The best she could do was to toss his blanket over him. From the hallway came the slap of slippers and the rustle of robes.

Hannah leaned over the next group of cots. "'Hear, O Israel . . .'" she began again. Something grazed her cheek— a cobweb perhaps? Then a hand reached up and clasped her skirts. She bent toward it. The hand patted her cheek like a baker patting dough.

"'*Baruch shem kevod mal'khoo'to le'olam va'ed,*'" a voice whispered.

"Matteo?" The hand left her face and two small arms pulled her down; they encircled her neck so tightly she had difficulty breathing. Then a tiny mouth brushed her cheek, as softly as the wings of a dove.

"Ama," a clear, sweet voice said. "I knew you would come for me."

CHAPTER 21

Ospedale della Pietà,
Castello, Venice

ANNAH SNATCHED UP Matteo and wrapped
him in his blanket as best she could. He had
grown in the months they had been apart. His
legs were longer, his arms rounder. She ran down the
dormitory aisle toward the door opening onto the street.
When she was almost there—so close she could feel cool
street air from beneath the door jamb—she heard more
footsteps. Turning, Hannah saw a bobbing candle
approaching as though moving of its own accord. She set
Matteo down and fumbled with the door. She cursed
herself for re-fastening the bolt when she entered. The
iron bar would not budge.

The candle flickered, nearly extinguished by the draft from the street. Hannah managed to shove the bolt back halfway. One more heave and the door would swing open.

The black figure holding the candle walked toward Hannah. There was no side corridor to duck down, no closet or alcove to hide in, no table or statue to conceal her and Matteo behind. Just this door to freedom held fast by a rusty bar. Matteo whimpered, his arms around her waist. "Shh," she said, holding him tight.

The figure drew closer. "I am the abbess of this convent. Who, pray tell, are you?" The accent was Venetian, the voice low and well modulated.

Hannah turned to the abbess and said, "I am Sister Benedicta."

"And where do you think you are taking this child?"

Hannah was shaking so much that she could not speak. Matteo hid behind her and buried his face in her robe.

The abbess held her candle aloft and peered at Hannah, squinting near-sightedly. "From what convent are you?"

"Saint Ursula in Malta." Hannah's face turned crimson with shame for pretending to be something she was not. She was glad it was too dark for this austere woman to notice. Hannah felt no better than a common pickpocket in a market caught red-handed stealing fruit.

"Come with me to the *parlatorio*. I do not wish to wake the other children." The abbess was thick bodied and tall, with a strong brow and square shoulders. A handsome ivory rosary dangled from her waist. She resembled Sister Assunta. Hannah picked up Matteo and followed the nun.

The abbess's left foot turned outward at a right angle, making her progress down the hallway slow. Even with Matteo in her arms, Hannah could have outrun her. But she considered the night watchman and his dog at the entrance-way and thought better of it. As if reading her mind, the abbess linked her arm through Hannah's, gripping Hannah's forearm with such firmness it began to grow numb. Slowing her pace to match the nun's, Hannah walked down the cor-ridor, along the loggia and through a garden. The abbess reached a door on the other side of the garden, opened it and ushered Hannah and Matteo into a small room contain-ing a long table, an iron chest and, in the corner, a *prie-dieu*.

The nun inclined her head toward a chair with a woven rush seat. Hannah sat with her back to the wall. The abbess threw open the shutters of the large, grated windows, let-ting in the chill of early dawn. Hannah pulled Matteo into her lap, where he patted her face with glad little cries and wriggled gleefully, refusing to be still.

He was wearing a too-small pair of breeches so tattered his pink knees poked through. A stained shirt missing most of its buttons hung limp from his shoulders. Older, stronger boys must have stolen his good clothes. Or were these the clothes—little better than street urchins' rags—that Cesca had dressed him in? What did it matter? His cheek was cool, free of fever. His eyes were free of discharge. She ran a hand over his head, beribboned with the fresh marks of a barber's razor. Never mind; his hair would grow back. She felt under his shirt for a rash or pustules. His skin was unblemished. At least for now, Matteo was free of the dreaded smallpox. Hannah had found him before he had contracted a disease in this wretched place. But of his spirit, there was no telling. Had Cesca and Foscari and this dreadful orphanage crushed Matteo's kind, generous nature?

"Give an account of yourself."

The abbess's voice was deep and strong, a voice one could better imagine issuing orders to servants than reciting prayers. Except for her white wimple, she was clothed in black from head to ankle. The tips of her dark slippers thrust from under her robes as she stood in front of the open window.

Hannah would not cower before this woman. "I am here," she began, keeping her voice steady, "to collect my son, Matteo." Somehow she would convince the abbess of her good intentions.

"*Your* son?"

"Yes, I know," said Hannah, attempting a smile. "'A woman may have either a husband or a convent cell, but she may not have both.'" Assunta had often repeated this phrase. "After my husband died, I entered Saint Ursula's, a convent that permits nuns to bring their young children with them." *Would* a convent tolerate the presence of children? She had no idea.

The abbess limped over to the table, pulled out a chair and sat. "I cannot have strangers, even nuns, breaking into my convent and helping themselves to my children."

"'Bless me, Holy Mother, for I have sinned.'" The words came surprisingly easy. "I beg your forgiveness. I have acted

sinfully, but when I tell you my story, I think you will understand my desperation." *And what is my story? And how to make it
credible enough to win the sympathy of this formidable woman?*

The abbess folded her arms, waiting.

Hannah cleared her throat. "My late husband and I were
both from wealthy Jewish families in Malta." *May God not
be listening to what I am about to say.* "I always longed to embrace
Christ as my Saviour, but my husband was opposed. After
he died, I converted to Christianity and joined the Carmelite
order of Saint Ursula's as a novice. After years of study and
praying for God's guidance, I took my vows. I have been
living at the convent with my son." Hannah paused, waiting for God to smite her.

The abbess said, "Your husband's family approved of
you becoming a *converso*?"

"On the contrary. They were distraught their grandson
and sole heir was being raised in the Holy Roman Church.
My father-in-law hired the Marquis Foscari and his con-
sort, a woman named Francesca. They kidnapped Matteo
from me at Saint Ursula's, taking him one evening when
I was at Vespers. When I discovered he was in Venice, I
sailed on the first ship."

The abbess regarded her skeptically. "Francesca sent this
boy with two men who informed me Matteo was her son
and she required temporary care for him. It is a common
enough situation. Parents entrust their children to me for
a few weeks or months while they arrange their affairs."

"Francesca and Foscari will return the boy to his
paternal grandparents," Hannah replied, "and cut him

off from any possibility of life everlasting as a Christian." If God had not struck her down yet, He understood and forgave.

The abbess narrowed her eyes. "Not if I have anything to say in the matter."

"My wish is to go back to Saint Ursula's with my son. My family is well-to-do, but my convent is poor. I am sure you understand how costly it is to maintain such a place. When I return with Matteo, my family, even though they are Jews, have promised to give thanks to the Virgin Mary by building a chapel in Her honour."

"I must not interfere with such a generous plan," said the nun.

"I thank you, Abbess. And forgive me for my presumption in entering your convent without invitation." Now she must retreat before her tongue got her in trouble. "I may take my son with God's blessing?"

"Not just yet. Francesca will be here this morning to pick up the boy. In fairness, I should hear what she has to say. You and Matteo shall stay in one of the nunnery cells until she arrives."

Hannah had no choice but to comply. She took Matteo by the hand and rose, turning her back to the abbess to hide her rounded belly. The abbess showed them to a bare room with a crucifix over the bed. There, on the tiny cot, Hannah and Matteo managed to sleep, wrapped in each other's arms. Knowing what lay ahead, Hannah savoured the sound of Matteo's gentle snoring, the feeling of his body still plump with vestiges of baby flesh.

A few hours later, Hannah heard footsteps in the corridor then a rap on the door. A fresh-faced postulate ushered them to the *parlatorio*.

Cesca sat next to the abbess, her back not touching the rear of the chair, a smile on her face. It was the first time Hannah had seen her since Constantinople. She looked just as beautiful. Neither time nor treachery had muddied her clear skin nor wrinkled her throat nor blackened her teeth. How satisfying it would be were it otherwise.

The abbess said, "Francesca, this is Sister Benedicta, who tells me she is Matteo's mother. She is here to take him back to Malta. She claims you kidnapped him."

"Hannah! Here you are in your ridiculous disguise," said Cesca.

From a basket on her arm, Cesca took several dried peaches and placed them on the table in front of the abbess. "I am so grateful to you, Abbess, for looking after Matteo." She gave the abbess a beatific smile. "I hope you were not deceived by this Jewess." Before Hannah could duck, Cesca tugged at Hannah's wimple. "Look at that face, the dark skin and eyes, the clever mouth, the long nose—a Hebrew face."

For a moment Hannah was tempted to grab one of the peaches and fling it at Cesca, or better still, jam it down her throat so she could not breathe, much less speak. "I have already explained—"

"I shall have him now, Abbess," Cesca said.

Hannah put an arm around Matteo. "Abbess, Cesca is a liar."

The abbess raised a hand. "Let us discuss this situation rationally. Francesca, I believe this woman to be a nun. Of course she has the face of an Israelite. She is a *converso*, who has bent her knee to Our Saviour. The Church welcomes such people." She spoke calmly, but her eyes darkened— the ominous grey of storm clouds and roiling seas.

"Nonsense. Her name is Hannah Levi. She is no more a nun than I am."

Cesca was leaner now. She seemed all hard edges—her jaw, her elbows, even the collarbone outlined under her green dress.

"Cesca stole Matteo and now plots to steal his fortune," said Hannah.

The abbess cast her eyes to the ceiling, as though conferring with God. "Francesca entrusted him to my care, claiming to be his mother. Sister Benedicta also claims the boy. Which of you am I to believe?"

"I have risked my life for him many times. I have been a mother to him in every sense of the word." Hannah acknowledged the beseeching quality of her own voice, which she could not help and which embarrassed her.

Cesca smiled and wiggled her fingers at Matteo. "Darling boy, come and sit on my lap." She reached in her basket, took out a peach and held it out to him.

Matteo jumped off Hannah's lap and over to Cesca, who swooped him up and cradled him in her arms. "Such a lovely boy," she cooed.

Hannah studied the abbess's face, trying to divine her expression. Matteo nestled into Cesca's arms and parted his lips as she held the peach to his mouth.

"This is my ama," Matteo said, putting his hand on Hannah's knee. "She has always been my ama." He clutched Hannah's skirts. Hannah let out a sigh of relief.

The abbess clasped her hands together and was about to speak, when Matteo placed a hand on Cesca's cheek. "Cesca is my ama, too."

The abbess frowned as she regarded both women. "In truth," she said to Hannah, "although my eye sight is not much good to me anymore, I venture that the boy resembles Francesca more than he does you." The nun drummed her fingers on the table. "We are a poor convent. To my regret, we cannot offer the children as much in the way of food and clothing as some of the more prosperous orders, but in spiritual sustenance, we are the best in the city. I shall keep Matteo until I have had time to pray and ask God's divine guidance."

Cesca said, "No, the boy must come with me. I am sure his guardian, the Marquis Foscari, will make a generous donation to your *oespedale*."

The abbess's stomach, pressing against the cord around her waist, gurgled loudly.

"Please," Hannah said, "I have arranged ship's passage. I must be at the docks with Matteo before the next morning tide." What was one more falsehood amid so many?

The abbess beckoned to Matteo, "Come here, child."

Matteo crawled onto the abbess's lap. She gave him her rosary beads to play with. Matteo let the ivory beads trickle through his chubby fingers, glancing from one to the other. It unsettled Hannah to see him playing with this Christian article Jews were forbidden to touch. Not to snatch the rosary from him took all her self-control.

The abbess's tapered fingers, which looked better suited to holding a violin or playing the harpsichord, stroked Matteo's shaved head. "Unclench your fists, Sister," the abbess said to Hannah. "He is a clever, handsome boy. I understand why you are both so fond of him." She looked at each of them. "You shall have my answer in due course. In the meantime, Matteo will remain here."

Hannah said, "Abbess, you and the other Sisters have done your best to care for all of these boys. On very little money."

"And when pestilence stalks the city for victims, the *oespedale* is the first place it calls," the abbess said.

"Yes," Hannah said. "But as you yourself have said, it is difficult to provide for the children." This was the most tactful way she could think of to describe the appalling conditions. "I wish to make a donation to the convent to alleviate some of the hardships I have noticed." Hannah picked up the hem of her habit. "If I may have the use of a knife?"

The abbess reached into the drawer of the table then handed her an ivory letter opener. "All donations are most welcome."

The good woman settled back in her chair with Matteo, patting his back. Soon his eyelids drooped and he was dozing against her shoulder. In the distance, the choir commenced a doleful chant. It was Terce, the mid-morning prayers.

With the tip of the opener, Hannah began unpicking the stitches in her hem.

"You must not give the boy to this imposter," Cesca said. "She will run back to Constantinople with him. The child must be in court to claim his estate." She touched the abbess on the arm. "Surely you cannot be deceived by this Jewess."

Cesca leaned over and, before Hannah could stop her, tugged off her wimple. Hannah's dark hair cascaded over her shoulders.

There was a collective intake of breath.

Cesca laughed triumphantly. "You see, Abbess? Is it not a rule that all nuns cut their hair when they take their vow of chastity, obedience and poverty?"

"It is an offence to God to masquerade as a Bride of Christ. You desecrate the nun's habit," the abbess said, rising to her feet and causing Matteo to topple to the floor. "Why was your hair not shorn when you renounced all earthly pleasures?"

"Because . . ." Hannah could think of nothing to say.

An ominous silence descended on the room, the kind that prevailed at public hangings the moment just after the noose is placed around the accused's neck and just before the hangman lays whip to the horse's rump. Even Matteo stopped wriggling and sat with his eyes cast to the floor.

The abbess grew white with anger. She flicked the rosary at her waist back and forth, the beads clicking against her robe. "I can guess what you are up to. There is more at stake than just the fate of this boy."

"What do you mean?"

"How many other children have you stolen?" asked the abbess.

"No, you misunderstand!"

"Do not play the innocent. You know exactly what I am talking about."

Hannah could not believe what she was hearing. In her state of shock, at first she thought the abbess was making a jest—a stupid, untimely jest, but a jest just the same. "I do not understand."

But Hannah did understand. And the certainty of what would come next had her wanting to run as fast as she could from this forbidding woman.

"Confess! Get on your knees. Make your peace with God. You are part of a plot to steal Christian children who have no parents to defend them. Children you will hand over to your Rabbi, who will—"

"No, absolutely not! You are mad."

"You are a procuress for your people. How many other children are part of your diabolical scheme?" The abbess stared, eyes narrowed, at Hannah then quickly looked away, as though Hannah was a repulsive object she had tripped over on the street.

"This is absurd." Here it was. The rekindling of the ancient fires, the fanning of the embers of the age-old grudges. From the set of the abbess's jaw and the twitch of her beads Hannah knew that no argument would convince the abbess otherwise.

"I wager that at this very moment your Rabbi is sharpening his knife to slit this boy's throat."

The abbess's fury grew like a conflagration that begins with a mere spark escaping a fireplace grate. The spark ignites a nearby rag, which sets aflame curtains and bedding and clothing, until the entire house is burning so fiercely that surrounding houses take flame. Soon the entire district is engulfed.

Hannah had no idea how to quench the flames.

"And isn't the holiday of Passover nearly upon us—when you Jews drain the blood of Christian children to make your bread?" asked the abbess.

The *parlatorio* felt as hot as the inside of an oven. Hannah feared she was going to faint. Hannah's mother, who was from Frankfurt am-Main, had told her of an incident: a child found dead—stuffed down the well of a Jewish moneylender, the accusation of blood libel, a confession obtained by torture. And then the entire Jewish quarter banished, hastily fastened bundles on bent backs, children straggling behind, the stink of scorched timbers and burned crops, horsemen with staves urging them on. "Abbess, I did not expect a woman of your obvious breeding and education would believe in such nonsense."

The abbess gave a grim smile. "You are a clever woman. I will grant you that. Where better to find helpless young souls than here in my orphanage?"

Cesca said, "How many ducats have you secreted away? With such a healthy pile, why don't you buy your sacrificial lambs instead of stealing them?" She grabbed at Hannah's skirt, but Hannah slapped her hand away.

"I am going to summon the soldiers of the Prosecuti and have you arrested," said the abbess. "A Jewess raising a Christian boy is a serious offence and I believe your crime to be much worse than simply that. The Prosecuti will investigate. They will find out exactly what your scheme is."

"You have misjudged me. I have no scheme other than to get my son back. I—"

"I do not want to hear another word from you. This is a matter for the courts."

"Well said, Abbess," Cesca said. "Now may I have my son?"

"Both of you be quiet." The abbess scowled at Cesca. "I shall keep Matteo here. The Lord in His wisdom will guide me to the right path. Until then, the boy will be safe and well cared for."

But he is not safe and well cared for. He is in rags, eating poor victuals. How long in this orphanage before Matteo was covered in pustules, writhing in pain from lesions in his mouth and nose? He could be dead within a month of any of the diseases rife in places such as this—the pox, scarlet fever, diphtheria. Wasn't anything better than Matteo remaining here?

There was affection in Cesca's eyes when she held Matteo on her lap. He had stretched out his arms to her. He had called her "Ama Cesca." It pained Hannah to hear the love in his voice, just as it would pain her if Isaac spoke lovingly to another woman.

"Abbess," said Hannah, "give my son to Francesca."

Cesca said, "She is right, Abbess. You have so many mouths to feed. Let me take one off your hands."

"That is the only reasonable thing I have heard since I had the misfortune to lay eyes on the two of you." The abbess pondered the matter for a moment and then nodded. "Fine, take him."

Matteo screamed in protest and clung to Hannah, who said in a soothing voice, "Loosen your grip, my son." He continued to cry and struggle. The faster it could be done, the better. Hannah tickled him and he dropped his arms. Matteo must not see her weeping. How upset Hannah had been as a child when her mother cried; how her weeping had made it seem nothing was right in the world, nothing certain or predictable or secure. "Be a brave boy," she said. "Do not fret. I will be back for you soon." She kissed Matteo's cheek as Cesca hurried him out of the *parlatorio*. The door of the main entrance groaned open then closed.

Much later, after Hannah had been locked in a cell, she wondered if her last sight of Matteo would be his red face bobbing over Cesca's shoulder, crying and calling for her, waving as he struggled in Cesca's arms.

CHAPTER 22

Pozzi Prison, Venice

ONLY ONE THING MATTERED: escape. Hannah was up to her ankles in salt water from the lagoon. The prison was known as Pozzi, meaning "wells," because it filled twice a day with the tides. The flooding was at its worst at high tide. Hannah's feet were numb from the icy water. She stumbled to the waste bucket, leaning on the wall for support, banging her wounded arm. The lice made her frantic. She had bitten her nails to prevent herself from scratching, but it was no use. Her legs and arms had red marks so angry a swarm of cats might have attacked her. She fumbled in her linen bag, but Tzipporah's tin of ointment was empty. What Hannah wouldn't give for a bath in clean hot water to rid herself of the lice. Even sprinkling her mattress with orris root, a gift from another prisoner, did not help.

From the cells farther down the corridors she heard the cries of the other women and the sloshing of sea water entering the cells. The lack of sleep—for who could sleep when rats jumped on one's face and mice burrowed into the folds of one's cloak and hair—had driven many of them mad. It took all of Hannah's self-control not to fling herself on her waterlogged pallet and scream and claw and rage, tearing at her face and hair as she had heard some prisoners do.

The bells of San Marco rang in the piazza, on the other side of the wall. When she had first arrived, she had recoiled at their loudness. Now she found comfort in the rich pealing. The noise masked the skittering of rodents.

Hannah forced herself to rise. She took pains with her appearance, although her back ached and she felt a fever coming on. She wanted nothing so much as to remain on her pallet and never rise again, but for the baby's sake she dipped a filthy rag into a bowl of water and scrubbed her hands and face as best she could with the brackish water, careful to keep her mouth closed. The small discipline of caring for herself made life more bearable. Those prisoners who made an effort—who washed, who darned their clothing, who busied themselves with tatting lace or nursing sick prisoners—fared better at the hands of the guards than did prisoners who appeared unkempt and listless.

She dried her hands and face on the hem of her habit

then ran her fingers though her hair. Her ivory comb had long ago disappeared. Without its aid her dark hair was more unruly than ever. Thank God, she had managed to hold on to her fourteen ducats. When the soldiers had searched her for valuables, they had not thought to check the hem of her nun's habit scrunched up in the bottom of her valise. Those ducats must buy her freedom.

Yesterday she had propositioned the guard Guido. The ring of keys tied around his waist resembled a rosary. Guido was in charge of the women's section of the jail. A large man with one eye crossed, he had probably not been a bad sort once. Now he ruled the jail with a heavy hand. He was not a jailer by choice. Years ago he had been a carpenter, he told her, but had fallen through the joists of a barn. His arm had knitted badly and his employer had cast him out to find what work he could.

They had been speaking in the courtyard. Would Guido leave her cell door unlocked and the outer door to the street ajar in exchange for her precious ducats? Hannah had lied, saying her brother was safeguarding ten ducats and would deliver them to Guido upon her escape. His small, malevolent eyes had lit up at the sum—for it was a goodly one, enough to buy a farm on the Terra Firma or prosperous tavern near the docks—but he shook his head. "I cannot do it, *bella*. If you had stolen a glassblower's *borsella* or broken into a church poor box, I would take fistfuls of your ducats and carry you over the threshold like a bridegroom, but the head jailer warned me to keep a weather eye on you. I don't know what you've done, but he warned me that if you escaped, *I* would be put to the *strappado*. Me, with Bianca and a flock of hungry mouths at home to feed. No, you will remain here until your belly ceases to shield you. Then you will be hanged."

With Guido's refusal came a feeling of misery so profound she had no way to express it. Hannah wanted to howl like a dog, fling herself on the ground, tear her clothes from her body and rip them to shreds. But she did none of those things. She followed Guido back to her cell, where, unless she could think of a way to escape, her baby would be born.

"But first there will be a trial? I will have a chance to defend myself?"

Guido grinned, showing teeth little more than brown stubs. "The Prosecuti do not trouble themselves with such niceties. The abbess denounced you and that's all they require." He turned away, muttering the word *trial* and shaking his head at the absurdity of the notion. "A judge would not listen to the likes of you."

"Suppose I was in court, testifying in another trial, what then?"

But Guido was already well out of earshot.

Have heart, she counselled herself. *These ducats will buy liberty.* There would be another guard with another set of keys. She would watch and wait. Yet, despair gripped her like a strangler vine, squeezing her so that the simple act of breathing required conscious effort. She lay on her pallet, hands clasped over her belly, trying to feel the baby within her quicken. The straw jabbed her through the thin cloth of her shift. The baby gave a quick kick. A welcome distraction. She stroked her belly in response. *I will protect you, little one, as you protect me.*

An hour later Guido unlocked the cell door and motioned her to the courtyard for her morning meal. His wife, Bianca, pregnant, with hair so blond it was nearly white, earned a few coins each day cooking for the prisoners. The guards, to Hannah's surprise, had allowed her to keep a handful of *scudi* in her linen bag to buy necessaries. She had saved them for Bianca, and parcelled them out one or two at a time. Soon there would be none left, and she would have only her gold ducats.

The other prisoners lined up as Bianca ladled out her watery stew. Each day Hannah fretted about whether she would find a shred of chicken gizzard in the soup, or a turnip floating in the broth, or a piece of bread soft enough to chew without breaking her teeth. Last week she had uncovered a morsel of shellfish; it had had a whiff of the sewer about it.

If Hannah did not get more food, her baby would starve. Bianca stood with a wooden spoon in one hand, her other hand balled into a fist pressing into her lower back. Maybe Bianca had been lucky enough to find a piece of beef or mutton fat in the market to flavour the broth. How much better than meat that would be. Fat melted and gave flavour to the entire stew, whereas a morsel of meat satisfied only one or two prisoners. Would the bread be without weevils this morning?

A common expression came to mind: "A tooth for every pregnancy." Bianca had only a few fist-broken teeth left in her head. Her thin hair, patches of pink scalp visible, was plaited into a braid and secured with a stick of polished bone. She was a ray of sunshine on this cold, damp morning, although she had no reason to be of good cheer, poor as she was, no doubt with a flock of children at home, and an ill-tempered husband like Guido.

"It will not be long now, will it?" said Hannah, glancing at Bianca's belly.

"Mother of God, won't I be glad when this one is out!" A sweet-faced little girl of about two years, with blond curls and dimples, clung to Bianca's skirts. "Pass us your bowl, then," Bianca said, holding out a hand, then lowered her voice. "Hannah, I'll give you a nice piece of meat, not too much gristle."

Bianca's arm, the elbow sticking out like the plucked wing of a chicken, spooned a goodly portion into Hannah's bowl. Hannah's eyes filled; she slipped a silver coin into Bianca's palm. The mutton looked fatty, the skin not crisp and the carrots an orange mush, but Hannah accepted the stew with gratitude.

"Your back is bothering you?" Hannah asked.

"It started this morning. Like someone was pressing hot coals to it. No matter, I'll soon be home. My mother has promised to come help with the children, God bless her."

"Maybe your time is here. Labour often begins this way."

"No, 'tis too early. I have another fortnight at least."

"I might have something to help you bear the pain." At the bottom of her linen bag Hannah had a ball of opium paste wrapped in gold foil. She had been saving it for her own confinement.

Bianca was about to reply, but the next prisoner in line, an old woman with wild grey hair and an unsteady balance, tugged at her sleeve.

Hannah carried her bowl deeper into the courtyard, the common area where all the female prisoners gathered to eat, a rough patch of mud and broken bricks and the leavings of fruit and vegetables. At least the sky overhead was blue and the air in the yard better than in the cells. She squatted on the ground next to the others, her back braced against the wall and her bowl in her lap.

Bianca finished serving and walked over to Hannah. She eased herself to the ground. "Guido said you were a midwife."

Hannah nodded.

"And that you are the best in Venice."

"That is for others to judge."

"This will be my . . ." She trailed off. "I think . . . my fifteenth confinement."

"How hard it must be for you." The poor soul looked as though the baby had sucked all the colour and strength from her. Hannah could not imagine where she got the energy to cook up a huge cauldron of soup and then cart it to the prison each day.

"If not for the young ones at home and this one—" she put her arm around her little girl, who had flopped down next to her "—I would throw myself in the lagoon. How can I face the pain of another birth, and another baby to nurse and clean up after?"

It was not the first time Hannah had heard such a sentiment from a worn-out mother. She took Bianca's callused hand in her own. "May God give you courage." Hannah dropped her voice. "And may this be your last pregnancy."

Bianca sighed. "It won't be. Guido will be in my bed again before my bleeding stops."

Marital relations when the wife was unclean shocked Hannah. Jewish law required the woman to cleanse herself at the ritual bath, the *mikvah*, after her bleeding had stopped, to remove all traces of blood. Although Hannah made allowances for some Christian ways, she assumed even gentiles refrained from coupling when a woman was bleeding. It was common knowledge conception at such times could result in a baby born with animal parts—hooves or snouts or scales or curling horns. She hoped Guido was not too rough in his concupiscence.

Bianca said, "My last child was born ten months ago. The unfortunate mite didn't live long enough for the priest to christen her."

Hannah turned her head so none of the other prisoners could hear. "I can fashion a device for you that will prevent further babies if you use it every time you and your husband join together." A pessary of washed and carded sheep's wool soaked in a seed-slowing compound such as olive oil infused with rosemary would work.

Bianca drew back. "That is blasphemy. I must accept all the children God, in His wisdom, sends me."

"Of course you must. I should not have spoken." Hannah glanced up at the high, unbreachable wall. She thought of the iron locks on all the doors, the stocky guards all around. And yet, freedom was so near. The street, just on the other side of the wall, was a rich compost of noise and commotion. Carts rumbled by on cobblestones; gondoliers importuned passengers; hucksters cried out the virtues of their remedies for impotence and carbuncles. How easy to get lost in the press of the crowds. "If your travail proves too great for you to bear, send Guido to fetch me. I have a compound to deaden the pain."

"Such a thing exists?" Bianca let the soup ladle hang at her side.

"When your pangs start, I will deliver your baby." Hannah held out her hands, fingers spread. "See how small my hands are? How nimble?" She took Bianca's ladle, bent it in half, then straightened it. "And how strong?" Touching Bianca's cheek, she said, "The Angel of Death flees when I am present."

"But you are a prisoner. You cannot leave."

Hannah could not survive in this grim, filthy place with rainwater coursing down the walls and foul smells rising from buckets without lids. This might be her only chance for her, her baby and, God willing, Matteo.

Hannah leaned over to pat Bianca's belly. "What husband can resist the pleas of a wife suffering the agonies of childbirth?"

CHAPTER 23

Pozzi Prison,
Venice

TINY CLAWS SPRINGING off her cheeks, followed by excited squeaking, jerked Hannah awake. She had not the will to throw off her blanket, stand and stomp about to send the creatures skittering back to the corners of her cell.

The bolt on her cell rasped and the door creaked open. Guido stumbled in. He was rough of tongue when sober and unpredictable when drunk. Hannah recoiled and shrank as far as possible from him into a corner, where she wrapped her arms around her belly. He had been bold with some of the other women—groping their laces and lifting their skirts to pinch their thighs in exchange for clean water or a fresh pile of straw—but had been decent to her, perhaps out of respect for her condition. Now he crouched over her, fingers digging into her shoulders. He reeked of sour wine and onions and his words were so slurred she could not make out what he was saying. Hannah tried to push him away, but he cupped the back of her head and pulled it close. "Come with me," he whispered. "Bianca is calling for you."

"So soon? But her time is not for a fortnight."

"Come."

Hannah grabbed her linen bag, which by some miracle still contained her birthing spoons—matching soup ladles fastened together with a hinge, which she had designed and a silversmith had fabricated—her almond oil and a river reed splayed at one end. She ran her fingers along the hem of her skirt to ensure the ducats sewn into it were still there. She had made the transfer from the hem of the nun's habit to the hem of her *cioppà* last night when no one was about.

There was no need to slip on her sandals—she slept with them strapped to her feet to guard against thieves, not to mention the scorpions in the cracks in the floor, where they sat poised, ready to sting. Guido took her arm and pushed her from her cell and down the corridor.

After many twists and turns and much scrabbling with locks—Guido was clumsy with drink—they were outside. He hurried her along a side street. Up one *calle*, down another, past churches, over bridges, under this *sotoportego* and that. Night noises filled the air: the drip of water off oars, the slamming of shutters and the groaning of the wood-keeled boats. Hannah soon lost track of where they were, although it seemed they were heading east to the *sestiere* of Dorsoduro. What a fine thing to be striding along in the open air.

Guido guided her to a low dwelling wedged between a cheese maker's store and a chandler's workshop. There was no proper door, just a length of soiled burlap to keep out the rain and the grunting, snuffling pigs foraging for garbage. He held the burlap to one side and pushed her inside.

"I'll wait out here under the eaves until the baby is born then take you back to the prison. And don't try anything clever. I must have you back by sunrise when the head jailer makes his rounds."

"You will be waiting in this filthy weather a long time," said Hannah, knowing full well a woman who had borne fifteen children would not take long to deliver her sixteenth but that a husband such as Guido, who no doubt saw childbirth as an occasion to get drunk, would not realize such a fact.

Rain bounced off his hat, a felt affair, misshapen from years of hard use. Hannah fumbled in the pocket of her *cioppà* and extracted the last of her *scudi*. "Here, Guido, find a snug, dry wine shop. Childbirth is women's work. Your task is to pray for your child's safe arrival." Was there a Christian born who could refuse the temptation of wine? "Never fear, I shall be here when you return."

Guido glanced at the coins in her outstretched hand, weighing the risk. "You won't run off? Do that and my head is on the chopping block. Without me, Bianca and the children will starve."

"Where have I to go?" That, at least, was true.

He snatched her coins and shoved her through the doorway, letting the burlap fall on her head in his haste to be gone. Off he lurched into the night, heading west, hanging on to the walls of neighbouring houses for support. She watched until he had disappeared. Stepping back into the street, she pulled her shawl higher against the rain. Hannah would head north. Before he drank up her *scudi,* she would have disappeared like steam from a kettle of soup.

From behind her, louder than the splash of overflowing street gutters, came Bianca's moans. Hannah hesitated. She owed nothing to this woman. Bianca was not a sister, not a neighbour, not a Jew. Fate had decreed that women like her would always be poor, ignorant and helpless, with or without Hannah's assistance. Hannah stood outside Guido's hovel, water dripping down her neck and soaking her clothing.

It was well after midnight. The streets were empty of all but milk-souring demons and fever-making goblins. Hannah would put as much distance as possible between herself and Guido. The sound of Bianca's weeping and what seemed a young girl's voice trying to comfort her interrupted Hannah's thoughts. Unyielding, she took a few steps down the street.

Many births went badly in spite of Hannah's skill and experience. Even if she stayed, there might be little she could do. Lilith, the Angel of Death, was a mighty foe. There had never been a birth when Hannah did not look over her shoulder, certain Lilith had come to claim mother or babe. She could enter with ease the grandest mansion. No iron lock was so well fashioned, no porter so vigilant, that Lilith could not glide in. This strip of dirty burlap that served as a door would not slow the angel's progress. Lilith hovered, invisible in her black cloak, ears pricked for the slightest mewling of exhaustion from small bodies. Her nose twitched at the coppery smell of blood. Bianca, weakened from too many pregnancies, would present no challenge.

So what if Guido was hanged for Hannah's escape? So what if Bianca and her children starved? If Hannah were free, meat fed, fire warmed and well shod, she would follow the dictates of her conscience. In her present circumstances she had not the luxury of compassion.

She sidestepped a mound of manure and stumbled into a deep rut in the street. Bianca's cry came again, more anguished this time. Hannah would go back and check on her, no more than that. After all, Bianca's only sin was to have been born poor. After so many pregnancies, she could bleed to death if her matrix refused to contract. Years ago Hannah had witnessed such flooding, the childbed a lake of blood pouring faster than could be absorbed into a dirt floor. Hannah skidding on the blood, sticky and warm, not knowing a body contained so much of it. A fifteen-year-old girl buried in the dress she had worn the previous year when she had danced at her wedding.

A simple examination; then Hannah would be on her way. She returned to the hut, held the burlap to one side and groped her way in.

Dear God. A sack suspended from the low ceiling, stiff with smoke and grease from the cooking fire, smacked her in the face. Other sacks—grease-stained canvas bags containing unwashed wool, awaiting washing and carding—hung like stalactites in a cave. A chimney-less fire smouldered in the middle of the floor. Sour air like old cheese pervaded everything. The stink of unwashed bodies and unclean linen made her eyes tear.

Hannah fumbled around until she found, in a hollowed-out piece of limestone, a lump of fat with a twist of linen as a wick. She managed to ignite the wick with an ember from the fire then wished she hadn't. Lard. The smell made her nauseous, though the pork fat gave enough light to view the room.

Young children slumbered in cots and baskets and packing crates tucked onto shelves projecting from the walls. Older children slept on the floor in twos and threes, lying head to foot. The walls of the hut seemed to contract and expand with the inhaling and exhaling of the roiling mass of children. It was as though the abode was not an ordinary one fashioned of bricks and mortar and wood beams but an edifice built from the parts of children—of the skin and blood and bones of children, lining the walls, shoring up the ceiling. The dwelling reminded her of Asher's, but without the strong-willed Tzipporah to maintain order. Hannah reached up to bat away what felt like a cobweb enmeshed in her hair. It was a child's tiny hand stroking her head.

Amid the snoring and heavy breathing came Bianca's cries. Hannah took the woman's cold hand and rubbed her wrists. A pool of blood had gathered between Bianca's skinny legs. "Hello, *cara*, I am here to get this baby out of you." She remembered saying the same words to the Contessa Lucia, Matteo's mother, years before. How different this was from Matteo's birth in the di Padovani palazzo on the Grand Canal—the sway of the damask curtains around the Contessa's bed, the casement windows with glass from Murano, the fragrant tea and rich broth awaiting the Contessa when the ordeal was over.

"Thank God you are here. I begged Guido just as you told me."

Before Guido left, Hannah should have insisted on a proper candle—rush, perhaps; beeswax would have been an unthinkable luxury. She wanted to view Bianca's belly as well as palpate it for the position of the infant. Bianca's cheeks were red from exertion. She grunted with pain. No birthing stool, no comfortable bed, no clean linens; just a heap of straw not much better than the one Hannah slept on in prison. Cows in the field gave birth in more wholesome surroundings. With Guido gone to the nearest wine shop—he would not return until his money ran out—Hannah had some time. Not much, but some. Her *scudi* would buy him two or three mugs of sour wine—maybe an hour's worth.

Hannah took the almond oil from her bag and applied a drop to her hands then rubbed them together to warm them. She touched Bianca's belly—and breathed a sigh of relief. Next, Hannah removed from her bag the hollow river reed, which she had cut into sections and serrated at one end. She placed the splayed portion on Bianca's stomach and put her ear to the other end, listening. The reed amplified the sound of the baby's heartbeat.

When Hannah was a girl, she and her sister, Jessica, used to lie together in bed, a river reed pressed to the plaster wall to eavesdrop on the young couple in the next apartment. They would take turns listening to their night noises—the man's soft entreaties; the woman's sighs; and sometimes moans and groans and wet, thrusting noises, which for reasons she and Jessica did not understand made them giggle as they fought for their turn with the reed. The "listener," Jessica had called it. When Hannah was an apprentice midwife, it occurred to her that a hollow reed might be useful in hearing an unborn baby's heartbeat. Indeed, it had proven so. By experimenting, Hannah learned to make the reeds sturdier through applications of linseed oil and beeswax. With this simple device, even the weakest heartbeat was audible.

This baby's heart was as rhythmic and strong as a smithy's hammer, although it seemed to have an almost imperceptible echo. God was on Hannah's side. The head was descended into the wreath of sharing bones. Such a sturdy child would be born quickly. With so many births, Bianca's passage would be slack. With the help of her eldest daughter, who hovered nearby, she would survive. Bianca's colour was healthy, and her clasp on Hannah's forearm firm.

Bianca whispered, "You were good to come, Hannah. It is such a comfort to know I am not alone. Some of the other babies I delivered myself. Even the monstrosity born three winters ago. Little more than toes and fingers woven together like a cat's hairball." She winced as a pang took hold of her. She waited for it to pass before saying, "I had to fling the poor thing into the fire myself."

Hannah had heard such tales before. Born-too-early babies tossed onto the fire, forgotten by all except their mothers. She pressed Bianca's hand. "You are doing fine, *cara*. It will not be long now."

"During this pregnancy, I have felt so tired. I hardly had the strength to make soup for my family and the prisoners."

"And very good soup it was," said Hannah. She reached for her linen bag, about to tuck her reed back inside next to her birthing spoons. "Of course you are exhausted. You work hard and have borne so many children."

Bianca closed her eyes, dozing between pangs. Hannah continued to hold her hand. Bianca had hands worse than those of a laundress, chapped from lye soap, with swollen red knuckles and calluses so thick Hannah wondered if Bianca even registered her touch. *Forgive me*, cara. She unclasped Bianca's hand and rose. It was time to leave.

Bianca began to pant. Hannah crouched again. She would stay long enough to cut the cord. As Hannah urged her to push, the baby's head crowned—pliable and wet, covered in blood. Hannah freed the shoulders and pulled the infant out. A healthy, surprisingly fat little thing, as white as a winter rabbit, almost translucent in its paleness. The baby was a girl. There was no mistaking the swollen lips of the vulva. She gave a shrill, startled cry as Hannah set her in the basin of water one of Bianca's older girls had the presence of mind to fetch. One of the guards had seized Hannah's iron-bladed knife, but there was a rusty gutting knife within arm's reach and she employed it to sever the cord. Hannah had not even had to use her birthing spoons. A girl of about ten years got up and took the wailing newborn into bed with her. All travails should be so easy, although the birth cake had not come slithering out as it should have.

Hannah wished she could stay and rub warm oil into Bianca's painful-looking fingers or, better still, some of Tzipporah's salve, if only she had some left, then sheath them in cotton gloves, but now was the time to escape. The birth cake would fall out of its own accord by morning.

More than an hour had passed since Guido had left. Hannah's ducats clanked as she knocked against a wall on her way to the makeshift door. She must leave this poor, dangerous district. She would hug the sides of buildings and scurry under the *sotoportegi* to avoid the gangs of young men who roamed the street. No woman, not even a pregnant one, was safe at night.

Once outside, she gathered her legs under her to dash into the darkness. The rain would obliterate her muddy footprints. Guido would not be able to track her. She was halfway down the street when she felt a tug on her arm.

"*Signora! Signora!*"

It was one of Bianca's girls, a pale, sad-eyed creature.

"You must come back. Mama is having more pains."

"I must continue on my way." *I have been imprisoned in a hellish jail. My son is with a woman who will likely kill him either deliberately or through neglect. My husband no longer loves me. I am scant weeks from my own confinement.* "You must take care of her now. You're a big girl."

If Bianca died, would it be so terrible a fate? The pitiable creature would find rest for the first time in her life. To conceal Hannah's escape, Guido could tell the head jailer Hannah had died in the night and he had disposed of her body before the rats ate it. As for the newborn and other children, Guido would soon find another woman foolish enough to raise his brood.

"There is so much blood. Please!" The girl pulled on Hannah's arm, her eyes wide with fright.

Had Hannah looked so terrified when, as a young girl, her mother had died giving birth to her sister, Jessica?

Reluctantly, Hannah followed her back to Bianca's hut, pushed aside the burlap and entered.

From a corner, Bianca moaned, "Something is wrong. I am still in so much pain." Her children stood in a semicircle watching, eyes as round with fear as those of colts in a stable fire. No doubt the children wondered if they would soon be motherless.

Hannah reached into her bag. Her hands touched the reed; she removed it and placed it on the floor next to her in order to get at the opium paste at the bottom of the bag. After lifting Bianca into a sitting position, Hannah held a mug of water to Bianca's lips and helped her to swallow the ball of paste. She waited a few minutes for it to take effect.

"I will never forget your kindness. As soon as I am able, I will send food to you and urge Guido to treat you with kindness."

"Never mind that now. Try to relax and let the opium do its work."

Opium sometimes slowed the mother's heartbeat. Hannah positioned the reed on Bianca's chest to listen to her heart. For several minutes, she moved the reed from above to below the umbilicus, afraid of what she was hearing. Bianca's heart beat strongly, but Hannah also seemed to hear a reverberation. *Please God, may I be mistaken.* Hannah moved the reed to the other side of the umbilicus. There it was again. A soft echo. She shifted the reed higher up. Again she heard it—like the fluttering of a barn swallow's wing in a snare.

It was the too-rapid heartbeat of another baby.

Hannah reached between Bianca's legs. Instead of a head well descended into the sharing bones, she felt the baby's buttocks. The first twin had been an easy birth, but this second birth would be fraught with every difficulty. The child must be rotated within the womb, or else it could not emerge and Bianca might struggle for days until she died of exhaustion and loss of blood.

"Bianca, there is something I must do."

Bianca lay groggy from opium. Hannah thought Bianca had not heard her, but Bianca turned her head. "Will it hurt?"

"It might be uncomfortable. You must help by relaxing. Breathe deeply. The opium will help."

Hannah spread several drops of oil on the white hillock of Bianca's belly. Then she pressed, massaged, searching. Her hands were her eyes, reading what was going on within the womb. Yes, the head, soft and symmetrical, was just below Bianca's heart. Hannah rotated her hands in tandem, thumb to thumb over the belly, as though compelling forward the stubborn hands of a clock. After a number of these rotations, the head was persuaded into position. "Good, Bianca. The baby is ready now. Now you must push." But Bianca's head lolled to one side. Her eyes were closed, her breathing slow and shallow. The opium was too powerful for her, worn down as she was from too many children and too little food.

"Come on, *cara*. You can do it. I know you are tired, but you must try. The baby must not linger too long in your passage."

It was no use. Bianca lay motionless; not even her eyelids flickered. Hannah took out her birthing spoons from her linen bag. She fitted them together so that they resembled the jaws of a small silver dragon. "I will pull the baby from you." When Bianca made no response, Hannah repeated her words, but Bianca was long past hearing.

One of the children, a girl of about eight with Bianca's pale hair and eyes, began to cry. "Go back to bed, all of you. Your mama will be fine." But whatever strength Bianca had once had was gone. Her legs flopped open. Hannah applied oil to the birthing spoons and inserted them into Bianca's passage. She fumbled for the baby's head. Once she found it, she cupped it with the spoons. The head seemed small. She pulled with a steady pressure, trying to harmonize her tugs with the birth pangs, but no ripples moved across Bianca's belly. The pangs had ceased. Hannah continued. A head emerged, then shoulders, then torso and legs, all blue and unresisting. It was another girl. She lay slack, not breathing.

In the poor light Hannah could not make out the baby's features, but by running her fingers gently over the face, she could feel that the nose and mouth were disfigured. The lips connected with the nose in a way that made it impossible for the poor infant to suckle. Even if Hannah could revive her, this baby would not live beyond sunrise.

There was a shift in the air, a slight current, not strong enough to be a breeze, although the candle flickered. *Lilith, the Angel of Death. Do not pass by. Stop here. We are in need of you.*

A moment later, Guido reeled into the hut. Hannah wrapped the baby in a cloth and thrust it at him. "I did my best, Guido, but it was no use."

He grabbed Hannah, and with her in tow, he lurched out into the night, the dead baby tucked under his arm like a loaf of bread. They followed a pathway alongside a canal back to Pozzi Prison. When there was a splash of something hitting the water, Hannah did not look.

CHAPTER 24

Pozzi Prison,
Venice

G UIDO—SOBER, CHASTENED, eyes red rimmed—
slipped a piece of chicken wrapped in a greasy
cloth through the slot in the door of Hannah's
cell. How shocked he had been last night to have his daughter's corpse shoved at him, and to hear the vigorous cries
of the surviving twin, not in the least dismayed to find
herself born into such wretched conditions. This twin was
promptly named Hannah by the weary Bianca.

It had been well past first dawn by the time Guido escorted
Hannah back to Pozzi Prison and locked the door of her
cell. Throughout the morning, as she tried to get some
sleep, Hannah tossed and turned, berating herself for not

fleeing when she had had the chance. If not for her hollow reed and the second baby's weak, irregular heartbeat, Hannah would be a free woman, somewhere safe and dry, perhaps eating roasted peppers and sheep's cheese on crusty bread.

Hannah felt her baby stir within her and was grateful. When she went for long periods without feeling the child move, she became fearful the infant had died. She dozed, trying not to think of the dampness of her cell, its musty smell that permeated everything, her despair so profound she felt boneless. She tried not to think of Isaac. *Divorce.* Before she was fully awake and had the consciousness to push the word away, it rose in her throat.

She awoke to footsteps on the stone floor, one set brisk, light and decisive, the other with a slight hesitation. The latter must belong to the other jailer, Sergio, a gangling man with one arm shorter than the other, who leered at the female prisoners.

"There is a lady to see you," Sergio called through the door.

The door creaked open and there was Cesca, a green bonnet on her blond head and a smile on her face. Hannah glanced around for Matteo, but Cesca was alone.

Cesca's teeth, as white as the inside of an apple, gleamed. She looked every bit as lovely as she had in the abbess's *parlatorio.* Hannah could not reconcile the absolute prettiness of Cesca—her unblemished skin, her blond hair like a nimbus of sunshine around her head, the grace of her figure—with her wickedness. Hers was a face made lovely by its animation—the widening of the blue eyes, the raised eyebrows, the rosy cheeks bunched in a smile. Without an audience to perform for, Cesca's face would be as blank as a hen's egg, Hannah thought spitefully.

Those who are starving do not smell just food—they also smell the perfume given off by those well-fed. With all who crossed her path, Hannah—stomach growling—played a guessing game. What did they eat? Beef? Venison? Oranges? How often? How much? How recently? Hannah inhaled. Cesca had a basket of food tucked under her arm.

"Hello, Hannah," she said. "You look like a cat after a pack of dogs has savaged it."

The remark did not sting. Hannah was far too dispirited to care what Cesca thought of her appearance.

Cesca held out the basket, which emitted a heavenly aroma. "Before you rail at me, I have a peace offering—a blanket, and wrapped inside, some baked fish and slices of beef joint and fruit. Eat and be well."

"An unexpected kindness, coming from you."

"I am a true Christian and the Bible teaches us charity for those in need." Fluttering her hand, she giggled, giving a self-deprecating grin. "Oh, and Foscari and I must keep you alive until the trial."

To Hannah's mortification, she could not stop herself from grabbing the basket from Cesca. "How is Matteo?" she asked, tearing the blanket open.

"As difficult as ever."

"Where is he?"

"With a woman who takes in children. You need not worry about him. Her husband is teaching Matteo to read and to form his letters. You must approve of that. You Jews set such store in that kind of thing."

At least he was not in the *oespedale*. There was comfort in that. Hannah bit into a slice of beef. It was juicy, and still warm; here and there a clove of garlic pierced its flesh. Strength flowed into her body. Cesca picked up the blanket from the floor where Hannah had dropped it in her haste to get at the meat and draped it over Hannah's shoulders. "Why are you here, other than to assure yourself I am still alive?" Hannah asked between more mouthfuls of beef. She chewed, trying to slow down, wanting the flavour of the meat to last as long as possible.

"I feel some responsibility for your present circumstances. If I hadn't denounced you to the abbess, you would be walking the streets of Venice a free woman."

"In other words you are here because you still need my testimony."

"Don't we both want what is best for Matteo?" Cesca said.

"If you wanted what was best for him, you would never have left him with the abbess."

"Do not take that tone with the only friend you have."

"We have never been friends."

Cesca glanced around the cell, looking for a place to sit. Seeing none, she stood with her arms crossed over her chest. "Let us be allies then, if not friends."

"You betrayed Isaac and me. You stole my son. Now you come here to mock me. I do not trust you any more than I would trust a serpent." Hannah peeled an orange—so ripe and succulent she thought her heart would break. Her fingers grew shiny from the fragrant oil of the peel. She wiped them on her blue skirt, hoping the scent would linger.

"Calm yourself. I would not allow Matteo to come to harm." Cesca drew a vial of smelling salts from her pocket and held it to her nose. "The stink of your waste bucket is making me feel faint. Doesn't the guard empty it from time to time?"

Good. Now you know what it is like for me. "All I want is to take Matteo back to Constantinople and live in peace."

"Once you testify. Our trial is next week. After that you may take him anywhere you please," said Cesca.

"I may be dead by then. You see the appalling conditions in which I live. This is the first decent food I have had since my arrest. And I cannot see why they would release me after your trial."

"Then we must get you out," Cesca said.

"Don't you think I have tried? I offered the guard Guido a bribe, but he refused." No need to mention her foolish decision to return to Bianca and assist with her second delivery. "Guido said my crime was too serious. That he would be hanged if I escaped."

The memory of the night she had killed Niccolò resurfaced. It was the night she feared the Prosecuti, with their network of informers, would discover during their investigation. The night Asher had witnessed everything and done nothing to help.

"I just had a little talk with another guard—Sergio, I believe is his name—as he walked me to your cell. For a price, he will leave your cell door ajar. Then, little canary, you need only to fly out."

"I don't believe you. Guido said the risk was too great."

"Then you approached the wrong guard. Sergio promises an unlocked cell and a ladder against the wall. He says you must flee at midnight this evening."

"How much will this unfastened door and ladder cost?"

Cesca said, "I suspect every ducat you've got. Give them to me. I shall act as your go-between."

"You, my dear Cesca, suffer from a disease for which gold is the only cure. I remember only too well how your eyes lit up in the abbess's *parlatorio* at the mention of my ducats." Watching Cesca now pace back and forth in the small cell put Hannah, already light-headed from eating too rapidly, in a daze. The pendant around Cesca's neck moved in time with her breathing. The longer Cesca talked, her voice rising and falling with sincerity, her blue eyes wide, the more alone and abandoned Hannah felt. Weeks ago, swallowing her pride, she had smuggled out a message to Asher, begging him to come, but she had received no reply.

Cesca said, "This guard Guido—how much did you offer him?"

Hannah hesitated, not wanting Cesca to know how much money she had.

"Well?" Cesca said.

"A few ducats."

"How many?"

"Two."

"No wonder he would not help you."

"I offered him five," Hannah amended.

"The money is still here?" Cesca raised an eyebrow, waiting for an answer. When Hannah did not reply, she went on, "Sergio will cooperate for—" she paused a second too long "—ten ducats, not a *scudo* less."

Guido must have told Sergio of her offer to him. "Please, stop talking so I can concentrate on this delicious beef." The meat was giving her strength. She no longer felt so disoriented and weak.

"Hannah, give the money to me, I'll arrange everything."

"If Sergio will accept ten ducats from you, he will accept them from me."

"Not unless you are prepared to offer him a little dish of something his wife refuses him at home." Cesca rolled her eyes and giggled. "He's not a bad-looking fellow. I am willing to oblige him for your sake. I will close my eyes and think of my lovely villa and consider whether I shall plant roses or dahlias in the *jardinières* on the north portico. By the time the Marangona rings again, you shall be free."

"How can you be so casual about such matters?"

"Bah! You Jews are such a stiff-necked race. What do you say? Are you prepared to have a frolic with our friend Sergio, or shall I?" Cesca opened her mouth and waggled her tongue.

"It's unthinkable."

"Such acts not only avoid a pregnancy but firm the jawline." Cesca tapped the top of her hand under her chin, turned her head sideways and pursed her lips. "A remarkable profile, would you not agree?"

Desperation could make the worst scoundrel credible, but Cesca had no reason to help Hannah escape. What better way to secure Hannah's appearance at trial than to keep her in prison? She shook her head.

"At least pay me for these victuals I brought you."

"You owe me a great deal more than a few morsels of meat," Hannah said, turning back to the food.

"I guess there is nothing more to be said, then. I shall see you at the trial," said Cesca.

"God willing."

After Cesca departed, her skirts swishing on the stone paving, Hannah dozed, her stomach pleasantly full for the first time in what seemed like years. A few hours later, she awoke to a lewd chuckle. Her eyes flew to the cell door. Sergio peered through the bars. "Your friend is a pretty filly. She'll be back soon."

"What makes you think so?"

"Because we have an understanding. She told me to fetch something from you and I am a man of my word."

"Leave me in peace." Hannah glanced around the cell for something to protect herself with. She had nothing but mouldy straw and her valise with the nun's habit rolled up in the bottom. Her ducats were still in the blue *cioppà* she wore, as snug as unborn eggs in the passage of a laying hen.

"Aren't you a high-spirited little thing?" Sergio selected a key from the collection at his waist and unlocked her door. "Cesca gave me what she called an 'advance on our understanding.' That isn't what they call it down by the docks, but a duck by any other name quacks the same."

He stepped into her cell then turned back to lock the

door, even testing the handle to make sure it was securely fastened. Satisfied, he strode over to her valise.

The baby within her gave her a kick, as though telling Hannah to tread cautiously. "Please, get out."

He reached into her valise.

Sergio was powerfully built, with sloping shoulders and a head shaped like an anvil. No way on earth could she overpower him. "Get out!" she repeated. Where was Guido? He might help her.

Sergio dumped the contents of her valise on the floor and pawed through the pile of garments until he found the nun's habit. Then he squatted on his haunches, feeling the clothing for the coins. When he felt nothing, he grabbed for her. "Where did you put the ducats?" She tried to push him away, but he was too strong. He picked up the hem of her *cioppà*, put it to his mouth and began ripping at the stitches with his teeth. Gold coins fell to the floor, some rolling a few feet. He got down on all fours and plucked them up; then he dropped them into a greasy leather pouch around his neck. Hannah looked away, unable to watch the disappearance of the only thing she had that might buy her freedom.

And then he came at her, animal excitement on his face. Hannah had seen the same expression on male dogs before they mounted a bitch. Soon, she feared, he would wrestle her to the floor and be on top of her. Rutting like a beast in the field. Thrusting into her.

"You have my ducats—isn't that enough? Leave me."

"There's something else I want."

Should she go limp to avoid injury to herself and the baby? Weep? Beg for mercy? Pretend to faint? Shout for Guido?

As if reading her mind, Sergio said, "Never mind yelling for Guido. He's not here."

"Please go."

"Not just yet." He was fumbling with his breeches and unfastening his fly with the anticipation of a starving man about to devour a feast.

Sergio could toss her to the floor and have her skirts over her head in a flash. Before she had time to scream, he would have his forearm across her windpipe, cutting off her breath.

How could an act inflicting pain give satisfaction? Was there any connection between what Sergio was about to do and what Isaac did? None that she could think of. The guard lunged for her, hands outstretched to grab at her breasts. When she ducked to one side, he followed her movement, arms out wide to cut off escape.

At night men roamed the bridges and canals of Venice, hunting for a woman unlucky enough to be abroad. They wove their drunken way back from the wine shops. Hannah had heard of a midwife hurrying along the street late one night from attending a birth. The unfortunate woman never arrived home. She was found naked, tossed behind a heap of rubbish, her throat a necklace of bruises, her body ravaged.

Hannah studied Sergio's grin, his blackened teeth stubs, his chin covered with stubble. He was close enough that she could smell his breath made foul from stewed cabbage and garlic. As he backed her into the corner, her heels hit the waste bucket, causing its contents to slosh. Without stopping to think, moving as quickly as her belly would permit, she pivoted, grasped the bucket with both hands and hurled it at Sergio.

God was with her. The bucket hit Sergio full in the face; its contents cascaded down his nose and cheeks then his chest. The iron bands holding the staves together slipped free with the force of the impact. An iron band gashed his cheek, adding blood to the tide of excrement and urine.

Hannah stood, sides heaving, breathless from exertion, unable to believe she had thrown the bucket with such vigour. She was terrified as she looked at Sergio, afraid this rash act would incite such fury he would kill her on the spot.

But Sergio appeared as stunned as she, his face contorted in disgust.

Then he fumbled for the key at his waist, unlocked her cell and walked out.

CHAPTER 25

Palazzo di Padovani,
Venice

FOSCARI'S PALAZZO—of course, it was not his palazzo any more than the villa belonged to Cesca—was elegant. Although not as spacious as her country villa, she could not help being impressed by the palazzo's lacy Gothic stone facade and graceful windows, reflecting dancing waves of the Grand Canal.

She had never been to the theatre—when would she have had the chance—but she could not imagine a play more diverting than the Grand Canal, which was as unlike the Tiber River in Rome as a silk ribbon is from a hemp rope. She sat on the balcony with Foscari, her hands folded in her lap, as though she had not a care in the world, and watched gondolas and barges drift by.

From inside the house came the giggling of Lucca and Matteo as they played cards, the game of Trappola. Lucca had proven to be a quiet, obedient boy and a useful companion to Matteo, entertaining him with stories and all manner of games.

Cesca wore *chopines* today, the dangerously high wooden shoes favoured by Venetian women of fashion, and a newly purchased dress of green velvet she bought from one of the *strazzaria*, a second-hand clothing dealer in the ghetto. The dress was so marvellously made it must have belonged to a noblewoman. Cesca doubted the woman had looked as good in it as Cesca did. Best of all, her new attire had cost only two of Hannah's ducats.

Foscari tapping his fingers on the arm of his chair signalled he would soon say something to shatter her feeling of well-being.

"I yield to no one in my appreciation of a well-dressed woman," he began, "but your weakness for velvet sleeve insets and *chopines* that threaten to buck you off like a frisky horse and pitch you into the nearest canal does you no credit." There was the tinkle of china as he replaced his cup in the saucer. "I know you are trying to emulate a grand lady, but you look like nothing so much as a housemaid who has stolen the key to her mistress's cupboard. Too much *décolletage* for the morning, too much ankle for any time of day. You aspire to be the *castellana* of your villa, not the wife of a newly wealthy green grocer."

To demonstrate she still cared for his opinion, Cesca

knew this comment must reduce her to heaving sobs. When Foscari glanced at her to judge the effect of his words, she hid her face in her handkerchief and made tiny, shaking movements with her shoulders.

Foscari said, "Oh, my dear, I am sorry. I have rendered you unhappy, haven't I?"

The skin around Foscari's nose looked inflamed. He leaned over and gave her knee a squeeze.

"Now, now. I am sorry."

How Cesca longed to boast of her adventures at Pozzi Prison. How he would admire her shrewdness. But she could not allow herself the satisfaction or he would immediately have his hand out for a share of her ducats.

It had taken so little effort to orchestrate the theft. A small service granted beforehand to Sergio to seal their arrangement and he had sworn on his mother's grave he would hand the ducats over, keeping only two for himself. Somewhat to her surprise, he had done just that, although when she went to the prison to collect them, he had requested an additional ducat for "inconveniences." Whatever he meant by that, she was happy to oblige.

Sergio proved easy to satisfy in every respect. All that had been required of Cesca was to take the jailer's ample shaft into her mouth. His groans and supplications to the Holy Virgin and Lord Jesus mingled with the cries of the prison's lunatics and halfwits. God answered her prayers, and in His mercy, allowed Sergio to spend himself quickly. Now Hannah's ducats glinted unseen in the sleeves of the very dress Foscari mocked.

When would this incessant game of brinksmanship be over? Cesca was not by nature deceitful—unless circumstances demanded—but Foscari forced her to be always on her guard. In a manner meant to convey forgiveness, she smiled at him through her shuddering. "You are right. I don't know what I was thinking."

She picked up a basket of apples, a gift from Palladio. "I will change out of this dress straightaway." Cesca selected an apple. She placed it between her lips, then took a small, sharp bite using just her front teeth, taking care not to drop juice on her skirt or smudge the mulberry staining her lips. She adored the dress and would not have it spoiled. The taste of the apple was like a warm August afternoon in the orchard, bees diving into fallen fruit and the air sweet with lavender. Between heaves of the breast, she took more bites, marvelling that Foscari, consummate actor that he was, gazed at her with concern. She extracted a piece of apple from her mouth and placed it between his lips.

"Here is something that will cheer you." Foscari took a sip of brandy from a flask in his waistcoat. "Your letter of intent—" He held up his index finger. "To seal our bargain." He extracted the parchment letter from his pocket and passed it to her. "Now that you have returned Matteo as I instructed, the letter is yours."

When Cesca had lived in Constantinople—a city of Mussulmen and Gypsies and thieves—she'd seen a man's hands hacked off by a baker who'd caught him stealing a loaf of bread. The baker had reached behind his counter, grabbed an axe, and two whacks later, the thief had stumbled toward

Cesca as though to embrace her, leaving a criss-crossing trail of blood behind him. Foscari had done far worse in stealing her villa.

What a pathetic idiot he was to suppose he had hoodwinked her. Tonight she would double the dose of peach kernel tincture she had added to his brandy. "Very kind of you, Foscari. I knew I could trust you." She refolded the parchment and tucked it into the pocket of her dress.

Cesca's mother used to admonish her: "Do not throw out your old boots until you have fetched home a new pair." Palladio was her new pair of boots, but he was far from being fetched home. On his last visit, although he brought her apples from his orchard, he showed little interest in her lowered bodice or sidelong glances. The frescoes were a subject they avoided in favour of mortars, terrazzo, facades, buttresses, arches, cruciform halls, architraves, gabled porticos, Ionic columns and the weight distribution of bearing walls. Palladio was teaching her a great deal but was deaf to her supplications that he serve as Matteo's guardian.

Foscari said, "Shall we go upstairs and dally for a bit? One of your playlets, perhaps, with an ancient Rome theme, complete with togas?"

How young and inexperienced Cesca had been when she and Foscari had first met. Although she had never enjoyed his attentions, when Foscari asked her to submit to certain acts, she had submitted. The occasional coupling had been little enough in exchange for the company of a sophisticated, well-connected nobleman who would make her rich. Now, as she grew less biddable, he became more demanding.

Foscari stood, extending his hand to her. She clasped it, allowing him to pull her upright. And soon he was mounting the stairs ahead of her, as eager as a curly-horned ram. It was not the gait of a man who was being poisoned, although the glassiness of his eyes, the greyish pallor of his skin and the tremor of his hands as he had held the brandy to his lips told her the peach kernel was working.

But poison, she was discovering, had a slow and unpredictable course.

A dagger was best. A quick, clean slice across the throat—

Except Cesca had never killed anything larger than a neighbour's rooster, which had the bad luck to wander into her garden.

One moonless night in Rome when she was a child whore entertaining men against the crumbling walls of the Coliseum, she had come close to killing a young man. On the advice of her mother, Cesca always carried a stiletto tucked in her garter. The customer, a drunken dyer's apprentice not much older than her, refused to pay, and began shouting insults and striking her about the head. As his face twisted in rage, the youth became no longer a person but an animal. She bent over and drew out her stiletto, and then lifted her arm to gut him like a mackerel. But her arm would not obey. Cesca ran down the street and ducked into the Basilica di San Clemente. There she crouched fearfully behind the baptismal font, her heart pounding so loudly she was certain God himself could hear.

Yet she had to overcome her squeamishness and kill Foscari. She did not want to but there was no help for it. And it must be done soon.

CHAPTER 26

Doge's Palace,
Law Courts,
Venice

A T DAWN THE SOLDIERS CAME for Hannah.
There were two of them, square shouldered and
tall, in the blue-and-gold uniform of the Doge.
Guido unlocked the door of her cell, explaining they were
there to escort her to the courtroom. Her presence was
required by the Marquis Foscari.

Wedged between the soldiers, Hannah walked as fast as
her girth would permit, across the Piazza San Marco to
the court. The sun cast a shimmering, unnatural light on
the square, making the brick walls and stone buildings
appear to oscillate as though underwater. Because she had
been confined for weeks in a tiny cell, the expanse of the

piazza disoriented her. She had difficulty seeing more than a few paces ahead. The sun made her eyes burn.

When she tripped on a cobblestone, one of the soldiers jerked her upright. The baby was pressing on her sharing bones, making them ache. Every step was a chore, every movement a task. She felt a pang in her lower belly. *Not now,* she prayed. *Stay within me a little while longer, I beg you. You are snug in the velvety darkness of my womb. The outside world is dangerous and contains nothing of interest.* The baby gave a protesting kick.

Hannah had on her plain blue *cioppà* and the red head scarf required of Jewish women. When she had worn the nun's habit, she had had to pad her sides with a pair of goose down pillows and make herself barrel shaped rather than reveal her true form, which was as though someone had thrust a large ball under her clothing. Some women could pass their entire pregnancy without anyone being the wiser—bellies delicately rounded, breasts a little fuller. Hannah was not one of those women.

To wear her own clothes should have been comforting—she had never been at ease pretending to be what she was not—but she felt exposed and uneasy. The nun's habit, for all that it had been a farce, had created an illusion of safety. Now it lay crumpled into a ball in the bottom of her valise, where she had stuffed it after Sergio's attack.

One of the soldiers gave her an impatient shove toward the *ad jus reddendum*, the law courts, with their colonnade on the ground floor and loggia opening on the first story. Hannah ascended the marble steps. Well before she reached the top of the stairs, her chest was heaving from the weight of the baby. The Sala della Quarantia, the courtroom where the Council of Ten dispensed decisions on every aspect of the lives of Venice's citizens, both civil and criminal, was on the first floor. A confusing throng was packed in like herring in a barrel. Dozens of men gathered in knots, talking. Petitioners stood with their lawyers, reading briefs. Some litigants acted on their own behalf, waving their petitions in the air. A fight broke out in a corner and two bailiffs stormed over to eject a pair of thuggish-looking dyers, their clothes stained blue from indigo, reeking of the stale sheep's piss used as a mordant to make fast their dyes.

Along one side of the room was a steep staircase leading to the balcony. Already it was crowded with people jostling for position at the low balustrade for a better view of the proceedings below. Hannah searched the crowd for Matteo and Cesca as the soldiers positioned her behind a pillar, one soldier on either side of her. She glanced up at the ceiling frescoes, which depicted scenes and people in the Christian Bible: the Miracle of the Loaves and Fishes, the Annunciation, the Madonna with the Christ child on her lap. What blasphemy to paint the human form. The brown nightingale that had flown in through an open clerestory window in a blind panic swooped from wall to wall, trilling. Hannah tugged at her dress, which stuck to her sides with perspiration.

The abbess was in the balcony, a great block of black doom, flanked by two novices. Their heads tilted toward one another as the nuns conferred. They were like three crows on a tree branch, eyeing a tasty bit of bread on the ground, each daring the others to swoop first.

Beginning at the entrance then working her way around until she reached the stairs to the balcony, Hannah scanned every face in the vast room. In the front row, which was reserved for noblemen and *cittadini* of importance, was a distinguished man with an alert air about him as he gazed not at the crowd but at the length and breadth of the room.

Palladio. When he cast his eyes to the ceiling, his mouth turned down as if in disgust. It seemed Hannah was not the only one who found the frescoes there abhorrent. She felt a rush of empathy with her companion from the barge. To her surprise, he rose and approached her.

"You are familiar to me, *signora*, but—"

"You have a good eye for faces." Hannah felt herself flush. "I was dressed as a nun the last time you saw me."

This statement did not seem to faze him in the least, for he merely said, "Of course. You made a good job of my hand." He stretched it toward her, flexing the fingers. "Scarred, but what do I care? I can still hold a chisel."

"I'm pleased to see that."

"But what possessed you to don a nun's garb?"

"It is a long story."

"Then we shall leave it for another time."

Hannah nodded, relieved.

"So you are the midwife who delivered the Contessa's baby?"

Hannah waited, wondering where this was leading.

"I was a dear friend of Lucia and the Conte's. She told me of your skill and kindness to her. She was nearly dead and yet you managed to deliver her child. You saved her life." He smiled at her. "Do you make a practice of that? Saving people, that is."

"God was with me. I never attended a more difficult birth. Many times I despaired, but the Contessa endured. After many hours, God permitted the baby to be born." There was no point in mentioning how she had cupped Matteo's head on either temple with her birthing spoons and drawn him out of the Contessa's exhausted body. Men were not fond of hearing such details. They preferred to think their precious offspring were delivered by fairies and left under toadstools and behind daffodils in the garden.

Palladio seemed to notice for the first time the soldiers on either side of her. "Why are you under arrest? I do not understand." He murmured something to the soldiers and they retreated a few paces but kept their eyes fixed on Hannah. "Is there something I can do to help you?"

How gentle his face; how well meaning he appeared. She had known benevolence from the Conte, as well—and had repaid that kindness by murdering his brother, Niccolò. "Thank you, but I am in a trap from which there is no escape."

"Foscari is the cause of your difficulty?"

Hannah nodded, catching a glimpse of the Marquis several feet away.

"His companion, Francesca, has urged me repeatedly to be guardian, but I have refused," said Palladio. "I did not even wish to be in court today, but my wife insisted. She said it was the least I could do to honour the memory of the Conte and Contessa. I explained to Francesca I cannot act as guardian because—"

Impulsively, Hannah grasped his hand. "If only you would, sir."

"I cannot. You see——"

Just then the bailiff, resplendent in red and gold livery, entered and called for silence. The cacophony, amplified by the stone walls and marble floor and loud enough to mask the firing of a cannonball, ceased.

Palladio gave her arm a quick squeeze and resumed his place.

"Order, if you please," shouted the bailiff. "The court of Judge Abarbanel is now in session." The judge entered, leaning on a cane as he made his way across the dais. With some difficulty, he eased himself onto his chair of gilded wood set high above the floor. Hannah tried to shrink behind the soldiers. The judge was tall and spare. If they had been in Constantinople, people would have referred to him as a "walking minaret"—though not to his face. His beard was white and his fingers as crooked as twigs on a witch-hazel tree. He had the look of an aristocrat—the pampered air of a well-tended man aging with grace. Abarbanel was a common *converso* name, the surname of a Jewish family who had converted to Christianity. Was it too much to hope he might have compassion for Jews?

Hannah turned her attention to looking for Matteo in the throng again. Occasionally, the flash of a red hat signalled the presence of other Jews. She spied Asher's black beard and red cap. There was nothing reassuring in the sight of Asher's familiar face. He waved to her. She did not wave back. Her brother was here to ensure she testified as

Foscari wished. She had no illusions he had come to lend her support.

Judge Abarbanel wore a robe of red silk, embroidered with gold thread, trimmed with sable. His boots—she had to crane her neck to see them—were of the finest kidskin. He had a thin Venetian nose, rather like a hatchet dividing his face in half. His ears were pointed, giving him the look of an intelligent wolf. His fingers curling around the arm of his chair, he appraised the crowd, as though calculat ing how long it would take to hear everyone's plaints and render decisions.

Abarbanel, in spite of his age, sat erectly, his ledger in front of him, his quill and ink pot neatly aligned with a hinged container of sand for blotting. He did not give the appearance of a judge who would overlook a serious offence such as raising a Christian child as a Jew. His mouth was as tight as the seam of a walnut. The clerk, wearing a blue robe and holding a sceptre, called the first case—that of a Jew Hannah knew by sight. The bailiff signalled him to enter the witness box. There the accused stood wiping his sweaty hands on his breeches.

"Your name is Avram Foà?"

"I am an honest moneylender," the man said. "Ask any-one in the ghetto."

"You are charged with receiving and selling stolen prop-erty, to wit, a silver necklace. What have you to say for yourself?" asked the judge.

Foà began a tortuous explanation of how he had come into possession of the necklace.

The judge interrupted his recital and barked impatiently, "It is clear to me, sir. You were unconcerned as to the provenance of this piece of jewellery. You seized upon a chance to procure it cheaply then sell it for a profit. For your carelessness—or should I say your indifference to the true owner—you shall serve five years in prison and pay a fine of five ducats. If you cannot pay, you shall serve an additional year."

A Christian woman standing nearby—the rightful owner of the necklace, perhaps—smiled in satisfaction at the harsh sentence. Had the owner been another Jew, then likely the Rabbi would have dealt with the matter. Cheating a Christian made the offence a public affair.

The judge motioned to the bailiff. "Call the next case, if you please." In quick succession, dozens of cases proceeded—robbery, assault, disturbing the peace, whoring and sodomy.

"How nice to see you again, my dear," said a voice at Hannah's side, diverting Hannah's attention from the legal proceedings.

Foscari stood with Lucca next to him. The boy smiled at her and touched her arm. "How convenient I was able to have you brought to court so quickly! Why, you were right across the Piazza San Marco in Pozzi Prison!" He smiled. "A few *scudi* to the bailiff. And poof! *Che miracolo!*"

Foscari smiled anew at Hannah, his silver nose in position, his eyes shining with an unhealthy moistness—the irises too blue, the whites the yolky yellow of a man too fond of drink. He did not look half so well as when she had seen him at the villa.

"What a busy place this morning. See those men there?"

Foscari pointed to a group of coarse-looking men slouched near the prisoners' box. "Those are the bo's'ns from the galley boats, seeking criminals to row their masters' ships." He lowered his voice. "You are ready? You will not disappoint me?" The parchment document in his hands trembled. His skin was an unhealthy grey. "We shall be called very soon."

"Where is Matteo?" asked Hannah.

"All in good time. First, you must do your part."

"Is he with Cesca?"

"Lucca has been well schooled. He knows everything down to the smallest detail about his past life in Constantinople. All you need to do is to tell the judge he is the rightful heir."

"And the judge's promise of leniency for my offences? Do I have your assurance on that?" Not for the first time she felt this judge had the look of a man who would delight in sending a witness to the gallows, even a pregnant woman. There was no clemency in his eyes, or in the set of his shoulders, or in the pale fingers stroking his white beard. With nothing more than a flourish of his pen he could order her death.

"Of course, my dear. It is all settled," said Foscari.

Waves of contempt roiled off him—for her, the judge, the courts, everyone who would thwart him. It was evident in the curl of his lips, the arrogant set of his shoulders, the swaggering manner in which he strode away. He trailed behind him the odour of greed—a pig's greed to consume everything in its path, the greed of a scoundrel for the wealth of a little boy who had done him no harm.

"I will say nothing until I see Matteo," she said.

Foscari and Lucca melted into the crowd.

People came and went. After the shorter cases were disposed of, the crowd thinned out. At last the clerk called, "In the matter of the di Padovani estate."

Foscari stepped forward. In a voice like syrup dripping over fresh berries, Foscari reminded the judge he had been before the court months earlier and been ordered to produce Matteo for the judge's inspection. Foscari nodded and pranced like a shopkeeper displaying a bolt of cloth to a rich nobleman. Showing his perfect teeth, Foscari answered the judge's questions with a bow and a flourish. The judge took up his quill and made notes in the red book in front of him. Was he deceived by Foscari, who gestured with his plumed hat, or was the judge as wise as his profession demanded? Who could divine the workings of the gentile mind? With Jews you knew where you stood. If a Jew did not believe you, he would tell you so straight out. Jews had none of the misleading civility of Christians, who said one thing while thinking another.

Lucca stood, eyes darting, as if he, too, were looking for Matteo. He shifted his weight from one leg to the other, his street-wise blue eyes taking in everything: judge, vast high-ceilinged room, crowd, Hannah. His hands were clasped behind his back, in a sweet imitation of how he must imagine a high-born boy should act. Hannah remembered how callused Lucca's hands were that night he had crawled into her bed in the villa and gripped her hand under the covers. Now they appeared smooth. That night he had looked as wan as if a barber had bled him. Now his cheeks were pink and round.

The judge interrupted Foscari's recital of the assets of the di Padovani estate with an impatient wave of his hand. "Yes, yes, I have a note of all that from the last time you were before me. Proceed with your witnesses."

Foscari nodded at Lucca. The boy marched forward, appearing touchingly adult for his age, the very picture of noble smartness in his blue satin breeches and matching rabbit-trimmed waistcoat. Silver buckles adorned the breeches. From a distance Lucca seemed the scion of a vast fortune, but his costume would not stand up to nearer inspection. The jacket was frayed and threadbare at the elbows. The buckles on his shoes were not silver but some baser metal. Lucca's finery was probably rented. In the ghetto were second-hand clothing dealers capable of dressing an entire army.

The judge peered down. "This is the boy you claim is the di Padovani heir?"

"I shall *prove* he is, Your Grace."

"And what is your name, lad?" asked the judge, leaning forward to better see Lucca.

"Matteo, sir."

The little boy blushed and glanced around the room, as though searching out Matteo to beg his pardon. Hannah followed his gaze but saw no child resembling her boy.

"How old are you, my son?" asked Judge Abarbanel.

"Five, but big for my age."

The judge spoke to Foscari. "He is too young to understand the meaning of an oath, so I cannot swear him in." Turning to Lucca, he said, "You know what it means to tell the truth?"

Lucca nodded.

"You know that boys who tell lies are consigned forever to the fires of hell, where they remain for all eternity?"

Again Lucca nodded.

"Very well. I am satisfied he is a bright lad and will tell me the truth." The judge bent toward him and smiled, cupping a hand around his ear. "You will have to speak up if I am to hear you. I don't eat little boys—at least not during Lent." He nodded encouragingly. "Do you know why you are here?"

"I am to be an heir."

"And what does that mean?"

"It means I shall have my own boat, a *trireme* with a battering ram, and a bow-mounted cannon and a—"

"What else?"

"I shall never have to eat turnips again—"

"I quite agree. Turnips are fit only for swine."

"And everyone must be kind to me because I shall be so rich. If they are not, I shall chop off their heads." Lucca's hand flew up to cover his mouth. "Or maybe just make them oarsmen on my galley then free them if they promise to be good."

The judge laughed. "And it means you shall live with the Marquis Foscari in your villa."

Did the judge believe Foscari's version of Lucca—a young nobleman, well dressed and confident? Or did the judge see Lucca as she did—a child of the streets, his bones freshly buttered with a layer of flesh, second-hand fur trimming his cloak? Out of the corner of his eye, Lucca looked at Hannah, at the soldiers on either side of her standing about ten paces away. "And can I live with Hannah, too? I like her very much."

Despite her anxiety Hannah smiled. There was a lovely earnestness about the child, a desire to please and be pleased that charmed her. Assuredly, some kind woman had once loved this boy. It was a comforting thought, if true. Lucca did not smile back but looked questioningly at Foscari.

"He refers to the Jewish midwife who attended his birth, my lord."

The judge nodded.

"And your parents—do you know who they were?" asked the judge.

Lucca's shoulders tensed. "My father was Conte—" his voice wavered "—di Padovani and my mother was—" He frowned, for a moment, glancing at the floor. "The Contessa Lucia. They died when I was no bigger than a two-week-old shoat."

Foscari shot the boy a look of approval.

The judge said, "I was acquainted with both the Conte and Contessa."

The remark did not surprise Hannah. High-born gentiles all knew one another just as Jews in the ghetto all knew one another, at least by sight.

"You seem to have inherited your mother's red hair, though I do not see much else of her in you," said Judge Abarbanel.

The judge's memory of the Conte and the Contessa Lucia would provoke him to be harsh to one who had, in his eyes, stolen Matteo and raised him as a Jew. Here was yet another reason for Hannah to despair.

With a flourish, Foscari reached into a bag at his side and, like a magician pulling a coin out from behind a child's ear, produced a well-worn blanket. He held it up, a corner in each hand, then waved it about for the judge to see. "This, my lord, is the child's christening blanket. You will notice the di Padovani crest embroidered in gold thread."

"Yes, you showed me that the last time you were before me." The judge turned to Lucca. "Is this your blanket?"

Lucca hesitated. Foscari cleared his throat to regain the boy's attention and gave an almost imperceptible nod.

"Yes, it is," said Lucca.

The judge said, "That is all I need to hear from this young man." He opened the large red book in front of him and flipped back through the pages. He dipped his quill in ink, made a note and then sprinkled the page with sand. He reread his notes. "The midwife who delivered the boy? I asked that she be brought before me."

"She is here under unusual circumstances, Your Grace." Foscari cleared his throat. "She is currently a prisoner in Pozzi Prison."

The judge frowned. "So I must base my decision on the word of a criminal?" Irritated, he gave a wave of his hand. "What is her offence?"

Foscari said, "I do not know, Your Grace."

The judge beckoned to the clerk. "Can you assist?"

"One moment, my lord." The clerk flipped through the pages of a large red book.

The offence that weighs most heavily on my conscience is one the Prosecuti know nothing of. Yes, I acted in self-defence. Niccolò would have killed me with no more thought than he would have given to shooting a pheasant. But even when one does the right thing, the only possible thing, one cannot escape the guilt of taking another person's life.

What the lagoon swallows, it also vomits back. Suppose Asher betrayed me? Or suppose Niccolò's remains were found? He would not be the first richly dressed corpse to be snared in a net of silvery sea bream. Murder of a nobleman is an offence so grave not even my belly would protect me from being hanged forthwith.

CHAPTER 27

Doge's Palace,
Law Courts,
Venice

WHY HADN'T CESCA stabbed Foscari when she had had the chance? She had refrained because, to her regret, she had not been able to enlist Palladio. The greatest architect in the Veneto had proven mulish. Any judge in the world would appoint such a distinguished and well-liked man, but Palladio continued to refuse her entreaties.

How her fingers itched to wrap themselves around Foscari's throat as he danced attendance on the judge, waving about some bogus document purporting to prove he was a first cousin to the late Conte. Thanks to the peach kernel infusion, Foscari looked frightful. Even from the balcony she could see his skin was as grey as river clay. Sweat dripped from his cheeks.

Foscari led Lucca by the hand out of the witness box and patted him on the shoulder.

The boy looked smart in his finery. Rented, of course. Foscari was not one to squander money on rapidly growing urchins. The boy had told his tale well. He was a wonderful little liar, and had spoken in a strong, clear voice from which the harsh vowels of the gutter had been erased, thanks to Foscari's tutoring.

The judge ruffled Lucca's red hair as he left the witness box. "Good luck to you, my lad."

How could the judge believe this undersized, overdressed little guttersnipe was the son of nobility? Foscari slipped a caramel from his waistcoat and slid it into the boy's mouth. Foscari seemed to feel genuine affection for the child. Matteo annoyed him, but Foscari had patience for Lucca. Now, seeing Lucca and Foscari from this distance, their heads bent at the same angle, their hands gesturing with the same airy motion, the details of their forms blurring together, she wondered if what she had told Palladio was true. Perhaps Lucca *was* Foscari's bastard son.

Not that it mattered a fig. The important thing was Foscari had no idea Palladio had met Matteo. No idea Palladio had chucked Matteo under the chin and told him how much he resembled his lovely mother, the Contessa.

Cesca pushed Matteo from her lap and smoothed the wrinkles out of her velvet skirt. He should have been grateful to her for rescuing him from the orphanage and that ogre of an abbess, but instead he had been demanding and fretful, asking for soup and then, when she brought it, shoving the bowl away with an ill-tempered grunt. Now on the balcony he kept stepping on her skirts and asking a dozen pointless questions. The orphanage might be an appalling place—Hannah had been aghast at it—but the pious *sorellas* understood how to keep children quiet, obedient and out of sight.

Matteo propped an elbow on her shoulder and leaned into her, staining her dress with a blob of the porridge she had prepared for him this morning. "See what you have done?" She set him a few paces away, behind a pillar. "Stand there and be a good boy."

Of course he did not obey. He leaned over the railing and, spotting Hannah below, waved gleefully, before Cesca jerked him back. "Not just yet. Let us surprise your mama. You may wave to her later."

There was Palladio, useless as a barnacle on the hull of a boat. He must understand the farce unfolding in front of him. To her frustration, rather than being horrified by the lies pouring out of Foscari's mouth, Palladio, seated in the front row of high-backed chairs reserved for dignitaries, was gazing at the ceiling.

Cesca studied his upturned face—the heavy, fleshy nose; the sensual mouth; the massive chest; and the strong fingers wrapped around his walking cane. She waved, trying to catch his attention, but to no avail.

In supporting Foscari's plan to use Lucca as heir, Cesca was certain she would force Palladio to act as guardian.

Why did he do nothing? The architect had met Matteo, seen the resemblance to the Contessa and knew Lucca was an imposter. Now he had a sketchbook open in his lap and was drawing with a stick of charcoal. Some capital had caught his eye. Damn him! The time had come for him to toss down his sketchbook and spring to his feet.

The egg-and-dart moulding on the friezes transfixed him. He would rather gawp at mouldings and wall reliefs done in *marmorino* or *scagliola* than stare at anything else in the world, including Cesca. What an exasperating man—and what a victory it would have been had she managed to captivate him.

A few paces from Palladio, and wearing the compulsory red hat, was Asher, the Jew moneylender—standing up very straight, neck craned, to better watch the proceedings. Little wonder he was observing Foscari so intently. When Cesca had arrived at Foscari's palazzo in Venice last week and seen the gilded chairs, the embossed leather hangings in the reception room, the sterling silver, the glassware, the gold forks, the chandelier and damask curtains surrounding the bed, she had done a quick calculation. Foscari must have borrowed at least fifty ducats. There was only one place in Venice to borrow money. A few discreet questions to the black-bearded men under the ghetto's *sotoportego* and they nodded at Asher.

A group of Franciscan monks, their black hoods raised, making them look like a flock of vultures, hovered around Foscari, demanding to examine his papers.

The judge motioned them away. His back was so straight that Cesca thought he looked as though he had a poker up his arse.

Hannah stood between two soldiers in the same dress she always wore, now tattered. Her pregnancy stretched it too tightly, destroying all modesty, outlining her navel for all the world to see. It was embarrassingly clear she was close to her confinement.

Hannah kept glancing around the vast room, dark eyes frantically darting this way and that, searching for Matteo. Well, she could search all she wished. The boy would remain behind the pillar, invisible to everyone on the floor below. Cesca would hear what Hannah had to say for herself. Then, she would decide when the moment was right.

CHAPTER 28

Doge's Palace,
Law Courts,
Venice

"THE JEWESS IS CHARGED with two crimes, my lord," said the clerk. He took a piece of parchment and studied it with the aid of a magnifying glass. "The abbess of the Oespedale della Pietà in the *sestiere* of Castello alleges that Hannah Levi kidnapped a Christian boy from his natural parents and raised him for many years as a Jew. Subsequently the child was rescued and placed in the care of the abbess by one Francesca Trevare. The afore-mentioned Jewess then attempted to steal this unfortunate child from the convent. The abbess believes Hannah Levi to be a procuress of Christian children for use in various rituals practised by the Hebrews."

At least there was no mention of Niccolò di Padovani. Was that something to be grateful for? Perhaps not. Did it matter if she was hanged for a sheep or hanged for a lamb?

Judge Abarbanel stared down his long Venetian nose at Hannah. He turned to Foscari. "You rest your case on a witness who is accused, and most probably guilty, of serious allegations. Are you trying to make a mockery of this court or are you a simpleton?"

Foscari began to stammer, "Y-Your Grace. This is Hannah Levi. She is the Jewish midwife who has testimony vital to my case. May I remind your lordship, you ordered her—"

"But, sir, you should have had the decency to tell me she was a criminal."

"At the time of the last hearing she had not been arrested. She was living as a free citizen in Constantinople. I sent for her."

The judge said, "In support of your case you present me with some hapless prisoner you have given a few *scudi* to deliver a well-rehearsed speech? How dare you, sir?"

Hannah took a deep breath, grateful she was supported on either side by the two soldiers. Her head was spinning. "I can explain." To her embarrassment, her voice came out in a high squeak. She would have traded a great deal for a drink of water.

May it please God, I cannot give birth on a straw mattress. I cannot place my baby in a convent, to be banished from the outside world to the misery of the orphanage like other unwanted babies. My child cannot die of disease and neglect before I have even put him to breast.

Judge Abarbanel scrutinized her then glanced away. In

the judge's eyes she wanted to find kindness and patience and a desire to discover the truth, but she found only coldness. Hannah saw herself as he must see her: uncomfortable with the weight of the baby, clothed in a worn blue dress with puckered seams.

There was a voice from the balcony. Heart sinking, Hannah recognized it as the abbess's. The nun lumbered to her feet and began making her way toward the judge, clutching at the balustrade as she hobbled down the stairs, her club foot splayed to the side.

The judge said, "Have a seat, Abbess. I shall hear from you in a moment."

She sat down in the front row, looking none too pleased at having to wait.

"The abbess has accused me of abducting the di Padovani heir and raising him as a Jew," Hannah said. "I hope, Your Grace, that when I explain the circumstances, you will realize I acted honourably."

"So you admit to the crime?"

"I saved the child's life."

"You must speak up, madam," said the judge. "My hearing is not what it used to be."

Hannah repeated what she had said.

The judge motioned to the soldiers. "Put her in the witness box."

He waited while Hannah climbed the three stairs leading to the box. Her legs trembled so violently she might have been climbing the steps of a gallows.

"You are a Jewess?" the judge asked.

Hannah nodded, her throat still so dry that she could hardly get out the words "I am." From this vantage point she might be able to see Matteo in the crowd—her vision was acute. But the room was vast. She squinted to squeeze a tear into one eye to clarify her sight. She saw no red-haired boy in the balcony.

"Do you promise to tell the truth?" the judge asked.

"Yes."

"This oath is binding on your conscience?"

No, it is not. Asher is right. I have no use for the laws of the gentiles, or for judges and lawyers or fresco-ceilinged courtrooms. I will say whatever is necessary to win my freedom and my son.

"It is," she said.

"The Marquis—" the judge coughed out the word as though it was a fish bone lodged in his throat "—Foscari wishes me to appoint him guardian of the di Padovani estate. Before I can do so, I need the child to be properly identified. I am prepared to overlook the fact that you are a Jewess, but I cannot overlook the fact that you are charged with two grave offences. If I find you not guilty, I shall hear your testimony. If I find you guilty, I must return you at once to Pozzi Prison." Judge Abarbanel picked up his quill pen and turned to a fresh page in his ledger. "Now, *signora*, what do you have to say for yourself?"

Hannah, in the high-sided witness box, its gate latched, soldiers on either side blocking her escape, felt as she had as a young girl when one of her brothers stuffed her in a blanket chest so small that even though she was only four and tiny for her age, she'd had to wrap her arms around her legs and bend her neck to breaking. Elbows jammed into corners, she'd breathed in her own peaty smell of fear.

"Five years ago," said Hannah, "the Conte di Padovani came to my house in the middle of the night and begged me to attend to his wife, who had been in travail for three days without result."

"You must have known it is against the law for a Jewish midwife to deliver a Christian baby."

"I did it out of pity, Your Grace. The Conte was desperate."

And I was desperate, as well—for money to ransom Isaac.

"The Contessa nearly died. The baby was blue—I had difficulty getting him to breathe. Nothing at his birth happened as it should. I was—"

The judge's face flushed. "I need not trouble you with the details of the birth, *signora*." He fingered the heavy gold chain around his neck. "Please continue with what is relevant."

In the front row Palladio half rose to his feet as though to speak. Then, thinking better of it, he sat down again.

"Foscari has presented me with a boy he claims is the heir," the judge said. "But the residuary legatees, the monks of the Monasterio San Francisco de Rosas, who have a competing claim on the estate, contend Matteo di Padovani died years ago of the plague. Their advocates tell me they will call upon a family servant, Giovanna, to swear she last saw the boy stricken with buboes and lesions, more dead than alive in the arms of a Jewish midwife who, I presume, was you."

"It was, Your Grace."

"Surely you do not expect me to believe the infant recovered from the plague?"

A child's cry of merriment filled the air. There was no mistaking that voice. Matteo, still dressed in the breeches and dirty linen shirt he had worn in the convent, grinned, flailing his arms like a miniature windmill as he waved from the balcony. Hannah gave a tiny wave and pressed her finger to her lips to admonish him to be still. *Please, dear God, for once in his life make him obey.*

"Matteo never suffered from the plague."

"I do not understand."

"I went to his family's palazzo. Giovanna refused to take Matteo. She slammed the door in my face."

"Why would she do that?"

"She believed the child suffered from the plague."

"And why did she think that?" the judge asked, with growing impatience. "Must I drag every word out of you?"

"Because . . ." Hannah hesitated. What explanation could she offer? The soldiers of the Prosecuti had been pursuing her. "I painted the baby and myself with buboes and lesions in the manner of a plague victim in order to . . ."

Matteo sat on the edge of the balustrade, legs dangling twenty feet to the floor below. Cesca stood behind him.

"Continue."

Lucca, breaking his grip on Foscari's hand, climbed the stairs to the witness box. Hannah reached forward and lifted him over the gate. Lucca must have sensed her misery, because he put an arm around her neck. One of the soldiers tried to wrest him away from her, but Hannah held him fast.

The judge said, "You may remain there, young man, if you are quiet."

"In order to . . ." An idea was forming. "I am sure Your Grace remembers how devastating the plague was that year. How a third of the population of the city perished overnight. How the canals were filled with bodies, the barges laden with corpses. How mothers were deserting their children, husbands their wives, priests their parishes. Like everyone else, I was frightened."

"*Signora,*" the judge said, "I remember it all too well."

"Looters were roaming the streets, robbing everyone they came across, breaking into houses. Lawlessness prevailed. Gangs of ruffians violated unaccompanied women."

"Please get to the point."

"I wanted to escape on the next ship, leave Venice altogether. I was terrified to be abroad at night, but I had passage to Constantinople the following morning at dawn. I needed to return Matteo before I set sail. I thought the best way to move about the city unmolested was in disguise. I painted myself and Matteo as plague victims so we could pass through the street safely."

The judge's quill scratched as he made note of her words.

"My ruse worked only too well." Hannah paused to let him finish writing. "Giovanna was terrified at the sight of us. Before she closed the door, she told me the Conte and Contessa had died of the plague, along with the Conte's brothers." She held up her hands. "You see, Your Grace, I had no choice but to take Matteo with me."

"Surely there were other relatives. Another uncle? Cousins? Aunts?"

"No one I knew of," Hannah said. In truth, she had had

no time to consider alternatives. After her murder of Niccolò, she had lost no time in departing Venice.

"*Signora*, I am tempted to believe this fanciful tale of yours. You have a plain way of speaking and a frank manner. But there is one thing I do not understand."

"Yes?"

"Why did you have the baby in the first place?"

Hannah had anticipated this question, but her imagination had not yet provided her with a plausible answer. She tried to think but could not concentrate with Matteo fidgeting with increasing liveliness on the balustrade above. Finally, she said, "I was suckling him. Matteo's own wet nurse was feverish with mastitis. Treatment of the yellow discharge from the nipples is painful, requiring a lancet to be inserted in—"

"You may spare me further details of this unfortunate woman."

"I sailed with Matteo to Malta, where my husband, Isaac, was being held as a slave. I ransomed him and then together we sailed to Constantinople. We have lived there ever since. My husband and I have loved Matteo as we would have loved our own son." She need not bore the judge with the horrors of the voyage, the hard work of setting up the silk business in Constantinople, the challenge of an impossible language and unfamiliar customs.

On the balcony, Cesca was gesturing to her, releasing her hands from around Matteo then replacing them. The judge was asking her something, but Hannah, distracted by Cesca, could not make sense of his words. Foscari came forward to stand next to her.

"The judge asked you to confirm for the record that this child—" he touched Lucca's shoulder "—is Matteo di Padovani."

Hannah brushed his words aside. She wanted to shout: *there is a child on the balcony about to drop to the floor and split open his head.*

The judge rapped a gavel on his writing table. "Please direct your attention to me. My query is a simple one. Confirm whether the boy in your lap is the child you delivered of the Contessa and the child you have raised since infancy."

Hannah felt an urgent little kick as her infant moved within her. She opened and closed her lips. No words came out.

Lucca shifted on her lap, staring at his new calfskin shoes that no doubt pained him. He looked up and stroked her face. She hugged him. In the back of the courtroom stood Asher, his black eyes fixed on her.

The judge said in an exasperated voice, "Is this the child you delivered? The child you raised in Constantinople? Once and for all, is this the di Padovani heir?"

Words formed in her mind but would not issue forth: *no, Matteo is on the balcony, about to topple to his death.*

Before she could say this to the judge, Foscari said, "My lord, if I may have a minute to remind this witness of her duty to the court?"

"You may."

Foscari leaned an elbow on the witness box. He was so close she could smell the fish gall glue holding his nose in place, and see herself in the nose's polished silver surface. The face reflected back at her—skin as white as paste, cheekbones jutting, eyes red from weeping—could not be hers.

Something bright blue fell from far above and snagged on a chandelier, where it swayed, until it drifted free and landed a few paces from her chair. It was Matteo's felt hat, one she had sewn for him. From far above came the glint of red hair. The brown nightingale alighted on the railing near Matteo's hand. Cesca smiled, as Matteo jiggled, waving down at Hannah with Lucca on her lap. Why did not anyone notice? But every eye in the courtroom was trained on her. Matteo continued to jiggle in Cesca's arms, calling joyfully, "Ama! Ama!"

Foscari crooked a finger to indicate Hannah must bend her head to hear him.

"I await your answer," said the judge.

CHAPTER 29

Doge's Palace,
Law Courts,
Venice

FOSCARI WHISPERED, "If I wave my handkerchief in the sign of the cross, Cesca will, with one push, send Matteo to his death." He took his handkerchief from his pocket and played with it, letting it drift through his fingers. Two flashes of white silk—one vertical, one horizontal—and there would be the whoosh of an object falling, a child's scream—then a thud like a melon hitting the floor.

What shall it be? Shall I give him a shove or will you obey?

Judge Abarbanel, eyebrows raised, quill pen poised, said, "*Signora*, do you swear on the life of your unborn child that the boy you hold in your lap is Matteo di Padovani?"

Hannah's tongue stuck to the roof of her mouth. She opened her lips to speak, but still her voice would not serve her. Lucca buried his face in her shoulder and snuggled into her as though he had been doing so for years, his breath collecting where her collarbone met her throat. What a convincing tableau of son and mother they made. How ready the judge was to believe the little boy she held was Matteo. She did not even have to speak. A nod would suffice.

Had Hannah risked everything, only to watch Matteo shatter on the terrazzo floor? Even if she tossed Lucca from her lap, raced across the room and bounded up the stairs two together, by the time her ungainly body reached the balcony she would be snatching at empty air. She sat frozen, gripping Lucca so tightly he cried out. From the balustrade Matteo sang "Here I am" in his high, childlike voice, thrusting his feet in front of him and clapping his palms. "'High as a steeple, high as a crow, high as a thrush. I think no bird as mighty as me!'" He flapped his arms and wriggled his bottom in rhythm to his song.

Cesca stepped back, hairpins in her mouth, hands at her sides. The nightingale, trilling merrily, flew close to Matteo, who reached for it, calling out, "Ama! Ama! Watch me catch the bird. Pretty bird, pretty bird, come to me. Teach me to fly like you."

May Matteo sprout wings; may he drift to the ground feather-light, gentle as a turtle dove, Hannah prayed. If God obliged, she would fall to her knees, would kiss the cross around the judge's neck.

Hannah must lie just one more time, just about this one

small matter. Still, she felt her face grow hot as she opened her mouth to speak. Asher was wrong. Bearing false witness, even in the courts of the gentiles, was a shameful act. But what choice had she? Would not any mother do as much to save her child?

Her lie would have no consequence, she told herself. Two people in the courtroom knew the truth. One of them would surely step forward to expose her falsehood. Yes, the judge would vilify her, perhaps send her back to prison forthwith, but as she watched Matteo teeter thirty feet above the cold marble floor, she knew she had no choice.

"This child," she said, touching Lucca's head, "is the boy I delivered of the Contessa. This is the heir to the di Padovani fortune."

The bird flew at Matteo's head. He stretched up his hands to catch it, just as Cesca swept him off the balustrade and into her lap, her arms safely around his waist. Before Hannah could let out a breath of relief, the abbess lumbered to her feet.

"Your Grace, may I address the court?"

The abbess came forward and stood before the judge, puffing out her chest and smoothing the folds of her habit, looking rather like a self-important pouter pigeon.

"Of course, Abbess. Tell me what you know of this matter," said the judge.

"Your Grace, the tale you have heard from this Jewess is very different from the one she told me when she tried to steal a boy from my convent." The abbess repeated Hannah's story of her being a nun in Malta. "This boy—"

she gestured to Lucca "—is not the child this midwife claims she raised as her own." She flung a hand toward the ceiling. "I suspect the di Padovani heir is that little scallywag up in the balcony, calling for her."

"Somebody bring that boy down here," the judge ordered, "so that I may take a closer look at him."

Cesca stood at the head of the stairs and placed a hand on Matteo's shoulders like a mother cajoling a child into a river to bathe. Matteo bounced down the steps. Cesca started to follow him; then, apparently thinking better of the idea, resumed her seat by the balustrade.

"I'm here, sir," announced Matteo when he arrived on the bottom floor. He marched over to the judge, hands on his hips, and stood squarely in front of the judge's high-backed chair. "All by myself."

"So you are," said the judge. "Come closer, young man, so I may get a good look."

Matteo moved a few feet closer. He stood head cocked, regarding the judge's quill and pot of ink with interest.

"Yes, I see a resemblance to both your parents. You have your mother's red hair and your father's eyes."

"My ama does not have red hair," said Matteo. "She has black curly hair, as you can plainly see." Matteo ran over to the witness box and tried to scramble in. He had just thrown a leg over the gate, when one of the soldiers grabbed him and carried him back to the judge.

The judge picked up the blanket lying crumpled on the table next to him and held it up. "Is this your blanket?"

In answer, Matteo tried to jump out of the soldier's

arms. "Yes! Where did you find it? I have been so sad without it." The judge handed it to him. Matteo rubbed the grimy square of fine wool against his cheek and stuck his thumb in his mouth.

"I am grateful to you, Abbess. Thank you for clarifying matters." The judge turned to Hannah. "You have lied to me about the identity of this child. What else have you lied about?"

She felt the soft kick of her baby, but it gave her no pleasure. Perhaps it would have been better if the infant had suffocated months ago. Hannah would be giving birth on a soiled prison pallet. She had saved Matteo but had failed to save herself.

If only Isaac were here, to hold her in his arms and tell her all would be well. But he was not, and when he did arrive, it remained to be seen what his feelings toward her would be. "Your Grace, I had no choice. Francesca, Foscari's accomplice, had the boy in the balcony and would have hurled him to his death if I had not lied."

"You, *signora*, have proven to be a most unreliable witness. I do not believe you. I do not believe Foscari. I have the difficult task of appointing a guardian. Do I have reliable witnesses to guide me in this decision? No, I am surrounded by liars and mountebanks."

"If I may, my lord," interjected a voice. "I wish to address the court."

A chair scraped the floor. From the front row Palladio crossed the room. He paused in front of the judge, waiting for permission to speak.

The judge smiled at him and nodded genially.

"My lord, I am Andrea Palladio, the architect." He removed his hat and bowed.

"I know very well who you are, sir. I am honoured to have you in my courtroom."

"I did not step forward earlier because I wanted to give Foscari a chance to put his head in the noose. Now that he has succeeded in doing so, I would like to address your lordship."

"Please do," said the judge.

"I was studying the ceiling—vaulting is one of my passions, and quite extraordinary in this building—and yes, Hannah Levi is quite correct. Matteo was balanced most precariously on the balustrade. I was about to send my valet—" he gestured to a young man in red livery, standing nearby "—to intervene, when the young woman, Francesca, secured him on her lap." He placed a hand on Matteo's shoulder. "In fairness, I think the *signora* Levi must be forgiven for lying. Had she not done so, there is no doubt in my mind Francesca would have sent the child to his death."

"Thank you for your observation. Is there anything else you wish to say?"

"Yes, my lord. I would like to assure you of the good character of Hannah Levi. Conte di Padovani was a dear friend. He was a just man. His wife, the Contessa, a worthy woman. Shortly before her death, the Contessa confided in me that this midwife had saved her life. She said most emphatically that without Hannah Levi's skill both she and her baby would have perished. She felt deeply indebted to the *signora* Levi."

"For performing a criminal act," said the judge.

"And was not the Conte equally culpable? Consider this, my lord. All parents do desperate, sometimes foolish things. The Conte went to the ghetto at midnight and bribed the guard to gain admission. He promised Hannah an extraordinary amount of money, two hundred ducats, if she could save his wife and child. He broke the law. I did the same when my eldest son lay dying of scarlet fever. I summoned a Jewish physician."

How kind Palladio was to step forward on her behalf. He was a prominent man, a man of influence.

The judge said, "*Il signor* Palladio, thank you for your evidence. I am prepared to accept that Hannah Levi lied under threat of harm to the child."

"I can further vouch for her character," said Palladio. "I first met Hannah Levi when we travelled together on a barge along the Brenta—"

"With all respect, *signor*, I have your point. I have heard enough about the midwife and her character. We must press on or we will be here all day and night. Now I wish to hear the details of the abbess's denunciation."

The abbess stepped forward with an agility Hannah had not thought her capable of.

Foscari cut in. "May I speak, my lord?"

"No, I will hear from the abbess first. Then you shall have your turn."

Foscari sat back down in his chair, a bad-tempered look on his face.

The abbess swore her oath on the Bible and the judge said, "Proceed, Abbess. What can you tell me in this matter?"

"I believe, my lord, that Hannah Levi is a procuress of Christian babies. The Hebrew practice of using Christian blood is well known. Who can forget the story of little Saint Simon of Trent, who was kidnapped and murdered by Jews on the eve of Passover in 1475? They crucified him upside down. The boy's flesh was pierced with needles. His blood was drained to use in making unleavened bread and for unnatural rituals. The Jews' lust for Christian blood is boundless."

Hannah had heard these slanders many times, spouted by idlers in the *campo* or ranting priests in stained robes. But the abbess was a respected and educated woman of the Church. If she persuaded the judge of the rightness of her allegations, he could order not only Hannah's execution but also the destruction of the ghetto.

"And who is better positioned to steal babies than a midwife?" The abbess paused to let her words settle in the judge's mind. "But this was Hannah Levi's blunder. In her thirst for Christian blood, thought by the Jews to possess curative powers, she grew careless and greedy. As her people clamoured for more children to satisfy their blood lust, she needed to search more aggressively. And so she dared to enter my convent in the middle of the night, disguised as a nun."

The abbess spoke with absolute conviction and the judge nodded intently. At first Hannah felt nothing but fury and blind panic. Then she thought of Isaac, the old Isaac, the rational Isaac, the one who still loved her, and her mind raced to cobble together a rebuttal.

"My lord." Palladio stepped forward. "I know something of the customs of the Jews. I am acquainted with a family of brick makers who used to be Jews but who converted. This I learned from them: there is nothing in the Jewish Bible that would make Jews desirous of human blood. On the contrary, they scrupulously avoid contamination with *any* type of blood, human or animal."

Hannah found her voice. She stood, Lucca's hand in hers. "My lord, Jews believe blood contains the spirit of living beings. We are forbidden to taste blood. Our dietary laws are strict. We take great care in the preparation of meat to avoid eating blood. Slaughtered animals are drained of their blood. Any blood that remains is removed by soaking or salting the meat. If I crack an egg and it contains a speck of blood, I am obliged to throw it out."

"Nonsense," the abbess said. "Jews have for hundreds of years considered blood an elixir. Herod, king of the ancient Jews, bathed in blood to preserve his youth. Jews use blood to bring down divine vengeance on we Christians."

The abbess paused, from the look on her face clearly about to deliver the crushing point of her argument. "The Jews have another use for Christian blood. Jewish alchemists and sorceresses take the blood and turn it into gold."

Palladio spoke. "My lord, you and I are rational men, men of wisdom and learning. We do not believe such superstitions any more than we believe in the ability of wolves to speak or fires to ignite themselves."

The abbess was undaunted. "Who better, my lord, to understand the perfidy of the Jews than a member of the Church?"

The judge held out his hands, palms forward. "I accept your eloquent submission, Palladio. I do not believe

Hannah Levi guilty of stealing Matteo di Padovani for ritual purposes. Like you, Palladio, I am not prepared to brand the Jews with the notion of blood libel. I have heard all the stories from years ago. Saint Simon of Trent, Little Saint Hugh of Lincoln who was murdered by the Jews, his body stuffed down a well, and so on. To me, these tales have always seemed nothing more than self-serving gossip put about by those who wish to pillory the Hebrews and thereby expunge their outstanding debts." He coughed into a silk handkerchief. "But the fact remains that Hannah Levi acted in a suspicious manner. She stole into the orphanage in the habit of a nun and would have taken Matteo di Padovani if the abbess had not intervened. *La signora* Levi gives no explanation for her actions. I dismiss the charge of procuring the child for ritual purposes. But as to the rest, I would like an explanation."

Hannah spoke. "I shouldn't have stolen in to the convent, but I did it to protect Matteo. I feared for his life. Do you not see it, my lord? If Foscari had succeeded and Lucca had been designated heir, then what further use would Foscari have had for Matteo? He would either have left him in the orphanage or killed him."

Foscari said, "That is a terrible slander, my lord. Shall I tell you what this midwife has been plotting for years? She is biding her time, waiting for the boy to reach his majority. Then she will come forward to claim his fortune. With God's help, I perceived from the first what she has in mind and intervened."

"I hardly think you have the right to make accusations

against the *signora*," said the judge. "You presented to me a counterfeit boy. A boy with no connection to the family whatsoever."

Foscari was undeterred. "I can explain. I am not to blame. I was misled by my maid servant, Francesca, into thinking this boy—" he pointed to Lucca, still on Hannah's lap "—was the heir. I now see my mistake, a mistake that does not detract from my suitability to act as guardian."

The judge looked at him, a pained expression on his face. "I think you knew very well what you were about, sir. Now that I have had a chance to study you and this boy, Lucca, I believe I see a family resemblance between the two of you."

"With all due respect, my lord, you are wrong."

"Sir," the judge said, "I charge you with submitting a false case with the intent of deceiving the court. I find nothing credible about you, sir. The midwife says she feared you planned to kill Matteo. While there is no evidence to support her claim, you deliberately deceived this court. I sentence you to ten years in prison." The clerk made a note in his ledger.

"Show some mercy," said Foscari. "I am an old man, and my health is failing. Prison will mean my death."

"I am being lenient, Foscari. Any other judge of this court would order you put to the *strappado*."

"And my partner, my lord? What of her?" Foscari gestured at Cesca, who was leaning over the balustrade. "I had the able assistance of that lady in the green velvet dress."

The judge beckoned to Cesca, who then picked her way down the stairs on her *chopines*. When she reached the main floor, she curtsied to the judge and said, "My name is Francesca Trevare."

"How are you involved in this lamentable affair?" the judge asked.

Before Cesca could reply, Foscari said, "The entire plan was her idea. She had the absurd notion she could be the *castellana* of Matteo's villa. She forced me to sign a letter of intent promising that when I was appointed guardian, I would transfer title of the child's villa into her name." Foscari riffled through the stack of papers in front of him. "I apologize, my lord. I cannot seem to lay my hands on the document, but I assure you it is clear evidence of her culpability."

"Step forward, *signora*," said the judge.

Cesca, dimples and velvet flounces, and bodice pulled low, approached the judge. "Foscari is a scoundrel," she said in her clear, lilting voice. "I was a simply a nursemaid to Lucca and Matteo. I know nothing of the law and have no understanding of what a guardianship order is. Foscari used me shamefully, and threatened to turn me out into the street if I did not comply with his every wish. Since I have no friends, no family, no money, I had no choice but to continue in his service." She dabbed her eyes with a handkerchief. "If you will take the time to read this so-called letter of intent, you will see it is nothing more than a contract for sale of livestock." She removed a piece of parchment from her pocket and held it out.

Foscari grunted in surprise. "She has stolen that document from my personal papers. She has absolutely no right to—"

"Proceed, *signora*," said the judge.

"—I knew very well which of the boys Matteo was since I was the one who rescued him in Constantinople. It was Foscari's idea to substitute his own son as heir."

At the word *son*, Foscari sputtered indignantly.

The clerk took the parchment from Cesca and presented it to the judge with a bow. When the judge finished reading the letter, he said dryly to Foscari, "You offer the lady a good price on the veal but not such an advantageous one on the mutton." There was a murmur of protest from Foscari, but Cesca ignored him.

The judge's face softened as he regarded Cesca's blond hair, caught in a chignon at her nape and snared in a gold net; her breasts, as shapely as wine goblets. *How childlike men are when confronted with the parts of females that glisten and glow and flash and are as fragrant as nectar,* mused Hannah.

Cesca said, "Without me, Matteo would have died." She glanced at the judge from under her eyelashes. "I sent him to the abbess for the sole purpose of protecting him from Foscari."

"I do not entirely believe your protestations of innocence, *signora*. But I am loath to send you to prison. I will show clemency. I order you banished from the Republic of Venice. You will have a fortnight to put your affairs in order and depart."

"As you wish, my lord." Cesca walked out of the courtroom, looking neither left nor right, back straight, head held high. A newcomer who had not heard the exchange might think she was departing after winning a great victory.

Foscari watched her go with a look of loathing on his face as two soldiers dragged him out of the courtroom.

The judge turned to Hannah. "As for you, *signora*," he said, "I find your behaviour in this matter foolish, misguided, reckless and impulsive to a degree that steals my breath away. However, I do not believe you were evil intentioned. If you were a man, I would not hesitate to sentence you to a galley for six months. Because you are a woman and carrying a child, with some reservations I find you not guilty of the charges brought against you by the abbess. You are free to go."

Hannah stepped out of the witness box and took a seat in the public gallery.

The judge scratched a note in his book. "I shall now proceed in the matter of Matteo di Padovani's guardianship. It appears the only choice left to me is to make an order for the Office of the Public Trustee to manage Matteo's considerable fortune." A long moment elapsed as the judge, clearly unhappy with such an alternative, studied the courtroom.

"I would like to put myself forward for the position." Palladio rose to his feet. "My wife, Allegradonna, and I will raise Matteo as a Christian. I will manage his estate and oversee the repairs to his villa on the Brenta."

"I think you would be an admirable choice," said the judge, with evident relief. He pounded his gavel on the table in front of him. "I shall so order."

Hannah should have felt joy at Palladio's appointment. She knew from her encounter with him on the boat ride up the Brenta that he was a benevolent man and a kind man, if the crinkles at the corners of his eyes from smiling were any indication. He was a man of dignity and a defender of the Jews. She wondered what manner of woman his wife was. Would she be kind to Matteo? Treat him like a son? Comfort him when he awoke from nightmares, cook his favourite foods, not force him to eat victuals he considered disagreeable? Or was she a woman who found the company of young children irksome? Hannah wished to meet her to assure herself of the woman's character, but of course she could not.

The judge stood and bowed to the crowd, which gave a collective bob in turn. He walked to the back of the room and disappeared through a small door.

Palladio ambled over to Hannah and patted Matteo on the head. Matteo clung to her. "Now, my son," he said, holding out his arms, "come with me. My wife and I shall do what we can to make you happy. You shall see. It will all work out for the best."

Matteo wrapped his legs around Hannah's waist. "Go with this gentleman, Matteo."

He screamed until Asher, who had been standing nearby, pulled the boy off and handed him to Palladio. Hannah hurried outside the Doge's Palace, Matteo's sobs echoing in her ears. Asher walked ahead of her, not with his usual brisk stride but slowly, his head sunk on his chest. Hannah could not look at him.

Hannah had done her best for Matteo, but there was no joy to be had in the result. She must find the well of strength she had deep within her, dip into the waters of courage and drink fully. Grieving would only harm her unborn baby.

CHAPTER 30

Villa di Padovani,
San Lorenzo, the Veneto

HOW IT BROKE CESCA's heart to leave her villa. Her trunk was packed. A bailiff would arrive soon to make sure she was on the boat to Rome. She padded across the terrazzo floor of the drawing room in her bare feet, leaving behind moist, high-arched prints. In front of the fresco of the *castellana*, Cesca clasped her hands and bowed her head.

Once, she had imagined herself in a velvet dress, presiding at a dinner party in the loggia, diamonds in her ears, a rope of pearls around her neck, the table gleaming with silver platters, the glow from dozens of beeswax candles making her eyes sparkle.

Her plans had failed, thanks to Foscari's bungling, but she need not trouble herself about revenge. The judge, that skinny steeple of a man in fur-trimmed robes, had saved her the task and—she must admit—the joy of watching the peach kernel tincture finish its work. Cesca genuflected to the *castellana* then gazed up for a farewell glance. She expected to see the wise, all-knowing eyes and the face of brilliant competence smiling down at her, but all was not as it should have been with her beloved *castellana*. At first, the white skin, violet eyes and heart-shaped face appeared unchanged. Pearls the size of grapes still hung from the *castellana's* plump neck, her face still radiated kindness. But something was amiss.

Cesca moved closer then dragged a stool from a corner of the room to climb up for a better look. The colours in the face and dress had grown fainter. Cesca peered from different angles to catch the light from the window. A bloom of fungus had crept across the *castellana's* figure, rendering the tempera—once vibrant—dull and tinged the colour of tea. The *castellana's* eyes were like a candle that had been blown out. Her complexion, formerly pink and gold, now resembled the skin of a corpse. Cesca stood on tiptoe on the stool and, with a section of her petticoat moistened with spit, rubbed the once-green drapery of the *castellana's* skirts. A patch of the original rich viridian rewarded her efforts. If Cesca could find a ladder, she could bathe the *castellana* with soapy lye water and rub her dry with a soft linen cloth. There was time.

Cesca went to the kitchen and returned with a bucket of lye water, soap and a rag. Standing on a ladder she had hauled in from the stable, she scrubbed, losing track of time, fixated on cleaning the fresco. For the hundredth time she rinsed out her rag in the bucket of filthy water and wrung it out, scouring faster, so fast her hand was a blur against the plastered surface. But it was no good. All this work and she had cleaned only the hem of the *castellana*'s skirts. The rest of the fresco remained overcast in an unpleasant shade of milky brown. Cesca's arm ached; her hands stung from the lye. Even with the ladder the *castellana*'s face remained beyond reach.

The fresco could not be put right. None of her efforts here had been of the slightest use. What a naive idiot she was.

A wooden-hulled barge thumped against the villa's dock. The voices of the bailiff and the bargemen come to take her away drifted into the drawing room through the open windows.

Cesca raised the bucket of dirty lye water over her head. Her arms trembled from the weight of it, and she almost lost her balance on the ladder. With a grunt she heaved it, filthy water and all, at the fresco. The iron rim of the bucket gouged a hole in the wall. The lye ate into the exposed plaster. The *castellana*'s face got the worst of the assault. The water ran in rivulets down her nose and eyes. The bucket crashed to the floor and rolled until it came to rest in the centre of the room. Cesca looked away, wiping her hands on her skirt. She climbed down from the ladder and gave the overturned bucket a kick. Not even the great Palladio could put right this wretched villa.

The architect must be counted as another addition to her

long list of failures. She had misjudged the depth of his affection for her and underestimated his loyalty to his sickly wife. Yet she could not hate him. He had been generous to her yesterday, when he had dropped in to say goodbye and dribbled into her pocket a tidy stream of ducats.

Cesca must not begin her journey to Rome with her hands caked in filth and gritty with plaster dust. She picked up the rag and rubbed them with long, pitiless strokes, over and over, first the palms, then the backs, then the palms again. But though her hands turned red and raw, they would not come clean.

There were footsteps on the front stairs.

Cesca made her way to the reception room and pulled on her travel boots. How delicate were her feet; how slender her ankles. Beauty—her fresh prettiness—was a wonderful consolation. Beauty and money—Hannah's and Palladio's ducats snuggled in her purse—were her stepping stones to a new life in Rome.

The bailiff called to her from the front door. When she did not respond, he entered the reception room, nodding to indicate he was keen to be off. She walked over to greet him. He slammed shut the lid of her trunk, hoisted it onto his shoulder. With an appraising glance, he motioned for her to follow him to the boat.

He was a short but well-proportioned young man, with a moustache and confident swagger. Together he and Cesca walked out the front door and along the loggia. They descended the steps of the portico. As they traversed the lawn to the waiting barge, Cesca stumbled on the uneven, rock-strewn lawn. She had to pull her skirts away from the wild rose bushes that grabbed at them.

White swans lumbered on the near banks of the water. Splay-legged creatures, with grey webbed feet and odd orange bills. Yet when they heaved themselves into the Brenta, they were transformed into creatures of grace and beauty. In chevron formation they glided away from Cesca and the bailiff toward the fresh grass and juicy bugs that awaited them on the other side. There they waddled up the bank, shaking off the muddy water from their white feathers.

There was a great deal to be said for shaking off muck and striking out for fresh meadows. With her ducats, Cesca would set herself up in a townhouse in a prosperous part of Rome. She would have intrigues with rich men. As a girl, she had allowed poor priests and half-starved, itinerant masons to steal what little innocence she was born with. Now she would set her sights on wealthy churchmen—prelates, and abbots, perhaps even a scarlet-robed cardinal. Why not? Behind their pious smiles, under their stiff robes, beneath their starched cassocks and between their legs, their pricks were no different from any other man's.

Cesca would be the most sought after courtesan in the city. Poems would be written to her. Men would pay tribute to her beauty with costly gems. One day she would wear a pearl necklace like the *castellana*'s. With patience, she would accumulate a fortune and invest it in well-situated properties. She would live out her days as a *signora d'affari*, the income from her properties keeping her in luxury. When she was old, she would recline on a purple divan like one she had seen in Constantinople and grow portly nibbling Turkish delight.

She turned, cast one last look at the villa, gave a smile and waved. Harebells and daisies bent their heads toward her. A canal pony lifted its head, snorted and shuffled its hooves. The bailiff, whose name he confided was Luigi, placed his arm around her waist to steady her as she stepped into the boat.

CHAPTER 31

Jewish Ghetto,
Venice

H ANNAH TURNED OVER in bed, awakened by the gates of the ghetto groaning in protest as Vicente swung them open. It was the noise that had greeted her every sunrise since moving in with Asher and Tzipporah a few months ago. Tzipporah had insisted she join the household. "One more pickle into the barrel," she had said, repeating Asher's favourite expression.

Hannah had needed shelter, at least until the baby came. Yet she would rather have slept in a pig sty than in the same house as Asher, if not for her conversation with Tzipporah, who had been waiting for her in the Piazza San Marco after the trial.

Tzipporah had drawn Hannah out of earshot from Asher and said, "Asher wasn't there, Hannah."

"But he described exactly what happened—the butcher shop, the knife upraised, the struggle."

"He wasn't there," Tzipporah repeated. "I was."

"But . . ."

"I was coming home late that night from helping at my sister's confinement on Calle Farnese. I saw everything. I was too frightened of getting stabbed—either accidentally by you, or by the nobleman—to intervene. So I rushed home to fetch Asher. By the time we returned, it was too late. The nobleman was dead."

"But why did Asher say *he* had witnessed the murder?"

"To protect me." Tzipporah took Hannah's hand and held it to her cheek.

"I did a stupid thing, which I hope you can forgive. You and Isaac are prosperous now. Perhaps you cannot comprehend how difficult it is to keep five sons and a husband fed and clothed. We are always short of food, no matter how I skimp. I water the soup. I seldom buy meat and when I do, only the cheapest cuts. I buy week-old bread and soak it in water. I make my creams and unguents to sell. But there is never enough money to go around."

"Isaac and I have struggled, too."

"That dreadful night, I seized a chance to make a few *scudi*. For once I wanted enough lamb on the table for every-one to eat their fill. Before Asher loaded the body of di Padovani onto the boat, I stripped off his fine cloak, leather boots, linen shirt and breeches. I sold them to a second-hand clothing dealer."

"So that is what started the rumours?"

"Murdered men do not undress themselves. If I had thrown everything in the fire, as Asher told me to, everyone would have assumed Niccolò had died of the plague and his body heaved in the lagoon like so many others during that terrible time." Tzipporah glanced at the ground. "Neither of us breathed a word. But you know how people gossip. There *were* questions about his death, but in the absence of a body and witnesses, nothing could be proven."

"I am glad you told me," said Hannah. Yet none of this excused Asher from threatening to expose her part in the murder.

"Asher is not perfect. What man is? But he is not the villain you think him."

Hannah took Tzipporah's arm and together they walked across San Marco.

It had begun to rain. The skies opened up, tipping out heavy buckets of water. The rain tasted salty on Hannah's lips. When they arrived back in the ghetto, Hannah embraced Tzipporah. She did not know of Asher's threats to denounce his sister. And Hannah would never tell her.

Now it was morning, weeks later, and Hannah struggled to awaken. The apartment in the old wood-frame building was so stuffy and hot that every day she awoke with swollen eyes and a leaden feeling in her limbs. The bed sheets clung to her. The early-morning humidity presaged rain. Hannah dressed and, with a squirming bundle in her arms, walked down three flights of shaky stairs to the *campo*. Isaac followed, carrying a wooden stool.

The rain-swollen clouds cast a pallor on the cobbles, even as morning sun peered through. The *campo* was nearly empty. Most of the men were in *shul*, the women inside preparing breakfast. Isaac should have been in *shul*, prayer shawl on his shoulders, *kippah* on his head, as he *davened* in time to the Rabbi's prayers, but ten men to make up the *minyan* had been present this morning and so Isaac, to her delight, had decided to sit chatting with her while she nursed the baby. Since his arrival Isaac had left her side only to fetch provisions from the market or to go to *shul*.

Two months ago when Hannah felt her first birth pang— she had doubled over from the shocking intensity of it— there had been a knock on Asher's door. When she flung it open, Isaac stood there, leaning against the door jamb, still ship sick from his journey. Jessica was in his arms. The little girl gave a glad cry when she saw Hannah. They entered the room. There was no more meat on Isaac than on a Shabbat pullet on Sunday morning. His shirt, the one Hannah had made for him out of fine cotton lawn, hung in folds. But when he opened his mouth to grin at her, she saw he still had all his teeth. There were a few strands of white in his beard that had not been there last year.

"Are you still angry with me?" she said. "If you are, I do not want you here. I cannot bring forth our child in an atmosphere of strife and disapproval."

Isaac closed the door behind them and put his arms around her. "I am so sorry, Hannah. When you left with

Assunta in the middle of the night, I thought you loved Matteo more than you loved me. I thought you had renounced our marriage, that you wanted to be free of me, free even of Jessica, so you could live once again in Venice. I thought, forgive me, that you no longer wanted me as your husband."

He looked at her with such an expression of joy she had to glance away from the heat of it. "I could not be at peace until I knew what had happened to Matteo. I wanted you to sail with me. But you—" she gave a sharp cry as another pang ripped through her and she handed Jessica to Isaac, then gripped the back of a chair "—would not leave your precious silkworms." Hannah knew these words were unfair and she would regret them, but the pain in her belly was too great to filter her thoughts.

"We will argue later. You have something more important to do now."

The tenderness in his voice gave her hope things would be well between them once more.

"We are both stubborn as peasants, aren't we?" said Hannah.

Yet another pang seized Hannah.

"Who shall I fetch for you?" asked Isaac.

"Tzipporah. She's visiting her sister on Farnese."

Tzipporah came running, along with her mother, who made sure all drawers and valises, windows and doors were open to encourage the safe passage of the child. Tzipporah sprinkled a circle of salt around the bed to keep at bay Lilith, the Angel of Death.

Childbirth was like being astride a wild bull. No amount of shouting, imploring or groaning made the slightest difference. Pain after pain bucked through her, squeezing her middle like a too-tight girth, making her twist and moan, causing her to cry out to God for mercy then howl like a beast in the fields. At last she understood what other women endured and it made her wonder at the forbearance of those like Bianca, who had had so many pregnancies.

After several hours of labour, Hannah vowed to Tzipporah, who was holding her hand, that if she survived, and she must for the sake of the infant and Jessica, she would never lie with Isaac again. He could be as handsome as he liked, with his muscular back, curly black beard and lean torso, but she would not be persuaded. If he had had the decency to be present and see her suffering, she would have screamed this at him for all the world to hear.

Tzipporah nodded, amused, and wiped Hannah's forehead with a damp cloth. "I always say that when I am in labour. And then, Asher always manages to change my mind. Give one last push, Hannah—you are almost there."

Finally, it was over.

Daniel emerged pink and kicking as Hannah groaned and thrashed in Tzipporah and Asher's bed. Isaac, with Jessica and the wet nurse, fretted in the *campo* below with Asher, who, many times a father, had tried to distract Isaac with a game of chess. But it was no use. Isaac, Asher reported later, had insisted on wearing a new path in the cobblestones with his pacing.

Forgiveness—what a long and bumpy road. After

Daniel's birth, a chilly formality descended between Hannah and Isaac, and beneath its surface, anger. But anger requires energy. Hannah had none. She was exhausted from the confinement, her lack of nourishment while in jail, and then from nightly feedings and daytime nursing, worrying and washing. Then, before Daniel was circumcised on the eighth day, Hannah forgave Isaac for the harsh words of his letter; he forgave her for leaving.

Daniel was as perfect an infant as Hannah and Isaac had ever seen. A round face, pink bow of a mouth, hair as downy as the first fine feathers of a duckling. Even the old *mohel* who circumcised him remarked on his comeliness.

Hannah planted herself on a bench near the wellhead. She tucked the baby under her shawl and began to suckle him. Although less than an hour ago Hannah had spooned gruel into his bird-hungry mouth, Daniel now latched on to her nipple as though he had not eaten since the day he was born. If Hannah had not been so tired, she would have told Daniel how impossibly beautiful he was. Isaac hunkered down next to her, munching on a piece of bread dipped in honey and sipping a cup of tea. Jessica played nearby. She was walking well now, hardly tottering on her sturdy legs. With her green eyes and black hair, she showed every sign of growing up to be as lovely as her mother, Leah. A few women smiled and nodded at them as they lowered wooden buckets into the well, heaved them up and then trudged back to their quarters.

When he had drunk his fill, Daniel gurgled and batted at her breast, his brown eyes following Jessica as she shrieked and ran with other children. Hannah cupped Daniel's cap of black hair and smoothed it off his forehead. Isaac cooed to him and murmured nonsense in his ear. Two dark concentric circles, a large one bent over the smaller. How much Daniel resembled Isaac—the same generous mouth, well-shaped head and long legs, but Daniel's eyes were brown like hers. This lucky baby had inherited the best of each of them.

Matteo's memory hung between them like a heavy tapestry. When they spoke of their son, Isaac recalled the good memories from Constantinople; Hannah remembered only Matteo being torn from her arms in the courthouse.

Isaac clasped Daniel's foot in his hand and jiggled it.

"He is a stout little man. Such a desire for food! You don't think he has worms?"

"Only his father's appetite." Behind Isaac's jest was an anxiety neither of them could give voice to. They had lost Matteo. Would they lose Daniel, as well? Not to a stranger but to disease or accident? The ghetto, with its charcoal braziers that could tip over at any time, canal rats, dank air and families living twenty to a room, was a hazardous place for babies. An infant could be robust at dawn and a stiff, grey corpse by sunset. A goodly portion of children born in the ghetto never lived to see their fifth birthday. The stealers of babies were numerous: the pox, bloody flux, breeding teeth, scarlet fever, measles, whooping cough, worms, diphtheria, typhus, rickets and measles.

"Matteo demanded any number of delicacies we were hard-pressed to supply. Do you remember, Hannah?

Things like quails' eggs, oranges and cherries. This baby would eat table legs and cobblestones and the lids from cook pots if we let him."

It was better to talk of Matteo than pretend he had never existed. But it was difficult not to tear up at the mention of his name. Hannah smiled and hugged Daniel, thinking how strong his suck was and how vigorously he kicked at the air.

Would she and Isaac always compare one son with the other? Would there ever be a time when she could look at Daniel without imagining how Matteo would have enjoyed the role of older brother, how he would have caught bugs for him to examine, held his hand while he took his first steps, helped him form his letters?

Jessica wandered over, unwrapped the blanket from around Daniel's feet and began to tickle his toes.

A gentile, dressed in black, walked in through the gates and came toward them, peering at the buildings surrounding the *campo* as though taking measure of them. As he drew nearer, Hannah recognized him as Palladio. The architect had the look of a man with no one to tend to him. Gone were his gloves, his brushed jacket and patterned velvet waistcoat. His shoulders slumped. He leaned on his cane. His mouth looked caved in, as though a barber surgeon had pulled a number of teeth. His belt drooped below a shrunken belly. A small figure skipped at his side. A figure dressed in new clothes. A red-haired boy. It was Matteo.

When Matteo caught sight of Hannah, he broke free of Palladio's grasp, raced to her side and threw his arms around her neck, pressing Daniel against her. His arms felt like iron bands so fiercely was he embracing her. Hannah laughed. "Do not strangle me. Or smother your brother. Let me look at you. How are you faring in your fine villa? Give me a turnaround." When he relaxed his arms and stood back so she could inspect him, she saw the answer. Pale skin, purple shadows under reddened eyes, cheeks no longer dimpled.

Palladio caught up with Matteo. "I thought I would find you here."

Hannah said, "I am so happy. Thank you for coming."

Isaac gathered Matteo to his chest and held him close, ruffling his hair, rubbing his knuckles along his cheek. He stood, keeping one arm around Matteo, and extended a hand to Palladio. "Isaac Levi, sir, at your service. You must be the *signor* Palladio about whom I have heard so much."

Palladio nodded. "A pleasure, Isaac." They shook hands. "May I join you?" Without waiting for an answer, he lowered himself between Hannah and Isaac. Jessica stood to one side, her thumb in her mouth as she gazed shyly at Matteo.

"I thank you for assuming the responsibility of Matteo and his estate. My wife has told me how you interceded on our son's . . . on Matteo's behalf in court," said Isaac.

"I confess it was your wife who convinced me, Isaac."

"I did nothing of the sort," said Hannah.

"Cesca implored me to act as guardian, but I was suspicious of her. I made inquiries about Foscari and concluded he was a rogue. I wanted nothing to do with either of them, not even for the sake of the Conte. It was your presence, Hannah, your longing, your eyes as you looked at the judge and at Matteo high in the balcony. You risked everything to save Matteo. I thought the least I could do was to step into the breach."

"How kind you are. And how is Matteo faring?" asked Hannah.

Palladio cleared his throat and spoke with evident reluctance. "He is a brave little boy, but he misses you."

"Yes, I understand," said Hannah. Boys did not need their mothers forever. But Matteo was a sensitive child. Things that came easily to other children—using the chamber pot, walking on his own, leaving their mothers' side for a few hours so she could go to market—he found difficult and would do only with the greatest reluctance.

"I can see he is pale."

"The only time he seems truly happy is when he is playing outside."

"And you, sir?" asked Hannah, looking at his wispy grey hair, which fluttered about his face and shoulders. "How are you managing?"

"In truth, not well. A fine pair we are, Matteo and me. A couple of lost souls. My wife died soon after the judge made the court order."

"I am very sorry to hear that. *Aleha HaShalom*. Peace be upon her," said Isaac.

Matteo pulled back Daniel's blanket and peered at the baby. "He is my brother?"

"Would you like to hold him?" inquired Hannah.

Matteo fell cross-legged to the cobblestones and stretched up his hands, and sat still as Hannah placed the new child in his arms. "What a good, calm brother you are. Hold him well." Matteo brushed a fly off Daniel's cheek and kissed his forehead.

"And Lucca? What news of him?" asked Hannah, thinking of his gravely whispered confidences. Without Lucca's help she would never have found Matteo in the *oespedale*. Lucca had trailed after Palladio that day in court like a puppy. She had wanted to hug Lucca goodbye, but he was gone before she had the chance.

Matteo's face brightened. He grinned up at her. "Lucca rides his pony up and down the towpath along the canal with a sword he fashioned from a barrel stave. Everyone in the district knows him because he is so brave. We pick grapes in the neighbours' vineyards and catch *pesce persico* in the canal. Sometimes it is dark when we get home and Marie—our housekeeper—scolds us."

"In other words," said Palladio, "they are a couple of savages, running wild. Soon they will be painting their faces blue and swinging like apes from the willow trees along the canal."

Matteo said, "Lucca needs his own pony. Apollo is too fat and old to carry both of us."

"Matteo's days are happy, but his sleep is full of night terrors," Palladio said. "His nurse tells me he has trouble sleeping."

"Have you given him warm milk with a little brandy? That might help." But Hannah knew it would not.

Isaac stroked her hand. "Matteo must learn to be without us. There is nothing to be done. Would you prefer him to grow up here in the ghetto like Asher's boys? Never seeing more of the world than what is outside their window? Never seeing the sweeping fields, the birds in the sky, or having a chance to pursue a vocation other than dealer in second-hand clothing or moneylender because those are the only occupations the law permits Jews?"

Isaac was right, but she could not help wondering if Matteo had forgotten all his prayers; his Hebrew; the lovely letters Isaac taught him to form. Was he growing up uneducated? And she could hardly give voice to her worst fear. Was he growing up, as most Christians did, to hate Jews?

Hannah put a hand on Matteo's head. "How nice that you have a companion." The children of the ghetto had no fields to play in, no ponies to ride. Most were working when they were little older than Matteo, fetching and carrying, loading and unloading barges, delivering bolts of cloth, working as porters in the Rialto market, firing the brick makers' kilns, stoking the bakery fires.

Palladio said, "Every day I oversee the improvements to Matteo's villa. The corner of the loggia is now true. Those vexing frescoes have been plastered over. The drawing room is now as white as a nun's cell. The dovecote is scraped out and the guano spread on the fields."

"All that must please you," said Isaac.

But Palladio did not look pleased.

"Every time I finish an improvement, instead of taking pleasure in it, I think, *Allegra is not here to enjoy this.* She knew how to divert me when I became too serious, to comfort me when I was puzzling out how to best distribute the weight of a roof. Now there are no dinner parties, no smells of her stews and barley soup drifting from the kitchen, no smile as she comes and goes in the garden, no scent of lavender from her bedclothes. I have only the thundering of Lucca and Matteo as they rampage through the halls. Lucca rides Apollo along the loggia, which vexes the masons and makes them shout at the boys." He paused; then, with the air of a man about to say something he knew he would regret and didn't mean, he said, "By the blood of the Virgin, I wish I had never attended court that day."

"Is it unthinkable you will someday remarry? It would lessen your burden," said Hannah.

He faced away from her, toward the gates where Vicente was oiling the hinges with goose grease. Hers was a tactless question, one she wished she had not asked.

"I am too old and crotchety to inflict myself on another wife. I would compare another woman's looks and cooking and dress to Allegra's."

"We have this in common, sir. The ache in the heart, that missing place, that hole that cannot be filled." Hannah put a hand on his knee but then, embarrassed, withdrew it. To change the subject, she said, "And what of Cesca? What has become of her?"

Palladio's face softened and a hint of pink crept up his cheeks.

Another man with an eye for a pretty face and narrow waist.

Tossing his cane to one side, Palladio said, "Gone to Rome."

With my ducats tucked in her pocket.

Hannah waited. There was more. When he said nothing, she prompted, "What will she do there?"

"Cesca has a scheme to set herself up as a courtesan in a townhouse near the Tiber."

"A costly enterprise," Isaac remarked.

Palladio looked sheepish. "Life is difficult for a woman with no funds and no friends. I hated to see her banished without a *crudo* to her name. I gave a few ducats to help her get established. She promises to repay me."

Yes, when octopuses pull carriages fashioned of peridot and mother-of-pearl.

"And Foscari?"

"He cheated the hangman of his fee. He grew ill in prison. He insisted he had been poisoned by Cesca, which I do not for one moment believe. He got into a scuffle with another prisoner over a piece of gristle. In his weakened condition Foscari got the worst of it—a stab wound in the belly, which became pus ridden."

Hannah could not help a feeling of relief.

Isaac spoke. "'Do not rejoice when your enemy falls.'" It was a quote from the Torah.

"But a difficult rule to obey, is it not?" Hannah looked across the *campo* to where Asher sat at his moneylender's table. Losing such a huge sum to Foscari had chastened him. For the first time in his marriage, he was beholden to Tzipporah. Her salves and creams were selling well enough to support the family, a fact she never let him forget.

Forgiveness is the glue that holds all families together. Hannah's first thought was that Asher must bear the consequences of his folly. She would not smooth his path, no matter how grievous his situation. But she refused to bear a grudge like Asher. Without his disposal of Niccolò's body, she might have been charged with murder. She loved Tzipporah and their children. And so Hannah convinced Isaac to make Asher a loan. Tzipporah, at last, had borne a daughter.

"We leave soon for Constantinople," said Hannah. "It was so kind of you to bring Matteo all this way from San Lorenzo to bid us farewell." She would be glad to quit the ghetto. Its shadow-filled alleys reminded her at every turn of her murder of Niccolò. To take the life of another, even when justified, is a hard memory to live with. Perhaps in another place, another setting, her guilt would lessen. Until then she was doing her best to make her peace with herself and God.

Palladio shook his head. "You misunderstand. I came on an altogether different errand."

CHAPTER 32

Jewish Ghetto,
Venice

"I HAVE A PROPOSAL to discuss," said Palladio. "I want you to join me at the villa and assume the rearing of Matteo." He leaned over and tousled Matteo's hair. "And Lucca, as well. I have grown fond of that boy. He is intelligent and has a talent for drawing, as well as an interest in designing boats. I suspect that someday he will make a fine ship's architect."

Hannah was taken aback. "There is nothing I would like more, but as I have said, we are soon leaving Venice."

Isaac said, "We have a silk workshop and house waiting for us."

"But what of Matteo?" Palladio said. "You see him at his

best. For your benefit he puts on a brave face. But he is a different boy at the villa. Some nights, he awakens screaming. Red foxes live under his bed. Wolves lurk outside his door. Vultures roost in the trees outside his window. He will not rise to use the chamber pot and soaks his bed."

"Our life is in Constantinople," Isaac said.

Isaac loved his workshop. He loved Constantinople. He did not find the Ottoman language impossible, or the customs of the other Jews strange.

"And you?" Palladio looked at Hannah.

Surely he was not suggesting the unthinkable: that she remain behind without her husband. Isaac looked at her. He did not need to speak the words aloud: *we must never again be parted.*

"We have a prosperous workshop, a house, an orchard," said Isaac.

Hannah began, "The two of us could—"

"Life is good for the Jews in the Ottoman Empire," Isaac interrupted. "We can work at whatever pleases us. We own property. The Ottomans do not vilify us as casters of spells, poisoners of wells and child murderers." He took Hannah's hand and kissed it. "We have already been apart too long."

Hannah sat thinking. "What of the management of the estate? Are you faring any better with that than you are with the raising of two high-spirited boys?"

"I have as much skill for commerce as the baby you have recently borne. I fear that by the time Matteo is of legal age there will be no more left of the estate than if Foscari had been put in charge. The way matters are proceeding, the boy will not have a *scudo*. Trade debts go uncollected because I cannot find anyone to collect them. The tenant farmers refuse to pay their rents because their cottages are falling down. I cannot find anyone to repair them because I have no access to the estate funds until the court order is confirmed by one of the judge's clerks. And I have no time to attend court because I am busy in San Lorenzo overseeing the improvements to the villa. Even if I did get the court order, I have no time to travel to the Fugger bank in Augsburg where the Conte kept his money on deposit."

"You must have a manager?" said Isaac.

"The Conte's steward—he's been robbing the family for years. More barrels of wine end up in his cellars than in the villa's. I cannot think why the Conte did not send him packing years ago. I'm too lily-livered to fire him and too busy to find someone to replace him. And worst of all—" Palladio pulled a handkerchief out of his pocket and mopped his brow "—the ground floor rooms of the di Padovani palazzo on the Grand Canal are filling with water because some of the oak foundation timbers need replacing. As for the Conte's brigantines? Are they transporting peppercorns and cinnamon from the Levant, their sails bellied out with good strong winds? No, both ships have sprung leaks and are rotting in dry dock. The caulkers won't lift a finger unless I pay them in advance."

"A sad state of affairs," said Isaac.

"It never occurred to me that having a great deal of money could be as difficult as having none at all," said

Hannah. She could see an arrangement cobbled together that would suit them. The best course was to gently guide Isaac in the right direction. But if he came to the opposite conclusion, there was nothing to be done. To change Isaac's mind was like trying to unbake a kugel.

Hannah held out her arms to take Daniel from Matteo, who was growing restless. Matteo scrambled to his feet and raced to the wellhead, slapped it with his hand and raced back to Hannah. He grabbed Jessica and dragged her away to look at a man selling cakes.

Hannah put a hand on Palladio's sleeve. "You need someone like Isaac."

"Can you read, sir? Have you a head for figures?" asked Palladio.

"Can he read!" said Hannah. "With the speed of a goshawk taking a rabbit from the undergrowth. There is nothing he cannot decipher, from a bill of lading in Latin to a marriage contract in Aramaic."

Isaac opened his mouth, but before he could speak, Hannah forged on. "He is the cleverest of men. Undaunted by any column of figures you care to place in front of him. Unfazed by the wordiest passage in any book. Able to write as well as a scribe." Hannah tucked Daniel's head under her shawl again and gave a little jump as he rooted around, found her nipple and began to suck. "Isaac would do nicely for you."

"What do you say, Isaac?" asked Palladio. "I am certain I can obtain permission from the Council of Ten for you and your family to live outside the ghetto."

Hannah waited while Isaac pondered Palladio's offer.

At last Isaac said, "It is an inviting proposition, sir, and I am honoured you think me capable." He cleared his throat. "To change our lives so drastically is not a step to be undertaken lightly." Isaac glanced at Daniel, lying peacefully in Hannah's arms.

Palladio said, "And you, Hannah? What is your opinion? There is a stone cottage on the grounds of the villa, fair size, snug, with its own sweet water well and kitchen garden. The place could be reroofed and whitewashed, and turned into a dwelling for you and your family."

How unusual that a man, especially one as celebrated as Palladio, would ask the opinion of a woman. "And Matteo?" inquired Hannah.

"He could live with you," said Palladio.

"Then of course we can come to an arrangement," said Hannah.

"Could we raise him as a Jew?" asked Isaac.

"I could not as his guardian permit it," Palladio replied.

Still, in the country there would be few neighbours to object to a few lessons in Hebrew, a few prayers whispered over candles and *challah* on Shabbat. Hannah posed the question she dreaded hearing the answer to: "Has Matteo been christened?"

"Another task left uncompleted, I am afraid. Soon I must. The village priest hangs about, pestering me as to when it shall be done. When Matteo is ten years old, the priest insists that the boy be sent to the Franciscans to be educated."

"Where his primary lesson will be to learn to hate the Jews," said Isaac.

Palladio shrugged. "But what is to be done? The boy must be schooled."

Hannah said, "Would you excuse Isaac and me a moment while we talk?"

"Of course." Palladio walked to the other side of the *campo*.

"It is a bitter thing to know Matteo will be raised as a Christian . . ." Isaac trailed off.

"Yes, but it cannot be helped." She moved closer to her husband. "This could be a new start for us, Isaac. Together we will raise Jessica, Daniel and Matteo. They will grow up rosy cheeked and straight limbed in the country. We have had so many struggles. On Matteo's estate, we will have peace at last. We will pull together once again like two horses hitched to the same cart."

With the money from selling our silk business, who knows? Maybe someday we will have our own estate, she thought.

"I have never lived in the country," said Isaac. "I understand raising silkworms, and unreeling cocoons, and printing silk cloth. I know nothing of the rustic life." He shook his head. "I am unfit for what Palladio has in mind."

"You are so quick-witted, Isaac. Everything you turn your hand to is a success. Look how well you have done with our silk workshop. Would you try for my sake? Only for the next year or two. If you are unhappy, I promise we will return to Constantinople." Hannah searched her mind for further arguments. "You are so good at teasing order out of chaos. I know that in a short time you will have Matteo's estate operating as smoothly as a well-oiled gate." Hannah wrapped Daniel more tightly in his blanket. "It will be an opportunity for you to learn new things."

"Draining swampy fields?"

"Double-entry bookkeeping of the sort they do in Venice."

"Growing winter wheat and rye?"

"Discussing Petrarch with an educated man like Palladio."

"Collecting rents from unhappy tenants?"

"Pressing golden olive oil, fermenting wine."

"Watching sheep bloat from grazing on new meadow and crops wither from insects and lack of rain?"

"Having Matteo back. All of us together as a family again."

There was a long pause.

Isaac said, "Hannah, you are right."

Was there a sweeter sentence in the universe than this one?

"Who knows?" said Hannah. "We have one baby." She looked down and stroked Daniel's cheek with her finger. "Maybe there will be more."

"And to be with Matteo again, safeguarding his fortune, would be a wonderful thing."

Hannah felt something loosen in her breast that had nothing to do with the rich milk flowing into Daniel.

Isaac said, "I know you have never felt at home in Constantinople." He toyed with Daniel's foot, unwrapping the swaddling, thinking out loud. "I can write to our Armenian neighbour and ask him to manage the workshop. He will do a good job. He has always had his eye on it. But only for a year or so, mind."

"You are certain?" Now that she had succeeded in convincing Isaac, Hannah wanted to make sure he was acting on his own desires, not to please her.

"No, I am not certain. The offer is so unexpected. But I am willing to try. I am restless here in the ghetto. There is little for me to do to occupy myself. Asher is busy. The other men all are occupied with their own affairs. I feel useless."

"Jessica would thrive, as well."

Matteo came over and climbed into Isaac's lap. Turning to Hannah, Isaac said, "What use are a house and a business if the people you love are not present?"

"Will it be enough for us simply to raise Matteo without having the power to decide his religion or whom he marries or what profession he follows?" asked Hannah.

"Yes," said Isaac, "Matteo's sweet company will be enough. He is not too young to learn to read and reckon. He is a clever boy. I will teach him."

"I love you, Isaac." But one thing continued to trouble her. "Are you still angry with me for leaving Constantinople against your wishes?"

When Isaac said nothing, Hannah said, recalling a passage from the Christian Bible, "'Love keeps no record of wrongs. It does not delight in evil but rejoices in the truth. Love always perseveres.'"

Isaac smiled. "May I quote from the Song of Solomon?" He took her in his arms. "'Many waters cannot quench love, neither can the floods drown it.'"

Hannah settled back against Isaac as she regarded the

campo and the surrounding wood frame structures. Through a space between Asher's building and its neighbour, she glimpsed the blue of the Rio del Ghetto. *Yes*, she thought, *there is no woman as fortunate as I.*

ACKNOWLEDGEMENTS

I wish to thank the many people who helped in the conception and bringing forth of this book.

To my editor, Kiara Kent, for her astute direction, and to Rachel Cooper for the lovely cover. To Beverley Sotolov, copy editor, whose attention to detail and insistence on historical verisimilitude is admirable, and to everyone at Doubleday Canada and Penguin Random House Canada.

To Beverley Slopen, my agent extraordinaire, for her limitless wisdom, insight, unconditional support and guidance.

To Jordan Hall, my wonderful mentor and insightful critic.

To my friends Shel and Marv Shaffer, Canan Ozbek, Beryl Young, Kate Rose and Linda Holeman for their warmth and support. And to Ruth Peacock, Marcia Jacobs, Gay Ludlow, Roland Lougheed and Susan Barclay-Nichols for being good and generous listeners.

A wistful thanks to Nita Pronovost and Adria Iwasutiak, whom I continue to miss.

To my family, I thank in particular my wonderful sister, Alice Rich, for her caring and clever artistic eye, and to Kerstin Peterson, for her invaluable editing suggestions as well as her formidable formulating skills.

Special thanks to Nicholas Terpstra, Department of History, University of Toronto, for his patience in answering my questions on orphanages in Venice.

And to Ken Peterson, my wise and wonderful husband, without whom life would not mean a hill of beans.

RECIPES

A word of caution, gentle reader: formulating creams and soaps is a highly engaging pastime. As a result of my research for *A Trial in Venice*, I became addicted to making soaps and creams. I now spend my free time stirring vats of soap, experimenting with colour, scents and moulds. I test creams for consistency, fragrance and colour; shop for exquisite containers when I travel; and give my creations to friends for birthdays and holidays.

Soap and cream making in Hannah's day was a messy, inexact and sometimes dangerous endeavour. Lye was prepared from soaking wood ashes in rainwater until the solution reached a concentration sufficient enough to float an egg. Luckily for us, lye is now readily available in most hardware stores. Hannah would have used beef or sheep tallow and olive oil. Her soap may have been, by modern standards, quite harsh. We will use modern versions of Hannah's ingredients: manufactured lye, beef tallow, olive oil and coconut oil.

In the old, pre-emulsifier days, Tzipporah would have heated almond oil, tallow, olive oil and wax together, relying on beeswax to make a firm cream. We are fortunate now to have a variety of emulsifiers, such as Polawax and e-wax, to bind our ingredients together.

I have included my two favourite recipes—modern versions of what Hannah and Tzipporah prepared. Both formulae will produce good, useable products. I like to think Hannah and Tzipporah would approve of the results.

Tzipporah's Night Cream

EQUIPMENT NEEDED: digital scale, large cook pot, immersion blender, two heat-proof glass beakers or Pyrex measuring cups, small food scale, spatulas and spoons, jars to contain the final product (you will need about 5 jars of 50-ml size).

QUANTITY: 200 grams

PART A:
Water Phase:
58% water . . . . 117 grams
2% sodium lactate (humectant) . . . . 4 grams

PART B:
Oils, Butters and Waxes:
10% almond oil . . . . 20 grams
5% shea butter . . . . 10 grams
10% cocoa butter . . . . 20 grams

8% Polawax (emulsifier) . . . . 16 grams

3% cetyl alcohol (thickening agent) . . . . 6 grams

PART C:

Cool-down Phase:

1% fragrance . . . . 2 grams

0.5% Germol Plus (preservative) . . . . 1 gram

2% panthenol (humectant) . . . . 4 grams

1% vitamin E . . . . 2 grams

2% cyclomethicone (gives a silky feel) . . . . 4 grams

2% dimethicone (glide, protective barrier) . . . . 4 grams

INSTRUCTIONS:

1. Weigh out the Part A ingredients in a heat-proof container, such as a Pyrex measuring cup. Weigh out the Part B ingredients in a separate heat-proof container. Place both containers into a double boiler or large cook pot filled with water. Heat to 70°C and hold at this temperature for 20 minutes.

2. Weigh Part A again and add a touch to compensate for evaporation.

3. Combine Parts A and B and blend with an immersion blender for at least 3 minutes. Continue blending now and then until the mixture cools to 45°C.

4. Add the Part C ingredients. Mix well with the immersion blender. Let cool to room temperature.

5. Scoop into sterile jars.

6. Ingredients are available from online soap and cream supply companies such as www.voyageursoapandcandle.com or

www.brambleberry.com. For further information and recipes, I highly recommend www.swiftcraftymonkey.blogspot.ca.

Hannah's Hand Soap

Soap making is not for sissies. Hannah made soap outside so she didn't breathe in the fumes from the lye. She wore gloves to protect her hands. She banished children and animals. She would have worn safety glasses if they had been available. So should you. Handling lye is a serious business.

EQUIPMENT NEEDED: digital scale, digital thermometer, large cook pot (not aluminum), stick blender, spatulas, a mould, container for mixing lye and water (a large glass measuring cup or a plastic juice jug will do), container for weighing out the lye (a clean yoghurt container works well), gloves, safety goggles.

Until you decide whether you are a committed *saponificatrice*, use a small wooden or cardboard box lined with freezer paper as a soap mould. The Soap Queen (www.soapqueen.com) has excellent videos on YouTube to guide you through the process.

You can order beef tallow online or render your own in a slow cooker on low heat. Buy ground beef suet from the butcher or buy it in chunks and cut it into 1/4-inch cubes for rendering.

QUANTITY: 3 pounds or approximately 10 bars of soap

Beef tallow . . . . 400 grams
Olive oil . . . . 50 grams

Coconut oil .... 250 grams

Lye .... 143 grams

Distilled water .... 380 grams

INSTRUCTIONS:

1. Slowly and carefully add the lye to the water in a container.
   Gently stir until the lye has dissolved and the liquid is
   clear. When mixed with water, lye becomes hot and active
   very quickly. Set aside to cool to approximately 50°C.
   (Always add the lye to the water, never the other way
   around. To remember, think "snow falls on the lake.")

2. Weigh out the oils and tallow. Add to the cooking pot and
   melt on low heat.

3. Remove from heat and allow the lye water and oil/tallow
   mixture to cool to about 50°C.

4. Slowly pour the lye mixture into the oil/tallow mixture
   and mix with your stick blender. The mixture will turn a
   creamy yellow color. Continue to mix with the stick
   blender for about 5 minutes. When the mixture is thick
   enough to support your initials on the top of the mixture,
   you have achieved "trace."

5. Pour it into the mould.

6. Let the soap sit in the mould for 36-48 hours. Press out of
   the mould and cut into bars. If the soap sticks in the
   mould, put it in the freezer for 1 hour, then press out.

7. Allow the soap to cure for 4-6 weeks.

8. Rejoice!

FURTHER READING

While this is a work of fiction, I have tried to be as accurate as possible in recreating the atmosphere of sixteenth-century Venice. Some of the books that I used in my research that I found helpful, informative and entertaining include:

Ackroyd, Peter. *Venice: Pure City*. Random House. 2009.

Baron, Salo. *A Social and Religious History of the Jews: Late Middle Ages and Era of European Expansion (1200–1650): The Ottoman Empire, Persia, Ethiopia, India, and China*. Columbia University Press. 1983.

Beltramini, Guido. *The Private Palladio*. Lars Müller Publishers. 2008.

Brooks, Andrée Aelion. *The Woman Who Defied Kings: The Life and Times of Doña Gracia Nasi*. Paragon House. 2002.

Crowley, Roger. *City of Fortune: How Venice Won and Lost a Naval Empire*. Faber & Faber. 2011.

Gable, Sally, and Carl I. Gable. *Palladian Days: Finding a New Life in a Venetian Country House*. Random House. 2005.

King, Ross. *Brunelleschi's Dome: How a Renaissance Genius Reinvented Architecture.* Bloomsbury Publishing. 2000.

Laven, Mary. *Virgins of Venice: Enclosed Lives and Broken Vows in the Renaissance Convent.* Viking Press. 2002.

Menuge, Noël James. *Medieval English Wardship in Romance and Law.* D.S. Brewer. 2001.

Monson, Craig A. *Nuns Behaving Badly: Tales of Music, Magic, Art, and Arson in the Convents of Italy.* The University of Chicago Press. 2011.

Roth, Cecil. *The House of Nasi: Doña Gracia.* Greenwood Publishing Group. 1948.

Salomon, Herman Prins, and Aron di Leone Leoni. "Mendes, Benveniste, de Luna, Micas, Nasci: The State of the Art (1532–1558)." *The Jewish Quarterly Review.* 1998.

Terpstra, Nicholas. *Abandoned Children of the Italian Renaissance: Orphan Care in Florence and Bologna.* Johns Hopkins University Press. 2005.

Terpstra, Nicholas. *Lost Girls: Sex and Death in Renaissance Florence.* Johns Hopkins University Press. 2010.